Some days I wonder if those that are accused were only placed in the position for do do so because maybe a once now retired higher power lost faith in them and left them to be that way as not only an example of what not to do but to know the difference and some day praise the

grace that was so
forsakenly lost. or
quite possibly never
Only free will found.
ans the
sacrafice of
those willing.

Gadji

Gadji

Louise Domaratius

QUALITY WORDS IN PRINT
QWP
Costa Mesa, California

Copyright © 2002 by Louise Domaratius

All rights reserved. No part of this book may be reproduced in any form without permission in writing from the publisher.

This is a work of fiction. The names, characters, places and incidents are products of the author's imagination, and any resemblance to actual persons or events is coincidental.

Quality Words in Print, LLC
P.O. Box 2704
Costa Mesa, CA 92628–2704
www.qwipbooks.com

Library of Congress Catalog Number (LCCN)
2001 126979

FIRST EDITION

Publisher's Cataloging-in-Publication
(Provided by Quality Books, Inc.)

Domaratius, Louise.
    Gadji / Louise Domaratius. — 1st ed.
    p. cm.
    ISBN 0-9713160-0-7
    1. Asylum, Right of—Fiction. 2. Refugees—Fiction.
3. Romanies—Fiction. 4. France—Fiction. I. Title.
PS3604.O6237D66   2002   813'.6
                                                      QCI01-701308

To asylum seekers everywhere.
To my great-grandmothers and great-grandfathers,
for whom the golden syllables, America, spelled refuge.

Then the king said, . . . "Why do you also go with us? Go back, and stay with the king; for you are a foreigner, and also an exile from your home."

2 SAMUEL 15:19

PROLOGUE

Château Lore
Meho

1989. Peacetime. At eight o'clock in the morning, Sarajevo lay under a blanket of fog like a sleeper unwilling to emerge. Meho pushed open the door to the cluttered grocery shop, where he had just been hired. The sleeping pills made him groggy mornings, and the entire world seemed muffled and indistinct. He was to carry in the stocks, replenish the shelves, mark the prices, keep order. This part-time job would help make ends meet, since the symphony orchestra paid poorly. A second oboist is not a rich man. But the shop mornings and the accordion certain evenings rounded out his monthly income neatly.

He was beginning to work again, and the paralysis he had felt since Samira's departure was slowly waning.

"I wouldn't want to hurt you, Meho, but I saw Samira with a guy at The Morava last night. What's the matter? Aren't you a man for her?"

That was how he had found out. He'd been earning their living playing the accordion for diners and tourists, and she'd been off flirting. Worse, perhaps. He called her: "If you want to go out, I'll take you. You ask me!"

"Well, what do you expect? You're never home. You know I like to get around. You can't begrudge me a little fun." Her eyes were as black as her hair. *Ochi chërnye:* "Dark Eyes", just as the song had it. Hers was the slim beauty of Indian women, with their chiseled cheekbones and mauve-gray hollows beneath their eyes. She was as tall as he, 5 feet 6 inches, and, when she wore heels, her sleek head was slightly higher than his. She had outlined her eyes with kohl, and her lips shone with dark red lipstick. She beckoned him to her, but he was hurt, suspicious. Then he questioned her and questioned her, until she admitted all of it: her betrayal, the other men. She promised it was over, but Meho's world was shattered.

They had been married for nine years. She had been eighteen, he twenty-one: teenage sweethearts. An adolescent passion, still his passion. Two years after their marriage, Nadir was born, his son and only child. Meho couldn't speak for the humiliation and the anger and the shock at her deception. And so he had sued for divorce, but, of course, the child was to stay with his mother. Meho wandered the streets of Sarajevo like a lost soul. His life with Samira passed time and again before his eyes like a film he could not choose but watch: Samira bathing Nadir, Samira in his arms; how she came, calling his name, when they made love. He became enthralled by the images to the point where he lost his way, didn't recognize the neighborhoods, forgot which streets he had taken. The medicine he took released the knot in his stomach but didn't stop the scenes from unfolding over and over, each accompanied by the acute consciousness that all of it was past, finished, irredeemable.

His memories spun within him, a bobbin of pain, palpable, but he wanted to overcome, and he would fight it. And so, each box, tin, bottle he placed on a shelf became a small buoy, pulling him up and forward.

When he first saw Gordana, she was leading a small girl by the hand toward the cash register of the shop. The child, like her mother, had wavy, black hair cut short, almost wiry in its thickness. Dark shadows underscored the clear green eyes of the young woman, and her complexion was sallow. She was tired. Her shirt was partially unbuttoned, and the swelling of her chest beneath the cotton material caught his attention. He found himself hoping she would come another time.

She did. Two mornings a week, after her duty at the hospital was over, she would come for fresh milk, and he spoke to her. When he asked her what her husband did, her voice was sharp.

"Husband?" she said. "He's remarried. I have Latifa, only Latifa." Then, she sensed his interest, and she smiled at him.

When he started having sex again, he felt resuscitated, even if he had to conjure up the image of Samira each time. He brought Gordana to his house, where she cooked for him and watched over his medical treatment. She nursed him, and he felt more secure. The four-year-old child was lissome, affectionate, and her presence comforted him. She would nestle in his arms, trusting him completely. He felt he had a family again, and he let himself be cared for.

Meho remained in the simple cinder block house his father had helped him build for Samira, Nadir, and himself. He went daily to visit his mother, Zlatija, a squarely built, energetic woman. Her graying hair was caught up in a black scarf, printed with bright red roses and knotted at the nape of her neck. Meho's father had left her one day, years ago, after the two boys were out of school. The constant quarreling with his wife had been too much in the end.

Zlatija trained her astonishing blue eyes on Gordana. She liked this serious-minded girl. She was less flighty than her previous daughter-in-law and would stabilize Meho. "If you want to stay with him," Zlatija told her, "it's simple. Get pregnant!"

Good Muslim men accept their responsibilities, and three months later he married her, still in a daze over the events of the past year.

His love for children was sincere, and he held his tiny new daughter in his arms, covering her with kisses. His tenderness surprised Gordana, so withdrawn that she did not even kiss her own child. She loved him the more for his effusiveness and imitated him, hugging the little Suada. Two years later, just as the shelling began, Amina, their second daughter, was born.

Gordana, happy in her new life, happy in Samira's former home, never counted on the return of her husband's first wife. She learned from the neighbors that Samira had been to the house and so started watching Meho, anger and anxiety pressing within, constricting her breathing.

"We could try getting back together," Samira suggested. They made love several times, but for Meho something was definitively spoiled. He reminded her he had a new wife, new responsibilities. He desired Samira as never before, but when the first rush of his passion had subsided, he felt repelled. The humiliation she had caused him came flooding back, and, although he held her brown, naked body against his, the pressure and lifting he usually felt did not occur.

"What's wrong with you?" she mocked.

"You hurt me too much, Samira. I don't want you any more."

For three years he had never ceased thinking of her. Now, he understood he was cured.

Gordana, alone in her fear, remained unsure of this.

ONE

"*Tu es morrte, morrte!*"

"You are deeaad!" Gordana's imprecation went on echoing in my ear, long after I had hung up the phone, the abrasive, rolled "r", the hysterical rise on the last note, as she spat out the plosive. *Morrte!* And I was dead. I deserved to die, for I had slept with her husband, and she had known that now for, perhaps, all of fifteen murderous minutes.

That was last year. Had I not met her first, I would never have known Meho nor brought that havoc on myself, my marriage, and on the family I wished only well.

It began, surprisingly enough, with *Le Comité d'Entr'aide Catholique,* the Catholic Aid Committee. Surprisingly, in that I am not Catholic, nor are such organizations meant as breeding grounds for adulterous relationships.

I have sometimes wondered what brings people to commit themselves to long hours of humanitarian devotion. What demons are they conjuring, what satisfactions, moral compensations, reassurances are they seeking? From what compunctions are they freeing themselves?

For me, it was the obscure but continual need to come into contact with other foreigners, the search for the common experience, the shared viewpoint of the outsider. To that I added the desire to be useful, appreciated, thanked, perhaps even admired. I was hoping much, but, in fact, expecting little.

Gordana, then, appeared to me for the first time on an October morning in the half-open doorway to the Saint Barnabbas' Parish catechism room. She cocked her dark head slyly and flashed the full force of her black-lashed, sea-green eyes. She was not beautiful, but her eyes were luminous against the deep olive of her skin. She smiled, uncovering a gap where her right eyetooth should have been. Its emptiness spoke of deprivation. She was a young woman in her early thirties.

She had come to me to learn French, the language of my adopted country. I spoke it fluently. Degrees from French and American universities had ensured me employment and respect. My husband was French. My children had been born in France. My life was in France.

Still, I was a usurper. Should I tell her? Perhaps the refugee I had volunteered to teach would feel disappointed to learn that her tutor was not French. I decided to reveal my non-Frenchness later. I felt compelled to redouble my efforts of kindness and attention to make up for this lack of authenticity.

Gordana, herself, was not as I had expected. "She's a Bulgarian woman," I'd been told. "So, you're Bulgarian?" I asked her.

Gordana corrected me: "No, I Bosnian *madame.*"

Marie-Toussainte, of the so-Catholic name, head of the program, had, as usual, everything confused. Her matronly heart was all-encompassing and her geography vague: Bosnia? Bulgaria? What difference? It was she who assigned me to Gordana. "She's willing," she said, "and she knows a few words."

Our first lesson brought acquaintance with Gordana's family. Personal pronouns, then proper names, her family's and mine, headed our first sentences. Photographs were brought and shyly spread over the table: three dark-skinned daughters; the disorder of an apartment where they had found refuge; Gordana on the train; flight to Croatia; her husband, Meho, as a street musician, playing with friends on a busy corner in Zagreb. Zagreb? A distant city that meant little to me, a dot in the atlas, evocative of nothing.

"I am nurse," Gordana told me. "It is the most beautiful work, because you can people *helfen.*" I learned to decipher her limping mixture of French and German.

One day, she failed to come to her lesson. When I called the Home for Refugees, I learned that she'd been ill. I thought I should visit her. I headed my car out of the city toward *Le Château,* as the place was known, both ironically and factually. In former times it had, indeed, been a castle. It was one of those imposing eighteenth-century structures that cap promontories in the French countryside. Here, the town encroached on the country as it crept toward the *Château,* its houses thinning out, its streets more rural, less evenly paved. A chapel jutted from one end of the building, displaying arched windows boarded over.

The interior, however, had the ingenuous air of a nursery school about it. The roughcast walls were pastel, and a sign of welcome, decorated with butterflies and flowers had been cut from cardboard and colored. At first sight, the cheerfulness was convincing. A secretary, busying herself with a photocopier in a glass-walled office, told me that Madame Kozić had gone out. I left a tin box of butter cookies from the supermarket.

If I had known that modest present was to bear the foretaste of poison for both you and me, I would never have come, dear Gordana, never have brought it, never have printed that note in simple French words expressing concern.

What right did I have to think I could bring any sort of comfort to someone who had been forced to flee to Croatia in 1993?

She hadn't told me what it had been like, of course. She didn't have the means, and, had she had them, her natural modesty would have kept her silent. But I could imagine. I could piece together the magazine articles with their heart-rending illustrations, the newspaper stories, the eyewitness reports, the films, documentaries, chronicles. And I could see it so well. Not at first; the seriousness of the matter hadn't struck me as yet. Gordana should have been enchanted with our provincial French town, should have felt privileged, should have been motivated to learn the prestigious language and culture, should have been grateful. Instead, she was depressed, sullen. Something heavier than the memory of war lay in the back of her mind.

Gordana attended her next lesson, thanking me offhandedly for the cookies. Her husband's lesson time had coincided that day with hers, and she introduced us on the way out. The gravel of the courtyard crunched beneath our footsteps, and the air was warm and dusty with the smell of dry leaves. A large linden tree stood between the priests' residence, a rustic, seventeenth-century building, and the low, prefabricated classrooms. I turned to her husband. "I hear you're a professional musician," I said. I'm a musician too, but not professional."

"That make no difference," he said, smiling up at me as we walked. I was several inches taller. I saw a squarish man, who seemed quite young, in his late thirties, perhaps. He didn't take his eyes off me, and his insistent grin was charming. One front tooth was chipped and slightly discolored, the others white against a dark complexion. His eyes were black, his hair too, thick on the sides, thinning at the crown. He wore the carefully trimmed beard and mustache of Muslims. I hadn't expected Bosnians to be so dark. Turkish blood, I imagined, trying to remember what I had read about the Ottoman Empire and the Balkans.

> *Dear Meho, that first meeting signified nothing in particular to me. How could I have known that it impressed you so strongly? That the tall, fair-haired teacher with the suit and glasses and attaché case had stunned you? That she was the exotic one, the other? It is no simple thing to see oneself as the other.*

I met Gordana regularly in a small, chill room of the parish hall. The cutouts and collages of the children who came there for their catechism covered the walls. The gas stove would groan, resist, and finally allow itself to be lit. I kept on my long, black coat, and she her cherry parka. "From Sarajevo," she said.

A cherry-colored parka from Sarajevo, and my imagination took off. Had she bought it before the war? Was it a gift from the Red Cross? *Rote Kreuz*: a basic in her vocabulary. She never could remember the French words, *Croix Rouge*. What miseries had that short coat traversed? And how had the family managed to salvage so many things: clothes, a radio-cassette player, souvenirs, photographs? Whenever there was a question of Sarajevo, the war, or the camps, my imagination jumped to fill in the blanks. I pieced the living fabric of their lives together as I once had a quilt. I could see Gordana huddled in that cherry coat in a refugee camp in Croatia, could visualize her in the minus twenty weather, shivering in spite of it. I could imagine it serving as a blanket for tiny Veronika, her youngest daughter.

Their vocabularies were inadequate, and a seal of secrecy seemed to lie over whatever ordeals they had known. I ascribed it to embarrassment, reserve, unwillingness to burden anyone with such narratives, perhaps first of all themselves. I would not have dreamed of insisting, and it certainly never occurred to me that they might have something to hide.

Meho informed me one November Monday of a death in the family. "Madame Ellen," he said gently, "Gordana not well, she not coming today. Papa dead."

"Her father is dead? Suddenly? What happened?"

"Heart attack. In Sarajevo. On way to doctor."

"How old was he?"

"Fifty-three."

"Oh God, that's my age," I said, but Meho was staring at me without understanding, a flicker of a smile behind his solemnity. "Do you think it would be all right if I went to the home to visit her? Shall I drive you back there?" I didn't know how to comfort people, and I felt panicked. Not going would have been cowardly.

Meho leaned toward me and carefully removed a blond hair from the black wool of my coat. Many times afterward I was to see this as an obsessional gesture in him. I found it odd and amusing, an unexpected familiarity, just then particularly out of place. Unlike me, however, he was untroubled by our errand.

Gordana appeared in answer to her husband's summons in the long communal dining room of the *Château*. I wrapped my arms around her. "My heart is with you," I managed to get out, as we both burst into tears. Meho watched us attentively, moved or unmoved, I could not tell. I saw their little Veronika for the first time outside of a snapshot, a scowl darkening her forehead, her bottom weighted down by diapers. Her mother's tears upset her, and she held out her arms to her father. Her black eyes and long lashes were precisely his.

Near the end of Gordana's mourning period, she, Meho, and their three daughters came to our house. They had no vehicle and no right to drive, so I met them at the Tulipes bus stop, a five-minutes' drive from our village suburb. I had misgivings: Would the sight of our spacious, middle-class house and all the inaccessible comforts it contained leave them more discouraged than before? Was this invitation tactless, or would they take it for what it was, a gesture of welcome?

Their carefully circumspect expressions gave no answers to my questions, and their stay was brief. The children sat obediently on the brown leather sofa in their good dresses, Amina's and Veronika's legs dangling. They politely refused to examine the contents of the toy box I brought down from the attic.

Meho was not ill at ease. His eyes shone as he pulled a bottle of cheap wine from a plastic bag. As we drank it, we conversed in approximate French. "We wait for summons to *Recours*." Their grammar was chaotic but their vocabularies rich in the legal jargon of the refugee. The Recourse, or Appeal, was that of the decision refusing them the right to political asylum. Their initial request had been denied, as was the case with nearly everyone. The Appeal was the leitmotif of their existence. Each family at the *Château* tensely awaited the day when they would be summoned to appeal the government decision that condemned them to undocumented errancy. For some, that decision meant forced return to their homeland, where imprisonment, torture, and even death might be waiting. Their lives hung in the balance of the Appeal.

Gordana paled when she spoke of the Appeal: *"Kom négatif? Kom positif?"* she would repeat.

Meho's eyes would darken. "We need lawyer, and lawyer cost three thousand francs. Where we ever get three thousand francs?"

Their Appeal rejected, they would be, as the polite administrative terms put it, "invited to leave the national territory" within a given time limit. If the deadline were not respected, they would be escorted to the border: the language of living rooms for the fate of families.

Meho and Gordana could barely conjugate the simplest of verbs, but they handled expressions such as "The National Office for Refugees and Stateless Persons", "letter of acknowledgment", *"Préfecture"*, "territorial asylum". Some, they taught me.

My first contact with the drama of the Appeal took place just prior to my first meeting with Gordana. Leila, a young Chechen, was to have been my student, not Gordana. But on the morning of the appointed day of our first lesson, Marie-Toussainte, beside herself, had called me. "Don't come! Something dreadful has happened."

"What . . . ?"

"Leila and Aslan have been rejected. You know, at the Appeal. She tried to commit suicide last night. Thank heaven she's all right! He has begun a hunger strike."

This matter of the Appeal was not to be taken lightly.

Dear Gordana, it is because of Leila's rejection that I met you. Drama building on drama, tragedy on tragedy.

Jacques had the intuition, when Gordana and Meho came that first time, that they would bring us bad luck. He did not mention it at the time, and, in fact, probably stored the reflection away in some small mental closet. He welcomed them courteously and seemed touched by their plight. We didn't speak much about it afterward. In fact, we never spoke much about anything together. But I could see he had been charmed by Meho's grin and offering of wine. That explained, no doubt, why he accepted Meho's coming to the house to build the wall in the kitchen. It was a suggestion of Gordana's. As I filled in my conversation lessons with the minor bric-a-brac of daily life, I told her how Jacques, my husband, had been planning to build a low separation between two parts of our kitchen. "The problem is time," I said. "He can never find the time." I had in no way meant it as a hint, but Gordana seized on the idea.

"That is work for Meho! Why you not ask Meho? He so nervous at home. No work, nothing to do! He will be so happy!"

Jacques was a perfectionist and trusted no one else to do work in the house as he wanted it done. This time, for some unknown reason, he agreed to let Meho, a perfect stranger, build his brick wall for him. Was it charity? Real trust? Or was he feeling, at that time, so overwhelmed with fatigue and apathy that he relinquished his hold on work he normally guarded so closely?

Jacques' job in the fiscal administration, at the *Hôtel des Impôts* in town, devoured the better of his time, sapping even the energy he usually found for building and repairing. At any rate, this once, he seemed prepared to take a risk. I was to pick up Meho and drive him home. On Wednesdays, I had no classes at the *collège,* the junior high school, where I taught English part-time to fourteen-year-olds, twelve hours a week.

Meho worked hard and conscientiously. His father had been a mason, he told me, and so he knew what to do. At noon, I prepared a hot lunch for the two of us, with wide, buttered noodles, chopped beef, and salad. I was careful to avoid pork, for I knew Bosnians were Muslims. In France, the midday meal is hallowed. That this might not be the case in his country did not occur to me.

Meho submitted to my ministering, surprised, perhaps, by the intimacy of the warm food between us. As we sat opposite each other at the kitchen table, I attempted mundane conversation, showing him pictures of our children, grown up now, then some sheet music.

Language was difficult, so I found props. I explained about the town orchestra, where I played the violin. He looked with interest at the *William Tell Overture,* the *Radetzky March,* excerpts from

Dvořák and Shostakovich, but, to my surprise, he was not sure whether Shostakovich was a Russian composer or not. He hummed a few measures, only more or less respecting the rhythm.

Meho presented himself as a professional musician, an oboist. In France that had definite meaning. Knowing music history was part of it, as was surefire sight-reading. He didn't seem to possess that, either. Requirements could be different in other countries, of course.

"Madame Ellen," he said suddenly, "won't you go out sometimes with my wife? She so worried, always nervous. She nervous at me!" He smiled appealingly with the look of the nagged at but forbearing husband.

"Of course, Meho. I'll be glad to."

When Meho spoke my name, it sounded like *AY-lenn*. His use of my first name with *Madame* in front amused me. *Madame Aylenn*. I did not bother to tell him that this was not French usage. He meant well, after all. I knew he wouldn't dare call me simply Ellen, and I didn't really want to hear the more formal Madame Aubert, or just plain *Madame,* distant and courteous.

"She could come help you with housework. I think you have very much to do with job, big house."

"I have a neighbor to help me."

"But you pay her?"

"Yes, I do."

"My wife help you for nothing."

"I couldn't accept that."

When the work was finished, a strong, heavy-sweet odor of sweat filled the kitchen. I opened the window to air the room, while Meho showered in our bathroom, opposite the kitchen where we had eaten together.

> It was the first time, Meho. I'm sure you never thought there would be others. You shut the door, of course. Later, you wouldn't do that.

I was struck by his gentle, uncomprehending expression, when I offered him some money in an envelope. His eyes spoke for him: No, I don't want money. Can't you see I have done this for you?

"Get something for the children . . ." I stopped short, fearing I would hurt his pride.

Marie-Toussainte insisted that a lawyer wasn't necessary for the Appeal. "They only exploit the weak," she said flatly. Her round face was flat too, a crêpe with glasses. But goodness and dedication were written all over it. Occasionally she dropped by at our lessons at the parish hall, making sure everyone was busy, distributing hugs. Leila had returned to the classroom and could be heard hiccuping next door, as she spelled out French words with Sister Agnès de Jésus. Leila was a congenital hiccupper. The more nervous she was, the more the hiccups shook her.

"Her husband is a saint," Marie-Toussainte said, rolling her eyes. The saint had been a freedom fighter, she explained, whom Leila's parents had hidden in their home. He had been compelled to marry her out of gratitude to the family, and together they had escaped. A child had been born and danced involuntarily on Leila's knee with each jerk of her mother's body. Despite their official rejection by France, they hoped to gain time. The need for medical help was a valid excuse, and, so, Leila continued to hiccup through her French lessons. Marie-Toussainte called me from time to time to translate something for her, since I could speak a little Russian.

"I'll never learn," Leila wailed, on one of these occasions.

"Of course you will," Marie-Toussainte replied, while I blundered about for the Russian words. "Can a child be born in less than nine months? Are bridges built overnight?"

Violette Delambre shook her pale, gray-streaked red hair and disagreed with Marie-Toussainte about the lawyer. "Sending those poor refugees to the Appeal without a lawyer is like sending a lamb to slaughter," she said. "They are totally defenseless. They may have the right to an interpreter, but they don't know what arguments to put forth." Madame Delambre headed another humanitarian association (*Assokation,* Gordana pronounced it), this one called "Support for the

Balkans". Like Marie-Toussainte, she was retired, filling her life now with the suspenseful struggles of the asylum seeker.

I learned from Meho that the Balkan support "assokation" sometimes met on Wednesday evenings, as did our orchestra. He played with us now on an oboe lent by the local *Conservatoire de Musique*. His own instrument had burned with the rest of their belongings in Sarajevo, he said. A few weeks after building the wall in our kitchen, he approached me in front of the parish schoolrooms: "Madame Ellen, about that orchestra . . ." Gérard, the conductor, or *dirigent,* in Meho's word, had been happy to enroll another oboist. We were amateurs, all welcome. I felt proud to introduce a former member of the Sarajevo Symphony Orchestra. The mere mention of Sarajevo brought a hush of respect.

After the rehearsal, Meho informed me that Support for the Balkans was meeting that very evening and might still be in session, although it was ten o'clock. I noticed he had chosen orchestra at the conservatory over the association. Couldn't the meeting have been important for him, help somehow to advance his case, or did he assume it was for some useless, routine business?

He looked at his watch as we left the music building together in the autumn night, then broke into a run despite the cobblestones of the old town. I ran alongside him. "Am I going too fast?" he asked, as we sped down the stone steps by the cathedral to the parking lot beyond it.

"I may be old, but I can still run," I laughed.

"I didn't mean you were old! But you might be out of practice running."

I intended to leave him at his meeting, but he suggested I might want to come too. I was prepared to humor him, so I entered, my violin case strapped over my shoulder. Six or seven dark-skinned men sat in a semi-circle, all inhabitants of the *Château,* all subject to the dread Appeal.

Madame Delambre and her friends presided. A young black-haired Albanian woman from Kosovo interpreted. Like Gordana, she had been a nurse in the former Yugoslavia. Her request for political asylum had been granted earlier, and her French was fluent now.

"*Pozdravi Gordanu,*" she said when we left: "Greet Gordana for me." Thanks to my Russian, I picked up the Serbo-Croatian, or Yugoslavian, as the Kozićs called their language. I was being drawn into a new world now, where anxious, dark-complexioned people, invisible to the rest of our town, awaited fateful decisions and pondered momentous choices. A lawyer: Couldn't you do without one? And what if you didn't even speak three words of French? How could you explain your predicament to him anyway? And suppose you did decide to hire one. Where, God help you, would you find the funds?

"*Pozdravi Gordanu,*" I said to Meho, as I dropped him off at the home. I didn't have the tonic accent right. He corrected me with a smile, repeating the word: "Po*zdravi . . . Jacques!*"

Château Lore
Leila

Leila shed bitter tears, sniveling noisily and taking pleasure in it. Aslan was not speaking to her again. All right, she got nervous when that Kozić woman knocked her pan of hot milk off the stove so close to Marie's little face. Marie: She had wanted a French name for her baby, the most typical French name she could think of. Who cared if it was a Christian name? Maybe that would impress them, those authorities. And she had screamed, and, yes, maybe cursed a little. True, she had promised to watch her tongue, but a mother could be anxious for her daughter, couldn't she? Leila ran a hand through her heavy black hair. She had never worn a headscarf, and she never would. Her father set no store by things like that. A girl's virtue is in herself, not in her scarf, he said. Her virtue is in her upbringing and her education.

But Leila had no success at school. The lessons, she understood well enough, but she never could remember them from one time to the next. They were like the soap bubbles children blow. One minute they were there, bright, multicolored; then you put your hand on them, and your fingers clenched against nothing, a bare remembrance of wetness. "I hate school," Leila told her parents. The mistress kept her in the back of the room, distracted as she was by her hiccuping. The other children, tired of mocking her, ignored her.

At recreations, Leila sat in the courtyard with a rag doll tight against her chest, just at the place where the hiccups burst out and shook her. If the others would not play with her, then she would show them how she felt about them. She would say the nastiest words she knew, and she knew plenty. "Bitch, swine, may Allah strike down your grandmother; may your father's seed dry up and your mother's womb shrivel!" She left school as soon as the law permitted.

Leila kept to her mother's skirts, stirring kasha, walking to the bakery occasionally for *sushki* to dunk in her tea. She kept an eye on her younger brother Shamil, but even he mocked her: "Leave me alone, hic, hic," he mimicked. She thrashed out at him but got sent packing to her room if ever her mother caught her.

Her mother and father exchanged doleful looks. "We'll never marry off this one," they lamented. Who would want a hiccuping shrew? Were it not for her handicap, Leila was a handsome enough young woman, with a round face and hips, and the point of a widow's peak above arched eyebrows.

It was the war for independence that had brought her Aslan, and, although she knew that, she entertained the idea that he had married her for love. Her father had saved Aslan's life by hiding him in the coal shed, when the Russian Army swept through their quarter of Grozny. Ten days and nights he had spent there behind the winter's supply of coal, choking in the dust and the airless cabin, the black so ingrained in his pores, he thought he would be black forever.

It was Leila who took him water and bread and emptied his pail. "I, too, am a rebel," she told herself. "I am fighting for our independence and risking my life each time I cross this damned courtyard."

The bombing drove her parents and Shamil to the hills, but she said she would stay with Aslan. There was a price on his head. Without that price, perhaps she would not have noticed him, skinny as a scarecrow, high cheek-boned, with brown hair already thinning despite his young age.

Leila's parents returned to a charred shell of a house, the coal shed still intact. Their daughter huddled with Aslan, both as black as chimney sweeps, thinner than before, wan, anguished, alive. Aslan thanked

Leila profusely. Without her, he recognized, he would have died of thirst. Without her parents' hospitality, he would be a dead man.

"I would like a word with you, young man," Leila's father said.

The marriage was celebrated in haste and simplicity. Leila had no wedding ornaments beyond her own cinder-black hair, falling like a veil on her shoulders.

Her wedding night was a nightmare, for her husband did not want her. Aslan gritted his teeth, trying to feel only the warm, round hips, to forget the nervous hiccups that shook his bride. He resolved to force loving words to his lips: "Calm, my dove, my dark-eyed one!" He had to prove himself a man. He shut his eyes. If only he could shut his ears. They lay side by side in the ruins of a burned-out flat. A sofa remained, the better part of a roof.

When Leila finally slept, hot with spite and disappointment, her hiccups subsided. Aslan, leaning above her on one elbow, stroked her bare thighs. At last, he felt a swelling, a rising. His hand found her curly, black mound and gently pushed open the labia.

Leila awoke screaming, but she clung to him. If only she could master the jagged jerking of her breathing, if only this once. Marie was conceived that sweaty dawn, and Aslan had not touched Leila since.

Two

The Slavic Society where I studied Russian decided on a Christmas party. Plans were made; each member was to bring food or drink. Cédric, the spirited young man who headed the group, thought we ought to have some live music, but that would be too much for our budget. Meho immediately came to mind; he could play the accordion. I knew that from the photographs Gordana had shown me. He would surely be content with whatever our budget permitted, and this work needn't be declared. The problem would be finding an instrument. I promised to ask him.

The Kozić family sat in a row once again on our sofa. Suada was the image of her mother, olive skin, strong chin. Amina, the shy one, was porcelain pale, with Gordana's transparent, green gaze under straight, black bangs. "She just like my mother," Gordana said.

"I can see your mother is very beautiful."

"Yes, very beautiful."

Veronika, two now, made faces. She mimed and mimicked, giggled and squirmed next to her two sisters. Her hair was a tangle of shiny onyx-black curls. Meho was pleased with the job offer and thought he could borrow an accordion, but Gordana's reaction puzzled me.

"Why job for Meho? Why everything for Meho?"

"But Gordana," I said, "it's because Meho is the one who plays music. If I get sick, it's you I'll call to help me, not Meho."

This appeared to mollify her, but before our next lesson, I looked carefully through my clothing to see what I could give her. I found a black skirt, perfectly new, that I had never been able to wear; it was too small. I told her she needn't accept, if it didn't please her. She might know someone at the *Château* who could use it. She glanced at the skirt and pushed the plastic bag to one side but carried it off with her after the lesson.

> *Gordana, why were you jealous of your own husband's good fortune? You weren't rivals, were you? So, you thought I was favoring him? I wasn't, you know. To me, helping one meant helping the other. What did you sense?*

Jacques and I went to the *Château* to pick up Meho and his borrowed accordion for the party. "However did you get one?" I asked, intrigued by his resourcefulness.

"Yugoslav I know in town lend it," he said. "Didn't want to at first. Not really very nice man."

"But you talked him into it?"

"He finally say OK, if I bring back tomorrow."

Gordana and the girls came down to say good-bye in the hall. Suada danced up and down, pleading to come to the party with us. Meho was ready to give in, but Gordana's frown said no. Her black eyebrows furrowed the skin between and scolded them both. Bedtime was bedtime.

I was a little nervous about my musician; I had never heard him play. "Perhaps you should begin now," I said, after the guests had begun milling about with their glasses of pale Vouvray. There had been no need for doubt. Meho's fingers sped unhesitatingly over the keys, pushing, pulling, cajoling the instrument, while sweat poured from his forehead. He hadn't played in years, perhaps. I wondered, in fact, when he had last had an accordion in hand.

I danced to the slower melodies with Jacques, while Meho watched us, his expression benign. He played with a half-smile and a distant look, apparently searching his memory for the tunes or seeking variations. He must be remembering, I imagined, other festivities in other places, other musicians, the music of other tongues.

His eyes twinkled with unspoken laughter as we left. He moved in confidently between Jacques and me, taking my arm, leading me down the steps.

> *That movement, Meho: taking possession. What pleased you the most that evening? The folk songs you played? The attention you received? Or taking my arm that way?*

On the afternoon of Christmas Eve, the Kozić family announced that we should be their guests. We had already dropped by the *Château*, where communal rooms could be used for receiving guests. Under no circumstances were we allowed to visit the families in their private rooms. Gordana laid the table in a corner of the former chapel, which served as a living room. "Happy New Year" in a variety of languages and alphabets had been printed by hand across a banner that hung above the low table, while a tall pine tree stood in a corner opposite. Children of all shades and accents skipped in and out of the room.

Our son Jeremy and his wife, Adeline, accompanied us with their blond little Léo, six months old, in their arms. Meho seized upon Léo, cradling him, feeding the child his bottle. He never let go of him during our visit. Suada grabbed Adeline and led her around the *Château* in defiance of the rules.

"She is not little girl," Meho reprimanded. "She the mother of baby!" Adeline, her glasses halfway down her nose, pushing aside a lock of straight, dark hair, grasped Suada's hand, following her patiently upstairs to where Pierre, the children's pigeon, flew around the room. Meho had trapped him in the park, and he had become their mascot, free in their tight quarters, until I brought our old blue birdcage to Gordana one day.

The table was covered with soft drinks, tea, coffee, crackers, and a variety of cakes, some iced in bright colors. "Did you make all these, Gordana?" I was ready to show how impressed I was.

"Yes!" she declared proudly.

"She didn't make them," Suada piped up, scornful. "They were left over from the party the home organized yesterday. The other ladies made them."

Gordana said nothing, nor did I.

> *What's a little white lie, if it made you feel better, Gordana? But, you know I would never have held it against you, if you'd admitted the truth about the cakes. It was such an unimportant thing. Lying isn't unimportant, though. Lying can be a way of life. Omitting the truth can be another way, subtle, hypocritical. I never thought it could become my own familiar way.*

It was Sunday afternoon, and the orchestra was leaving for a concert in another town, two hours away by coach. Our instruments in the hold, we climbed on, a noisy group of mixed ages, most of us in our formal, black and white dress. There was Meho, already tranquilly seated when I arrived. He was wearing jeans and a colored shirt. I hesitated. Should I sit next to him or take a place next to Yvonne, a violinist too?

She was short and heavy-bottomed, her mahogany-dyed curls in a tight permanent. Below thick, gold-rimmed glasses, her cheeks were falling to jowls. How I hoped I did not resemble this patently middle-aged woman, who was, I had to admit, younger than I. I suspected she was watching what I would do. I forced myself to choose her, and we chatted idly.

We were casual friends, although I had never really penetrated the chilly armor that protected her. She spurned anyone who did not meet her musical standards. I suspected I did not make the grade myself. Her husband, Frédéric, taught the clarinet and composition at the conservatory, and her only daughter, a clarinetist too, had steamed brilliantly through to national first prizes and to work as a professional.

"Aren't you sitting with your Croatian friend?" Yvonne asked. No one could get his origins straight.

"I thought someone else might sit with him, and that way he could make a new acquaintance."

No one had, however, and he rode with a calm, expectant look on his face. His clothing worried me; would he have the necessary formal wear? "Meho, have you got a white shirt?" I finally ventured, as we were getting off. He nodded toward the plastic bag he was carrying.

"Don't worry!" He didn't own a suit, but that, he apparently thought, would be all right.

I decided to introduce him to Yvonne. "The Sarajevo Symphony?" She was duly impressed. "My daughter was there with a group of musicians, when Zubin Mehta made an appearance at the city hall."

"Zubin Mehta?" He didn't appear to recognize the name.

"Who was conducting when you played?" she asked.

Meho was evasive. "We always changed conductors," he said. I knew, as she did, that this was quite plausible.

Meho was obviously not eager to discuss the symphony, just as he never discussed the war nor made any mention of the ethnic rivalries involved. I found him detached and impartial. A Bosnian Muslim, I thought, would harbor some hard feelings toward the Serbs, but Meho seemed above that. He pulled a bright red apple out of his plastic bag and insisted I eat it. "But, Meho, I'm not hungry. Not now." I had to promise I would eat it after the concert. "Don't forget to remind Gordana she has a lesson tomorrow morning."

"Can I come too?" he asked playfully. It didn't occur to me he might be serious.

At the meal after the concert, the orchestra members were invited to seat themselves at long tables in a municipal dining hall. Yvonne sat on one side of me; I saved a place for Meho this time, on the other side. I noticed a silver identity bracelet, slack around his wrist, with "Nadir" engraved on it. "Who is Nadir?" I asked.

"My brother."

Why would he be wearing his brother's bracelet? Dead in the war, no doubt, and that I did not dare ask. I squirmed a little on my chair. My back hurt after playing. Meho noticed immediately and began massaging my back, rubbing his hand up and down my spinal column, over the bump where my bra fastened.

"Well, well, we're being spoiled, aren't we?" said Yvonne, lifting a reddish-brown eyebrow.

What would she think of that? What on earth had got into him? I was surprised, uncomfortable, yet pleased. Some nerve he had, but he obviously liked me, even felt proprietary toward me, or he wouldn't be doing that.

As soon as the others had dispersed from the coach, at last back in our quiet town of Laudes-la-Romaine, he took my arm and pulled me close to him. "Well, are we going to your place?" he quipped.

Melisand, I think I've got myself an admirer. You know, Meho, our Bosnian friend? It's so funny, how he tries to flirt with me.

Melisand was my twenty-five-year old daughter, my child and yet my closest confidante. She was married and worked in Brussels. We kept in touch daily, thanks to the lightning miracle of e-mail. I was going to tell Jacques, too, about my new fan, but something stopped me at the last second. I could have an admirer, couldn't I? What difference did it make? Jacques spoke to me so little, anyway. I didn't think he would care.

Gordana and Meho opted for the lawyer. She was interested in human rights cases. She wouldn't defend them for nothing but agreed that they should pay her in modest, monthly installments. She would study their dossier and make the best of it. The money they paid her would come from the weekly stipend they received from the association that housed them, France-Sanctuaire. Since refugees were not allowed to work, they would just have to pull their belts a little tighter.

When the summons before the Appeals Commission in Paris finally came, the lawyer requested a postponement; she wasn't free that day. The wait continued, and Meho seemed to take it in stride. If they were to be sent back, that was time gained, after all. How can they stand it, I wondered. How can they get up each morning without knowing where they will live in a year?

Gordana told me she had no appetite: "Coffee, cigarettes, that's all. I very nervous." Except during her lessons, Gordana always had a cigarette in hand, and her teeth were slightly stained. "Meho not so nervous, but he think a lot. He think," she said, touching her temple with her forefinger.

He put his anxiety into activity. Mornings, he went running, she told me. Twice a week he took a special French course for foreigners at the university, and, twice more, lessons with Sister Agnès de Jésus at the parish hall. He practiced his borrowed oboe at the conservatory, "getting his fingers back," as he called it.

Gordana sniffed at this. "I tell him life is for him, not me." She said she was bored with the home where the children kept her captive, tired of keeping their two rooms neat, of cooking in the communal kitchen, taking her turn at the housework, nursing the baby. At two, Veronika still screamed for her mother's breast every evening, and Gordana would not wean her. More likely, it was she, in her insecurity, who could not wean herself from the child.

Gordana described for me the atmosphere of the kitchen, where the *Château* women worked. Leila would shriek in defense of her burner and have them all damned to hell. Gordana said she and the other mothers kept their children as far from her as possible. They'd be learning all the worst words in the Russian language, the worst brand of vulgarity.

I could see the scene, the large stoves with multiple electric burners lining one wall. On another, I imagined rows of smudgy, once white cupboards, each labeled with a family name and padlocked. The women would come and go, some in aprons, others with their heads covered. At all hours, odors of onions and frying emanated from the kitchen and filled the *Château* with a masquerade of hominess.

The communal dining room had its own pervasive odor, too. It was there that I always found someone to fetch the Kozić family for me, frequently Smaïl, a young compatriot of theirs, who bounded up willingly to the second floor. A television set in one corner was on continually, a group of men in front of it. Other men sat together at the long, Formica-topped tables, their voices low in a mélange of languages, Russian, Albanian, Serbo-Croatian, and a sort of semi-French lingo: *Château* French, I called it. Their wives were close to invisible. Occasionally I would glimpse one gliding like a shadow along a corridor or entering the small library, a child in tow.

Although I had not seen their rooms, I knew Gordana and Meho were privileged. They had two, thanks to their three children. Families with one or two children had to make do with only one room. Marie-Toussainte told me how one father of two teenagers had lamented to her that he would give anything for one night alone with his wife, only one. Such was *la vie de Château*.

Gordana confided to me that Meho was a spendthrift. "He not realize. He wanted to buy carpet for our room, to sit on in front of TV. Imagine! We no need carpet!" This seemed surprising, indeed, as did the very fact that they had a TV. A basic necessity, assuredly.

I had seen the *Château* toilets. These, too, were communal, rows of narrow cabins, like the ones in schools. The odor was sharp, even though the women took turns cleaning them.

One can catch infections in a place like that, Gordana. You said you got that infection from me, but I never, never had any infection.

Château Lore
Leila

Aslan and Leila conspired as to how they could move the cold heart of the French authorities. There was no going back to Chechnya now, nothing but ruins for Marie to call home.

Aslan had broken with the Islamic forces shortly before the air attacks and the pursuit of the Russian soldiers that took him to Leila's home. He had disagreed sharply about the kidnapping of a young Russian private. There would be a ransom posted, and it would bring money for the cause, his chiefs argued, but Aslan realized they were corrupt. The money would be shared between the Russian officer who facilitated the kidnapping and his own chief.

Disgusted, Aslan had fled, kalashnikov in hand, fled from his own as from the Russians. But no official paper could possibly exist to prove this. The Appeals Commission had turned a deaf ear to his explanations. Here was another foreigner with no special qualifications, no tangible proof of persecution, nothing but one more wearying story of rebellion and a war-torn city. "France cannot host all the misery of the world," one politician had resoundingly proclaimed on national television. It was not about to.

Leila gestured in the direction of the shoebox that served as their medicine cabinet. "I'll swallow them all tonight," she said, "but promise me you'll call someone!"

"Of course I will," Aslan replied. "You'll be all right. You haven't got half the bottle left anyway. And tomorrow I'll announce a hunger strike. I'll hold out. You'll see."

That night Aslan ran to get the night attendant, Madame Charpentier. She arrived at nine each evening and watched television for some time in the dining room with the refugees, then settled in the little office with the low cot, where she could read and knit. The home was like a dormitory, with a concierge always on guard, a native speaker in case of emergency, making sure the rules were respected. No one was allowed upstairs, and all visitors were to leave the common rooms by ten o'clock. Madame Charpentier was a plump, middle-aged woman, dressed in a light blue smock, her hair carefully curled and sprayed. She was a naturally compassionate soul and never without a kind word for the pensioners. She was alarmed at the sight of Aslan, disheveled, his pajama bottoms askew, as he panted out the news: "It's my wife. She took all of her tranquilizers at once. She couldn't bear the news. The Appeal, you know; we've been rejected. The letter came this morning. Please, Madame, call a doctor!"

The number of pills swallowed and their strength was not dangerous, but Leila slept soundly, the wretched letter clutched in her hand. Her hiccups had ceased. The doctor slapped her awake and ordered Aslan to ply her with great quantities of strong tea all night. In the morning, pale and exhausted, he announced his hunger strike to Elisabeth, the secretary, who called Marie-Toussainte.

Leila, propped on pillows, was pouting when she arrived. "My poor child! You must pull yourselves together, both of you." She hugged Leila, then kissed little Marie, who played at the foot of the bed, twisting fringe from the bedspread. "You came to France to live, not to die!"

"They no want us here." Leila spoke in a peeved tone. The usual fire had gone out of her voice.

"It's not a question of wanting or not wanting," said Marie-Toussainte. "It's not personal, against you, don't you see that? There are so many, many requests. Nearly everyone is rejected at the first Appeal.

Afterward, you can request territorial asylum. You'll see. You have your chances just as much as anyone else. You've got to believe it. Look at your Marie there, so darling. What would she do without a mother, without a father? Did you think of her when you took those pills last night, Leila? Did you?" Leila sulked.

"And you, Aslan, don't you see your women need a strong, healthy man to look after them? That's enough about this not eating."

Aslan didn't like being scolded by a woman, even if she could easily have been his mother. There was truth to her words, though. Suicide was cowardly; playing at suicide was foolish and theatrical. Besides, the Appeals Commission would never even hear about it. He sighed, swallowing the bitterness of defeat and more waiting. If only he could stay in France, he could be freed from the punishing misery that crushed his broken country, freed too from his obligations in the eyes of all those that remained there and knew him, freed, he had begun to hope, from Leila and her infernal ill-temper.

"Take heart, dears," Marie-Toussainte comforted, as she left. "I'll call the new volunteer who was to give you your French lesson today, Leila, and tell her you're not up to it. You can start when you're feeling better."

Three

The administration that ruled on the fate of foreigners proceeded to the case of Meho and Gordana Kozić and their three children. They were notified of the date of their Appeal. The director of the Refugee Home, Monsieur Lenoir, made plans to drive them to Paris, where their lawyer would join them between two other appointments in a busy schedule. It was a gray day in February, and it rained. I waited until the following Monday to ask Gordana how it had gone.

Meho was with her in the parish classroom. They looked somber. "We won't get the answer for awhile," Gordana said.

"But your impression? What is your feeling about it?"

"The lawyer just said, 'I'm sorry, I'm so very sorry.'"

Veronika kicked in her stroller and screamed. A tear pearled on Gordana's sallow cheek, settled in the dark hollow beneath her eye, then made its way slowly down, spreading, wetting. "Three of children, three. Where we go with three of children?"

"Have you finished?" Meho was brusque with her. I had never seen him like this. "Madame Ellen," he said, "it's no good to cry. Crying very bad for the health." I pressed Gordana's hand. Her husband wasn't going to comfort her.

"There one thing we did not tell them. Maybe we should have. I did not tell, but I never try to hide it either."

"Meho, what?"

"Where we come from."

"Don't you come from Sarajevo?"

"Yes, from Sarajevo, from Bosnia. But we not really Bosnian. We Rom."

"Rom? You mean you're Gypsies? What difference does it make?" I did not want them to think it made any for me.

"Everyone Bosnian, Croat, Serb, and me, who am I, me?" asked Gordana. "I *Gypsy.*" She used the European word that I had spoken. The syllables rang with despair.

"I was *intellectuall* for Gypsies in Sarajevo," said Meho. His Yugoslavian accent made the word stand out. "I wanted to make school for Roma children. I have troubles with city hall in Sarajevo, with Bosnian government."

I had no advice. I was a teacher, not a lawyer, and the problems of asylum seekers were new to me. The only thing I could offer was comfort. Meho walked ahead of us as we left the building. Gordana held back next to me. I put my arm around her shoulders in the cherry parka. Together, we pushed Veronika.

The skirting at the bottom of our corridor was made up of tiles. Jacques spent some time repairing it, gluing back the tiles that had come loose. He worked carefully, holding the newly glued tiles in place with rods of wood that crossed the hall. "Watch out for them," he warned me, before going to the back room where we kept our television, to watch the evening news.

I finished cleaning the kitchen, then turned out the lights. I didn't need light to find my way around my own house. I knew it by heart. My ankles caught in the first rod, and, trying to regain my balance, I only twisted my feet, stuck in the forgotten trap. I fell so abruptly and so hard that I let out a cry. The length of me, 5 feet 9 inches, was stretched out on the floor. I was too dazed to move. Pain shot through my legs.

Jacques came through the kitchen. "What now? Oh, you fell. I told you to be careful." He turned and went back to his program.

It was another pretext for something to talk about at my lesson with Gordana. I made light of it, but I showed her the black and blue marks on my feet, ankles and shin. She recommended compresses of bread soaked in red wine, a good Bosnian remedy, she assured me. I tried it, so I could tell her I had.

Meho telephoned that afternoon. He was concerned, he said. "Are you all right? Are you sure you're all right?"

"I'll survive, honestly! It's nothing at all!" I laughed it off, although my shin still hurt. Apparently he needed an excuse to talk to someone.

Was that it, Meho? You wanted to make conversation with someone?

How lonely to be a refugee, I thought, and Meho was a sociable sort. I was glad he at least knew the Aubert family, Jacques and Ellen, now.

Jacques, it was Meho who asked those simple words, 'Are you all right?' You turned away, disgusted one more time with my awkwardness. You never even held out your hand to help me up. A bruise on my leg, another on my soul. You didn't know it, nor did I, but when I fell that day, it was into his arms that I fell.

A barrier of depression separated Jacques from me. Some inner, incommunicable pain deprived him of words. Not the everyday words with which we go about our business, but the words of life and love. We talked, indeed, at least occasionally, about a current event, a film on TV, even about the people we knew. Jacques was harsh, critical; no one ever reached his standards. He, himself, of course, did not reach his standards. We cannot love others, when we despise ourselves.

Jacques was tall, refined, a real intellectual, as I imagined one to be. His wavy, chestnut hair was graying, now that he had reached his early fifties. His hazel eyes were his most expressive feature, but, for the better part of a decade, a dark curtain had been drawn across the back of them. I couldn't get through it, not for any lack of trying. I had grown accustomed to his closed face at mealtimes. "Please," I would beg, "speak to a doctor!"

"I have nothing to say to a doctor," he would reply. "Why should I see a doctor when I'm perfectly fine?"

What could I say to that, when everything belied it? He who had been so gentle a young man became irritable, cutting, aggressive. I cringed when I approached him. His inner demons snapped out at the world around him.

Melisand would fly to my side: "It's not Mom's fault," she would say, putting her arms around me, defender of the oppressed, straightening her back and glaring at her father. She and I would go out to cafés and talk for hours in the warm, smoky atmospheres about what was happening to him, and what we could do about it.

"What have I done?" I would ask her. "What have I not done? What should I do?"

We imagined slipping anti-depressants into his food. My unflinching ally, she would say, "Whatever happens, Mom, I will always be on your side."

Finally one day, gathering my courage, I suggested to Jacques that we might separate. He never had anything to say to me; we had nothing to say to each other. My voice was shaky and, no doubt, unconvincing. Did he assume I was just overwrought that day? Playacting? Nothing in his attitude indicated that he felt threatened by my words. I was a child brandishing a water pistol, drumming it against an adult's strong thigh. Enveloped in his familiar *tenebrae*, Jacques scarcely paid attention.

I was not one to make scenes. The incredible powers of adaptation I had, adapting to a new language, country, culture, played their part here too. I made a habit of being rejected, without measuring the emotional attrition.

Pressed by Melisand, Jacques finally agreed to see a psychiatrist. "Love, as far as I understand it, means that people talk to each other," she said one day, surprising him as he brooded. "I love you, Daddy, but you won't ever let us share what's wrong. Don't think we can't see it, either. Please stop shutting us all out! Please do something!"

He looked away, moved, not wanting us to see the tears welling in the shadows of his eyes. When I made an appointment with a psychiatrist, he wrote down the date without comment and went to the consultation.

Jacques began a tentative voyage of reconciliation with himself. After months of trial and error, the doctor hit upon Prozac, which suited his moody patient, reawakening some of his former kindness. Our bonds, however, had been distended, if not cut. Silence had given birth to silence, and I kept quiet now, too. Meeting his indifference year after desolate year had hurt too much. I had taught myself to react in kind and could not undo that lesson overnight. I had banished the words of affection from my vocabulary. The language of love must travel a two-way road. We lived side by side.

Gordana recommended honey and grated lemon rind for the asthma that left Jacques breathless, begging for air that scraped and hurt as it fought its way in. The stricture of his vital passages mimicked that of his soul, too raw and shrunken to let the full flow of life through. His attacks were frequent.

"Have you made my remedy?" she asked me.

"No, not yet."

The next time, she held out a jam jar to me. It contained her mixture. "One spoonful every day at breakfast," she prescribed.

"Well, have you given Jacques the lemon-honey?" Meho asked. I was driving him back to the *Château* after a Wednesday evening orchestra rehearsal.

"Oh, I forgot!"

"That's not good," he smiled. "If my wife not take care of me when I'm sick, I would not stay with her."

"You mean Jacques ought to leave me?" My tone was light-hearted.

"No, that's not what I wanted to say." He paused, earnest: "Who takes care of you, Madame Ellen, when you are sick?"

I thought an instant. "My daughter," I replied.

"But your daughter is not with you," he said gently.
"True. I take care of myself when I'm sick."

From my schoolroom chats with Gordana, I got a good idea of the tension that prevailed at the Refugee Home. Each family eyed the others, wondering which ones would come to be counted in the lucky statistics of the accepted. Jealousy and rivalry were nourished by the forced idleness, the inescapable promiscuity of the common rooms. Secrets were carefully guarded, but gossip flourished. The tidbits Gordana reported to me made a doleful collection:

"She only lives with him; he's not her husband."

"Would you believe it? And they call themselves good Muslims!"

"He says he's Turkish. So why does he understand us when we speak Romany?"

"They say they'll be persecuted if they go back. They just want a free lunch."

"Their son is always picking on my daughter. I'm going to see the director about it."

"Have you seen what she feeds her children?"

"They're always trying to get in favor with Monsieur Lenoir. Did you notice? They invited him for coffee again today."

"I don't like him. He's a black."

This last term, directly out of the Balkans, referred to Meho and was related to me by an outraged Marie-Toussainte, hard put to understand that racism could continue to prevail among the downtrodden. Meho's Gypsy origins were not a secret for everyone. The age-old prejudices were imported along with the worn suitcases and tenuous hopes.

Even *Château* personnel were not immune to the high voltage of the atmosphere and sometimes took sides or succumbed to bursts of rage or annoyance. Such was the case with Elisabeth, secretary at our local branch of France-Sanctuaire.

A young woman in her mid-thirties, she was sitting one day at a table in the dining room with the Kozić family, her long chestnut hair flowing down the back of her chair. Suddenly tempted, her eyes brimming with mischief, little Veronika ran to her and pulled it with all her two-year-old might.

Elisabeth bounded from her chair, caught Veronika by her short black pigtails and held her up by them until the child screamed with pain. "I'll teach you to pull people's hair," she scolded. Meho, already overwrought, snatched his daughter away, tears in his eyes.

"Leave her alone!" he shouted. "She only a baby."

"Go back to your country!" Elisabeth sneered. "We don't need you here."

"France is my country now," he shouted, raising his voice another notch. "And you, old maid, go back to your father's house!"

Gordana recounted this incident to me with obvious pride. "Meho cry," she said, touching her cheek where the tears had overflowed, "and he turn over the table. But Mademoiselle Elisabeth very nasty girl. She know just what to say to hurt us. She know we have no more country."

Meho and I were riding once again to the *Château* in my little Peugeot. He wondered that I never locked it. "Really, Meho, if you wanted to steal a car, would you take this one?" It was an old model 205, with a grinning radiator grill, its pistachio-green flanks marred by numerous scars and scratches, its motor showing the first chugging signs of senility. The evening was chilly; the town lighting got dimmer as we began our climb toward the home.

"It is hard, Madame Ellen, to be a foreigner." It was the only time I had seen Meho discouraged, short, bitter lines at each corner of his mouth.

"I know, I really know. But you won't always be a foreigner here." I didn't know what else to say. Meho had fled a hostile environment for an unwelcoming one, one hell for another, albeit lesser. Mine was the outheld hand.

We were players in a drama whose final act I could never guess, although I thought I knew the roles, his and mine:

> "In the charcoal of my eyes burn the embers of roadside fires; your pretty streets hold no stopping place for a poor man with the dust of war and sorrow clinging to his feet. Like all of my people, wherever I turn my Bohemian step, I am an outcast."
>
> "No, abide with us, and let me speak the language to you until it rings true and familiar. Abide, and I will make this your home."

How could he not cling to me? Seeker of asylum, seeker of consolation.

A public demonstration in defense of the undocumented was organized in front of the *Préfecture,* the regional headquarters of the Republic, by a number of anti-racist, anti-fascist associations. "The Communist League is participating," said Marie-Toussainte. "We must be sure to keep away from this." The *Comité d'Entr'aide Catholique* was strictly apolitical. We had to bide our time, Marie-Toussainte told us, and avoid the crowd in front of the eighteenth-century government building.

Despite her warning, I watched from a safe distance the assembled militants and onlookers, the convinced and the curious. The imposing *Préfecture* structure, sober in red-tinged brownstone, stood back from the street, isolated by gardens and a parking lot. The crowd amassed before the gold-tipped, wrought iron gates, close to the sidewalk. Placards proclaimed: "Support the Undocumented!", "Papers for All Asylum Seekers", "Grant Papers to Foreign Students!".

Oleg Petrov, the pale blond theology student from Russia, held up a sign of his own making: "The Prefect Says NO". He too lived in the *Château* with his thin, worried-looking, young wife and their little son, Vania, born since their arrival. Their requests for asylum had been refused successively, down to the last, the one for territorial asylum. This one was the Prefect's to grant or refuse, but, as Oleg's sign proclaimed, he had said no. The official decision was unswayed, although it might have been influenced by the birth of their child on French national territory, "on French soil", as the articles of a decree read. Oleg Petrov scowled beneath his homemade placard, while a journalist focused on him.

The people in front of the gates came and went with their signs held high, grouping and regrouping according to their associations or political leanings, talking, moving, letting themselves be photographed.

Meho scrupulously avoided the gathering as he did any occasion that attracted public notice.

Suleyman Osayin had apparently had his fill of demonstrations back home in Sofia and kept to the *Château*.

The women left this sort of politics up to their men, and Gordana agreed with Meho: "We want no trouble, no offend anybody. We wait, just wait."

You, the sans-papiers, *the undocumented, the faceless, the identity-less, the country-less: Wait, wait out your lives! Your country will not have you, nor will ours. Your only land is the heart of your friends. I am your friend, Gordana. I am your friend, Meho.*

A short time after the demonstration, Gordana consented to leave the *Château* and come to the house again. She had made Bosnian *pita* for us, wrapping it carefully in a white dishtowel and carrying it on the bus the family took. I met them at the bus stop, and they piled into my car. Gordana had been promising to make this Bosnian specialty for us. Moreover, it was a way of honoring her father. The Muslim (*Musleemish*) custom, she explained, when you have lost someone dear to you, is to prepare a meal for friends with his favorite food.

In the kitchen, as we set the table, Gordana told me how strange Meho had been about her father's death. "He call friend in Yugoslavia. Friend tell him about my papa, and Meho say nothing for one week. Then he ask me, 'You miss mama and papa? You like to see them?' I say, of course I want to see mama and papa. When he tell me my papa dead, I faint."

What was it, Meho? Cowardice? You didn't know how to tell her? You didn't dare to tell her? You knew how sensitive she was, didn't you?

Jacques and I respectfully tasted her father's favorite dish, coils of bread dough wound into a flat, oily disc, a suggestion of ground beef filling the intervals. It must be difficult to pay a lawyer and buy meat too, I thought. This offering was a rare one, though, for Gordana didn't go out of her rooms willingly. She chafed at the *Château* and its constraints yet clung to its sturdy walls as her only home port. As the winter wore on, she found increasingly frequent excuses for missing her lessons. One of the girls had a cold, the flu; she herself had a cough. Amina needed an operation on her teeth, spoiled by too many sweets, too many years of fanciful diet and Red Cross packages.

"Why did you give them so many sweets?" I asked Meho.

"The children, they wanted."

"Of course they wanted them, but you are the parents, aren't you?"

In this culture, children had the freedom of their whims. Meho's and Gordana's were astonishingly good for being so rarely scolded. A natural reserve kept them in check. Their parents' circumspect behavior had penetrated their young minds. They knew without knowing that when your fate is undecided, the best is to behave.

Veronika, I found out later, was running a fever the day I invited the family for dinner with my friend Thérèse. She and I had struggled over Russian together, groaning at its multitude of declensions, its infinity of hard and soft nouns, masculine, feminine and neuter, resolutely requiring, we would laugh, the minds of chess champions or violin virtuosi to master.

Then, her marriage in tatters, Thérèse had suddenly moved to the south of France, in need of a new job, ready, despite her fifty-six years, to turn a page and fill in a blank leaf in her life. I nearly envied her, admiring her courage and initiative. I, too, I thought, should pack up and move away. I was too passive, too resigned. Like the true Frenchwoman she was, Thérèse was loath to discuss her personal problems in detail, but we shared a complicity that was not fully dependent on words.

That evening, she had helped me prepare the *pot-au-feu* and lay the table for seven. She counted herself, Jacques and me, and the Kozić family. Meho appeared on the doorstep with Suada and Amina. "Gordana, she not want to go out," he said, offering no further explanation.

"Let's go and get her! We'll convince her," Jacques suggested. He wanted to help. He could surely perceive and comprehend Gordana's feelings of depression, the no-future bleakness, the impulse to withdraw, to shun the company that would thrust its cheerfulness at her like a bitter challenge. But he had begun his own upward climb and was ready to proffer a hand.

Meho shrugged. "She won't change her mind."

> *Meho, why didn't you tell us everything? The fever, the doctor who had come in the night? Didn't you know how to say all that in our language? Or was it just your way with half-truths?*

Thérèse and Meho exchanged a few polite words, she in her schoolgirl Russian, he in Serbo-Croatian, each understanding the other. I caught: "Sarajevo is a big town": *grad,* he said. "Ah yes, *gorod,*" Thérèse replied, using the word we had learned. Her face crinkled into a broad smile. She was slight, with sunny curls, and a wide sweatshirt overlapping tight jeans.

At eight o'clock, our French dinnertime, we sat down to a meal. Meho and Suada allowed me to serve them, pushed the morsels of beef and the vegetables around on their plates and sent them back full.

They had already eaten, I guessed. "Meho, I told you it was for dinner!" He smiled, chagrined. He had not understood me.

After dinner, we moved to the living room and sat around the piano, urging Meho to play for us. I wanted to show him off, to impress Thérèse with my find, this refugee with the hidden talents. I knew he was no wind-up, music box toy in embroidered vest, but I wanted him to be the center of attention, to warm himself in our smiling approval.

He must have felt my confidence. At ease for the first time in front of our piano, he improvised accompaniments to songs we all knew, American, French, even Russian ones. "Oh, When the saints . . .", "Oh, Susanna!", *"La vie en rose"*, *"Chevaliers de la table ronde . . ."*, "Moscow Nights", "Katiusha".

"How you do play!" Thérèse told him, and I basked in her pleasure. Meho and Suada departed with a bouquet of our first daffodils for Gordana.

Meho had appeared totally carefree that evening, in spite of Gordana's repetitive, somber moods and the children's illnesses. This buoyant cheerfulness persisted through the following days, as he applied himself to our orchestra program. During a break at rehearsal, he sat behind my chair in the first violin section. "I see at university, for music group there, they need oboist and violinists. Let's go! We go, yes?"

"Meho, I haven't got the time," I replied, amused by his childish enthusiasm. The campus orchestra was bound to be disparate and highly amateur.

Did you like playing so?

February: I was taking stock again. Two years before, on Valentine's Day, I had left a letter of seven pages, handwritten in black ink, for Jacques to find when I returned home, later that day than he. I had to be sure he would have time to think my words over, words too full of tears for me to voice. Now I read over parts of what I had written:

I have been excluded, Jacques, from your life, to the point of having no more name, let alone a name of endearment. Names and words, you will tell me, are only words; it is our acts that speak. So then, where is the gesture of tenderness, the comfort, the interest one has in the other, the solace, the encouragement, the occasional compliment, the thanks, the concern for the health of that person with whom we are one flesh?

In a moment of inspiration, Melisand and I found what we thought might be the key: acting, that passion of your younger days! I do not recall which of us had the idea first, but I immediately put myself to it, while we crossed our fingers. You would participate in the amateur theater group I had found. To our joy, you accepted. I believed for a time that you were saved, but your night was too dark, and acting cannot cure everything.

You cannot imagine my relief, when, after your first meeting with a psychiatrist, you said he had prescribed lithium for you. Lithium! A metal. A chemical. A substance which aids in depression. What if, finally, it was not your character which had altered irremediably? What if we did not have to go on in ineluctable, bleak indifference one to the other?

What if, in fact, you were ill? I saw there an immense hope, because, if you say illness, then you say treatment; if you say treatment, you say betterment, healing. A love that is gone cannot be rekindled, but an illness can be cured. How could I not have reacted earlier? But then, how can the layman discern the fine line that separates personality from pathology? The word illness gives me hope.

I will always be there, if you accept this evident thing: to seek help for your illness. I have borne much and I will bear more, again and as much as I must, because I love you, because I cannot stay without hope. For too long now I have had the impression that all of my being is an open wound. I want to make mine the plea: Say the word only, and my soul shall be healed.

Jacques had been moved by this, admitted that he believed he was alone in his claustrophobic night of suffering. I waited, but nothing changed. He continued to see the doctor, who tried different medicines with varying results. He continued to act with the theatrical group, too, conscientiously, as everything he did, but without enthusiasm.

Years of habit had established our relationship of cool cohabitation. Occasionally, I broke out in screams. "Why should we go on living together? You take one floor; I'll take the other!" When this happened, he was gentle with me for a day. Then he forgot.

Château Lore
Smaïl

The shell that fell on the Markale market in Sarajevo at five minutes past twelve on that snowy February day was the beginning of the end for Smaïl, and the end of the beginning. With the death of his parents in one devastating swoop of history and tragedy searing together in a lightning flash, he entered a period of overlapping in his young life: too much suffering for him to be a child any more but not enough years to make a man. The neighbors sheltered him; no one would let him out of the apartment building until the sirens had stopped, and the vehicles, cars, trucks, ambulances had ceased their incessant racing back and forth, their bearing of the dead and their hastening of the wounded to whatever help could be availed.

His own mother and father were among those for whom nothing more could be done. In one last hope-suffused trip out of doors, for Sarajevo was calm that day, they unwittingly abandoned their boy to the tides of exile and uncertainty. They must have been optimistic, indeed, to have stepped out into the icy white air together, but the water jerry-cans were heavy, and Džana was hoping to find potatoes at the market, plus whatever else good fortune and a little trickery might bring. Death, however, was eyeing them from Lukavica that day, and it bore a Serbian name.

Smaïl called her Tetka Maja, Aunt Maja, but she was their sixty-year-old neighbor, a strong, white-haired woman taken to wearing gray scarves and shawls, since the snipers trained their weapons on anything bright and colorful. Tetka Maja cradled Smaïl and told him how happy his parents had been that day, how cheerful, how they had died without a second's suffering, thinking all was well. He would keep their memory always as a precious flower in the garden of his mind, to be tended and loved, to be watered by the pride they would have in him, if only they could see how he was going to succeed in life and honor his father's name. She put him on a waiting list with the United Nations High Commission for Refugees, to be taken out of that hellhole of Sarajevo.

He remembered this overlapping time as a period of anesthesia. His mind seemed to stop, like a clock that has ceased ticking, and it was a godsend, for if his thoughts had run on, they would have driven him mad. Instead, he was fully absorbed by the present, by the daily scramble for food and water for himself and Tetka Maja, by the brisk walks to the UNHCR headquarters, to see if his name was nearing the top of the list for the next coach out of town.

At last, his turn came, and he pressed forehead and nose against the steamed-up pane, forcing a smile at Tetka Maja, as she waved from the sidewalk, pulling her gray shawl tighter, then hugging her breasts as the overcrowded vehicle lumbered out of its parking place. The supplies he clutched in a worn net bag were her last for the week.

Four

The February school holiday took us to Brussels. We sat in the streamlined French high-speed train, as the russets and greens of the countryside streaked past. Although it was unusual for me, I felt the first signs of motion sickness, my stomach beginning to churn. I tried to read, but the lines would not stay straight, and the more I ignored my stomach, the higher it seemed to rise toward my throat.

"I'm sick at my stomach," I said to Jacques, reading beside me. "I'm going to the restaurant car to get a coke."

Without a word, he moved his legs so I could get out. *And you thought he would offer to get it for you; you're an idiot as usual.* I always chided myself, never him.

I clung to the corners of headrests, one side, then the other, as I made my way, slightly dizzy, to the *wagon-bar*. The cold soda came just in time, the fizz calming my nausea. I sat a long time on the high stool in the coolness of the speeding car, then moved slowly back to our seats, where Jacques made room for me again, still wordlessly. *You could have fainted, you could have died; he would not have noticed.* The invisible wife.

The fields we passed brought to mind other, golden ones, prickly and perfumed in the late afternoons of summer. We had laughed and rolled together in those, made love furtively and delightedly, picking bits of dry grass from our clothing when we were sated, climbing back toward our car hand in hand, accomplices forever, lovers forever.

Forever, until nine years ago. Our own Berlin Wall had started to grow up then. The plea I had so carefully worded two years before had remained *lettre morte,* long forgotten, despite the crutch of antidepressants. Jacques had not even kept it; it lay in a folder on a corner of my desk.

Jacques had never been patient with my lack of manual dexterity. Now each clumsy gesture, each lack of know-how before the mechanical things of this world put him beside himself. One day I had invited a friend of his to dinner, Jean-Yves, his only friend, in fact. Jean-Yves, a *vieux garçon,* an "old boy" as the French say for bachelors, was one of those homely, gentle-mannered men who put their affections into dogs and the organization of cheerful church functions. He was patient and sensitive, liked long discussions fraught with careful analyzing and reflecting. Heavy black glasses with thick lenses rested on his cheeks. As usual, he'd been early, and I had still been getting ready.

Jacques had left the house hours before without saying why. He'd appeared suddenly, after Jean-Yves' arrival, carrying a crate of six wine bottles. I'd been struggling with the childproof cap of a potpourri bottle, about to give up. Jacques had snatched it from me. "How can you expect things to work if you don't observe them properly?" He'd sounded furious. Was it really so important? "Look, you line up this mark with the little arrow. Is that so difficult?"

"But it sticks. It wouldn't open for me."

"Of course it doesn't stick. It's just you! You've got to press down in the right spot." His voice had been tight with barely contained irritation. "And I've already showed you how these caps work."

Suddenly, I'd felt very weary of this. "You see, Jean-Yves," I'd sighed, "what I put up with all the time?"

Jean-Yves had smiled nervously. "Oh, come on now, I feel for you," he'd said, trying hard to sound jokingly ironic. His friend Jacques was a bit irascible, all right, but who isn't from time to time? We all know he's a good man, a kind man. But the unease was there; the atmosphere was heavy with it.

Jacques could ignore me all day except to berate me on one point or another, then, at bedtime, would pose his hand, square like a workingman's, on my thigh, my breast. I knew his intention. Usually I would submit, just hoping to get it over as quickly as possible, sometimes feigning satisfaction, often saying, "It doesn't matter about me; we'll see the next time." Once, after a particularly trying day, I had balked, pushing him away. "How can you insult me all day and then think I might conceivably want to sleep with you?"

"But it's you who made the overture," he had said, stunned.

"Overture? I?" I'd been flabbergasted. "What could you possibly have seen as an overture?" How could he know me so little, understand so little of what was happening between us? I'd started to cry, hating myself for it. Why couldn't I just get it out of me in words, all the anger I'd been building up against him in me? Make him understand what he was doing to us? And all I could do was sob like an imbecile. Meek, rebuffed, he'd turned on his side, thinking, no doubt, that there was no understanding women.

My periods had stopped at fifty-one; that made two years now. My vagina clenched up, refused him access. When he did penetrate me, I frequently felt pain. "It's the menopause," I would say. "I can't feel pleasure. It's the hormones that are not there any more." What could he say? Besides, I believed it myself.

Our train pulled into *Bruxelles Midi*. I felt the thrill I always did when I arrived somewhere, a train ride behind me, a city before me.

Melisand was waiting for us on the platform, tall, slim, dark-haired like her father, wrapped in a long, narrow-waisted black coat.

"Hi, kids!" she called to us, as she always did, hugging us, teasing. We climbed the slope to the street, tall, dingy houses on the opposite side, covered with wide, smutty billboards, advertising beers, *Spa* water. The dampness of the northern February, the dust-tinged light of the air were familiar to us now.

Melisand carried my suitcase. She was always carrying my burdens, whatever they were. If I did not have this strong, merry child, I thought, I would dry up and die. I usually spent a few days of each school vacation with her, sometimes with Jacques, when he was able to free himself too. I felt a fondness for this city of Brussels, where I came only for rest and change. I liked the pointy outlines of the sooty, gothic churches against a gray backdrop of damp twilight. I liked the decadent, gingerbread squares with their facades criss-crossed in dark strips of wood. I loved the violet glow of *Avenue Louise* at the end of a busy Saturday, shoppers rushing, couples strolling. A multitude of tiny, white lights, strung in garlands along the trees, remained from the Christmas season. Branches in the squares of Brussels were outlined in the crystalline fire of tiny diamonds.

At Melisand's apartment, Jacques and I shared the wide double bed on the mezzanine; Melisand and her young husband, Julien, would take the sofa below. We are at close quarters here, I thought. Jacques won't try to touch me.

On one wall of her living room, she had gathered photographs of all the family. My gaze rested on one of Jacques at thirty, his hair thick and dark, with sideburns and a mustache *à la* Beatles: the style then. He could be a Gypsy musician, I thought; only the violin or the guitar or the accordion is lacking. At his side I stood happily smiling, my hair a huge, honey-colored puff of curls.

I felt welded to him in those days, lost and inadequate without him. He sustained me materially, even intellectually, or at least helped me redefine my own thoughts in his penetrating French fashion. My American pragmatism blossomed into something deeper when it encountered the French art of abstraction he taught me, and we both felt richer for the heady cocktail of our cultures. We made bridges to each other and crossed them joyfully.

The pain, however, had come slowly, insidiously. Melisand had noticed it before I had. "I'm afraid Daddy is going to leave us," she'd said one day when she was fourteen. "He doesn't love us any more."

"Don't be silly, darling! Of course he loves us and needs us." Love us, he did, no doubt, but a great, black abyss had swallowed up his need and any expression of it and left him stranded on his own lonely island. Moodiness, neurasthenia, and chronic depression had always been his own father's lot, and yet I had not imagined they could one day be his. He had laughed and danced and clowned as a student. There could be no connection, could there, with the steely, hurt-filled, ice-blue eyes of his father?

"So, tell me about your Bosnian family," Melisand said, as we sat on her chintz-covered love seat. Her brown eyes were wide with sympathy. She was always quick to tune in to what preoccupied me the most. I explained the first rejection, then the summons to Paris to review their case, the anxiety of the wait.

"Meho keeps his morale up; it's harder for Gordana. She has her ups and downs."

"Give any of my old stuffed toys you want to the little girls," Melisand offered. I showed her a picture of the children sitting on our sofa, from one of their first, shy visits: three shiny, brown, little hazelnuts, with raven hair and starched white collars. I could see Veronika dumping her chocolate milk on her dress front, hear Gordana saying, *"C'est pas grrave"*: "It's all rright, all rright," with a trill on the "r".

We had scarcely unpacked after returning from Brussels, when the answer to Meho's and Gordana's Appeal came. It was Marie-Toussainte who gave me the news. "It's no. They've been rejected."

I sat in front of my computer, by the telephone, tears streaming down my face. Whom could I call for advice? Whom could I write to? I had a cause now, and I would not let it rest.

"What's the matter?" Jacques asked me, passing by on the way to his study, surprised by my stricken face. "Oh, I know! They've been rejected, have they?"

I didn't call Meho and Gordana. They must have been devastated, and I wanted to give them time to digest the news. Although it was Wednesday evening, Meho would surely not go out to the weekly orchestra rehearsal. I resolved to drive to the *Château* the following day.

I left my car near the door with a glance upward toward their rooms. I could see no one. Elisabeth, in her glass cage of an office, called their floor. "A visit for you, Monsieur and Madame Kozić."

Meho came down first, and, in the narrow hallway, we greeted each other in the French fashion, a kiss on each cheek, then held each other a moment longer, in recognition of this blow that had come to them. "Where were you last night?" he asked. "You didn't come to rehearsal."

Gordana joined us in the corridor, she, too, remarkably calm for the circumstances. They must have known it was coming, whereas I had continued to hope against hope. They led me into the tiny library. Tattered story books, dictionaries, and donated schoolbooks filled the shelves. An old Singer sewing machine stood in one corner, and a rectangular table, where the children came to do homework or play cards, took up the middle of the room.

"I will write letters for you, I promise. To Madame Mitterrand at *France Libertés*. You know? The wife of former *Président* Mitterrand? I will tell her all about you. Someone will help!"

They showed me their report, and I understood that the lawyer had not been able to make much of it. It had been written by Elisabeth, as she had deciphered Meho's broken language when he'd first arrived. Their house had been destroyed, it began, and they had fled to the camp of Kupljensko in Croatia, then to the home of friends in Zagreb. Mustafa and Sanela had kept them in their flat for long months. Meho had brought Gordana, pregnant with Veronika, back to Sarajevo in 1995, but he had lived clandestinely, like a rat, he said, in cellars. He did not explain why. He ended by saying that he would return to Bosnia only when the international community made it safe for his family to do so and could guarantee that safety.

Nothing proved that they had been the targets of government persecutions or government-tolerated persecutions. It was the report of thousands upon thousands of victims, for the dead were not the only victims of the Bosnian conflict.

When I left, they accompanied me to the parking lot as always, smiling affectionately; Gordana held Veronika in her arms. I drew them all to me. "You take everyone?" asked Meho.

If it were in my power, Meho, I would take everyone.

Six days later, the telephone rang. Meho's halting French came across the line: "You ask to call? You say Jacques' birthday?"

"Yes, Meho, but it was for last Saturday. I made a chocolate cake, and I told Gordana you were welcome, but she said you weren't home."

"I forgot to call when I got back. I go to town of Maubray-en-Vallée; I am so sorry!"

"That's all right. You have other worries!"

"Please say Jacques a very, very happy birthday!"

"Of course."

"You invite other people?"

"No, only you."

"You come here maybe? We give you tea, coffee."

Jacques was touched by this invitation in his honor. "He's a nice fellow, and he deserves a chance for a better life here," he remarked to me, as we drove to the *Château*. In their chapel living room, Gordana sat rocking Veronika in her stroller. She had been screaming for her mother's breast again.

"And while you here, we want ask you something . . ." Meho wrapped his strong arms around his stomach, as I had seen him do before. Anxiety pains, I thought. God forbid that this should give him an ulcer. "I have new report for file. I see Madame Vesna. She write with me, all in French, good French, I think. You type on computer?"

"So, I am Monsieur Kozić's secretary, am I?"

"Yes, good secretary," he grinned.

"Madame Vesna," as they called her with *Château* courtesy, was a dentist. She had come several years earlier from Yugoslavia to France. As Meho had learned from one of his Yugoslavian acquaintances, Vesna was something of an expert on writing reports that would move the indifferent hearts of the national commissions. She did not live in our town. Meho had had to ride the train to visit her, stay overnight, all at a considerable cost to him. They obviously thought this was worth it. He held out several sheets of manuscript, handwritten in blue, ballpoint pen. Here was, perhaps, their life buoy.

He and Gordana were filled with renewed optimism that night, cheerful, even teasing each other, catching hands in the corridor, as they accompanied us to the wide door. We passed the glassed-in office, the postcards from former inhabitants now enjoying luckier times, the yellowed notice advising: "Weekly Stipend to be Distributed on Fridays". Meho held my arm as usual, going down the steps into the cool dusk. Jacques, not wanting to be outdone in gallantry, took Gordana's. The lights of the town below us winked opposite, fireflies on a lavender spread.

> *I, Meho Kozić, have been informed by the Appeals Commission for Refugees of their decision to refuse my request for the status of political refugee in France. I wish nonetheless to renew this request and thereby solicit your good will in the re-examination of my application, fearful as I am of persecution on the part of the authorities and citizens of Bosnia-Herzegovina. At the time of my first appearance before the National Office for Refugees and Stateless Persons as well as before the Appeals Commission, I did not dare mention a detail of extreme importance in the history of my family: We belong to the Rom race.*

Here, I stopped, deleted "race" and put in "people". "Madame" Vesna's French was far from impeccable and her vocabulary sometimes unfortunate. I did not know quite whether she was a Serb, a Croat or a

Bosnian, but her mindset was ingrained in her prose. How much of this report was from Meho, how much from her, I could not tell.

> *When the war broke out in Bosnia, I was drafted into the army to defend Sarajevo, under the orders of Commander Halilović. I thought that I could, at this time, prove my loyalty to my country. However, due to the ever present racial prejudice against the Roma, I was sent to the front lines, without a uniform, and without nourishment. This was the same for other Roma. Bosnian soldiers asked us which nation we were defending, since we did not belong to any so-called pure ethnic group. They said we would be sure to defend the victors. They did not trust us, calling us* cigo, *an insulting and degrading term for Roma. When I complained about this to my commanding officer, he would not reply.*
>
> *On the rare occasions when I was on leave to visit my family, I was always accompanied by another Bosnian soldier, to prevent me from spying for the Serbs, they said.*
>
> *In ...., I had a serious quarrel with my commanding officer, after requesting military identification papers to prove my participation in this war. This request was denied, because the government had not yet decided on the status of minorities. Furious, I announced my decision to go home. I was then threatened, as were the members of my family. I spoke out against the politics of all the parties involved in the conflict but was informed I could be court-martialed because of my political opinions.*
>
> *The last contact I had with my commanding officer was in................., when I asked him to list my family among those sought for via radio broadcasts. When he refused, I decided to desert. How could I fight for people who refused to recognize my existence and my rights?*
>
> *My house had been burned down and part of my own family had disappeared. I was in despair. I found my wife and children, and we went from one refugee camp to the other. When we arrived, we were told there was no room left, that they were expecting Bosnians or Croats, according to the camp. As for us, it was as if we were no one.*

So, that was it. Meho was a deserter. It was not his war. Why should he have stayed? Why should he have risked his life for a people who looked on him and his with scorn? The rest of the report detailed the minor persecutions and the harassment he had suffered since his youth. Moslems, Croats, and Serbs had always rejected him, he wrote, and he had had to work twice as hard as the rest in order to pass his examinations. He had been insulted and rebuffed. When he had participated in the founding of a school for the children of nomadic Roma, he had been accused of anti-government activism. I read on to Gordana's testimony, also written in Vesna's hand, correcting it as I typed:

> *I, too, Gordana Kozić, née Orif, have the honor of requesting a re-examination of my application for the status of political refugee. I come from a country where human rights are not respected for minorities. In my work as a nurse, I was insulted and mistreated, especially by my male colleagues, and whenever I complained of their behavior to the administration, I was told that I should be happy to have work. The problem was never brought up in meetings, and the director explained that he could not give warning notices for fear of tarnishing the image of his establishment.*
>
> *The neighbor children spat on our house when they passed it. We were ill-received by government administrations, and in employment as in other domains, preference was systematically granted to citizens of the three main Yugoslavian communities: Bosnian, Croatian, or Serbian.*
>
> *When the war broke out, our situation worsened. The hospital director took on medical students to do the work of the nurses, and I was told that I would have to live on my husband's salary. Fortunately, the Red Cross put us on their waiting list for food supplies, so that we were able to eat from time to time.*
>
> *Our stays in refugee camps throughout Bosnia and Croatia were nightmares; men harassed me, calling me prostitute, which made my husband furious and frequently put us in a difficult position. Our lives were endangered. That is why I decided to leave this hell and flee to France.*

I had to see Meho and Gordana about the dates Vesna had left blank in Meho's report. On a Sunday afternoon at the *Château,* Jacques and I found Smaïl in the dining room, at his favorite occupation: watching a soccer match on the television set which overhung the corner of the room. He gave us each an energetic handshake, as usual, and said he would call the Kozićs.

Smaïl was eighteen, but he looked older. His hair was a light blond, always plastered with the gel in favor with young people. He had been orphaned in the Bosnian conflict. He, too, had known the camps, the hunger and the uncertainty. And, to all appearances, he was calmly waiting for the decision concerning him, playing soccer whenever he could and going regularly to French lessons. He was not enrolled in school.

Smaïl returned with Meho and Gordana, Meho in the navy tracksuit he wore at the *Château,* Gordana in slippers and socks falling about her ankles. As always, they lowered their voices when speaking of their experience, even though, for the time being, we alone occupied the chapel. Apparently, Meho was not sure of the missing date. "Please try to remember. I can't finish typing this part," I said.

"My quarrel with commander, it was when, Gordana?" he asked. I noticed she was wearing her tiny gold earrings.

"Ah, quarrel . . . ," she hesitated, narrowing her eyes. "Wasn't it in October of '92?"

He seemed relieved. "Yes, that's it! Gordana, go up to room, get my other papers, please!" She bounded up, ready as always to serve him.

Jacques and I sat once more before the low table, with cups of the hot, sweet coffee we hadn't dared to refuse. "What best for us?" Meho suddenly asked, "request for territorial asylum or see about to reopen case with national office?" His French stumbled into incoherence when he attempted to discuss these all-important matters.

We understood that here was another choice to be made. The Prefect could choose to grant them a year's asylum, to be renewed eventually, in the territory over which he had his jurisdiction. However, if Meho and Gordana chose to request a review of their case with the national office, they had to furnish new elements, new and convincing proof of the danger threatening them on their return to Bosnia. And, risking that procedure, they could then not ask for territorial asylum. Either way was a gamble.

Rexhep Jupaj and his wife ambled into the chapel with their newborn baby and took seats near us. Here was a couple who had chosen to reopen their case. They were ethnic Albanians from Kosovo, he dark-haired and cheerful, she a slim, gray-eyed blond. Rexhep carried an afternoon's supply of disposable diapers and formula.

France-Sanctuaire had put them out when their last request had been refused. They were housed somewhere in a room in town, guests of one of the human rights organizations. They missed the common rooms and the gossip of the *Château*. Dropping in on Sundays, they kept up on the proceedings and setbacks of their fellow asylum seekers. They watched the multihued *Château* children come and go, chasing toys and each other in the chapel parlor. Nothing in their appearance or attitude could differentiate them from any young French couple visiting friends for an afternoon's chat. If they felt any prejudice against Roma, it was not apparent. The Kozić children played at their feet and kissed the baby, while Rexhep and his wife smiled indulgently. A family of three Congolese children pushed Veronika's empty stroller, scrambled for a ball on the floor, and came one after the other to peek at Rexhep's baby.

Meho, who never could resist a child, bent over the small bundle. "*Khorosho!*" he called in Russian to Oleg Petrov's pale little boy, when he toddled into the chapel, and tossed Fatou, shiny black as a chunk of India ink, into the air, rubbing his face against her round baby stomach as he caught her.

I loved seeing you like this, with this small United Nations of children, Meho. Only a good-hearted man could love children so.

On a Wednesday morning, I took it upon myself to visit Monsieur Lenoir, director of the *Château*. Ostensibly, I was there to take a book to Gordana, but I shook Monsieur Lenoir's hand, businesslike in my black suit, attaché case in hand, meaning to impress. He was lounging in the dining room with Meho, his narrow form draped on a chair.

Gordana, in her old slippers and a shapeless pullover, ran between the laundry room and the dining room, where she served us coffee. Meho listened to our conversation, brows knitted, eyes darker than the black coffee, trying so hard to follow this talk between others which concerned only him. Gordana pulled up a chair by his side, her gaze vague and polite.

"The European Convention on Human Rights demands that they receive asylum if they have justifiable fears of persecution on returning," Monsieur Lenoir explained.

"So, you are a lawyer?" I sought to flatter.

"No, but as director, I will accompany them to their interview at the Prefect's Office. However, it is essential that Meho speak for himself."

He turned to Meho. "You must show you have learned French, that you can express yourself, even if you make mistakes. Show you are integrated, fitting in, eager to work. . ." Meho nodded.

I insisted. He was fitting in. I wanted Monsieur Lenoir to defend them, and I wanted him to explain it to me, this complex maneuvering that was needed to save a family.

"The Kozić family must present a good case," Monsieur Lenoir went on, "letters of recommendation, petitions, if possible, in their favor."

"Sister Agnès de Jésus write a letter for me," said Meho.

"Why didn't you tell me that? I didn't know we could do things like that! We'll get you more letters!" I exclaimed, seeing new possibilities.

"If I go back, they wait to put me in prison as soon as I get off plane," said Meho. I believed him. People said the Dayton Accords were not respected, that the amnesty went unapplied.

"Monsieur Kozić is in the difficult position of being a Bosnian citizen, without being a Bosnian," the director said. "Moreover, the lawyer made a mistake before the Appeals Commission. Monsieur Kozić presented himself as a Bosnian Muslim, and she told them he fought for the Bosnian Serbs."

God in heaven, so they had taken him for a traitor! And in fact, he was a deserter. I knew that now. He had fought for nothing but his own skin. What pity could he hope for from ethnic Bosnians? The Prefect's Office must be made to understand these things. I couldn't bear to think of my dear Gypsy family among the statistics of the rebuffed.

Little by little, Meho's file took form. The Slavic Society, remembering his playing and cheerful demeanor, sent a recommendation. Gérard, our portly orchestra conductor, beaming kindness, went in person to the *Préfecture* to say he needed this Bosnian oboist. "We don't just send people back like that," he was told. When I proposed a petition, the orchestra president, an ancient, doddering violist, who played with his mouth wide open, refused.

"We are a municipal association, and we cannot meddle in politics!" he declared. Had he not lived through World War II, seen the aftermath and the misery? But he was adamant. Nothing could be written with the goal of swaying the Prefect's decision. How can knowledge or an experience of suffering not give rise to compassion? Fear and selfishness, I found, are a formidable pair of harnesses.

I would fight on other battlefields, then, I decided. My black folder under my arm, my degrees and position announced, I requested an appointment with the local deputy to the French Parliament.

He was polite and noncommittal. "Nothing will move this Prefect," he said with his dandy's smirk. Thick, wavy, white hair billowed in a mane around the deputy's face. "In a former post, he was accused of laxism and of not applying the law to the letter. You remember the scandal in Saint-Tanguy?" I remembered. "He was Prefect there when it happened, and he bore the brunt of the responsibility. He will take no risks now to displease anyone in the government." He smiled unctuously. My hopes faltered.

Château Lore
Oleg

In Russia, they call it *dedovshchina,* the hazing, but the cruel practice has more to do with torture than with the taunting of new students. You are lucky if you come out alive. Oleg was drafted at eighteen, and his parents did not have the twelve hundred dollars required to get him declared unfit. That was half a year's salary for his father, and, on that, they never managed to save a kopek. He had no illusions about the honor of serving Mother Russia and her people. The fate that awaited young draftees was sadly well-known, but Oleg hoped somehow to pass between blows like a bird between hailstones.

There was something birdlike about him, indeed, with his wispy, ash-blond hair and his skinny limbs, his brusque movements and his rapidly blinking, pale blue eyes. He passed between nothing, however, and found himself bound for the sea at Vladivostok. What could he know about ships and the life of a sailor, when he had spent his life cooped up in his parents' two-room flat on the tenth floor of an apartment block in the city of Kaluga? He kissed his girlfriend Sveta goodbye there, leaving her in tears on the train platform along with his mother, as he boarded the crowded convoy.

At first he wrote that it was not so bad. The other, new, second-class soldiers were friendly enough; they were all in the same boat, after all, and helped each other out in small ways. He didn't mention the nightly lineup, when the officers went down the line punching them in turn in the stomach or kicking them in the genitals. As if breaking them in little by little, they made this ritual rougher as time went by; the officers filmed the soldiers as they doubled over after a blow, trying to get their wind back, fighting nausea, then laughed to humiliate them further.

Oleg froze in sheer panic, when he saw one particular, brooding Azerbaijani, whom the other officers unleashed on the draftees like a pit bull on thieves. His IQ could not have been normal, and the quantity of vodka he drank dulled whatever sense he had without weakening his muscles.

Oleg nursed his bruises and cramped abdomen on his pallet at night and turned to prayer. He had always had a feeling about that, even if attending the Divine Liturgy was not something easily compatible with passing exams or getting a job. He pressed his fingers hard against his closed eyes and imagined that the light this produced came from the golden onions of Saint-Sophie of Kiev, burnished to glowing by the rays of the lowering sun. *Lux ex oriente*. The light comes from the east. Not this east, where he was, which was a mockery of human society, but a mythical east of Resurrection. *Vo istinu voskres!*; in truth, He is risen. Oleg repeated the words to himself until he slept.

One night they came for him. Oleg felt himself being lifted from his thin mattress, and he recognized the vodka-breath stench of the powerful Azerbaijani. He clapped his hand over Oleg's mouth and dragged him, as he struggled silently but furiously, to a small cubicle beyond the dormitory. Here, an electric chair had been rigged and stood blindly waiting for him. Some of his comrades had hinted at this torture, but they had obviously been threatened into keeping their mouths shut. Oleg felt his limbs go weak, as waves of dread washed over his meager body. The Azerbaijani was unbuckling his khaki trousers.

"I want to have a little fun with you tonight, soldier," he sneered. "Take off your clothes!" Oleg blanched, his thin face nearly transparent, like an apparition's. If he had willed his hands to obey him, they would not have. They crucified Christ, so what is this, he thought briefly, but even his usual prayer did not form in his mind but remained stuck, paralyzed in some remote region of his brain.

"The chair is just in case you don't cooperate," added the Azerbaijani. He grabbed Oleg and held him against his sweaty body, back to front. He had taken off his pants and boots and was pushing down Oleg's underpants, when Oleg struck out his long arm and grabbed one of the heavy boots. The heel had metal spikes on it, and Oleg brought it down on the man's turgid, purple sex with every ounce of strength he could muster. If the cubicle had not been shut, the howl of curses the enraged Azerbaijani let out would have awakened the regiment. Oleg sank to the floor in weak relief, as the man bounded away, clutching himself.

Five

"Monsieur Lenoir, he likes Meho," Gordana told me. "Every day, he takes coffee with him and talks. He says, 'you and me, we brothers.' Monsieur Lenoir's grandpapa was immigrant from Yugoslavia." I learned this on one of the many afternoons I stopped by the *Château* for a chat with her. I became an expert at piecing together the puzzle of her sentences. I learned that the other boarders envied Gordana her visits.

Leila said she didn't want to study French with Sister Agnès de Jésus any more; it was Madame Ellen she wanted. "Because she thinks then you visit her too, you invite her too," said Gordana.

Sister Agnès de Jésus was seventy, white hair tucked under a gray scarf. She wore a gray street-length nun's habit and sensible black shoes. Her wrinkled face was plain, but her pale blue eyes smiled with goodness. She loved them all, her pupils. It would not do to take one away from her.

Marie-Toussainte had assigned Leila to her, after her suicide attempt. They labored over a first-grade ABC primer. Sister Agnès de Jésus had more heart than teaching skill. Marie-Toussainte, anyway, had vetoed a change of teachers. "But Madame Ellen know Russian; she help me more," Leila had pouted.

I discussed this with Marie-Toussainte, not because I wanted Leila for a student, but because I felt there must be some tactful way to make Sister Agnès de Jésus understand that the ABC book was inappropriate.

"What can I do about it?" Marie-Toussainte sighed. "Some of my volunteers can teach, others can't, but I don't want to hurt anyone's feelings. Anyway, our main purpose is to extend a welcoming hand to these people, not make scholars out of them. If they must leave France one day, let them at least remember that they met with some friendship here."

Marie-Toussainte was making her rounds at the parish hall, making sure that everyone was studying and happy, kissing us all roundly twice on each cheek. She did her best to make the refugees understand why it was so terribly difficult for them to be accepted. "France is like a mother," she said, "she has a big, big heart." She struck her own opulent chest. "But she must leave some children out, and so she weeps. It is because all her children do not have work, you understand? It is her French children who work, who are paying for you here: French taxes, yes?"

After my lesson, she spoke to me *aparté*. "No one knows Meho's story as well as Monsieur Lenoir," Marie-Toussainte said in a near whisper, "but there are things Meho won't divulge. He refuses to give any information to Madame Delambre at the Balkans Association. We wonder if he isn't. . . . There is something . . ."

This worried me until I finally confronted Meho with it at orchestra. "Marie-Toussainte says you won't talk to Madame Delambre." I could visualize this good lady's gold-rimmed glasses and straight, rust-colored hair: a well-intentioned busybody.

He was visibly annoyed. "I tell all my file to René. He is lawyer for Anti-Fascist Committee. But no one else except Monsieur Lenoir. It his work to defend us. He go to Prefect with us. If Madame Delambre she get mixed up in this, then Monsieur Lenoir, he'll say, OK she do it for you, and he'll drop us."

So, that was it. You were the wise one after all. All these well-wishers, meddling in your business, including me. But you knew what to do. I felt ashamed; I had let you see I did not trust you.

At her following lesson, Gordana told me, "Monsieur Lenoir, he talk a lot to the man." The "man" meant the Prefect's representative for affairs concerning foreigners and asylum seekers. "I don't know, but I feel good. I think, good interview."

I noticed she had on maroon lipstick. It underlined a small thickening of the flesh beneath the middle of her lower lip. Her skin retained its brownish-yellow hue, contrasting with her limpid eyes. We were reading *Tintin*, a comic book, in our little schoolroom, still chilly from a hesitant spring. Nonetheless, it was hard to keep up a pretense of gaiety. Gordana had little head for languages. When left to herself, she relapsed into the *Château* pidgin, even though she could say many things correctly, if she tried. She, Meho, and Monsieur Lenoir had been summoned to the *Préfecture,* where their story had once more been recounted, dissected, painfully relived. The "man" had listened sympathetically. Her intuition this time allowed her the luxury of hope.

That is why, perhaps, the new refusal was all the harder to accept. The interview at the *Préfecture* had been their last chance. The form letter reply came back swiftly, cold, polite, and negative. Meho brought it to Jacques and me, sitting on our leather sofa where we had tasted his wine together, where the children had sat huddled and shy, where the family had smiled on command for snapshots later shown and shared. He turned the paper this way and that, as if somehow the words might change with the direction of the paper. *Is there no other way to understand this?* his expression seemed to say. He wished for the miracle of a new interpretation. If only he had not understood it correctly, and we would tell him it was a mistake, that there were more steps to be taken and everything would be all right.

> Sir,
>
> *You were received by my Office at an interview during which you were able to put forward all arguments and to produce all documents*

> useful to the defense of your request. These have been examined with the utmost care and attention.
> It appears that you have not brought forth the evidence of a stay on French territory of more than five years nor proof of a stable income.

I was stunned. How could an undocumented alien prove he had been living in the country, when, precisely, he had no right to do so? And how could a war refugee, forbidden to work here, prove a stable income? Here was the squaring of the circle.

> It is therefore impossible to grant you further authorization to remain in France.
> This being the case, I must ask that you take all necessary measures to leave the country within one month from the date of the present decision.

The end of April. One month.

> Beyond this date, if you remain on French national territory, I will take a decision of accompaniment to the border, as specified in article...

I dared a look at Meho. He was observing Jacques and me out of the corner of his eye, his brow furrowed, beseeching. He watched us turn the page.

> If you wish to contest the present decision, you may formulate, within two months
> —either an appeal to my Services, including your arguments and all new facts capable of modifying your situation
> —or an appeal to the hierarchy, that is to say, the Ministry of the Interior.
> This appeal will not suspend the application of the present decision.

That meant continue trying; do something; do what you can, but you must leave. When you are back in the bombed-out streets of Sarajevo, with no place to go, no place to set down your bundles and no way to feed your family, then, a few months later, perhaps, France will decide you can stay here.

"There is nothing else to do now," Jacques told Meho. "You have done everything. Look into the money they give if you leave voluntarily. Call the toll-free number they give." Meho shook his head, his features stubborn. We showed him to the door, pressing his hands, embracing him. Like him, I knew I would not give up.

Gordana had been less ready for it this time than I had. She had soothed herself in a cradle of illusions, founded on nothing surer than the gentle manner of the civil servant they had met, while I went about contacting all the Gypsy associations I could.

Meho made an appointment to meet the pastor of the Light and Life Church, the Gypsy evangelical movement, who provided the names and telephone numbers of Rom lawyers in Paris. They went by first names that sounded like nicknames: Dédé, Rollo, Tom. Meho unfurled the stub of wrinkled paper he had scribbled them on. His pockets were always full of bits and scraps of information, telephone numbers, references gleaned here and there. He had ideas and connections he never bothered to explain to me. And what business were they of mine?

"Did you speak Romany with the pastor?" I asked, curious.

"No, he speak only French. Very nice man."

I thought of the caravans of the French Gypsy people parked in our town square. They came regularly, sometimes did the rounds of the neighborhood door-to-door, selling baskets or small wares, offering small services, begging. Sometimes they left as silently as they had come. I found them annoying, these fat Gypsy women with their unkempt hair, long skirts, mules, drawling accents, and insistent manners.

"Hello, dear. You mustn't be afraid of us."

"Don't worry, I'm not afraid of you."

"Oh, such a pretty lady! You're not from here, are you? I can see that right away!" How did they always spot me immediately for non-French?

"This is my eldest daughter." The Gypsy woman would gesture to a smirking, wall-eyed adolescent. "She's the first of thirteen. And she's just had twins. It's so hard for us, you know. Don't you have some men's clothes to spare?"

And when I brought packages of clothing from the attic, she would ask for coffee. If I gave her a package of coffee, she would ask for sugar. I shooed these women away, but I knew they'd be back. My house was marked.

These, I thought now, were Meho's and Gordana's brothers and sisters, although I could see no resemblance. My friends must have belonged to the Roma *bourgeoisie*. They were literate, had been sedentary.

"Why the moving? Why the caravan?" Gordana once said. "That is no life!" She distanced herself from these people, who nonetheless lived well in comparison to the roaming Gypsies of Yugoslavia.

"I don't know how they do it," Meho had wondered, shaking his head at the sight of their prosperity.

I had met some of his nomadic compatriots too, well before the Bosnian conflict. They would descend in swarms on the Paris *métro* or on towns, leaving unsolved house break-ins in the wake of their passing. Although anyone, of course, could have been responsible, it was handy to have Gypsies to blame. Thin, doe-eyed mothers sat with too-quiet babies swathed in rags on street corners. A scribbled sign was invariably propped in front of them, gray from age and use: "I am from Yugoslavia. I do not speak French. I am poor. Please give me something so that I can eat." Filthy, brown-skinned children, too old to sit with their mothers, stretched out their hands piteously: *"S'il vous plaît!"* They were among the most beautiful people I had ever seen, and the most wretched.

The shiny new caravans of the French *Gitans* bespoke another standard of living. Would they not have a feeling of solidarity toward a family of their own people stranded? Couldn't Meho and Gordana hide and travel with them, rather than be sent to the border? I mentioned this to Gordana.

"Then . . . us . . . perhaps, the caravan?" She was ready to grasp at any straw.

Meho tried to explain to us what Vesna had told him after this new refusal. Something about a Promise of Employment. She worked at her office and often did not return home until nearly ten. It did not matter, he said; it was not rude to call people late in Yugoslavia. "Up to midnight, OK!" I had to go out, so Jacques called her. Every minute counted now. We had one month.

"She holds Meho in high esteem," he reported back. "She says he is well educated."

Well educated? Not particularly, I thought. I knew he had left regular school at fifteen, then studied the oboe at the Academy of Music, where he had had some general subjects. But I supposed she meant well educated for a Rom. Still, I felt pleased my sympathy for him was being corroborated, and I was glad Jacques had heard this.

"In order to make a new appeal to the *Préfecture*," Jacques said, "he must provide a Promise of Employment. It is the only way. France may agree to keep him if he can prove he has a way to earn a living. He must find an employer who will sign an agreement to hire him if and when he obtains his papers."

Here was a daunting challenge. French people in great numbers went unemployed. What employer would risk signing such an agreement, when the fate of the future employee was uncertain? A vicious circle again.

Words that Cédric, from the Slavic Society, had spoken to me after a Russian lesson came back to me, repeating themselves with the strength of hope. "If ever he obtains his papers, I can find work for him. In metallurgy. There's a factory in search of help. It's tough work, though. Not for everyone." Cédric was brusque but good-hearted. A shock of brown hair fell over his forehead. He wore unrimmed glasses and carried a satchel in businesslike fashion, talked fast and with authority. I picked up the telephone.

"No employer is going to want to take a chance on someone who is not sure to be there," Cédric said.

"But the metallurgy? You said they needed people."

"I don't know if they still do. I'll have to see. And see to it he has a good résumé, and write up a summary of his life story and why he's seeking asylum." His tone was gruff, but I knew I could count on him. I called Meho to say I would be there the next day to help him write his résumé.

From their second-floor window, Meho saw me getting out of my decrepit Peugeot. A sticker from years before decorated the back window: *"Halte au massacre en Bosnie-Herzégovine!"*

"Helena!" he called to me, using what sounded like a Yugoslavian form of my name, maybe a Gypsy form. The "a" at the end made it a song. He was naming me anew, leaving off the usual, deferent *Madame*.

"Wait for me, I finish shaving; I'll be right down!" He used the familiar form of you. It sounded gentle and moving to my ears, a new intimacy, a gift and caress of the language. For months, I had been saying *tu* to Meho and Gordana, a sign of the friendship I felt for them, a signal, too, that I considered us equals, socially, if not in age. They had not dared or not known how to respond. Their *vous* showed respect and kept a distance, too.

There was no anxiety in Meho's voice. One could have thought a clean shave was his only preoccupation. He smelled of lavender, and his cheeks were white above the silky inverted crown of his beard.

He led me into the small, dingy library where we had already met, after their first rejection. People entered, excused themselves, tiptoed back out, as I sat with him, writing. Gordana brought us a plate of thin, rolled pancakes with sugar, and we ate them all.

"None for me," she said, "not hungry."

"I talked to Cédric last night," I told Meho. "You met him at the Slavic Society Christmas party. He's the president. Do you remember?

Glasses. In his late twenties. Efficient, businesslike." Meho frowned, then nodded.

"Do you know, he works for the National Employment Agency? He said that, maybe, if you had a good résumé . . . there's a factory . . . So, let's write it?"

"Mine too," said Gordana. "I can work too. Why not? Men and women equal." Her voice was high and sharp as it often could be, with a twinge of defiance.

"Your date of birth, Gordana?" She was twenty years younger than I. "You are a child," I said to her affectionately.

"A child, me, with three of children?" She shook her head, her expression sour.

They searched their memories for dates, those of her nursing qualifications, his first prize in oboe, former employment, what they could do, what they would do. "I can put things on shelf in grocery store," Meho said, remembering a former job.

"Where we met," Gordana added, a rare gleam of complicity with Meho in her eye.

Suddenly, he reached into his back pocket, pulling out a letter and questionnaire from the Canadian Embassy Immigration Service. "What you think of this?"

"Where did you get that?"

"Oleg Petrov, he give it to me."

"I don't know, Meho, but I think you need certain qualifications to emigrate to Canada. You need a little money in the bank, too, just in case. How could you even pay for the trip? But I'll look into it. I'll write the United States Embassy too, if you want."

He nodded his head enthusiastically. "Petrov always nice to me."

"Does he have a résumé? Does he know about that?"

"Oh, yes, he has that."

I was glad that Meho and Gordana were not snubbed by everyone at the *Château*. I'd heard from Marie-Toussainte that Oleg Petrov was a student of theology. He, at least, appeared to know the meaning of tolerance and solidarity.

As I left with my draft in hand to be typed on the computer, Meho looked at me long and hard. A fine black line circled the hazel of his irises. "I need of you," he said, simply.

"I need you, too," I answered, moved. "I need your friendship. Please stay here!"

There is need and need, Meho. You needed me to write French for you. You needed my moral support. When you needed me physically, you said the same sentence, the same way, with the same endearing mistake. Which need did you mean then? Or all of those things already?

I made polite conversation with Jacques. "My navy spring shoes were worn, so I bought these," I said, showing him, "but they were dreadfully expensive." I didn't usually buy sixty-dollar shoes.

"Really? How much?" he asked, knowing I was normally careful with money.

"Three hundred and fifty francs," I confessed. What I did not confess was that they were the only pretty ones I had found with low heels, heels that didn't make me much taller than I was, already taller than Meho.

"That's all right," he said, "if you like them." Jacques never reproached me with anything I bought, nor, in fact, congratulated or sympathized with me. He simply did not notice me.

It was school vacation time, a chance to visit Melisand and Julien. This time, we decided to take the car to Brussels. The miles sped by under the tires of Jacques' sleek, black Citroën, while I felt something leaden bearing down on my heart. Jacques, on the contrary, was unusually cheerful. When he spoke, I barely responded. He noticed my new shoes and asked if I were satisfied with them. This was uncanny. When had he last paid attention to what I wore? Was the Prozac really becoming effective now? Was there some chance he was emerging from his depression?

If he was, then I was sinking into one of my own. They will be sent back, I thought, over and over. They do not stand a chance. Gordana had told me all about what was awaiting them in Sarajevo, that is to say: destruction, desolation, ruins, danger. "Our house is gone, and everything we had in it. The children could step on a mine." Her brother, his companion and child, lived in one room with Gordana's mother.

"Does she work?" I had asked.

"No. No jobs."

"How do they eat?"

"*Rote Kreuz.*"

Humanitarian aid. Bosnia still lived like an orphaned child, fed with the spoon of international charity. I could see them going for their rations, hugging the carton, lugging it back to the room. What was in it? Tins of sardines, perhaps, flour, oil, rice, coffee. The basics for survival, nothing for dignity, less for pleasure.

Gordana and Meho could receive a sum of several thousand francs, should they decide to leave France of their own accord. It wouldn't last long, I thought. If they refused and were escorted to the border, as the official letter put it, it would not be the border of Bosnia, I fearfully assumed, but the nearest one, the Franco-German border. There, they would be illegal aliens, lost once more in a totally foreign environment, with no chance to ask for asylum again. The Schengen agreement, at least as I understood, rightly or wrongly, its maze of articles, forbade this. Once one had applied to a cosigning state, no other was supposed to accept a request. I didn't know if there could be exceptions, tolerance, or the closing of eyes. I imagined them in the street, without food or shelter, destitute, Veronika screeching.

Jacques snapped his fingers against my leg in jest. Numb with worry, I felt nothing.

When we visited the Sunday morning flea market in Ghent, I saw the accordion. It was lying on the ground amidst a jumble of lamps, dusty chairs, and chipped, china knickknacks. It was bruised and out of breath, but its shiny circus decorations still gleamed in the gray Belgian spring; its pleats still opened and shut. It had the piano keys used by accordionists from Eastern Europe, not the rows of buttons familiar to French players. The Flemish merchant was enthusiastic. Here indeed was the most worthwhile of purchases.

"Yesterday," he told us, speaking willing French to potential buyers, "this Russian fellow came by and borrowed it for the afternoon. Well, believe me if you will, he made an honest day's wages with it." He took off his navy blue Dutch cap, revealing a bald pate, and placed it on his heart, in token of his good faith.

My own heart was racing with the anxiety of desire, but I didn't have the thousand francs needed to buy this unhoped for treasure. Jacques agreed wordlessly, and my bankcard procured the sum. "At least he'll be able to stand on a corner and earn a meal for the family," I said.

"Gordana was so hopeful for awhile," I told Melisand, as we chatted in a corner of the apartment. She sat opposite me, holding my two hands. "She even started wearing lipstick and earrings and coming to her lesson every time. But now her hopes are all gone." My voice broke on "lipstick", and I burst into tears on "all gone". The memory of Gordana glowed in my mind, a bright pink blouse hugging the sandy brown of her chest. She had picked it out at the Catholic Aid Committee, along with clothes for the rest of the family.

"Oh, Mom, you are too tender-hearted. Dad was good, too, wasn't he, about the accordion?"

"Yes," I wept. "He was even ready to try it out. He lets me do what I want. He never says a word."

We drove to the *Château* immediately on our return, our hearts full of the accordion. Jacques dragged the heavy, worn, black case into the chapel. Meho looked at us, moved, incredulous. "But . . . it's not my birthday today!" A smile broke on his face, the sun after clouds.

He tried the instrument, squeaky with age and disuse, while we held our breath. Would it work? Could it be repaired? Of course, it wasn't the wonder the dealer had touted, but there was some hope.

"It's broken here." Meho touched the inner fixation of the keys with the hand of the connoisseur. "Some glue, perhaps?"

"I know!" said Jacques, peering at the worm-eaten wood. He was always clever at fixing. "Beeswax will do it!"

Meho looked at him appreciatively. Gordana busied herself bringing coffee and soda, biscuits, sweets, back and forth between the chapel and the communal kitchen.

"Didn't you want to ask them something?" Meho nudged Gordana, then looked at us. "You have meal with us here on Sunday?"

Gordana nodded her head up and down, obeying. We accepted. Sunday, for us, was Easter.

Château Lore
Smaïl

In the Kupljensko camp, Smaïl shared a tent with a number of other celibate men. They pushed their sleeping gear and meager possessions to make room for him, refraining from questions at the beginning, as the thin, blond youth took stock of his new surroundings. Smaïl did not speak either, although his gregarious nature led him to question them after a time. Thus he learned that his companions included a Bosnian journalist, an elementary school teacher from the suburbs of Sarajevo, an auto mechanic, and two peasants from Bijeljina.

"A cigarette, boy?" one of the peasants offered, as they sat outside the tent, hunched over their own knees. Cigarettes were precious fare, and Smaïl accepted, coughing as he attempted to draw the burning cloud into his lungs. Except for an occasional draft his father permitted from his own cigarette, Smaïl had never smoked. The man laughed, watching him out of the corner of his eye.

He had a scraggly black moustache, and a three-day beard put grubby punctuation marks on a rough, weather-beaten face. He smelled strongly of sweat and tobacco, but the air was sharp, and Smaïl didn't mind. A short, dark woman, pulling two thin, brown, little girls behind her, came into view. She was heading toward the pump, a bundle of laundry rolled up under her left arm, while the right pulled the children, one tripping behind the other, their arms hooked like a braid of wholemeal bread dough.

"Hey, *ciga!*" the peasant shouted, and the woman quickened her pace. "Not so fast! Come say hello to a friend! Haven't we met before? Didn't I see you in a brothel back home?"

"Do you know her?" Smaïl asked innocently.

"Sure don't," the man answered, "but I know her kind. All a bunch of whores, those Gypsies. I don't know why they let them in here. This is a respectable place for Bosnian Muslims. The Gypsies are Chetnik-lovers, anyway. Send them all to Serbia, is what I say."

Smaïl said nothing. He noticed only how the woman clenched her eldest child's hand, staring at the ground, pulling the girls behind her almost brutally, so that their small feet tangled and barely had time to touch the cold earth of the refugee camp.

Six

Meho called again. "Are you free this morning?"

"Yes, what's the matter?"

"I have French lesson at parish, then I must go to see René, Anti-Fascist Association lawyer. He give free consultations at noon. You help me?"

I always dropped what I was doing, if Meho needed me. My hours at the *collège* took up little of my time, although I worked on preparations and corrected papers at home. I shoved the grammar tests aside and hurried to get my car from the garage. As I approached the schoolroom, I caught sight of his dark head through the window. The thinning spot at the crown made me smile. Not such a young schoolboy, I thought.

I asked permission to enter during the lesson. Meho's tutor, a volunteer like me, was a retired accountant with little idea of what a language lesson might be. He appeared at ease and self-assured, however, standing in front of the blackboard, gesturing, listening to his own voice. For all his student could understand him, he might have been speaking Mandarin. Meho withstood it politely, nodded with the courtesy that was always his, but he winked at me when *Monsieur le professeur* turned his head.

Bits of gravel from the courtyard flew out from under our soles. When the schoolroom was a good distance behind us, we burst into laughter like a pair of teenagers.

"When you speak, or Jacques speak, we understand! Not him. He forgets I'm foreigner!"

"Why do you need me now?" I asked. It seemed clear he had been looking for an excuse to call me.

"René speak very fast. Better if you come too. He be there at twelve o'clock. No need for appointment."

René was not there and never came. We sat at a table outside his office, alone. Meho told me he was to have a musical audition in the early afternoon at *La Méduse,* an avant-garde theater company. The woman who administered the company had worked in Sarajevo and was still doing so indirectly. She did what she could for Meho. Now, she had arranged for him to send a recording of his accordion playing to Belgium, to a professional Gypsy orchestra that might hire him. He looked exhausted. He told me he had not slept the night before nor eaten a thing that day. I wondered how he could face an audition, but, for him, self-deprivation was undoubtedly a well-practiced skill. His heavy black jacket hung dejectedly on his square shoulders; the leather was scraped and worn, and it gave off a pungent smell. I noticed his threadbare shirt collar. His ebony hair was oily.

> *I felt sorry, Meho. You suddenly looked so disinherited, so utterly dependent on the alms of the Western world. You were a proud, energetic little man, but you were becoming weary, and you were entirely in our hands.*

"I'll be right back," I said. I ran out to the bakery on the corner and brought us each back a thick, yellow *flan*. Meho was still alone in the hall in front of the lawyer's empty office.

"Thank you for cake, Madame Aubert," he said, amused, standing very close to me, his head barely higher than my chin. The front of his jacket touched my white blouse.

"My head aches." I pressed my temples with my fingertips.

"Ah, you too? Family Kozić give you headache, maybe?"

"Yes, I guess so."

"I have bio-energy. I massage you."

"OK, Meho." I sat down, letting him take my head in his hands.

"And now I undress you." He slipped his hands down under my white polyester blouse and onto my shoulders, palms on my bra straps.

"Stop there, maybe Meho?" I suggested, smiling. He did so. I didn't take his remark seriously. I trusted him utterly, but the air had grown tense with something I had not felt before.

"Tomorrow night I play accordion for Cédric, thirty years birthday party. He liked how I played at Slavic Society Christmas party, so he call me for birthday."

"I know. I'm not invited. We know each other from Russian lessons, but I'm not a close friend."

"Me, I invite you to party!" he said, smiling.

"It would be nice if you could."

He suddenly looked at me intensely. "Ellen, you have mama in USA? Papa too?"

"A mama, yes. My papa is dead."

"Gordana, she wonder why you do all this for us."

Why indeed?

I paused. "Meho, I have no brothers, no sisters. I'm alone here in France too. I always wanted a little brother, a little sister . . ."

His eyes filled and he kissed my cheek. "You are nice, so very nice."

At the *Château,* the usual committee of swarthy, unshaven men sat in front of the television screen. In a corner of the dining room, two other men played chess. Their wives were on the floors or in the kitchen, doing what wives must. Gordana appeared and showed us into the small library, which she had transformed, covering the shabby tabletop with a paper cloth, china, and glasses set on it for three. Meho was out. He had played until dawn for Cédric's birthday, she said, had only slept a few hours, and now had gone out to get wine for the dinner.

He returned, perspiration making round droplets on his high forehead, soaking his black hair at the roots. Time was often elastic for him, but he had hurried. The buses were not running on Easter, and he had been lucky to find a grocery shop. The children circled the table. Suada leaned from time to time against her father's arm. Veronika fussed for her mother, who served us, her husband's guests, and him. She never sat, never stayed with us. Deferentially, she brought a piece of roast meat, vegetables *al dente,* chocolate éclairs from the pastry shop. A bouquet of three purple flowers on ragged, gray stems in a drinking glass tried hard to make the scene festive.

"My *maman* bought them," Suada said, "for you!" Gordana could have put the fifteen francs they must have cost into the till for the lawyer, but they were for me.

"A big kiss for Gordana!" Meho said, after the meal. She stayed impassive, a gilt heart pendant on a chain caught between the crests of her bosom. Her belly was still round and prominent from childbearing.

"Yes, thank you, Gordana!" we added quickly.

You were kind to her, Meho, then. Or were you showing us that you were kind? So sweet, I thought. My husband has never said thank you to me for a meal I have cooked.

"I get cassette recorder?" Meho asked. "Rom music? *Ty khochish? Ty liubish?*" Do you want some? Do you like it? There was the singular you form used for familiars in Russian. The words were for me, and I understood them. We smiled like accomplices, leaning slightly toward each other. Jacques spoke no Slavic languages.

The Gypsy voices despaired and cajoled, raspy, angry, pleading: love and reproach to oriental rhythms, the slow trilling of violin vibrato, then variations on the melodies accelerating to frenzy, fingers agitated on black and white keys. "Do you know those musicians personally?" I asked, trying to picture him in the midst of this fiery celebration.

"Yes, my Rom friends," he said. "You understand *Rom?* It is 'man,' and it is 'husband'. For example, Gordana, she can say, 'Meho, he is *moj Rom'* ." I glanced at Gordana. She said nothing, bending over the table, picking up a plate.

"Moj Rom?" I was surprised to feel a quick pang when you said this. But of course you were her Rom.

"What year you were born?" Meho asked me suddenly.
"That's classified information!"
"Well, then, how long you married?"
"Gordana, get him to leave me alone!"
"Stop asking things like that!" she scolded, but Meho wouldn't give up.
"We've been married thirty years," Jacques supplied, to my secret annoyance.
"But I was only seventeen when we got married!" I lied gaily. Meho raised his eyebrows. He didn't know whether to believe me or not.
"No," I admitted, "actually, I was twenty-three." He counted mentally for a moment, then looked at me, incredulous.
"But you look so young, so young!"
Meho was forty. "I think it is not so much," he said. Now, he held my arm tightly again as we left, pleased with his afternoon. To all appearances, he and Gordana, on that day, were oblivious to the sword of uncertainty swinging over their heads.

Marie-Toussainte's voice, on the telephone, was excited. "Thursday, the *Comité d'Entr'aide Catholique* is inaugurating its new annex. There'll be a reception; the Bishop is coming, and the Prefect is going to speak. We invited him, and he has accepted."
"No kidding! But..."
"Will you play? Could you do a duet with Meho?"
"And be ready in two days?"
"It's not a concert. You'll play while people are having their wine..."
"Violin and oboe? I don't have any repertoire... I suppose we could try to find something. Why not? Of course, we'll play!"
The Prefect. And if he knew the musician was Meho Kozić? We could not miss this opportunity. My heart raced. Meho and I agreed

to rehearse on Wednesday at the conservatory. We would look for music in the library there and practice in the oboe classroom.

The conservatory stood in the old town, set back on a square of lawn. The trees were dressed in the fresh green of their April leaves. Young people came and went from the stone building, all shapes and sizes of instrument cases in their hands. Meho was waiting for me in the entrance, when I arrived with my violin slung over my shoulder. We kissed, the ritual of four polite kisses, one cheek, then the other. In the oboe room, he held me to him. Meho, my dearest friend. If only this could help you!

We were both nervous. We searched the library and found Bach, Couperin, Haendel. We would have to do without the continuo. We chose our movements carefully, cutting out the riskier passages. There could be no getting lost in front of the Prefect. I knew we would play while people milled, but still, what if he listened to us?

The oboe teacher needed his room, and yet we were not ready. Meho packed his instrument in its rectangular, black case. It didn't seem to bother him that we carry it off with us, even though it had been lent for use in the conservatory practice rooms only. After all, we were to return two hours later for orchestra rehearsal. In the meantime, I drove Meho to our house, where we continued playing. We would have to break for supper, then hurry to orchestra.

Jacques returned from his office. "So, how are the musicians?" he asked. I made conversation with Meho in the kitchen, while Jacques showered. As I had that first time Meho had shared my meal, I brought out photographs. Jacques had been reframing them, and they lay on the table nearby. There was one of me as a nine-month-old baby. "Who is it?" I quizzed him.

"Ah, the little Léo!" he smiled, remembering my grandchild.

"No, it's me!" I laughed. He hadn't seen the age of the photograph. I showed Meho one of our wedding. Jacques and I were gazing into each other's eyes: two romantic children. He shook his head in admiration:

"Now I see how beautiful you were when you were twenty."

"And now?"

"Now, you are kind."

"Meho! That's not nice to say! I'm going to tell my husband!" I tried to joke, but I was vexed. Meho did not seem to understand.

"Well, will you show me a picture of your wedding one day?" I asked him. He looked thoughtful a moment. "Ellen, it's a second marriage. For both of us."

"Oh." What should I say? And what difference could that possibly make? He was confiding in me, though. Did second marriage mean second-class marriage by any chance?

"Did you have any children with your first wife?" I asked, as we drove back to the conservatory.

"No, no children," he answered simply.

I sighed, remembering what he had said about my being kind now. How could a fifty-three-year-old woman be beautiful to a man thirteen years younger? I was foolish to have been hurt. He caught my passing thought, pursed his lips as if to send me a kiss.

"Everything all right?"

"Yes, of course, everything is all right."

"Ellen, I understand now what stupid thing I say to you in kitchen. I didn't mean it, that you are not beautiful now."

"Oh, Meho, it's nothing. I don't mind what you said."

The April evening was cool with the fragrance of new vegetation in the air. After the rehearsal, my wheezing Peugeot climbed once more toward the *Château,* stopping at an intersection. Here, the streets were broad, leading to the outskirts of the town. A white billboard shone in the dim light; a sign pointed to the public hospital, another to the sports complex. I sat, pensive, waiting for the traffic light to change. Meho touched my hand.

"Ellen, *ma chérie,*" he said, unexpectedly. "You have changed my life. I need of you. I love you very much." His voice was deep, emotional, like waters overflowing. *My cup runneth over*. It was too much for him to keep inside any longer. I felt electrified.

"I love you too, Meho." What did one answer to a declaration of love? And was it one, or just a moment of gratitude from a drowning man in a sea of anxiety? Neither of us spoke until the car was parked in front of the entrance to the *Château*. My mind was racing. What did he mean exactly? He leaned forward to give me the *bises,* the four kisses we always exchanged. This time, he pressed forward so that our lips brushed as we moved from one cheek to the other.

"And you are beautiful. You are very beautiful," he said, getting out of the car.

I lay in my bed galvanized, unable to shut my eyes. I must have felt it coming. I should have known, and yet I had imagined nothing of the kind. I liked Meho immensely; I had never really thought of him as desirable. Had I been falling in love with him then? I thought one knew those things. Why this tension? I was like my own violin bow, tightened to the breaking. His words repeated themselves over and over again. I must tell Melisand, I thought. I must tell someone. I will never sleep tonight. Jacques breathed regularly by my side.

I made my way to the computer, where I typed a letter. This, I could not send by e-mail. What if, somehow, it couldn't be deleted? I couldn't tell Jacques, although my conscience hammered at me that I should. If he knew, then his knowledge would be a fortress between my seething emotions and myself. I decided not to.

We had one more practice session at the conservatory, just before playing for the Catholic Aid Committee. It was sprinkling, and Meho appeared in a tie and a flimsy suit jacket, another second-hand find of Gordana's. It was wrinkled from the damp.

"How nice you look!" I said, "but you must hang up your jacket and let it dry a little, or it will only get more rumpled." Obediently, he let me hang it over the back of a chair. He put his oboe reed into a little vial of water to soak and soften. We practiced until it was time to go, but we had to have the permission of the conservatory director to borrow the instrument. This time, Meho was scrupulous about his obligations. Perhaps he was proud to be seen in my company and to tell the director, Monsieur Rolland, that we were going to play for *Monsieur le Préfet*. He took advantage, at any rate, of the opportunity to ask for Monsieur Rolland's help.

"I risk very great danger, if I go back to Bosnia," he said. "Only negative answer so far from commission here. But I make file. I need letters. Maybe . . . you . . . ?" He did not know how to frame his request.

Monsieur Rolland picked up the telephone. "You live at the Refugee Home, at France-Sanctuaire, right?" Meho said he did.

"*Allô? Monsieur le Directeur?*" Monsieur Rolland was asking for Monsieur Lenoir. He explained who he was. "I have Monsieur Kozić here in my office at the moment. He has been asking me to do something to further his petition for asylum. Just what can I do to be of help?" He ran his left hand through his white hair as he listened. Meho's plight touched everyone, and here was a defender of musicians. Meho glanced at me as Monsieur Rolland spoke. We were sitting like two students in front of the principal.

"A paper certifying he has been practicing his oboe all year at the conservatory? And that I am prepared to enroll him next year in order for him to further his musical education in France?"

This last struck me as humiliating. Didn't Meho hold a first prize from Sarajevo? Was that not obvious to Monsieur Rolland? The French always did think that only their diplomas were valid. Well, pride would have to be tossed to the winds. Anything that favored his cause would be welcome.

Monsieur Rolland hung up the telephone. "I will write a letter for you and send it to the home."

Meho moved his foot over and pushed it against mine. "*Merci,*" he said to Monsieur Rolland, with an earnest, grateful smile.

"So that was you two I heard on the Bach?" The director was noncommittal about our playing. What does it matter, I thought. "The Prefect is a music-lover," he added. "I often see him at concerts."

Meho touched my shoe with his again, then winked at me when Monsieur Rolland turned a moment to look out of the wide window by his desk. The window opened onto a narrow street of the old town.

Now he is flirting with me like a teenager, I thought, as we left, armed with oboe and violin. Meho kissed me squarely on the mouth before we entered the premises of the Catholic Aid Committee.

"*Moj Rom . . . ?*" I said, testing the syllables. Meho beamed. Let *Monsieur le Préfet* listen, I told myself. We shall be superlative.

He did not listen, in fact. He arrived without warning, delivered his speech in an adjacent room, and disappeared as quickly as he had come. We barely glimpsed a tall, erect man in a dark suit, gray hair shaved close like an army officer's, a jutting chin. In front of the tables set with glasses and bottles of sparkling white wine, Meho and I played indefatigably, moving from Couperin's Concerto Royal to our favorite movements of Bach, and on to the folk songs we had sung with Thérèse. Then Meho played Mozart from his Sarajevo repertoire and would have gone on indefinitely; he radiated energy. Monsieur Lenoir stood by us, nodding approval, applauding noisily. I wondered whom or what he was applauding exactly.

"That will be fine, now," Marie-Toussainte whispered to me loudly. "You must meet *Monseigneur.*" The new Bishop was full of sympathy for the plight of the asylum seekers. He would go to see the Prefect personally, he promised. Relations between the *Comité d'Entr'aide Catholique* and the *Préfecture* were cordial. Could the Prefect risk appearing heartless?

And there was Sister Agnès de Jésus, quietly smiling in her gray dress. Meho hugged her in his warm, personable way. "I've never stopped praying for you and your lovely family," she said. "I tell Him, Dear God, just look at them! Surely You are going to help them!"

Marie-Toussainte, reigning over her little world like a mother superior, dropped the leftover petits-fours into a bag for the Kozićs. "They can kiss your feet," she said to me, "with all you do for them."

When we separated, Meho gave me a handful of chocolate cookies. "These good, Ellen. You like these."

"How is Gordana?" I asked, a bit guiltily.

"Tired," he said, "very tired."

And then, it was not my feet he kissed.

For weeks, Marie-Toussainte had been trying to obtain an audience with the Prefect. When his office finally said she could have five minutes of his time, she prepared herself carefully.

"*Monsieur le Préfet,*" she began, her voice deep and urgent, thinking she could envelop him in her matronly aura the way she did the refugees. "You know that the *Comite d'Entr'aide Catholique* has never taken sides. We are a strictly apolitical association. Never have you seen any of us in the unfortunate public demonstrations that may have taken place in this town. We fully understand the difficulty of your position. And yet, we must ask you, out of sheer considerations of humanity, to reconsider the applications of Messieurs Petrov, Kozić and Osayin. Believe me, they are worthy of your attention. The fate that awaits these families is dire and frightening. They are in inextricable difficulty . . ."

"Madame," the Prefect replied with cold courtesy, "I appreciate your concern. However, I am well acquainted with the case histories of each of these families."

"Then you know that Monsieur Petrov cannot return to his country . . ."

"I know also that Monsieur Petrov has demonstrated under the windows of this office with placards criticizing my judgment."

"You know that Monsieur Osayin has exhausted every possibility . . ."

"I have followed his dossier."

"And that Monsieur Kozić . . ."

"Useless to say any more; I know his history."

"*Monsieur le Préfet,* I beg of you on my knees . . ."

"That is not appropriate, Madame. Thank you for your visit."

Marie-Toussainte had put her full capacity for hope into this interview, from which she left in despair. She narrated the interview in detail to me that evening on the telephone. "He would not even hear me out," she lamented. "Well, so be it. Now I'll get an appointment with *Député* Lamotte; he is close to the Minister of the Interior, they say."

"You are brave, Marie-Toussainte. You are a mother to all of them."

"Listen, I was at the *Château* the other afternoon with Sister Agnès de Jésus. We talked with Gordana and Meho. He explained to us about the persecutions in Yugoslavia. He drew a map for us, showed us where they fled. You know what happened to Muslim women so often. He was so afraid for his wife. Honestly, tears came to his eyes when he told us about it. I don't know . . . if I'm any judge of character, he is a good man . . ."

> *Meho, I believe it too. And I must be falling in love with you. I need your warmth more than I have ever needed anything. Are you still afraid for your wife? Where am I in all this?*

Meho let me drive him to the *Château* again after rehearsal. When we stopped for a light, I couldn't help wondering why he didn't kiss me. He seemed abstracted, vaguely worried. My pulse sped as I pulled up in front of the home. This time I would show him I was ready to say good-bye. I pressed my mouth against his, hard, harder. He looked at me, thrilled. "Oh, big kiss!" he said, smiling.

"*Pozdravi Gordanu!*" I put in quickly.

"*Pozdravi Jacques!*" he laughed.

Occasionally Meho came to the house to play trios with Jacques and me. Jacques was an amateur pianist, although his years of study were far behind. Music, like reading, was a pleasure he allowed himself little time for. When Meho came, however, we would dig through piles of baroque music to find pieces we could play with some ease together. He was our professional. He set the tempos, corrected our mistakes. He seemed to find unending pleasure on Saturday afternoons in our living room, with the hard-backed chairs by the piano, two metal stands brought out and unfolded.

Jacques was vaguely flattered that a professional musician would play with him. He needed his Saturday afternoons for the innumerable odd jobs he undertook but managed to salvage a couple of hours for Meho. He said he understood Meho's need for company and recreation. Meho's dark eyes never left me. This last time, when Jacques went out of the room for a moment, we exchanged looks, happy and intimate, a special knowing between us. Then, triumphant, he brought out a pile of letters. "Promises of Employment" he said proudly. "Seven of them."

"Seven? Seven Promises of Employment? But how is it possible?"

"Look!"

We read through the pile. Each letter was typed in due form and offered employment as an accordion player for an evening, a weekend, or a festival of three days. His theater friends had obtained these engagements for him. "This is wonderful! It's remarkable! Still, it's not a regular job . . ."

"I get lot of little jobs. Then, maybe, big one."

"Of course. What does Monsieur Lenoir say?"

"He say 'crazy'! He never see anything like this! 'Every day Meho come to me with another letter.' He say he send them to Prefect on day before delay expires. He wrote letter, too, to say how I look for job all the time. Osayin and Petrov spend all their time on their backsides in front of TV. I am everyday in town, looking for work."

"You are strong, Meho," I told him, and he smiled at my approval. He never gave in to a moment's discouragement that I could see. "How is Gordana standing it?" I had not seen her for some days now.

"Gordana not so well. Very tired," he said. "Her dead papa came to her in a dream. Then she cried for two days. Now she worry about child she leave in Yugoslavia."

"A child? She has another child in Yugoslavia?"

"Yes, with papa, Gordana's first husband. She ask me all the time, 'Meho, bring Latifa here!'"

"And will you do it?"

"When I can. Now, I cannot ask for anything at *Préfecture*. No work, no papers."

"Why didn't she come with you?"

"Safer for her in Macedonia."

"Of course. How old is she?"

"Twelve."

"Twelve? Gordana had her so young! Do you know her?"

"Yes, very fond of this child. She lived with us when she was little."

Then why didn't she stay with you? How could you have left your daughter behind, Gordana? It was a question of life and death; I do not doubt it. There are so many things you have not told me. Will I ever know your lives? How can I ever fathom your suffering? What else have you kept to yourselves?

It was simple enough to imagine that when the first attacks began on Sarajevo, Gordana's eldest child had been packed off to her father. Better that than run the risks Gordana and Meho had run in fleeing. Still, what deprivation, what intolerable sacrifice! The war had brought them to France. The war had also separated mother and daughter. Would they find each other again? It could be years, Latifa's childhood gone, before her mother saw her again. Did she feel abandoned? Did she understand? Was she unhappy? Gordana must ask herself this last question every day of her life. I felt sick for her, sick for them, and here was Meho, begging solace with his ardent Romany eyes.

The answering machine often winked red when I got home. He had called and hung up. I erased the call each time. When he found me there, he always asked, "And Jacques? What is he doing?" He spoke gently, as if to a child. He wanted to know my schedule at school. I invented hours I did not have.

Meho, I wasn't afraid of you; I was afraid of myself. I had to make up those little lies about my schedule. I know you scarcely believed them. What if you had found a way to come to the house? How could I have said no to my insistent, dark-eyed Gypsy?

Château Lore
Murat

Murat stayed at study hall after school every day, because he needed extra help learning French. Mademoiselle dictated, and Murat leaned on his pencil, as if pressing it a little harder would get the words out. Sometimes the point broke, and then he would get the plastic sharpener out of his schoolbag and twist it around the tip. Murat liked watching the thin wooden curls float down to the desk. Mademoiselle would prod him, then, "Come on, Murat, we're not going to sleep here tonight, are we?"

When he was finished, he would skip back up to the home where *Maman* and *Papa* would be waiting. It amused him to call them by their French names. *Baba* didn't sound right here, anyway. Murat was a very important man in the family; when Monsieur Lenoir called them to explain something, he was called too, and he stood at his father's side and helped find the words in Turkish. Murat already knew plenty of words: Turkish, Bulgarian, French, even a few German ones from Switzerland, but those, he had mainly forgotten. He'd only been in Switzerland for two years, between the ages of three and five. He hadn't even gone to school then, but he remembered certain games he used to play. That was the first time they'd been abroad, after the Bulgarians had tried to make his papa take a Bulgarian name. Kossev, they said he had to be called. It was stupid; his name was Suleyman Osayin, and he was proud to be Turkish. When the regime softened up, as Papa said, they went back to Bulgaria. He wondered what softened up meant. Was it like a melon that was finally getting ripe and starting to smell good? His father's father had come from Turkey to Bulgaria, and he said they should always remember what they were.

Murat didn't really care if he was Turkish or Bulgarian or French, so long as they left him alone and let him play soccer. He had posters of his favorite soccer heroes on the wall of their room at the *Château*. They said you could, if you used that blue paste that comes off again.

Murat and his maman and papa lived all three in the same room. He liked it when Maman brushed her long hair and twisted it in the back, especially when she lifted her two arms to clasp on the barrette. He noticed there were a lot of gray strands in with the chestnut ones, but that was normal. She was old now, thirty-eight.

For his *goûter* after school, he had fresh bread his own papa made. That was the only work he did any more now, making the bread. Murat liked to watch his strong hands in the dough, kneading and patting, just the right amount. He wouldn't make the rest of their food, because that was a woman's job, but Papa was a baker.

Suada's mother made bread too, but it didn't look the same. She told him her mother did it the right way and called him a prick, so he hit her. All he did was shove her shoulders a little, but to hear her squawk you'd have thought he'd nearly killed her. Her mother came and hugged her and said, *"c'est pas grave"*, it doesn't matter, the way she always did when the baby spilled stuff, but it must have mattered, because then she said she'd get her husband to talk to the director. Suada was always making a stink anyway, like when she said she wouldn't go to school because the teacher slapped her, but the teacher never touched her. She just didn't want to get scolded for not doing her reading lessons at home. She was only in the first grade, anyway, even if she was already eight. She'd never even gone to school before. She said it was because of the war. But he had gone in Bulgaria up to last year, when he was eleven. Here they'd put him in elementary school instead of junior high school, because he had to learn the language. They lent him the books and everything, because Papa told the teacher about how they'd lost everything back home when the bakery had burned down.

His father said he couldn't figure out who'd burned the bakery. It began with an explosion, and there wasn't any bottled gas, because he used a real wood fire in his ovens. So they knew something had been planted. People didn't want a Turk making their bread, especially one that succeeded. Nobody died, because they did it on a holiday, but Papa said it was a message he was supposed to understand.

SEVEN

I accepted tea at the home *en famille*. That should be safe enough. "So, I get tea for you and your brother?" Gordana asked, cheerful. Meho had apparently reported what I had said that day in front of René's office, and she was joining the game. As soon as her back was turned, Meho seized me, sucking in and out my lower lip.

"Meho, stop it!" I whispered, scandalized. He pretended to sit obediently. I was blushing furiously when Gordana returned with the cups.

"Look at her dress!" Meho said to Gordana, pointing out my long, cotton print skirt. "The *gadja* don't usually wear long skirts. She's dressed like a *romani*." He spoke in his own language, but I understood him. *Gadje*, I knew, were non-Gypsies.

"We *gadje* wear whatever's in fashion, you know," I said. I had never paid attention to what I wore in his presence. Suddenly it seemed a matter of importance.

"Won't you have something to eat?" Meho asked. It was five p.m.; I assumed they meant a cookie with my tea, and I accepted.

"*Kushat?*" Gordana asked Meho. He nodded. She appeared a moment later with chopped meat and canned beans steaming on a plate, placing it before me on the low table. I had not realized, but this was their dinner time. They had not adopted French meal times, which was, after all, just as well, so long as they lived in the *Château*. Each family retained its habits, avoiding a crush in the kitchen.

"I am worry about the children," Gordana said. "They never want dinner."

"They're not hungry. They eat good at school," Meho reassured her. He seemed relaxed and happy. Gordana followed us to the car. "Your brother forget his umbrella in your car," she said, apparently happy too. She had picked up my fond name for Meho and was using it again, as if this were perfectly natural. I read neither jealousy nor suspicion in her seawater eyes. She did not refer to herself as my sister, however. I handed my little brother his umbrella and drove to the school meeting awaiting me, trying not to think of the kisses stolen while Gordana was working in the kitchen to feed me. They both seemed in excellent spirits. That was what counted.

Cédric was on the phone. "I've got the appointment at the foundry. I'm picking up Meho Monday and going with him. He's going to need help speaking. I'll let you know how it goes."

When Saturday came, and our rendezvous for trios, I was nearing a confession. Normally, it was I who would pick up Meho at the bus station, and I well knew what temptations would be mine during the ride. I summoned my courage. "Jacques?"

"Hmm?" He was absorbed in the local paper.

"Would you mind getting Meho? When he comes with me, he, uh . . . he has a tendency to flirt with me . . ." I listened to my own voice sounding matter-of-fact, detached.

"Is it time?"

"Yes."

He got up without a word and went to the car.

You never said a thing about it, Jacques. You never asked a question. You never wanted to know what I meant by 'flirt', and you never asked, later, if he was still doing it. I had done my part, had I not? I had warned you that the serpent was tendering the scarlet apple. To me, it was clear you were not interested.

Unexpectedly, Jacques kissed me twice that afternoon. He stood stiffly, his face somber. His kiss was cold and proprietary. It meant you are mine and do not forget it! There was no delight and no passion. I couldn't help comparing now.

Did you see me even for a fleeting moment? Having appeal for another man? You never would have thought so, would you? And you did not think he could have any appeal for me. I was married to you.

Cédric reported back as promised. "It's in the bag," he said. "The director wrote up the paper right away. If he gets his papers, he'll be hired at thirty-five hours per week, a three-month contract, renewable."

"So he made a good impression?"

"Yeah, especially that history you wrote. When he read about how Meho hasn't had any news of his parents and brother since 1993 and doesn't know what happened to them, his eyes even went misty. It's not so often you find a boss like that, with a heart."

"Thank God."

"Meho doesn't even seem to realize the importance of this."

"Maybe he doesn't get all the French. I hope he thanked you, Cédric. You've saved their lives with this."

"Yeah, well, he'd better work hard. I need to keep my credit with that director. I wouldn't go out on a branch like this for just anyone."

"Thanks, Cédric. Thanks so much."

Jacques was tense and preoccupied. The premiere for the play he was in was taking place that evening in a small art theater in town. It was a Wednesday night, and not many people were expected. There would be more at the Friday performance. But I knew this first evening was important for him, and, although he didn't expect me to attend, I resolved to dash to the theater as soon as my orchestra rehearsal was over, just to be there for the applause at the end.

As soon as Gérard put down his baton, I ran to the exit. I could not drive Meho, and I should not. I was running to Jacques, still running from Meho. As I fled the conservatory in the night, I heard him behind me, racing on the cobblestones: "Ellenna! Helena! Where are you going?" I explained.

"I'll come with you."

"Do you really think so, Meho? We have to run. I want to be there when Jacques gets out."

We got there in time. The little theater hadn't opened yet. Meho and I stood in front of it. He sprang up to kiss me from below the curb, landing back on his feet just as the doors flung open. His black eyes flamed with desire.

"Meho!" I was outraged. He was ready to kiss me on every street corner in town and seemed amused that I should mind. "But I know people in this town, don't you understand? It's not your town, but it's mine, and I don't need you kissing me everywhere in public!" This flouting of propriety amused and entertained him, the risk and the insolence of it.

Jacques, unsuspecting, was pleased to see us. "Meho certainly did look chipper tonight," he remarked later. "How does he have such a good morale?" It was agreed that Meho would attend the play with me the following evening.

He couldn't understand a word, of course. It was literary, with much dialogue and little action. He sat near me, and it was all I could do to keep from taking his hand. He sat frowning with the effort of the strange language.

After the play, the participants were reluctant to disband. Meho stayed close to Jacques and me, as we followed the group to a café in town. I wondered what he thought of this very French ambiance: a high-ceilinged, nineteenth-century apartment converted into an intimate café, with sculpted wainscoting, high-backed, plush Voltaire chairs. The air was smoky. Tall flutes of wine or heavy-bottomed glass mugs of beer stood on the round tables. I translated as much of the conversation as I could for Meho, sitting by him, even drinking once from his glass.

But when it was time to go, I asked Jacques to drive him home. I knew what would happen if I let Meho in the car with me, how fragile was my resolve to resist temptation. We had come in separate cars, since Jacques had been at the theater early to prepare for the performance. He said nothing to my request, assuming, no doubt, that I was simply tired. My words from Saturday had been forgotten. Meho climbed in with him. He will get the message, I thought. This is the second time Jacques has driven him. I had made up my mind to flee.

He knew I was running. On Sunday, we met for an orchestra concert in town. "How are you, Meho?"

"Not so good, not feel good."

"What?" I had never heard any admission of the kind from him. "What is it?" He merely shrugged in answer, but looked at me hard, as if I should understand.

"I don't feel quite right myself," I admitted. He nodded. We understood each other perfectly well.

Our orchestra was playing and Meho had the oboe solo. We were there early, Meho with Suada and Amina. Gordana, as usual, had decided to stay at home with Veronika. She said she didn't like music anyway.

You didn't appreciate him, did you? Married to a professional musician, and not like music, indeed? Not make the least effort to come, when he was playing a solo? You didn't deserve him, Gordana.

The weather was warm, and the trees in the public garden behind the concert hall were lush with the tender green of spring. Meho had a disposable camera, which he handed to Suada. "Take our picture!" he commanded. We had on our concert clothes, dark with white shirts, serious. He stood on a stone step to be as tall as I. This amused him. Suada squinted, obeyed her father, then grabbed his hand to pose with him for me. For her, it was all a game. He was storing memories.

We crossed the street in front of the concert hall, each holding a child by the hand, to see a roped-off, open-air exhibit of antique automobiles. Meho leaned forward enthusiastically, pointing out details to Suada. A Model-T Ford, red as a peony, shone in the sunlight. When we turned to cross back, the children skipped cheerily along with us. In the middle of the street, Meho turned to me suddenly. "Helena, what is forbidden is just what you want to do."

"That doesn't mean you should do it." I didn't think that wanting something, however, passionately, sufficed to make it right. Did he?

We didn't speak again until the intermission. I found him in a corner of the wings, pretending to study the silver keys of his oboe.

"Ah!" he smiled, as I approached. "At last! Here you are!"

"Meho, you've got to understand. I'm too fond of my husband."

"It's all right."

"And I'm too fond of Gordana, too. Do you love Gordana?"

He nodded affirmatively, his expression grave, but he did not speak. Then a broad grin lit his features, and he rolled his dark-lashed eyes at me, very much as Veronika did when she was playing at getting her mother's attention. "Honestly, I cannot stay serious with you."

You knew you'd get to the end of my resistance, didn't you? You were just biding your time! And you said you loved your wife. Then you could have been nicer to her, couldn't you? All you were thinking of was the forbidden fruit!

He climbed into my car as usual the Wednesday following. "And now, Helena," he announced solemnly. "I am going to give you a kiss." How did he always guess what was going on in my mind? He knew perfectly well what I wanted and would not allow myself. As we neared the entrance to the *Château*, he gestured toward the shadows farther down. Without speaking, I drove there and stopped. He enfolded me in his arms and kissed me now with real concentration, his dark beard rubbing my cheeks, his tongue traveling inside my mouth. I gave myself up to it, ran my fingers through his hair, disoriented by the feel of this alien skull, the implantation of the hair, the texture of it. We held each other for a long time, until I said good night.

At home, I panicked. I was fifty-three years old and probably more naive than the young teenagers I taught. I suddenly began to wonder if I could get AIDS from saliva, from a cut in the mouth. I e-mailed Melisand, who cool-headedly told me to calm down. She sent me the basics on AIDS, which I erased immediately from the screen and then wished I had not. I wanted to read it all again. My mind was racing like a timer out of order.

"Mom, if you're upset, tell Dad about Meho."

Melisand, I can't, I wrote back. *I'm too emotionally involved. I've thought about it, but there are certain things he can go without knowing. I do tell him certain things, for example: 'Meho called me again. He's got a real umbilical cord with me.' Your father doesn't react. He has no thought of being jealous. I take each day as it comes and live each instant as I can. If I told him, it's sure, he wouldn't want me to see the Kozićs again, and I can't bear giving up Meho's adoration of me. He tells me things I've never heard before in my life and certainly never will again. Of course it won't last. We each have our responsibilities. But maybe we each have a lack we need to fulfill, and if life gives us a little present, we shouldn't be too quick to toss it away. I won't cheat on your father. Your pre-Prozac father, maybe I could have, but the post-Prozac one is nicer. How could I live with myself if I thought I was making him unhappy? And Gordana. She's been through so much and still going through it.*

Melisand and tranquilizers kept me going. I had never felt such relief at school, either. It was a sheer diversion. The time I spent with my students, however unruly, was time I did not spend thinking of Meho, waiting for him to call or wondering where our relationship might lead. My youthful, clamoring pupils had become an oasis, an opiate of forgetfulness. When I shut the door to my classroom, I shut out the emotions boiling in my brain.

Marie-Toussainte and I discussed *Château* business on the telephone, as we often did. I learned from her that Monsieur Lenoir had not sent Meho's employment letters to the *Préfecture* as promised. He had finally done so, she said, but only at her insistence. She thought he was afraid of his superiors. If it was learned in high places that a house director was doing anything special to help a refugee, he could be reprimanded. A certain quota of refugees was accepted each year, and nothing was to be done to sway this in one direction or the other. He must not seem to favor anyone, she surmised.

Meho had added to his collection of documents for the new Appeal the letter from Monsieur Rolland, recommending him for his artistic ambition and promising that he would have a place at the conservatory the following year to work toward a French diploma. This too had been sent in the fat manila envelope *in extremis*.

According to Marie-Toussainte, Monsieur Lenoir was maneuvering between the hierarchy of France-Sanctuaire, the *Préfecture,* moral pressure from the Catholic Aid Committee, and his apparently real friendship for Meho. That personal politicking of any sort could take precedence over human distress was beyond my ken.

Marie-Toussainte called me again after her appointment with the deputy. "It is rumored that the Kozićs are going to be accepted."

"No? The employment promise did it, then?"

"It's not even that. It's apparently because they are Rom and stateless and have no place to go."

"Then the administration has a soul?"

"Apparently, but it's still unofficial, so I don't want to say a word to Meho about it. I wouldn't want them to get their hopes up and then have it fall through."

"Of course not." My skin tingled on my arms. "And Mr. Petrov? And Mr. Osayin?"

"Doesn't look so good for them. But there is a period of one month before the expulsion notices become effective."

One more month. The end of May now.

"By the way, you know that heavy blond Kosovar woman?" she asked.

"I see who you mean. Ferialle, I think she's called."

"She's been trying to 'buy' me. Every time I go up there, she has some present or other for me. Today, she wanted to give me a hairbrush. I told her to keep her things. I help everybody the same."

"What did she say to that?"

"Nothing, but she's very obsequious."

"That must be the way it works in their countries. The baksheesh, you know."

> *Meho, you weren't trying to buy me or pay me for anything, were you? The way to your papers could not pass through my bedroom. In that case, better to court the secretary at the Foreigners Bureau…*

La Méduse, the theater company which had helped Meho before, offered him the opportunity to play at a fair, some distance from us, not far from Paris. He was to be away the entire May Day holiday weekend, all of Friday, Saturday and Sunday. Eternity. If I couldn't see him, I would settle for someone close to him. I needed to hear his name, to see his smile on the children's faces. "Gordana, would you like Jacques and me to take you and the children to the country? It might be good to get away for a few hours."

Rather to my surprise, she accepted. The weather was cold, but the sky was clear. She borrowed a stroller from the *Château,* and we packed it into the back of the car. Gordana was wearing jeans. I had never seen her like that, like a young woman of her generation, in fact. She didn't wear the long skirts of the Romany women, but she wasn't usually in trousers, either. The roundness of her belly, left over from her last pregnancy, was flattening. Her short, thick hair was getting longer, and she tied it in back with a barrette. She had stuffed innumerable boxes of cookies into a knapsack for the children's afternoon snack. Their little faces were soon smeared with chocolate.

We drove to a nearby wood, where many apartment dwellers came on Sundays. Although the trees were burgeoning with new leaves, the chill of winter was in the air. "How cold it is here!" she said. I thought that spring in Sarajevo must be a gentler affair. Meho often shivered in his black leather jacket. They were used to warmer seasons. France was surely a cold place to them in more ways than one.

Jacques played the doting uncle. If he enjoyed it or was simply being a good sport, I wasn't sure. He tossed the children on his shoulders, feigned to run after them, while they squealed. Gordana smiled. "Just like Meho. He always play with the children like that." She told me how he was never at home back in Sarajevo, either. She was used to it. "Meho always work, only come home once in awhile." I wondered if he were running after women. Gordana's gaze was clear. She didn't appear to have those thoughts.

"Gordana," I said, as we drove back to the *Château,* "there's something I want you to know."

"Yes?"

"If . . . if your appeal for territorial asylum is rejected . . . if you have nowhere to go . . . I just want you to know, you can stay with us. You know, we have a whole floor upstairs that we don't need."

"Thank you." Her voice was calm. I didn't know if she realized what I was offering. But this time, she didn't seem to think their petition would be rejected.

When I made the same offer again in dead earnest to Meho, it amused him. "And what would I do on your second floor?" he said. "I'd come and get you!"

Marie-Toussainte, on the other hand, was impressed. "I will never have them on the street," I told her.

"But you aren't allowed to house undocumented persons."

"What do I care? I'm a respectable citizen. I would break a law for humanitarian reasons, if the law is inhumane."

She was surprised at my resolve. "But the police will come and get you."

"So, let them come! Just how much can they do to me?"

She took me for a Christian activist and almost convinced me I was. But I couldn't imagine that I risked a prison sentence for putting up a homeless family, aliens or not. She was right, however. A short time after our conversation, I read in the local newspaper that a militant in another city had been condemned to a suspended sentence and fined for "aiding and abetting the illegal stay of an undocumented alien".

Earlier that spring, a revised immigration law that gave us renewed hope had been adopted by the French government. It was no longer necessary to obtain a certificate from the town hall in order to house foreigners from certain, specified countries. Moreover, the right of asylum was extended to all people "persecuted in reason of their action in favor of liberty". Meho's work in defense of the Roma could perhaps be cited here. The law gave hope to students, too, as well as artists and people in cultural professions. Surely there would be some article of this law that could apply to him. I read and reread it, trying to squeeze water from the stone of its legalistic prose. It would not go into effect immediately, not soon enough for Meho.

It's the economy that remains the prime mover, I thought. "Forty-two percent of all requests for authorizations to remain in France have been refused so far this year," I read in the newspaper. Those people could not have had promises of employment . . . or could they? The government could not afford to let the population think it was too lenient on immigration. That would only give rise to increased influence on the extreme right. People like Meho and his family, each with its history of love and suffering, flight and despair, were numbers to the politicians, and these numbers were toys.

The long, chilly weekend drew to an end. On Monday morning, I found Gordana at the schoolroom. "So, how is Meho?" I asked. "Did it go all right?"

"Yes, but lots of work. Got back late last night. He tired, very, very tired."

I didn't dare hope to see him. He didn't usually meet Gordana after her lesson, and, if he was tired, he would surely stay at home. I felt a flicker of expectancy, nonetheless, but, as we left the room, the courtyard was empty in front of the classrooms. Then Gordana spied Veronika's empty stroller near a door. "Oh, look!" she cried, pleased, "Veronika!" Meho and his little girl emerged from a corner of the garden, each holding a small bunch of tiny wild jonquils. He stood in front of me, his head slightly lowered, and held out the bouquet. Then he motioned Veronika toward her mother.

"*Mamak!*" he said. Give it to Mama! The child smiled radiantly and handed the short-stemmed flowers to her mother. When he lifted his eyes and looked at me directly, I felt I was being burned. He was indeed tired, and a strand of black hair lay limply on his forehead. His face was unusually pale, his eyes smoldering. The air between us was electric, the current tangible. My God, I thought, can she feel it too? Can she feel how the air is inflammable? Can she see the expression in his eyes? Does she realize something or not?

Gordana was cheerful. She was pleased her husband had come to get her after her lesson.

> *Melisand, I have got to get away. I have to get away and think of other things. I cannot stay rational. I am on the verge of a nervous breakdown.*

Château Lore
Leila

The treatment of Madame Leila Zaraeva's congenital nervous illness requires prolonged medical care, and the necessity of hospitalization must be envisioned.

Thus concluded Aslan and Leila's passport to temporary asylum: a French medical report. She was hiccuping her way to freedom, for the ill in need of medical care were succored and detained. All right, it was for three months, but the other refugees didn't have to know that, and Leila could lord it over them. With luck, it would be extended anyway, and Aslan had the right to get a job now.

A social worker, a nice young woman, very gentle and friendly, had come and explained about the halfway house where they would be lodged. She would help Aslan, too, in his search for work. She explained how *Action-Travail* provided odd jobs for the unemployed: shutters to be painted, a hedge to trim, gardening, a fence to build. They had to contribute as much as they could to the rent, even if it was a charitable association that would lend them the two rooms, with a kitchen and a real bathroom, all their own: none of those stinky toilets to share any more and no more fighting over stove tops. Leila smiled to herself as she remembered Gordana Kozić's face when she'd heard the news, all of their faces, in fact. She had been a queen that day, basking in their envy and suspicion. How had she done it? If

France would keep Leila, it would take anyone, they thought. Their own hopes rose.

The social worker returned many times to visit Leila and Aslan, so many, in fact, that Leila no longer wanted to see her. She was a pretty *Mademoiselle* of Portuguese origin, or so she told them, but she could have been anything. Her thick, black curls danced on her shoulders, shinier than Leila's own. Marie ran to her and hugged her knees, and the first French words she spoke were to Mademoiselle Nathalie.

Leila herself was exasperated with French. Sister Agnès de Jésus taught her from an ABC book, and there was no making any sense of it. Bé, Ba, Bo: What could that mean? It was enough trouble, learning to write that Latin alphabet, but the syllables drove her mad. Sister Agnès de Jésus was all right when she explained useful things, like French meal times, but she would never learn to read with her. She asked Marie-Toussainte if she couldn't study with the woman who taught Gordana Kozić. "She can help me, because she know Russian," she had argued, but to no avail.

"You're not making progress because you don't learn your lessons," Marie-Toussainte had countered, and, as Leila had to admit to herself, it was true, but who wanted to recite syllables? Besides, Gordana's teacher invited her and her family to her home and did things for them. She wanted someone to visit her too and make much of her. Not Mademoiselle Nathalie. Her hair was far too beautiful, and she didn't like the way Aslan looked at it.

Eight

*T*he shadows near the *Château* hid us again as we found each other like a homecoming, lips on lips, hands stroking tenderness. Meho, intense and serious, kissed me passionately, staking out careful possession of each inch of my face and neck. "I have to go, Meho. Jacques is expecting me back."

My face was hot. My skin, sensitive and pale, turned red at the least touch. There was a risk this touch would show. Several miles separated the *Château* from the house, and my burning cheeks had just enough time to cool. Tingling with something unfulfilled, yet relieved to be back where it was safe, I plopped myself down next to Jaques on the sofa. Surprised, he put down his book.

"Have the Kozićs any answer yet?"

"When I asked Meho, he just smiled like the sphinx and said 'nothing official.'" We were one week into May now. The dreaded end of April had gone by, and no one had been evicted from the home nor sent to the border, any border.

Jacques helped me use the computer to make attractive notices, advertising Meho's recital at our school. "Meho Kozić, Accordion", they read, "Music of the Former Yugoslavia, May Seventh at 12:45 p.m.,

Auditorium". My colleague Nicole was pleased, helping me tape them to the library door and tack them to bulletin boards. Her shiny, platinum blond hair fitted her head like a mushroom cap. She was always busy, always organizing, always late.

"The Music Club students will be there, and probably a number of others. You know we can't pay him, don't you? We can give him a gift certificate, for example, to a shop in town for a CD or a book."

"That's fine, Nicole, whatever the school can do. But you know, he hasn't got a CD player, and he doesn't really read French."

"I'll see what we can do."

Meho was to meet me at the school. He carried a large, red Czech accordion that the *Méduse* Company had obtained for him, he explained, to compensate him for playing for them, since the law forbade him to accept any salary. This accordion was the real thing, worthy of a professional, not a broken antique like the one from the streets of Ghent. I showed him into the teachers' room, empty for the lunch period.

The *collège* had been a convent in the seventeenth century. Careful restoration had made it into an elegant edifice with vaulted ceilings, where bells rang out incongruously to mark the end of classes. In the teachers' room, modern, burgundy-upholstered armchairs and a coffee machine contrasted with austere stone arches.

"That is architecture!" said Meho, as he raised his eyes, then ran them over the rows of brown, wooden boxes on the walls, where the teachers kept their papers and received mail.

"What is your program? I'll have to announce it."

"First, *Jelem, Jelem*. Rom song. It tell of the Gypsies, they travel, they have no place to rest their heads."

"And then?"

"*Zelënkaia*"

"What's that?"

"Song of love for a girl with green eyes." He seized me and kissed me. Indeed, my eyes were green, but a murky, gray green, not limpid pools of black-fringed light, like Gordana's.

"I can see what you like!" I said.

He kissed me again, his own eyes flashing. "Meho! Anyone could come in! Be careful!"

He laughed. He was claiming possession of the English teacher on her own home ground, in a place where she was used to taking herself seriously. He was wild and outrageous and charming.

His playing left me speechless. I knew he was good, could improvise, but this was virtuosity. Here were no questions of sight-reading, but of the Yugoslavian soul. He passed from Gypsy music to Bosnian, Serbian, Albanian, Croatian, Russian, Polish, even Italian. There were fireworks and nostalgia, melodies in the minor key, then bursts of sun and laughter in the cascades of notes. *"Jelem, Jelem",* Meho sang, his voice not quite strong enough to cover the generous sound of the chords. "Let us go on!" I imagined I understood the words: "no place for the Gypsy to stay, no place of welcome for the man with no destination."

Meho was perfectly self-possessed on the stage. He smiled benevolently at the gathered youngsters, his black eyes velvety with affection. Was this look for his enthralled audience? For me?

When the program was finished, I asked him if he wouldn't like a cup of coffee or some lunch. It was clear that he wanted to stay with me. The weather was splendid, the May sun warm and golden. Where could we go without being on a terrace in view of all? "I know! Chez Mady, across the square," I suggested. "We can get anything you'd like there." It was a *brasserie,* and their veranda was entirely glassed-in.

Meho ordered an expensive concoction of ice cream, then proceeded to feed it to me. I remembered Jacques, who never suffered that I taste what was on his plate in restaurants. "You made your choice, and I made mine." My curiosity annoyed him. Meho gave himself to the sensuality of the shared spoon, the rich sweetness of the ice cream, this new intimacy between us.

The restaurant was crowded with people we neither knew nor cared about. Waiters in white shirts rushed past. Near the window sat a family before large plates of sauerkraut and sausage. The grandmother glanced at me. What do they think of this mature, fair-haired woman and her burly, dark companion in his tired leather jacket, feeding each other like a pair of young lovers? Nothing at all, probably.

Only I could be thinking anything of it. I pretended to read the lines of Meho's hand, Gypsy style.

"Your line of Laudes-la-Romaine is very, very long," I predicted, smiling. "You'll be staying here a long time!" I told him about the Gypsy I had met just before my dark-haired Melisand was born, and who had insisted on scrutinizing my palm. She had predicted that I would have a blond boy baby. "They don't know the first thing about it," he laughed. "They just pretend."

"That's what I thought! You know," I added, "you Gypsies, you don't have the same mentality as we *gadje*. You're so much more expressive. We keep things to ourselves more."

"And this love, you kept it to yourself then?"

"I didn't know I was in love with you."

Meho simply looked at me. "And you?" I asked. "Did you know you were in love with me?"

"I thought of you very, very soon, Ellen. My God, the first time I saw you in front of that church schoolroom . . . !" He shook his head in wonderment at this memory. "We take a walk?" He leaped up to call the waiter, his head high, snapping his fingers authoritatively. French people don't do that, I thought. The waiter materialized immediately and left the check, which I paid. I sat waiting for my change.

"Why wait for change? Only ten francs!"

"But ten francs are worth waiting for." I found him generous with my money. He left his expensive ice cream nearly untouched, too. Profligate and carefree, Meho was one to live for the treat of a moment. He had been ready to spend his family's weekly stipend on a throw rug. I had behind me a lifetime of saving and foresight. I called waiters courteously and tended to be intimidated by the French variety. His manners were new to me, but, if they surprised me, I did not love him the less for them.

"A walk" meant finding a bench in the public garden where we could be relatively alone. The ground was dappled with green and gold, as the sunlight penetrated the branches of the trees. Large diesel lawnmowers moaned, as municipal gardeners worked in the park. The sweet smell of newly cut grass mingled with fumes. Meho and I necked on a bench, like youngsters after school. His shoulders were strong and rather fleshy, his arms muscular. He gathered my upper body into them, holding me like a warm bundle, bringing his long, shapely musician's hands around to my breasts, soft under the cotton of my summer dress. I yearned for him to hold them. He seemed far away.

"I loved first wife very much," he said, "and you, I love like her."

"First wife?" It sounded Chinese. "Tell me about her."

"Serbo-Croatian woman."

"A Gypsy too?"

"Yes, Gypsy. So a beautiful woman."

"Will you show me her picture one day?"

"Impossible. Gordana cut her out of every snapshot. She say she's dead. The past is dead."

"Did she leave you?"

"I ask for divorce."

"Why?"

"When she say 'no' to me about something, then it was 'no'."

I was to get no more explanation than this for the moment. He told me he had a son, though, seventeen years old. I had thought it odd he would have had no children before his thirties, but so many shadows still waited to be lit up.

"Why did you say you had no children with her?"

"Not want to talk about that then."

"And your parents, Meho?"

"Dead."

"Both of them?"

"Yes, both." He didn't seem disposed to expand on this. It must hurt.

"The war . . . ?" I ventured. Meho nodded, then turned to kiss me again. "Meho, look at where the *Comité d'Entr'aide Catholique* has got me."

"This is real humanitarian aid," he joked. "Thank you Ellen!"

I felt a sudden doubt. "Did you ever kill anyone? In the war, I mean?"

"No," he shook his head, smiling.

"I want you to know something. I will never sleep with you, Meho."

"It doesn't matter."

We left the park hand in hand, and, despite the difference in our heights, my hand seemed to have found in his its rightful place. I withdrew it as we neared the street. Any number of my acquaintances, my students, could pass by here.

I drove him to the theater company, where he was to leave the accordion, not a gift outright, apparently, but specially lent for his use. As we waited at a traffic light, I asked, "Meho, why me?"

"I don't know Ellen. Marie-Toussainte says, '*L'amour, c'est l'amour.*' That's all . . . Ellen, are you satisfied with me? Is everything all right?"

"Yes, Meho, thank you for being you. Thank you for just being."

"Thank you, my Helena, thank you for just letting me love you."

This man with so few words at his disposal had charmed me by the sheer force of his emotion. The words that were his were the right ones. Between us could be none of the barriers that the mastery of language bestows on relationships.

I felt more peaceful after this. He wouldn't hound me. Jacques seemed to be awakening gradually from a sleep of many years. When I arose from bed in the morning, milk for my *café-au-lait* would be warming on the stove. I had never before obtained that small favor from him, although he was usually up before I was. It seemed strange he should have this attention for me. I needed Jacques physically more and more; he was reaping the benefits of my arousal. Thank God he was so thoroughly unaware.

Meho and I agreed to meet on Sunday at Life and Light, the Gypsy church. Jacques couldn't possibly have any misgivings about my attending a church service. I chose a long skirt from my closet, remembering his words about the *gadja*, the non-Gypsy women, and their clothes. A small Frenchwoman of indeterminate age, her thick, graying hair carefully tied in a bun, met me in front of the meeting-house door. She, too, wore a skirt that reached her ankles.

"Is it your first time here?"

"Yes. I'm meeting a friend. A Bosnian Gypsy. As you can see, I'm not one, though."

"I'm not a Gypsy either, but I love it here. There is so much warmth, enthusiasm like you'll find nowhere else."

I entered and chose a seat on a wooden bench. The room was long and spare with whitewashed walls. A door remained open to the outside, and children came and went freely. Some were blue-eyed and freckled with tanned faces and tawny spikes of hair. Others were dark with shiny night-black hair like Meho's girls. Couples and families sat closely side-by-side, some teenage girls arm-in-arm. All the women wore long skirts, some with glittery golden mules on brown, tough-skinned feet. The men had on jeans, wide leather belts and crisp cotton shirts. They stood with their legs slightly apart, thumbs in their belts, in the manner of cowboys. They had mustaches and weather-beaten faces. Meho entered, a courteous smile on his face, he too in his Sunday best, and shook the hands of the couple next to me. The pastor struck some chords on his guitar and the assembly began to sing.

"A lot of you remember how it used to be," he said, attacking his sermon. "You were lucky if you had some straw to sleep on! Now, it's the air-conditioned caravan! Ah, life is easier now, isn't it brothers and sisters? Maybe you did some things back then that you aren't so proud of now, and you'd just as soon forget. You were just like that image they have of us: chicken thief, and then say it was the fox that did it! Brothers and sisters, Jesus hasn't forgotten those things, but he will forgive you for them! All you have to do is call on His holy name . . ."

"Amen, Lord!" someone called in the assembly.

When it was time for prayer, some women sobbed, their colored shawls jerking. "Oh Lord, oh Lord, forgive us, Lord! Oh Lord, we love you; we love you so much!" They choked with emotion, hysteria not far.

The pastor greeted Meho and me cordially after the service. As we spoke, a girl with long, golden-brown hair stood looking at me in unconcealed surprise and admiration. Did she recognize Meho as one of theirs? She obviously saw the outsider in me. I smiled at her, and she gratified me with a look of rapture. She reminded me of a young *romani* who had rung the doorbell once, and I had opened a ground floor window to her, not wanting to go to the door. "I have only come to talk to you about Jesus," she had said, "and invite you to a prayer meeting."

I had thanked her, and she had pointed to a row of flacons that caught the morning light on a dresser. "If you have any old or near-empty perfume bottles you don't need . . ." I had swept up four or five and handed them to her, glad to be rid of her at so little cost.

"Be careful, Madame Aubert," my next-door neighbor had warned afterward. "*La Romanichelle* has taken something from you. I saw her cross your lawn with something shiny in her hands."

"She did not take anything," I had said, slightly annoyed. "She asked, and I gave it to her."

The pastor said they would continue to pray for Meho. "And those lawyers?" I asked. "The ones whose names you gave him?"

"They can't do anything for him in France, so long as he hasn't got his papers. However, if he has to go back, they could help him and his family get to a Gypsy village in Romania."

"A Gypsy village in Romania?" And live with the poorest of the poor? This was not Meho's aim, either for himself or for his children.

When we saw Gordana that evening, we told her about the emotional women, shouting and weeping their prayers. "Pfff, they not right here," she said in a disgusted tone, tapping her temple with her forefinger.

You, Gordana, did not seem so passionate then.

We didn't tell her about the time we'd spent in my car after the service, Meho pleading for another walk in the park. Scarlet with his kisses, I swore I would buy a spray for my complexion and keep it in my bag. How could I go home like this?

"*Ia liubliu tebia,*" I said to him in Russian before we separated. "*Dobro liubish?*"

"*Da, dobro.*" Yes, I love you dearly. He moaned with refrained desire, but he let me go.

"I'm out of a car," said Jules, the elderly violin player who sat at the stand in front of me. "It broke down this afternoon. My wife drove me to the rehearsal in her car, but now she's in bed. Would it be too much if I asked you to drive me home this evening?"

The answer caught in my throat. "Of course not, Jules. You know it's practically no detour at all. I'll be glad to. But you know I have to drive Meho Kozić back to the Refugee Home . . ."

"No problem. We'll take him first." It was, indeed, the only logical itinerary.

I was astonished at the strength of feeling that overwhelmed me. I wouldn't see Meho alone that evening. It was suddenly a tragedy; Othello had murdered Desdemona. It was irreparable, the end of the world. I felt as if I had been struck a blow, physically shaken. I played on without seeing the notes, everything a gray, fuddled haze of misery.

At the break, Meho said, "Something's wrong, Ellen. What is it?" He always caught my mood, even from a distance. I could tell Jacques in so many words that I wasn't feeling well, I thought bitterly, and it wouldn't register with him. To Meho, I didn't even have to speak.

"Oh, it's nothing. It's just that I have to drive that old Jules home, and I won't be alone with you."

"We'll take him first."

"We can't do that. It would look too strange. He lives right near me."

"Oh."

At the end of the rehearsal, Meho motioned me toward the exit. I followed him to the oboe classroom, where he put away his instrument. He shut the door and embraced me: coffee bean and tallowy candle. He put his arms around me and lifted his face to reach my lips with the utmost earnestness, a conscientious child applying himself to his lesson.

"We can't stay here," I said. "Jules is waiting."

"He can wait two minutes, can't he?"

"Couldn't you call me tomorrow?"

"Tomorrow holiday weekend begin, and I go near Paris to play for *Méduse*."

"Again? You won't be here all weekend? And we won't be able to go to the picnic together? The one the *Comité Catholique* is giving!"

"No. But I don't want to go to Paris."

"You must go, Meho! It's work for you!"

"I want to stay with you."

I did not take him seriously. But the three long days ahead would be a Sahara of deprivation. Resigned to it, I called Gordana, and we agreed on an afternoon chat. We sat opposite each other in the chapel, a pile of her crêpes between us.

"Eat! Have more!" she encouraged me. It was rumored more and more these days in *Château* lore that the Kozićs were going to be accepted. Monsieur Lenoir let it be inferred but would give them no confirmation. Finally, Gordana, her nerves frazzled, had cornered him in his office. "Why you play games with me, Monsieur Lenoir?" she had asked, exasperated and in tears.

He'd assured her that he had not received anything official yet. He was not playing with her and would let her know immediately if something came. For her part, she was sure he was playing cat and mouse with them, that he knew but wouldn't divulge the truth.

As Gordana was telling me her story, Meho appeared in the doorway and slowly entered the room, expressionless, beaten suitcase in hand. He was to have left hours before. "You did not leave!" she exclaimed triumphantly, her eyes sparkling with surprise and pleasure. He sat down beside me, saying nothing.

"Why you not leave?" Meho remained silent. His face had a closed look I had never seen. "I know!" Gordana snapped her fingers. "Yes, I know why you come back. You think, maybe, if today comes the answer, if something to sign . . ."

Still, he sat mute. Then he pulled a small sticker from his pocket, the kind one finds in cereal boxes. *You have won . . .* it proclaimed. "What have I won?" he grinned suddenly, turning toward me.

"Nothing, I'm afraid, Meho . . ."

"Won?" cried Gordana. "Who needs that? You, you win refugee status!" We all laughed, while she hurried to the kitchen for coffee.

Meho settled on his chair, smiling at me. He placed one hand on my belly, curved beneath the flimsy material of my blue summer dress. "Is there baby in there?"

"Oh come on, fat chance!" I said wryly. "Maybe if I go to Italy . . ." He did not catch the allusion. His hand remained, flat, warm and possessive below my abdomen. I felt myself go weak beneath the weight and authority of it. I wondered how I could go on saying no to him.

> *Why didn't you go to Paris, Meho? For the letter, as Gordana thought? Or because you couldn't bear to be away from me? Is that why you wouldn't answer her? Because it was something you couldn't admit?*

Meho pulled out his French exercises from the university course. "You help me?" he asked.

"Sure, why not?" We sat over grammar exercises for ten minutes.

"Why you steal my teacher?" Gordana asked when she returned, mock angry. "Ellen my teacher!"

"Never again, last time," Meho promised.

From the moment Meho placed his hand on my stomach, I was his in my mind. I entered a period of physical distress; my vagina ached. I was tense from head to foot. I lay on my bed prodding and pressing my own flesh until relief came and came again, my nerve endings tingling, my inner linings wet and raw. I thought I must be losing my mind; I was already losing my body. I swallowed tranquilizers, which brought temporary quiet until the waves of desire overwhelmed me again. I had never known suffering of this sort. You are nothing but a bitch in heat, I thought, but insulting myself was no help. My body would not be calmed. The wretched burning desert I had become cried out for quenching.

> *Melisand, I know what he wants, but I am not that kind of woman. I will not do it. I will not.*

Château Lore
Oleg

After his midnight adventure with the Azerbaijani, the military authorities slapped a damning report on Oleg and dispatched him to the front in Chechnya. They laughed at him, when he said he was a conscientious objector and would never aim a weapon at another man. There was no leisure for a conscience when you were cannon fodder, anyway, and enough weapons would be aimed at him. Oleg fingered the tiny crucifix he wore inside his shirt, a Christ carved in black resin, dangling from a grayish piece of string, and reflected that He cast a miraculous spell of protection around him. It must have been the intervention of his guardian angel that got the letter mailed to his parents, unless it was the hypocrisy of those at the command post, who simulated normalcy from time to time. Packages from home never seemed to reach their recipients, either, except the occasional one, to prove the rule false by its exception.

Oleg heard rumors of kidnappings. A boy seen one day would be gone the next, without having been in combat. The Chechens would ransom the family, while the Russians would decry the black-bearded bandits. This, at least, was how some families learned where their sons were. When Oleg began to suspect one of his chiefs of abetting this human trafficking, he made his plan to desert. If he were caught, it meant three years in the Gulag, followed by two more of the military.

It was not the sort of undertaking that could sustain failure, but Oleg could have saved himself the plotting and planning. His father arrived from Kaluga one day with a change of clothes and a ticket for him to escape to Moscow.

Where Papa had got the money for the train, Oleg could only conjecture. Once in Moscow, he lay low in the safe houses, where clandestine deserters could find a roof for a time and a meal a day. Sveta learned his whereabouts from the Committee of Soldiers' Mothers and joined him in the back bedroom of a dingy flat, where he was hiding and reading whatever he could get his hands on. She wept with relief to see him alive and well. They held each other for a time, two famished teenagers, speechless with emotion.

"Sveta," he said, "I swore that if I got out of that inferno alive, I would enter the priesthood." She said she would accompany him always. "If you marry me," he added, "you must know that my first love will always be my God." Sveta agreed, for she did not fear the rivalry of God. He told her about his plans to enter theological seminary, but abroad. In Russia, his future was lost, for deserters were tracked and hunted until they had paid the price. He put his hopes in Paris; there was an Orthodox seminary in Paris, and one could live as a free man.

Sveta embraced this plan eagerly. Her family would help with the funds for the trip, and he could leave the visas up to her. She would get them out of the country, but first, she would get a pope to marry them.

Nine

*C*édric told me on the phone how he had stopped at the *Château* with papers for Meho from his future employer. He was so annoyed, he apparently just had to tell Meho's sponsor. That girl, Elisabeth, he said, had intercepted him.

"You work for the National Employment Agency, don't you?" she had asked.

"I'm just a friend. Where I work is nobody's business but mine." He had been reluctant to admit it.

"Listen, can't you do something for Monsieur Petrov? He's really nice. Monsieur Kozić is not nice, but Monsieur Petrov is."

"I don't know Petrov and he's no concern of mine."

Moreover, Cédric had told Meho he would never set foot in the *Château* again. "Please, stay and have coffee with us!" Meho had insisted.

"I'll have coffee with you in your own apartment in town, when you get it. In the meantime, tell that secretary I can't be getting promises of employment for all the refugees in this place." He wanted me to know that, too, I figured, just in case I might decide to take another refugee under my wing. I could imagine Cédric speeding past Elisabeth's office on his way out. She would have been sulking near the photocopier. The episode of the pulled hair was one she had surely not forgotten.

On Sunday we drove all five Kozićs to the Catholic Aid picnic. Meho and Gordana crowded into the back, Suada beside them, Amina and Veronika on their knees. Gordana had on the pink blouse which glowed so against her sallow skin, descending just far enough on her skirt to underline the soft circumference of her stomach. "Big fight between us yesterday," she said. It must have been over, for both were smiling. The children chirped eagerly. We were riding toward a small castle, surrounded by a park, where animals roamed in wide enclosures.

We sat at long picnic tables, while volunteers from the society brought plates laden with ham, pâtés, slices of cold roast, then rice salads, dotted with the green and red of chopped bell peppers. I shivered at the coolness under the trees. "Your wife is cold," Meho said to Jacques, who didn't reply. Meho made the gesture of removing his shirt to give it to me.

"Are you really so cold?" asked Jacques, his voice a trifle derisive. "It's warm today."

"I'll be all right."

> *Why was it always you who noticed my needs, Meho? If Jacques felt it was warm, then it had to be warm for everyone.*

"Look! There is the Osayin family!" I nudged Jacques. "They're staying on illegally now, you know that, don't you? They've dared come out!"

"I guess they feel sure the police won't come for them here."

"How insecure they must be! It must be unbearable." The three Osayins sat at the end of our table, helping themselves to lavish plates of food. They smiled and nodded as though they hadn't a care in the world.

Marie-Toussainte embraced us all. "How wonderful to have you," she said. "And so much is happening now. I visited the Osayins yesterday at . . . at where they are staying." She moved on to greet others.

Gordana leaped up from her chair and sat beside me, gripping the side of my own chair, her eyes suddenly flaming green. "I know!" she said, looking me very closely in the face. "I know!" she repeated dramatically, as though a great secret had been revealed to her.

A wave of panic engulfed me. What did she know? What had their fight been about? So Meho had told her something about us. They had quarreled, and he had told her it was Ellen he loved. It was all I could think of. And all she said was "I know!" How tolerant she was, then! It could only mean that she did not really love him, didn't care any more. I didn't answer her but lowered my head, flooded with shame. Meho gazed at me affectionately, perceiving my distress.

"Go pick a flower for Madame Ellen," he whispered to Suada, who ran off, returning with a little bundle of dandelions.

Marie-Toussainte passed by our table once more. "My dear Ellen," she said, "won't you come and help me get the coffee?" Still speechless and dismayed, I got up to follow her. I found that the coffee had already been made.

Marie-Toussainte lowered her voice. "It's about the Kozićs. I know what good friends you are, and I wasn't sure whether I should tell you this, but . . ." She hesitated.

"What?"

"The things in their report. They're completely false. The *Préfecture* checks things with the Ministry of the Interior, you know, before they make any decisions. They're not Bosnians, first of all."

"What do you mean, not Bosnians?"

"They don't speak the language. Their interpreter at the first Appeal noticed that they couldn't understand it."

"That's not possible. Meho has a Croatian/French dictionary in his pocket all the time. I've seen it with my own eyes. He looks up the French words in it."

"Well, I don't know, but they're Gypsies and they're not from Sarajevo."

"Not from Sarajevo? From where then?"

"From nowhere. They're travelers."

"That's not so! They studied in Sarajevo. Both of them!"

Marie-Toussainte looked skeptical. "He said he fought in the Bosnian war, but it's not true. He never did." I didn't know what to say to this. Had he actually deserted or, in fact, never been drafted?

"Moreover, Meho was recently released from prison in Germany," she went on relentlessly. "He did four years there."

"Prison? Four years? But what for?"

"Theft."

"That's a lot for theft!"

"People have noticed; he speaks German."

"German, Marie-Toussainte? He knows about as much German as someone who's had a term of it in school. If he'd spent four years in Germany, he'd know more German, believe me!"

"That's not all. He's been married before and has a wife and son in Switzerland."

"OK, that I know. That's true enough. But is it a crime to get divorced and remarry? Don't you know anybody who has done that?"

"Yes, of course, perfectly good people . . ." she conceded, moving out of the kitchen tent, back toward the tables.

I made a pretense of drinking coffee, while my mind whirled. What did Gordana actually know? What was this about theft and prison? Where had Marie-Toussainte got her information from? If part of it was true, couldn't all of it be? If Meho had been in prison, was Veronika not his daughter then? At any rate, he could speak Serbo-Croatian, I was quite sure. Perhaps the interpreter had heard them speaking Romany. And if so, what crime was that?

We began a slow walk through the park, peering into the enclosures to see the goats, llamas, exotic birds.

"Superrr!" exclaimed Gordana, pointing out some furry creature to one of her daughters.

My throat was dry and taut. "Oh, look at this!" I said, forcing enthusiasm, while images jumbled in my head, my pulse racing. I ducked into a cabin marked *Toilettes*, fumbling in my bag for the shiny pink capsules of tranquilizer.

Twenty minutes. In twenty minutes they will take effect, I thought. Certain of that, I relaxed slightly. I must ask them if it is true. That's all. I cannot bear not knowing. I walked slowly beside Meho, who sent Suada to pick more wild flowers.

"We continue what we . . . started together? I meet you tomorrow?" he asked.

"Where?"

"I don't know. After your work? At your school?"

"Oh no, Meho, not there. I'll meet you in front of the cathedral, all right? After school, at four o'clock?"

He saw how nervous I was. "What's wrong?" Suada was back, listening closely. Something in our lowered voices caught her attention. "Suada! You go see your mother!" He spoke sharply. I let him walk on ahead of me. When he had joined Gordana, I caught up with them and sat beside them on a bench.

"Marie-Toussainte spoke to me. When we went for the coffee."

"What? What she say?" Gordana's voice was harsh. I could not get the words out without sobbing. Gordana stroked my forearm. "It's all right. All finished now."

"It's just that I love all of you so much. I don't care if Meho was in prison." Meho shook his head disgustedly. "I never see more of a prison than outside of door."

"I wonder how you could have made Veronika," I added.

"Aha! Yes!" Gordana cried. "Veronika two years old."

"Of course there are visits in prison . . ."

"Visits?" She was scornful. "Yes! Visits with *Polizei!*"

"I never set foot in Germany," Meho continued. "Sure, I speak three words German. We learn German at school. Where they get that I was in prison in Germany?"

"I know where!" Gordana cried out. "It's Osayin! He tell that to Marie-Toussainte, it's sure! He very jealous because he know we be accepted soon. He always against us, always listen. He say 'Turkish', but I know he is not. He understand *romani* very well."

"Gordana, what interest would he have in making false statements about you? And who would take him seriously?"

"Monsieur Lenoir. He always talk to Monsieur Lenoir! Now I know! He say bad things about us." I couldn't persuade her of the contrary. Life in the *Château* bred paranoia.

"Tomorrow, we speak to Marie-Toussainte," Meho said. "You come too, all right?"

Still petrified, I sat in front of my computer that evening, while Jacques read in his favorite armchair.

> *Melisand, she knows everything. He must have told her. And she doesn't seem to care. I don't know what to do. Should I tell your father about Meho and me? Should I just tell him part of it? That he's been flirting with me? Or nothing at all? Just keep it to myself?*
>
> *What he doesn't know won't hurt him,* she answered. *Telling part will only upset him and won't get you anywhere. If you have to say something, say the entire truth, not that it's just a little flirt, because that would be taking him for an idiot. If nothing important is going on, then of course you just don't mention it. But if you begin speaking about it, it can only mean that it is more important than what you are willing to say. As for telling the truth versus saying nothing, you would just be clearing your conscience, wouldn't you? That would be a selfish motive, not respect for him. Mom, don't feel guilty after all these years of the wretched relationship you've been having! You deserve some happiness. Just stop worrying! Things will take care of themselves.*

I read her message over and over. The last sentence repeated itself in my mind like an incantation.

> *Dearest child, you always knew what to tell me; your generation was not one of self-sacrifice. How satisfying to hear that confession would be selfish!*

The telephone rang a few minutes later. Marie-Toussainte's voice was perplexed: "Meho phoned. He wants to meet me tomorrow morning at the parish. Any idea why?"

"Of course I know why. I told them what you told me. He wants to put things straight with you."

"I'll be there. Are you coming too?"

"Yes. Just tell me, was it Monsieur Osayin who told you about the prison and all that?"

"Gracious, no!" she replied.

The four of us sat around the table in the room where Meho had listened politely to his tutor perorating only a few weeks earlier. In front of him he placed his and Gordana's Bosnian identity cards. These he pushed toward Marie-Toussainte like a card player bringing out a trump. They were shiny and new, with recent photographs, the sort of card the UNHCR might have made out for them, based on their own testimony. Gordana sat quietly listening, while Meho explained himself in ragged French.

"What you tell Ellen not true. She and Jacques good friends of ours, now what they think? Now they think I am thief; I stay in prison. Yes, I speak a little German. I speak it because I study it in school. Does that make me thief?"

"And I, maybe I used to be a prostitute!" said Marie-Toussainte. "But of course it makes no difference now if I have decided to lead an honest life. The past is the past." Good Christian that she was, Marie-Toussainte was willing to recognize that the past could be forgiven and transcended, but she was obviously not inclined to accept Meho's denial.

"And first wife in Switzerland, so what? That is my private life. That is no one's business."

"Of course." Marie-Toussainte was more conciliatory. "It's unimportant. Anyway, none of these things will keep you from being accepted. I have heard some encouraging rumors about you. You have good chances."

"And me? Maybe I want divorce now," Gordana interrupted. "My husband have other woman."

Ignoring this, Marie-Toussainte said she would call the Foreigners Bureau immediately and see how far their business had progressed. She hurried off to the priests' residence. Meho, Gordana, and I sat silently, waiting. In a very short time, she was back.

"My dear friends!" she cried, her voice husky, "they told me you have been accepted! They're making up your papers. You are French now! You are going to stay here!" She flung her hefty arms around Meho, then Gordana. We all embraced as if it were New Year's, but something was lacking. Gordana and Meho held back their usual warmth.

"Good-bye, then, dear French friends!" Marie-Toussainte left, full of her good news, sure she had been the herald of joy. The three of us remained seated.

"I believe it when I see document," said Meho.

"Me too." Gordana's voice was cold. "Who does she know at *Préfecture*? Where she get her information?"

And now I had to speak. I had to speak to you, Gordana.

"Gordana," I began tentatively. "You know, about our . . . our little problem, between us. Really, Gordana, believe me, I never wanted to take your husband from you . . ."

She smiled at me sweetly. I assumed she understood. I assumed I had been forgiven.

I didn't expect to see Meho later that day after school. I almost drove directly home, but something made me go to the cathedral anyway. It's a pleasant afternoon, I reasoned. A little walk will do no harm. I was no dupe to my own hypocrisy, however. I had to be clear in my mind about it; would he come or not? The asphalt turned to cobblestones near the massive, ancient structure. I walked slowly, the heels of my sandals catching between the stones. There was no one in front of the Romanesque facade. I stopped a moment to gaze at the huge doors. The carved Evangelists presided over them stiffly, in the more equivocal company of Solomon and the Queen of Sheba. Suddenly, Meho was beside me, smiling. He had come from the stone steps on the side, leading up from the parking lot below. "I didn't think you would come," I said.

"Why not? We have rendezvous!"

"Well, you know, after what Gordana said. She knows about us, doesn't she?"

"Knows what? What have we done, anyway? Only a few kisses."

"She spoke about a divorce this morning, about 'another woman'."

"She means Samira in Switzerland! She say that because mad at Marie-Toussainte."

"She didn't mean me?"

"Of course not!"

"But when I said I didn't want to take her husband from her . . ."

"Why you say that?" He shook his head. "But it doesn't matter! She not understand a word what you talk about!"

"And yesterday, at the picnic, when she said 'I know'?"

"She think you know about our answer from *Préfecture*."

"Oh, my God, I thought she was talking about us."

"Why you panic like that, Ellen?" He was laughing. I felt drained. I had been living in a film of my own creation.

"Come on," he said, taking my arm, "where we go?"

We entered the cool darkness of the huge church, found our way to a wooden bench near the back. Meho looked at the altar flanked by the wrought-iron grilles of the choir. "You want to make wedding here, maybe?" Then he began to kiss me, long draughts of intimacy. I tasted his tongue, the inside of his mouth, soft and warm. "Tomorrow I give you love, Ellen," he said.

"It's not possible," I whispered, looking past him at the stained glass windows, which made colored shadows in jigsaw patterns on the stone floor. This was St. Brice's Cathedral, and what was I doing here? God forbid anyone I know should enter here, I thought, and see me close to him like this.

"You want to go to hotel?" he asked.

"No!" I was horrified.

"Ellen, do you have sex with Jacques?"

"Well, yes. It's only normal, isn't it, I mean between man and wife?" He said nothing. "Are you jealous?" He nodded. "Meho, how many women have you slept with?"

He frowned at my question. "First wife, Samira, then Gordana. That's all. You know, I don't give that to just anybody!"

"But maybe you've slept with a prostitute? Maybe during the war?"

"No, never!" He was adamant. I saw I had offended him.

"Really? Never anyone else?"

"Ellen, I don't look at women. I loved Samira very much. If she stayed with me, I still be with her today. Gordana, she not seem to like sex very much. I don't know, but I thought . . . I thought I lose my desire until I see you."

"You just want to amuse yourself with me."

"No!" he repeated, vexed. "You, I love!"

"And sometimes I think every woman must be in love with you."

This brought a smile. "Maybe not every woman need of me!"

We sat glued together, my forehead pressing against his neck. I raised it to see a small group of tourists, guided by a librarian I knew well, walking briskly down the side aisle beneath the stained glass windows. Oh God, please let her not have seen me, I prayed, aghast. And if she has seen me, please let her not have seen me kissing Meho, please! What sort of prayers were these for a cathedral? "I must go, Meho. It's time, I'll be late, I really must."

A member of the clergy had spotted us. He walked to where we were sitting and remarked with a scowl, "There are other places for what you want." Waves of shame and anxiety swept over me. I fled the cathedral, fled Meho, wishing I could flee from myself.

As I walked through the old town, I passed my friend the librarian, alone now. Her straight brown hair framed her kind, studious face. One lock of white hair bobbed above her round, metal-rimmed glasses as she walked. What is she thinking of me? Is she shocked? Laughing at me? Maybe she can put herself in my place, who knows? Maybe she wouldn't throw the first stone. Maybe she thought I was explaining the history of St. Brice to a friend. Perhaps she never even noticed me.

"*Bonjour Hélène!*" She greeted me with a broad smile, the picture of unsuspecting candor.

Thank you, God, thank you!

Château Lore
Murat

His mother was called Fatma, and what was funny was that Murat was the one who helped her with her exercises and not the other way around. She wanted to sign up for the French lessons that Marie-Toussainte organized, just because everyone else did, but she hated them, so she usually made up excuses. The last one was that she had fallen down the stairs at the home and injured her foot, and when Marie-Toussainte came by, she pretended to be lame. But then something was boiling over in the kitchen, and his mother forgot to limp. She ran to get the pan, and Marie-Toussainte just sat there staring at her, her eyes this wide. Murat didn't think it mattered, so long as he and his father could manage to speak. Mothers didn't have to know that much.

His father was telling Marie-Toussainte about the anti-government demonstration and how they had dragged him to the police truck, but he'd managed to get away. Someone else kicked the policeman holding him, and so the guy lost his grasp. But they got his father's identification, and someone probably even took a picture, so Papa figured his name was down on a black list, and he could get sent to prison. That's what he told them at the Appeal, but they never paid attention or even acted like it was important. They said, can you prove it, and of course he couldn't prove it. And they also said, "Bulgaria is a democracy now. The Soviets are gone." So then Maman and Papa got the negative answers.

After the street demonstration that soured, his father got them on a Russian truck that was heading for France. It cost all of their savings, three thousand marks, plus some money for the trip. The truck stopped in Italy, and they had to get food there without being seen. Actually, the trucker got it for them. It was very uncomfortable, sitting on the floor of that huge trailer with a bunch of other people, and you could feel every bump in the road. When they were in Italy, the roads were smoother already, and they said those were highways for capitalist behinds. At the border with France, the trucker told them they had to get out, and they went to the police directly and got sent here to the Refugee Home in Laudes-la-Romaine. That was a year ago, and his mother and father were always fighting now. Papa was always at the home, because he didn't have any place to go except sometimes to meetings for asylum seekers, and Maman cleaned the room twice a day from top to bottom.

Murat liked it when Mademoiselle Elisabeth played games with the children. She did that after checking their homework on Wednesday afternoons. There wasn't any school on Wednesday afternoons, but there was always homework, and the parents spoke every language under the sun except French, so they needed Elisabeth. She had them study in the little library, with the sewing machine and the books, but no one ever sewed on Wednesdays, because the children were there. He was sure Suada cheated at Uno, but he wouldn't hit her again. Otherwise her father would be going to see Monsieur Lenoir and making a fuss like the last time. There were quotas, and not everybody could stay in France, his father told him, so they had to be really quiet and not be noticed.

Marie-Toussainte went to see the Prefect for them, but it didn't get them anywhere. She called embassies, too, like Brazil and South Africa, but they said they didn't have a need for Turkish bakers. In France they needed bakers all right, but the Bakers' Syndicate said they'd find a place for Papa to work when he had his papers, and now Marie-Toussainte was telling them he could only get his papers if he had work.

He wasn't expecting his father to pick him up after school on Tuesday. He never expected he would have to give back his books and his other supplies, too, when school wasn't even out yet for *les grandes vacances,* but Papa said he had to. His teacher looked really stricken, and she asked if there wasn't something she could do, but his father said no, it was definitive. They'd had the order of police escort to the border in the mail that morning.

Murat was scared to death they would meet a policeman on the way home, but it was silly, because there were never policemen on the road between the school and the Refugee Home. His mother said a reporter from the local paper had been there with Madame Anne-Laure from the Asylum Seekers Defense League, and tomorrow there would be an article all about them. She was going to organize a demonstration in their favor, too, in town on Saturday, but his father had better not go. A lawyer was going to appeal the Prefect's decision at some big Administrative Court in a city, and in two days, they would have the answer to that.

TEN

My desk was covered with papers to read and correct, but they blended before my eyes into an inky fog of scribbling. I read without understanding a word, went back to the beginning of the first one and still couldn't concentrate. Images of my meeting with Meho at the cathedral superimposed themselves over the lined, off-white, notebook paper. I could still taste his mouth, the fullness of his lips framed by the soft black of his mustache and beard. I shut my eyes to the papers and drifted.

The telephone rang. "Just calling to see how you are." Melisand's voice was cheerful. "Is Dad home?"

"No, darling, he has his play rehearsal on Tuesdays, you know."

"So, are you all right?"

"No, I'm not all right. I'm not all right at all."

"What is it, Mom?"

"You know what it is. He wants it and I want it, but I can't do it."

"Listen, if you really want it, I don't see where the problem is."

"I haven't got the right to hurt anyone."

"Who is going to be hurt?"

"Your father, if he ever finds out. Gordana . . ."

"There's no reason they'll ever find out. It's just between you two. You'll have a secret garden, that's all. Mom, be selfish for once!"

"I'm selfish all the time, Melisand."

"No, I don't mean stuff like buying new clothes. I mean do something for yourself as a person, for once!"

"I do lots of things for myself."

"Honestly, you don't. It's your 'only child' thing again. You're always so afraid people will think you're selfish that you deny yourself all the time. You do everything you can to make Dad feel better. Now, do something for you!"

> *Melisand, why did I listen to you? The child must listen to the mother, not the contrary. We are from two different generations. I should have listened to my own scruples. But I listened to what I wanted to hear.*

Tomorrow is Wednesday, and I will act. I will take it upon myself, I swore. Melisand's words echoed: "something for yourself as a person." Had not Jacques denied me existence as a person? He didn't even call me by my name. I had begun to like my name, now that Meho spoke it.

Wednesday night meant orchestra rehearsal and a new meeting with Meho. I had an excuse ready, in case Jules should ask me to drive him home again. I was prepared for everything this time. On a small piece of paper, I wrote in Russian, checking the words in my dictionary: *I have finished thinking it over. I love you. I want to sleep with you.* I carefully traced the Cyrillic letters. If this paper gets lost, I thought, not a soul at the town orchestra will make heads or tails of it. Bosnians, on the other hand, can read both the Cyrillic and Latin alphabets. I felt sure the Russian would be similar enough to Serbo-Croatian for him to catch the meaning. I slipped it into the pocket of my jacket and drove into town.

As I approached the conservatory, Yvonne's husband, Frédéric, dapper and brisk, his clarinet case in hand, was leaving. His classes were finished for the day. *"Bonjour belle dame!"* he called to me. "You look so pretty tonight! You always look so pretty!"

"Oh, come on, Fred," I said, "are you chatting me up?"

"No, but I wish you lots of happiness tonight," he said affectionately. I wondered if I didn't exude something. How could he perceive it?

Meho was not there. The orchestra attacked the theme from "Maria", from "West Side Story". At each page turn, I looked toward the door. No one. Fifteen minutes passed, and still he did not come. Tonight of all nights, would he be absent? He never missed a rehearsal. Even their rejection at the Appeal had not made him miss a rehearsal. My hands were clammy, and sweat trickled from my underarms. I nodded yes and no to the frail, white-haired lady sharing my music desk, hardly hearing what she said. He was sometimes a little late, but never so long. Thirty minutes now. It must mean he was not coming. I will resign myself to it. I will see him again some time. But what could keep him from coming? After nearly an hour of practice, Gérard announced we would break for a few minutes. I turned again, and there was Meho just moving into the woodwind section. As the other musicians got up to chat, he placed his music on the stand and joined them. I sidled through the crowded room, pushing the music desks, slipping between the flutes and the brass. "Meho, good evening."

"Good evening, Ellen."

I took the plunge. "I had some Russian exercises to do, you know, for my course? Would you mind checking if I've written this right?" He took the slip of paper. He looked at it for an eternity of seconds, frowning at the Cyrillic, the unfamiliar words, then, suddenly, opening wide his black eyes, questioning, astonished. He broke into an incredulous smile.

I snatched the paper back from him, wadding it, but he wouldn't let me keep it. "No! Let me take it!" I said.

"Oh no!" he insisted, still grinning, stuffing it into the pocket of his cotton shirt. He had told me he'd once kept a paper napkin from our house. How much more of a relic this would be! I didn't insist further.

As I regained my seat, Jules was still standing, pleased with what he was about to say. "Since you were so kind as to drive me home last time, I'm going to pay back the favor. Tonight, I will take Monsieur

Kozić back to his Refugee Home, and you can get home early for once!"

"Thank you so much, Jules," I said calmly, "but you won't have to do that. You see, Monsieur Kozić and his wife have invited me for a drink after the rehearsal this evening."

"Letter come today," said Meho, as we climbed into my car.
"From the *Préfecture?*"
"We are accepted. They give us documents."
"Then it's true! Oh, Meho, I'm so relieved! You must be so happy."
"We had little party at the home this evening."
"So that's why you were late?"
"Yes. Everyone drink wine, Monsieur Lenoir danced, I played accordion."
"But you came to orchestra anyway."
He just smiled. "Children's pigeon fly away, day before letter come for us. When I see it's gone, then I know, soon we leave *Château* too. Pigeon take his liberty. Us too."

Noah's dove, I thought. After the flood had subsided, the bird hadn't returned. Meho's family too could at last set foot on *terra firma*.

Meho touched his pocket. "How are we going to do?"
"I'm free on Friday afternoon. You take the bus to the Tulipes stop. I'll pick you up there at two o'clock, if that's all right. Then, we'll spend the afternoon at the house . . ."

He didn't want me to drive all the way to the *Château*. Instead, we parked in an unlit, adjacent street. Meho had received his green light. This time, when he kissed me, he shot his hand under my long, summer skirt, into my panties. A flash of lightning seared between my thighs. I gasped, shaken by immediate orgasm, once, twice, clutching at him. "I will not sleep tonight," he said, "I will not sleep."

On Thursday morning, I dropped by at the *Château* after my second morning class. I wanted to congratulate Gordana, or so I told myself.

"Meho out," she said apologetically, as if she realized it was he I was hoping to see and accepted that. But she repeated something he had said about me. "Ellen, she not really do anything to help us," he had told Gordana, and she reported his words. Why, I didn't know. Did she want to be sure I knew Meho didn't really appreciate me? Moreover, why had he said that to her? To deflect any ideas she might have that he was particularly grateful to me?

"It's true, Gordana," I admitted. "I didn't accomplish anything for you, but I have carried you in my heart for months."

"I know that," she said, serving me a cup of coffee.

"When letter come Tuesday, Meho and I stay awake talking till three o'clock in the morning. We think of big party we'll have, to celebrate. We invite you and Jacques, *dirigent* of orchestra, director of *Méduse* theater, Monsieur Lenoir . . ."

As much as I shared their joy and relief, I felt infinitely sad at the idea of the two of them, together in bed, sharing, planning. That was as it should have been. And I was no part of it.

Forgive me, Gordana, but I did not want you to be a part of it.

She invited me to return with Jacques that very evening. "We celebrate papers with you," she said. "I tell Monsieur Lenoir to come again tonight too."

At seven, Jacques and I rode to the home in his car. Gordana had prepared a small feast of chocolate ice cream cake and sweet white wine. I sat opposite Jacques in the chapel, while Monsieur Lenoir leaned back on a bench, and Meho played the accordion. He was dressed informally for the warm May weather in shorts and sandals, and never had he appeared so handsome to me. His tan face glowed with the triumph of the victor. He had won all he had competed for: his visa, his fair-skinned *gadji*. Meho hugged the red accordion, making it breathe like an organ, teasing the joy from it. Would I were that instrument in his arms, I thought. He bent toward me, singing, *Cigani liubiat zhenshini; Cigani liubiat konje.* Gypsies love women; Gypsies love horses. Gordana and I laughed together, as if we shared a joke. Jacques was silent, not understanding the words.

"Thank you, Ellen, for help!" said Gordana, jumping up suddenly and whisking a small package in gift paper from her apron pocket. "Thank you, too, Jacques, for help!" she added, placing a similar packet before him with a flourish of her hand. Inside mine lay a hematite necklace of the kind easily found at the marketplace. The gray stones shone darkly, like somber pearls. I put it on immediately. Jacques' package contained an imitation gold chain with an athlete in leaping position hanging from it. A Gypsy present, he must be thinking.

Melisand, don't bother sending any e-mail today. I have an appointment with him all afternoon.

Now that my mind was made up, I felt appeased. Beyond my marriage, I had no experience of sexual relations. On my wedding day, I was as virgin as an unwritten book, as virgin as good girls were meant to be, at that period of time when I reached my twenties. Never had I thought I would come to this, offering myself to another man. Jacques had been a part of me for thirty years, and, still, we remained shy with each other, something of our youthful inhibitions still intact. It must be some other Ellen who had written that message to Meho, who had decided of her own accord to give in to her instincts and accept another man's embrace. Besides, what did I know of him? His past was unclear. Communication was difficult. He might be a pervert, ill, a profiteer. Who knew what depravity lay behind him in Yugoslavia? Could I believe him when he said he had made love only to Samira and Gordana, when he said he loved *me,* or was I foolish, innocent, and naive?

I had decided, and I would take my chances. With perfect composure I had asked for condoms at the local pharmacy where I went regularly. I hid the packet in the bedside table drawer of the room which Julien and Melisand shared when they visited. If Jacques saw them, which was unlikely, he would think they were Julien's. Before I left the house, I placed them on the pillow of Jeremy's former bed, where I intended to receive Meho. Not in my marriage bed. That far, I could not go.

Still resolute, I drove to the Tulipes stop a few minutes before two o'clock, my heartbeat quickening as I approached, and parked the car within view of the area where the bus would come to stop. The two o'clock bus was punctual, its huge red and white bulk gliding to a halt in front of the shelter. Three teenagers and an old woman with a shopping bag got off. No one else. I will wait for the 2:10. A stone was pressing in the pit of my stomach. When he was not on the 2:10 bus, I decided to drive back to the house. I was now abiding in a no-man's land between anticipation, anxiety and disappointment. My mind was too numb even to conjecture about why he was not there. Changed his mind or held up? Held up, I guessed; I will give him the benefit of the doubt and return. The minutes stretched out with all the length of their uncertainty.

When I approached the bus stop again at half past two, he was sitting tailor fashion on the patch of lawn in front of the shelter. "Missed the two o'clock," he said simply. "I didn't see car, think maybe you not come after all."

"Oh, Meho, I was here and went home again! I thought *you* weren't coming!"

We climbed the stairs, and I showed him my computer, how the e-mail worked, and how I could write to my daughter and be received within the second. I showed him the note I had just got from Philippe, an English Department colleague. How trivial this conversation seemed, and how calm I felt, as if receiving a lover were a common occurrence for me. I sat on his lap facing him, my long legs circling his strong, square body. A great quantity of heat flowed from my abdomen to my thighs. He touched the shiny gray necklace on my throat. "When I saw that, I think, how very beautiful you will be with it!"

I took his hand and led him to the bedroom. Meho undressed himself and me in the blink of an eye, tossing our light summer clothes onto the floor. "Maybe you want to look at me?" he said coyly, and I smiled to see the long triangle of his back and tight male buttocks. I didn't find him beautiful, and yet I had never felt such a flood of desire. The pistil of his male flower was erect, its corolla black with tight curls above the dark, twin, aubergine-tinged purses. I caught the head of his penis in my hand, hard and clean and silky. Of course. Meho had been circumcised. "Please, will you use this?" I asked, showing him the pack of condoms. At first he did not comprehend, then raised his dark eyebrows in surprise.

"Better for you, perhaps? You have...*crème?*"

"No, I didn't think of that." He said nothing, neither yes nor no, but didn't take the package.

"I'm not so young. Of course you know that. I can't have children, so that's not the problem. But sometimes, also, I have to tell you this . . . the sex act hurts me."

Meho was inside me before I knew it; no condom, no pain either. He was in his place; we were joined as we should be, cleaving unto one another. It seemed right and good. But he had outsmarted me about the condom. Now I can get an illness, perhaps die. That is not a problem. What I am doing is morally wrong, and I deserve to die. But my husband does not deserve to die. I cannot bring him death. In the following second I found myself ridiculous and dramatic. Meho was the picture of health. How could I even think of his bringing me death, bringing Jacques death? But I retreated from the edge of pleasure, like an ocean wave that laps at the beach, then recedes. Meho came and came again. I clutched the thick black hair of his chest, caught my fingers in the golden chain with the "M" pendant he always wore.

What was I doing? Was this Ellen having sex with a hairy-chested man who wore a necklace? Was this the good student from the genteel, ivy-covered college, the good Episcopalian, the conscientious teacher? I didn't care. Somewhere she had to be me, and I was making her acquaintance, a Gypsy like Meho now, a wanderer entering exile.

"You come?" he asked.

"I don't know why . . . I want you so much, but I can't."

"You too much think." Meho turned himself on his knees, his head toward my blond, scant-haired mound, his eyebrows questioning. "You want?"

"If you do."

He kissed and nibbled at my labia until the volcano in me erupted, time after time, my pelvis rising and falling, the heat ebbing and flowing. "And now, together," he said, as we joined again, a spring set off, uncoiling and rebounding in unison inside our bodies. For two and a half hours Meho and I lay together, drenched in our mingled sweat, caught in the mesh of pleasure, the desire so long withheld now galloping free rein. Spent and satiated, we held each other, our heads touching on the pillow. He will think I am nothing but an easy woman. I must talk to him. "Meho, Jacques doesn't love me, you know?"

"Ah?"

"He doesn't speak to me. Sometimes he needs me physically, but it's not like this. He's ill, you see. It's mental. He goes to see a psychiatrist. He has medicine for depression. It helps a little but not very much. He is always withdrawn and he pays no attention to me." I started to cry silently, hot bitter tears flowing freely along my cheekbones, back onto the pillow, making little wet spots. Was I crying for the failure of my relationship with Jacques, for his coldness to me, for the blow I had just dealt him, for myself, for my fall? I did not know.

"My case is a little like yours," Meho said, touching my cheek, stroking away the tears. "Gordana, she never show she love me. She never say it and she never kiss me. Don't you think, if a wife love her husband, she want to kiss him?" I assumed loving wives kissed their husbands, but I didn't press this topic. I felt relieved Gordana didn't show him affection.

"Meho, I want to know more about you," I ventured. "The war in Bosnia, for example. Did you fight in it? Did you really desert?"

Meho's face took on that closed look I had seen once when we were together with Gordana, and he hadn't wanted to answer her. The light went out from his eyes.

"Meho, answer me!"

"Leave me alone, Ellen!"

"What, 'leave me alone'? Don't you see the gift I have just given you? I have loved you *so* much, I didn't know what more I could give you. So I have given you *myself*, and now you say to leave you alone? It is my right to know!"

He sighed. "All right, Ellen, you have told me about Jacques, so I tell you something about me." Meho was a bargainer, but he didn't seem to feel he owed me anything for a gift. He too had given a gift. "I never fought in war."

"Where were you then, during the war?"

"We ran away to Croatia."

"And how did you live?"

"Humanitarian aid."

"And how did you get here? I thought you'd been evacuated by the Red Cross or the UNHCR."

"No, we came in a truck, hidden in a truck, with other illegals. I knew someone who could get us out of the country."

Meho was no hero. He wasn't the human rights victim he would have liked people to believe, either. Was that a reason to reject him? He was just a human being who didn't want his life destroyed by a savage war in which he had no part. I could understand this.

"Ellen, I was so afraid we never get our papers to stay here."

"I know that. You had to get them to save your family."

"I was so afraid that I would lose *you*."

Jacques found me weary that evening. The truth was, I could hardly sit. Meho had, it seemed to me, the strength and staying power of a battering ram. My fragile tissues, unaccustomed, were pounded to a pulp. I lay exhausted but sleepless on our bed, reliving each moment of the afternoon. Why do we say that a man takes a woman? For I had taken Meho. I had taken him into me and held him and kept him. He had found his refuge, and I had welcomed him.

But his sullen silence after our lovemaking frightened me. Now you have made the mistake of your life, I repeated to myself. Not only have you committed adultery, but with a man whose life is woven with the stuff of shadow. His report, which I could recite by heart, was a fabric of lies; how much of it, I wasn't sure. I understood that he had to embellish his situation to elicit attention and compassion.

He, Gordana, and the children were the innocent victims of a cruel war that hadn't spared civilians. They had nothing to return to in Yugoslavia. What other lies or half-truths had he told me, though? What did I really know about his sex life except what I wanted to believe? I had surrendered to him the innermost sanctuary of my body, and, if he had defiled it? I reached for the pink capsules beside my bed. Lust hath murdered sleep, I thought. You entered into it with your eyes open. Now resign yourself and accept your failings.

His voice on the telephone was different, happier, reassured. "Can we meet this afternoon?" he asked. I told Jacques I was going into town to go shopping.

There is a high point in the botanical garden with a sundial, hidden by a mass of low bushes. We climbed to it. Only people on their balconies in the surrounding apartment houses could see us, a bit like spectators at some leafy Globe, if indeed they should happen to look down onto the garden. They would have seen a slim, fair woman on a bench, pressing close to a sturdy, dark-haired man. Meho placed my hand against his chest so that I could feel his heart racing. "See, Ellen, what a magnet you are for me?" I told him my fears, my misgivings.

"Ellen, I don't have AIDS," he said, naming it. "Just think, if I did, Gordana and the children would be infected too." It was true enough, Gordana breast-fed Veronika, and both were obviously fine. But I persisted in my anxiety.

"Then, I will go to public hospital and have test and give it to you," he promised. "By the way, Ellen, maybe *you* have AIDS?" He smiled at my expression: "If you do, then, dearest Ellen, please give me AIDS!"

"Meho, that is no subject for a joke."

"I understand you. You are intellectual woman and you worry and ask yourself questions. Maybe you feel better if you go talk to a psychiatrist." I thought that perhaps I would, although what neuroleptics might exist for the washing away of guilt, I could not imagine.

He placed his hand gently on my stomach. "You give me a baby? I'd like that."

A child. With Meho's dark eyes and my long-limbed body.

"You know I am an old lady, and that I cannot!"

"Ellen, please get idea out of your head that you are an old lady. You are nothing resembling an old lady! And for baby, are you sure? Ask your gynecologist doctor maybe? You are young, my Ellen. You are younger than me."

I shook my head, touched to tears. If years were measured by the suffering and difficulties a person had lived through, then Meho truly was older than I. He told me about Samira, how she had refused to follow him to Priština, when he had been assigned to the Kosovar Orchestra, how she had left him for another man, other men, then wanted to come back when he was already married to Gordana. He missed his son, Nadir, who was with his mother and the latest of her husbands. I asked him then if the name I had seen on his bracelet was his son's, not his brother's, but he said he had given his brother's name to his son. Above all, he told me how much he loved me.

"With Samira, I made great love, like with you now. It is a very great happiness. Who would ever have thought we would make love like this one day? It is God who gives us this love. We must not refuse it. Life is too short. What happens to us is wonderful, Ellen, no?"

Wonderful, perhaps, but terrifying. I want it more than anything. Why doesn't my wanting make it right?

"I think of you until I fall asleep at night," he said. "And in the morning, early, I look for you, but you are not there."

"Why must it be so difficult to love someone? Why can't we stay together? Why do we have to hide?"

"You are not happy, Ellen?"

"Meho, won't you just stop being kind to me? Erase that charming smile of yours. Stop looking at me with those eyes of liquid coal. My life would be so simple again!" My words pleased him.

"It heats me up, how you speak to me," he said.

From the moment my vigorous Gypsy brother encamped in my heart and body, I began a double life. Obsession, guilt and duplicity cohabited with summits of burning passion and bitter-sweet happiness. I went about my duties at the *collège* like an automaton, greeting colleagues in the teachers' room, dispensing lessons, filling in bulletins. The end of the school year was nearing, and the tying-up of a final term requires innumerable meetings.

I felt oddly estranged from all of it and wondered how those people whose paths I crossed daily could go on so obviously unperturbed, their lives regular and predictable. They lounged on the wine-red armchairs, plastic coffee cups in hand, discussing exams or the coming holidays. I composed a countenance, a studied appearance of ease, while my mind and body seethed.

Something seemed to be splitting in my brain. Outwardly my life went on, while day and night I thought of him, and when I didn't see him, my body begged for him, insatiably.

Jacques perceived something of my absence. I sat opposite him at the dinner table and made conversation, but sometimes I was elsewhere. "Are you thinking of the patio?" he asked.

"Yes," I replied, glad he had provided the answer. We had recently decided to add a flagstone terrace to the back of the house, and it was I who had wished for it. When the contract had been signed, I was already a different person, however, not the one who had dreamed of this project. We must go ahead with it, though, I said to myself. How can I say, let's stop building our house together, stop building our marriage together? We shall do it, and come what may! Still, I was not often thinking of the patio.

My meetings with Meho were a punishment and a celebration. Beforehand, I was sick with guilt and anxiety, afterward, liberated and relieved, reconciled with myself and the world. I would kiss his hands, famished for the feel of the curly hair on his chest, for the heavy scent of his sweat. Meho was careful of his person, but he perspired abundantly and had his own virile odor. I had never smelled anything like it before, could have got drunk on that wild scent of campfire and stable. His semen, on the other hand, was transparent and odorless. Was this, I wondered, the stuff of black-eyed Gypsy babies? I didn't wash for a long time after we made love. "I want to keep a little of you with me," I told him.

Meho asked if I would prefer him without his beard. I touched its black softness, flecked with tiny bits of white. He shaved his cheeks carefully before coming to me. His dark eyes, which flashed green and hazel in certain lights, had the long, black lashes of Hindu men: his forebears from India, who had charmed the serpents and dealt in sortilege. I didn't want any part of him to change. Below his left shoulder, a thicket of black hairs sprang from a brown beauty spot: hallmark of the Creator, the small seal of imperfection that binds one to the beloved. His long musician's fingers knew exactly where to touch the fount of music in my body.

Above all, he gave me the gift of self-acceptance. Jacques had convinced me that I was awkward, inept, and unlovable. In Meho I found a contradictor.

"*Me mangav tu,*" I told him; "*mangalu tu.*" He taught me the words of love in his own Gypsy language: "I love you."

"Yes," he answered, "but I will always love *you* more."

> That is what you said, then, Meho, our first times together. You even said that if ever I left you, you would kill yourself: 'I will give myself death.' Do all the Roma have so high a sense of melodrama?

Meho was my festival and it seemed right I should celebrate him, his success, the explosion of joy his family's acceptance to our country had brought, our own private apotheosis of joy, the release of those interminable months of anguish and tension. I prepared a meal for the

Kozićs, choosing my engraved crystal wineglasses, my yellow and red hand-painted plates, my embroidered, ivory linen tablecloth. If, before, I had feared to intimidate them with any show of wealth, now nothing could be too festive.

Meho came early, to work on the repair of the decrepit Belgian accordion. Jacques melted beeswax and painstakingly restored the inner workings of the broken keys, while Meho oversaw the operation, standing quietly by the workbench. He appeared helpless and admiring in the face of Jacques' skill. Once each part was in place and well consolidated, Jacques took the car to drive to the *Château* to pick up the rest of the family. Meho and I exchanged a meaningful look. We had twenty minutes. Jacques and Gordana trusted us, but had we not already betrayed that trust and amply? He held me to him, lifting my blue and white dress in the hall behind our kitchen, our bodies battered by wave after unfurling wave of acute pleasure.

"Why is what I feel for you so violent, so unbearably violent?" I couldn't fight it. There was some elemental force at work far stronger than my own will. "Jacques and Gordana are coming. Do you realize? Please, is it not possible that you be a little more my brother and a little less my lover?" He shook his head no. "If you are my little brother, is this not incest then?"

"No," he laughed. "You are my darling sister, but we didn't have the same mama and papa."

"We have papers now, we settle here, now we can make ourselves a boy," he said to Gordana in the course of the evening. A knife turned in my heart. Why was he talking of that?

"Oh no!" she replied sharply, "finished for children!"

"Why finished?" he said. "I'm forty. If we wait too long, I get to be too old to be papa."

"No more children!" she repeated, her voice acid. "Now I want to go to work. I want to live."

"Meho, Gordana is a modern wife," I ventured, even though this conversation was none of my business. "She doesn't want to spend her life changing diapers."

"I, too, am modern husband," he replied coolly.

"Besides, Gordana's tired. She needs to recuperate."

"She'll be OK. In camps, it was much harder. See how she lost tooth when Veronika born?" He pointed tactlessly to the gap in Gordana's mouth. "Not enough calcium, no magnesium in camp food."

"Why did you talk about having a son with her?" I whispered to him later. "It hurt."

"I know, Ellen. I just wanted you to hear how nasty she answers me."

"What do you do, anyway, not to have children?"

"No wife of mine ever take any medicine for that," he said, proud of his prowess. "Gypsies very good at sex, you notice? When I feel ejaculation coming, I get out."

"How do you know words like that, like 'ejaculation'?"

"Easy! *'Ejakulacje'* in Yugoslavian, *'éjaculation'* in French!"

Château Lore
Oleg

Sveta and Oleg disembarked at Paris-Charles de Gaulle, one battered suitcase in hand. Tense with the momentousness of the occasion, they presented themselves immediately to the border police and requested political asylum. Had they not been sent to the *Château* in Laudes-la-Romaine, they would have soon starved, for they were not the kind to beg on street corners or sing in the *métro*.

Their newest journey was to be down the corridors of the French administration. They learned quite soon that deserters from foreign military service with ideals of the Orthodox priesthood in their minds were not particularly desirable individuals, not even when a child born on hallowed French soil had come to round out the family. They exhausted the appeals, even the one to the regional Prefect for territorial asylum. The pealing and jingling of monastery bells that Oleg tended to hear in his dreams turned to a dull knelling.

"The Prefect Says NO", he printed in large, black letters on the sign he was taking to the demonstration in front of the *Préfecture* . This was democracy, Oleg thought to himself, and you could protest against leaders without the sky falling on you. On the contrary, people must know the injustice and unfairness that was being dealt him.

If Monsieur Dobrinine had known what Oleg was planning to do, he would, perhaps, have counseled greater circumspection, but, alas, he had not. Monsieur Dobrinine, retired from the *Beaux-Arts* School in Laudes-la-Romaine, was descended from a family of old Russian aristocracy, among those who had fled after Red October, and he devoted his retirement time to the defense of Russian-speaking asylum seekers. Oleg and Sveta were his protégés at present, but his cleverest pleading so far had been fruitless. He was, in fact, at his wit's end and had even petitioned the Canadian Embassy about immigration for the Petrovs. It was an uncertain business and beyond their means for the moment, anyway. Oleg would have to get work, but French law forbade that, so long as he did not have his papers.

The small but tightly knit Orthodox community stood behind them, giving gifts and praying. When he was not rereading the few books he had brought in his own language or studying French, Oleg spent considerable time in front of the television set at the *Château*. They were no longer entitled to stay there, but neither were they requested to leave. He and his wife got on well with the other residents; even Leila was appeased by Sveta's firm gentleness, and Gordana Kozić, who spoke to nearly no one, offered them coffee. They bided their time.

Eleven

*I*f Meho lived each day now in the glow of his accomplishments, for Gordana, this was not so. She wept with emotion the day a social worker visited the family in their rooms at the *Château*. "Social worker say, here you are very well, but when you have apartment in town, you be so much better," she reported. This visit had taken place before the arrival of the official letter. It was little wonder Gordana thought the authorities were playing with her. One day, an apartment in town was heavily hinted at; the next, the mails remained mute, and Monsieur Lenoir swore up and down that he hadn't received any confirmation. When the letter finally arrived, it offered refugee status for one year, renewable.

Their status achieved, they could not prolong their stay at the home too long; their rooms were required for new arrivals, for whom the well-worn cycle of wait, hope and despair would begin afresh.

The apartment became Gordana's newest obsession. She had reached the point where life in the *Château* was intolerable to her, the gossip, the pettiness, the jealousy, the rivalry.

"Why you? Why did *you* get refugee status?" asked Ferialle, the heavy-buttocked Kosovar, who had tried to bribe Marie-Toussainte with hairbrushes and trinkets. She made no effort to conceal her spite and envy.

Gordana was proud to narrate the repartee she'd had. "Well because," Gordana had put on her *bourgeois* airs, "you understand, *I* went to nursing school, and my husband to the Academy of Music."

"So, when are you leaving for the apartment?" Ferialle had added, insinuating that she could not wait.

"Not yet," Gordana had replied, "but when we are settled in the apartment, I'll call you. You can come be my *femme de ménage*, my maid."

Material conditions were difficult too, the communal kitchen at one end, their rooms at another, on another floor. She never stopped running. "I want that apartment!" She wrung each word out, her nerves near the breaking point. Low-rent, subsidized apartments could be obtained with the help of the local council, once certain conditions were met, and if a large enough one for their family were available. The time required for this was indeterminate. Another wait began, stretching forward in all its tantalizing torment before Gordana.

Dear little Melisand,

I think that if only conditions were looking up for the Kozićs, if only they could have a decent place to live, then maybe Gordana would relax and be able to satisfy her husband better. As for me, you know how tense I continue to be. Meho suggested I should see a psychiatrist, and it's not as if I hadn't thought of it myself, but a doctor cannot make your life choices for you. I told him I went to see my general practitioner, but she just told me to take more tranquilizers. I'm the overtaut violin string that is going to snap. Meho doesn't think it's a good idea for me to take so much medicine. He says he is my doctor and my medicine, that it was before I knew him that I was ill.

Do you realize, this is the first time since I left my mother's and father's house that anyone, except you, has ever expressed any interest in how I take care of myself?

Of course, I can't put all the blame on your father: Who hasn't got faults? And there's no denying he has many qualities. But you know, too, that before he started the Prozac, he left me not a battered wife, but a battered soul. I'm still afraid to speak to him half the time, because I dread the whiplash of his tongue, and yet, now, most often, he speaks to me nicely. Then, I tell myself, see how unjust you are; he's speaking to you altogether normally.

Your father has given me material security, the house, everything practical, but with Meho I have finally found someone who makes me feel loved, someone who actually worries about me. Remember how I told you once that if I ever became seriously ill, your father just would not be capable of accompanying me, and that, if you weren't there, I would be utterly and totally alone?

God help me, he just passed in front of the computer screen; I was paralyzed with fright! But he didn't read anything; he even kissed me. Whatever made him do that?

My heart is being torn in two like a rag.

P.S. From Wednesday on, I'll be giving exams in Champrichard. It will be a sort of retreat. Maybe I'll be able to think things over.

I wrote this letter to Melisand the day after my celebratory dinner with the Kozićs. To my profound relief, Jacques didn't read it when he passed behind me that evening on the way to his study. What I did not realize was that I had failed to delete it from the computer.

Meho and I made love when and where we could, sometimes in the country, usually in my little automobile. He would bend over me to grasp the round handle that made the driver's seat recline. Then, with studied application he would claim me, his tongue circling the volutes of my ear, his mouth on my nipples, sucking and nibbling.

Before my departure for Champrichard, we drove out of the town, past the university, past a Gypsy encampment in a vast, vacant lot. "Look, there are the Rom," said Meho, smiling. "Maybe they lend us nice caravan!" Their trailers were parked in a circle, some with satellite disks. Their laundry dangled from ropes like floppy, tired flags. He and Gordana would have no need now to ask them for refuge, I thought.

"Listen, Meho, I'm short of time," I protested. "I have to go home and get something to eat before my classes this afternoon." He fed me chocolate and peanuts from the grocery bags he had brought to take home to Gordana. "Peanuts good for love desire," he said. I didn't want to tell him I was leaving for the examination board, but, at the last minute, I scribbled the telephone number of the hotel where I would be staying. And now what will I do, I asked myself, if Jacques calls me and the phone is busy, because I am talking to Meho? I will have to tell him I called Melisand. I was learning to lie.

When Jacques did call, his tone of voice was tinged with reproach. "You didn't say good-bye to me this morning when you left. I missed that all day."

"I didn't want to wake you," I said. In my haste to escape from it all, I had not even had a thought for him. I wanted only to leave the house as quickly as possible, unnoticed. It was very early in the morning. I told him about the examinations, and we said good night.

Meho called later. "I love you and I miss you," was all he said. I wept on my hotel bed, a helpless jelly of sobs and spasms. Why was Jacques now, of all times, reproaching me with not speaking to him, when, for years, he hadn't greeted me, nor cared one way or the other. Was he waking up, now that it was too late? And, if he loved me, why didn't he say so? Meho had said so.

In Jacques' reproach I could hear my own voice: *You are guilty of infidelity and you know it.* But Meho's was the voice of love. When I made love to Meho, was I being unfaithful to Jacques or faithful to myself?

On my return from Champrichard, the table was set, a vase of red roses from the garden in the center. Jacques had placed the plates and napkins carefully and even prepared soup. Surprised, I thanked him. "Before we eat," he began, "I have something I would like to talk to you about." Something ominous in his tone panicked me. "It's . . . serious."

"Of course. Let's go sit down in the living room then," I said, trying to keep a hold on myself. I knew he knew, must know, somehow. "This isn't going to be easy," I added softly. My mind was galloping ahead; my hour of reckoning had arrived, and I would have to admit everything. Well, and so be it, I thought. Perhaps it is for the better.

"I have a heavy burden on my conscience," Jacques began. Here, the world was beginning to turn upside down. "I know that for a number of years now, I haven't been a good husband to you." He was saying his *mea culpa*.

And I, then? Was it possible he hadn't guessed after all? Should I speak or not? My throat tightened. The words I had immediately formulated mentally, "Then you know I am Meho's mistress," stuck there. I will wait, I decided. I will see what he tells me.

"I have the feeling that you are escaping from me. I have the feeling that I am losing you. Please, just tell me what to do. I would do *anything* to keep you." His voice was strained, his brown eyes full of pain.

My panic gave way to a feeling of reprieve. He didn't know then or didn't know everything. And if he were to learn, I would somehow be absolved. He had recognized his responsibility and put me into a position of strength. "You know that I've wanted to leave you," I admitted. "You remember that letter I wrote you one year on Valentine's Day? I've never stopped thinking about leaving. You should realize that. But you've made progress since the Prozac, and I've let more time go by. You know, in a certain way, I still love you. Intellectually, you give me a lot. But I don't ever feel that you love me. You never say it, and you don't show it. I'm just someone who's there in your way. You never use any term of endearment any more. Don't you remember how you used to?"

He hesitated. "I know," he said, "but now I believe I can say it." His face was ashen, the graying page of an old book. He too was making a huge effort at self-mastery, at giving birth to words. "I do love you, Ellen. My Ellen darling."

"I've been so lonely. I'm so alone, Jacques. If I hadn't had Melisand to confide in all these years, I don't know what I would have done. Neither of us knew what to do for you. When you were in your bad periods, I couldn't talk to you, because you were incapable of hearing me. When you were better, then I didn't dare speak. I didn't want to break the fragile peace."

"Please promise you will tell me when I am being unkind to you, or when I am speaking harshly." I said I would try.

"My only goal now in life is to make you happy." He looked stricken and contrite. For years, I would have given anything for him to speak those words. Now, they were the last thing I wanted to hear.

"He knows something," I told Meho, when we met on Saturday afternoon at our perch in the botanical garden. I repeated Jacques' plea.

"I'm glad for him if he has opened eyes and finally seen you," he said, looking at me, shaking his head slightly, his look tender. "I don't want to cause Jacques any pain. He's a good man. Been good to us. I will be very careful. I don't want to cause you any trouble with him."

I didn't expect that reaction, and I loved him the more for his generosity. Still, he had not said he would renounce me, only that he would be cautious. "I'm married, Meho. I can't give you my husband's place."

"I don't ask for it. I'll take second place, Ellen . . ."

Second place; easier to say than to accept.

"But I must tell you this," he went on. "You are my own heart. I looked into your soul and I saw that you were alone. I will keep you and protect you. *I* will never leave you to be alone. You have entered me now. You are a part of myself."

That night, when I finally slept, I dreamed that my name was being called, incessantly. I could not make out the voices.

Love digs in nails and thorns. It rends the flesh of the soul. I took my distress with me to the city of Aiguebonne, where my son Jeremy, Adeline, and their little boy lived. If I had thought one moment that I would escape for a few days, I soon found that one can run away from anyone but oneself. In Aiguebonne, I was to play the grandmother, when I was more shaken than a troubled adolescent. I was sick with desire and anguish, constantly on the edge of tears.

Jeremy and Adeline could see my thoughts were elsewhere. "Why are you so tired, Mom?" Jeremy asked. "Oh, I know," he provided the answer, "It's the end of the school year, and you've been so worried about your Bosnian friends."

Yes, so worried.

Jacques never stopped calling. During the day, he sent e-mail to me via Adeline's office. "How lovely to have such an attentive husband!" she said, delivering the messages. Yes, how lovely! His effusions made me uneasy, each declaration of affection a new thrust, a slap of self-reproach. I swam in a bath of culpability.

"So, what did you do this evening?" I asked him, making telephone conversation again. "Watch television?"

"No, I was up at the *Château*," he spoke casually. "Meho called. He said they had problems, so I dropped by."

"What problems?" My heart raced. Jacques at the *Château* without me? This was odd. What could Meho possibly have called him for, when he knew I wasn't there? Or was he being foxy, inviting us both, making it obvious *he* had no inkling I wasn't at home. Then again, could it have been Jacques the crafty one, going to the *Château* of his own accord and ascribing the request to Meho? I was too worried and confused to make sense of all this.

"So what did you do?" I forced myself to sound casual too, letting through just the spark of curiosity Jacques could legitimately expect.

"They need five thousand francs and they haven't got it."

"What? Five thousand? Whatever for?" This was a very large sum, about eight hundred dollars.

"Two thousand to conclude their debts with the lawyer and the national office, and three in order to have French identity papers made at the *Préfecture* for the whole family. So long as they don't pay, they won't have the papers, and without the papers, they can't apply for the apartment."

"Well, what did you do?"

"I would have written him a check, but I didn't have my checkbook with me. He never mentioned money on the phone."

I dared ask no more questions. Meho must have called him, taking advantage of my absence, perhaps, to bring up this financial matter. If Jacques had been prepared to give the Kozićs five thousand francs, then he couldn't suspect too much. He was a good man, indeed. Out of consideration for me, he was ready to succor those I had given my heart to. And what was I? A woman who had not respected her marriage vows, an adulteress. But had he respected his, to love and to cherish? He had abandoned them too long, and now there was the price to pay.

When I slept that night on Jeremy's couch, I dreamed I heard Meho's voice on the telephone, telling me he loved me in Romany. When I asked him to repeat it, he became inaudible. There were many, many people around him, and we were cut off. I awoke with my head splitting.

"Jacques was up at the *Château,* right?" I asked Meho. He didn't answer. We were sitting in a park again, this time near a cordoned-off area, where an archaeological dig had unearthed craggy Roman ruins, the broken foundations of houses and public baths. Meho kept trying to slide his hand inside the waistband of my jeans, and I kept removing it. "Sexy lady!" he said to me.

"Don't be silly! I'm a bookworm type, Meho!"

"For me," he persisted, "you are very sexy lady." A child in her First Communion outfit, white and frilly, played on the grass near us. Her parents chatted nearby.

"Listen, I know he went to see you. What did he say to you?"

"He was very nervous. I could see something not right. First, with Gordana, he smiled very much, then he came outside with me. It was very difficult for him to speak. He said . . . he said something like, 'Meho, stop to give happiness to Ellen . . .' or something, I can't remember words." For the life of him, the French words would not return.

"Wasn't it, maybe, 'you can't give happiness to Ellen'?" I asked.

"Perhaps. He told me to stay away from you. I said, 'Ellen and I just have friendship. Have you not friendship with my wife too?'"

Meho was never at a loss for an answer. Still, his insolence in denying any relations with me and asking more or less directly for money from the man whose very wife he was sleeping with struck me as exceptionally brazen. My husband was a gentleman, and my lover was not. Still, I desired him. The years of hurt that Jacques had inflicted on me welled up in me now and wouldn't be quieted. Meho was an explosion within me, physical and emotional. Which was stronger, my love or my desire? Was it possible to love someone and not desire him, or to desire a man without really loving him? So often we desire what we do not truly love.

"You and I are so different," I told Meho. "How is it possible for us to love each other?"

"To me, you are very much like a Gypsy woman, and, where you are different from me, I will change you," Meho said. I couldn't see this Gypsy in me, unless it were the new, reckless Ellen, tired of adapting to every situation, ready at more than fifty to follow her own *drom,* her own road. Was I unconsciously seeking in him some unknown part of myself?

"You and I are the same," he told me, and I laughed.

"It would be no fun if we were the same."

"Of course, I am a man, and you are a woman." He didn't really want to joke. "But fundamentally, we are the same."

What did you, my wanderer, see of yourself in me?

"Meho, I have spent many years building my life. I cannot throw it all away now."

"I understand. I will never ask you to do that."

I wanted to reassure Jacques that I wouldn't leave him, but that I had to live this new chapter in my life to the full. I wanted to move away, to live alone for some time. The passion I felt for Meho could not pass overnight. One might just as well ask the sap not to mount in the trees or the moon not to rise. It partook of a force that transcended me.

Jacques weighed on me with all the burden of his anxiety and chagrin. He lay in wait for my changes of mood, listened to each sigh, watched the very tremor of my eyelids.

I suffocated; my vital space was overtaken. For years I had played with the truth to spare him. I had kept to myself my pain and vexation, resigned to it, working above all else to preserve the peace of the household. Why had I not cried out more often, screamed the truth in his face, told him how he was making me hate him? I hadn't been fair to him, hadn't given him a chance to make amends, because I hadn't told him how great was the expanse of devastation within me. Once again, I found myself guilty. I renounced my fantasy of living alone; he wouldn't understand, and it would destroy him. He knew he must wait, but how long would he be willing to wait? I became frightened at the idea of losing him and just as frightened that Meho might turn away from me. I needed both of them.

The need that Meho, the refugee, and all his family had for me had become mutual, and now the balance tipped toward me. I needed his need. I had to nurture him or wither away myself. I worried about the sum of money Jacques hadn't lent or given him. I cast about for an idea: How could I give him money without wounding his pride?

For two weeks now, he had been working at the foundry, where Cédric had found him employment. One morning I drove to the foundry office, a neutral white envelope, with his name typed on the outside, in my hand. Inside I had placed eight one-hundred franc notes. I asked the secretary if she would transmit a message and left in all haste.

I teased Meho as we drank coffee together in my kitchen. The French window onto the back garden, where the patio would be built, was open. "You are really a Gypsy," I said. "The more I give, the more you ask for!"

"Are you a racist, Ellen?"

"Yes!" I said, seeing the surprise in his dark eyes. "I am partial to Gypsies!"

He smiled. "At any rate, I never stole you!"

"No, you are no thief, Meho. I gave myself."

He asked to see me more and more, and I was incapable of saying no. When he called me on the telephone, his voice melted my resolve. I ran to meet him, wherever he was, seized with a recklessness I had never known before. Thus, on the day of an important teachers' meeting, barely two hours before it was scheduled to begin, I found myself in an underground parking lot near the central marketplace. Meho's bank was near the marketplace, and he had some business there. He wanted me to meet him, and, of course, I left my books and went to him. The subterranean parking lot was cool and damp and smelled of gasoline fumes. It was low-ceilinged and dimly lit with tubular, infrared lamps.

"You are so beautiful today!" Meho exclaimed, his voice affectionate. Unlike Jacques, he had mastered the art of the compliment. He raised his black eyebrows in delight and mock amusement at the sight of my panties. For Meho, sex was a joy. One did not feel any burden of sin or guilt or embarrassment. "What happens between us is natural," he would say. "Ellen, stop fighting against yourself!"

He pulled down his trousers and penetrated me as I lay back in the driver's seat, perspiration raining down from him onto my blouse. The day was hot. Outside, the sun shone whitely. "With you, my little Helena, I am like sixteen years old."

"I wish I was . . . !"

"My *molodoshka!*" My young one. "I will keep you for twenty years!"

"How is it that you make love so well?"

He smiled indulgently. "Because I do it with my heart!" A car pulled into the spot next to ours; the driver looked over and winked at Meho as he rode me. *And now what have you come to,* my inner voice chided. I couldn't decide whether to feel despicably tawdry or incredibly daring.

Meho drew a bottle of port wine from his workbag. "For you and me," he said, "to make party together!" I guessed where he had found the money for the wine, although I was still unsure whether the secretary had given him the envelope.

"Meho," I ventured, "didn't you get any mail at work?"

"No, no mail," he said.

Eight hundred francs, lost, was all I could think. I felt a hot wave of anxiety rush over me. "Are you sure? Didn't the secretary give you a white envelope?"

He looked at me curiously. "Because that envelope . . . that envelope was . . . you?"

"Well, who did you think?"

"I didn't know. I think boss . . ."

"Meho, I gave that to you for the *Préfecture,* not to buy wine with."

"*You* gave me money?"

I nodded. My blouse was crushed from his perspiration and our embrace. "Can I go to the meeting like this?" I asked.

"No, not so good, you better change."

As I drove swiftly back home, he told me when to change gears. He put his hand on the horn of the car and honked when someone cut in front of me.

"Hey, cut that out!" I said. "You can drive when you have your own car. In the meantime, I do the driving."

"Sorry!" he said, laughing. "I thought I was speaking to Yugoslav woman. I forgot I was talking to American woman. To a free woman!"

I composed my best professional expression once again and entered the teachers' meeting, my blouse fresh, the smell of gasoline still clinging to my skirt.

Meho looked at Melisand's photograph on the bookcase in my living room. "She is beautiful girl. She is like you." I told him how I confided in her, how she encouraged me to live the life of a woman. "She is a very modern young woman, Meho, and she knows how her father is with me. In fact, he never speaks to her either. The girls in our family are second-class citizens." He seemed shocked, but, on second thought, pleased.

"I'd like to call her. I wish I could talk to her."

"What could you possibly say?"

"That I have another daughter now. And two boys."

"Two boys?"

"Nadir and Jeremy, of course. I love Jeremy very much."

Your children, Jacques. What would you say to that? Gypsy hospitality is legendary.

Indeed, since he had met Jeremy at the *Château* on Christmas Eve, he phoned him occasionally, about where to order oboe reeds, or where to find sheet music, for Jeremy too was a musician, a pianist like his father. Meho always found a good reason.

"My mother's eyes were as blue as the color in that painting you have there," he said, pointing to an abstract picture over the piano in bold lines and primary colors. "People think Gypsies have dark eyes, but lots have blue. My mother have so beautiful eyes."

"Is she still alive?" I knew I had asked this before, but I was hoping for more details.

"No."

"Because of the war, right?"

He shook his head. "Died of illness."

That was not what you had given me to understand that day in the park. Or had I jumped to conclusions?

"Were you close to her?"

"Yes, close. Good woman. A man must respect his mama. I tell Nadir, you go out with girls, OK, but first you tell mama where you're going."

You wanted him to be considerate of Samira. Whatever she had done. I liked that.

"Did your father die of illness too?"

"Him too. But they weren't together anymore. They fought all the time. It was just the sort of atmosphere I didn't want for my boy, for Nadir."

"And your brother, Nadir?"

"Disappeared."

"Was he married?"

"No, not married." Meho was taciturn. He preferred to let mystery prevail. It left more room, no doubt, for imagination and sympathy.

He studied Melisand's photograph again. "If I cut your hair," he said, and, indeed, he was very talented at cutting hair, "I make a little shorter, more modern cut."

I asked Jacques, "What would you say if I got my hair cut?"

"Why not? It looks limp."

I was to play the violin in a concert of baroque church music that evening, with a small detachment of musicians from the town orchestra. I spent the afternoon at the hairdresser's. "So, what do you think?" I asked Jacques, when I got home.

"It's not bad," he said. "She did a good job."

Meho was in the audience. I sought out his face, near the back of the church. His expression was neutral; he appeared to be watching the choir. He came forward to say a brief hello at the end of the concert, discreetly handing me a crumpled piece of paper. Inside were some words in Serbo-Croatian that I could not understand, and *Les Tulipes,* the bus stop where I sometimes met him. I guessed that *sutra* meant tomorrow.

He sat on our sofa, marveling: "When I see you last night with new haircut, all I can think is, my God, how beautiful Ellen is! Did Jacques tell you how beautiful you are?"

"No, but he said the hairdresser was good."

Meho's black eyes twinkled like a starry night. He knew he had scored a point. It was his natural gift to see me, my being, not just the outer trappings. Meho looked at Ellen. Jacques, now that he had begun to look, looked at Ellen's clothes, her hairdo, all these the work of others or of my own craft, but outside of me. In Meho's look, I existed.

He snatched his disposable camera from his pocket and snapped my picture as I sat on the sofa, my chin cupped in my hand. He caught me totally unsuspecting. Again, we found ourselves on Jeremy's bed. Meho in orgasm was ecstatic. "I love you, Ellen," he would repeat, "I love you, I love you." When his appetite was calmed, he would cover me with kisses and thank me. "Thank you, my dearest Ellen!" I was unused to effusion.

I lay on my back, naked, yielding. "If only I had not leave camera in bathroom," he said, shaking his head in wonderment at my long, pale body, offered up to him. We bathed together afterward, and I dried him as if he were my child, lingering on the curls around his sex, small now in its black nest. "All over already?" he asked regretfully. As we embraced before the mirror, a flash went off. Meho had set his camera at a distance, and we both would be in the picture.

I looked foolish, hugging you to my bare breast. When you showed me the picture later, I took it in my hand, and you thought I wanted to keep it. Why didn't I keep it?

Château Lore
Murat

So Maman and Papa went to that city, two hundred kilometers away. With the lawyer and Madame Anne-Laure and four other people from the Defense League. Murat couldn't go to school, because he was illegal now. He didn't like staying at the home without anybody to talk to except Elisabeth and the big guy who was guardian during the day. He was so tall and strong, he could crush Murat's father between his thumb and his forefinger. He usually just sat in his little office and watched TV, anyway, and Murat always hurried past when he was there. He bet the guy would be capable of calling the police, and they would come to get him and send him away, and he wouldn't even be able to say good-bye to his best friend at school.

When his parents got home, they told him the judge had decided the Prefect was right. They had to leave. But the order didn't say where they had to go, so maybe they wouldn't have to go to Bulgaria. Besides, they didn't have any money, so where could they go anyway? And then his mother cried and said that minors didn't have to be sent away, and he could stay in France. But they would be separated forever. Then she hugged him too tightly and said it was better that way, if he could have a better life. His father told her to stop being so dramatic, and of course they would never separate. The lawyer said he wouldn't give up, and there would be another appeal. But Monsieur

Lenoir said he didn't have the right to keep them at the home, so, anyway, they would be out on the street.

Murat didn't say anything to the other children at the home. He helped his mother pack their suitcases, and then they followed Madame Anne-Laure, who said she had a room for them in town. Actually, it was an attic, really long with mansard windows, and when his mother washed the clothes, she hung them up right there in the room. They couldn't go out at all, and when a reporter came to take their pictures again, they had to sit with their backs to the camera. He, Murat, was right between Maman and Papa, and the reporter said that looked really poignant, and there would be a lot of people at the demonstration the Defense League was organizing.

Madame Anne-Laure was always meeting important people to talk about their case, and she even got Murat back in school. She went to the school board and argued for hours, and the result was that Murat got permission to go back to his class, and the teacher gave him his same books back. The other kids didn't even notice he'd been gone, or, if they did, they probably just thought he'd had a cold. He never said a word about anything to them, but he ran really fast to the bus stop to catch his ride into town, because if there was a policeman around, he might get asked where his parents were, and that, he would never tell. Murat thought maybe he would be tortured in prison if the police caught him.

Marie-Toussainte knew where they were, and she came to see them. She said she would find another place for them to live, where his mother could wash dishes in the cafeteria, and they could earn their keep that way, at least for awhile. She said they ought to go out to the Catholic picnic on Sunday, because the police would never bother them there, and they had to get out a little, or they'd go crazy. She asked Murat if he wanted to stay on in France without his parents, but he thought that was the stupidest question he'd ever heard. She told his father he had to be really careful about people that employed clandestines, because he'd only earn a pittance for long, back-breaking hours of work, and he wouldn't have insurance or anything like that. But Papa said, what choice do I have?

Twelve

Seismic vibrations weary the psyche. When I didn't see Meho, I would lie on my bed, my senses exacerbated, endlessly seeking relief through my own fingers, the cotton crotch of my panties damp, the tender sheath of my vagina sore. Then tears would come, as images of Jacques, supplicating, would file past in my mind. His every gesture now was to placate, to repair, to restore. The kinder, the gentler he showed himself, the more wretched I grew in my guilt. I got up and went to my computer, typing rather than writing by hand so that the foreign words would be easier for him:

Beloved Meho,

I am writing to you, because I need to write. Sometimes it is easier for me than speaking. It relieves my heart. I spoke to you by telepathy on Sunday. Didn't you hear me? I guess I'm not very good at it.

I love you. Please do not doubt that, even if I do not come to you every time you would like. I love your family too and everything that touches them. I would never want to hurt any one of them.

This love between us is a great suffering for me. I cry all the day. I do not know how long I can continue this way. My heart used to be light, but now it is heavy. I have forgotten how to laugh.

I know that you understand the problem; before, my husband and I were friends, but we did not really love each other anymore from being to being, because his own being was ill.

You have given me such wonderful gifts. You have made me understand that I was a woman who could still be loved and desired. You saw my soul and you saw my body too.

I wanted to give many things to you too. I gave you everything I had to give.

It was then that my husband realized that something of my being was escaping and going toward another being. He awoke from a long, long sleep, and he saw me too.

He wants to rebuild a relationship with me, a profound and real one. I cannot refuse him that. We have been married for thirty years. He is my oldest friend. We have shared so much. For nothing in the world would I want to hurt him.

I do not want to hurt you either. You are so precious to me.

Meho, what can I do? Not to hurt you? Not to hurt Jacques? To stop suffering? Please tell me, if you know the answer!

If there is no answer, then let's let some time go by. Let's try to return to that simple friendship that held our two families close. I pray to God every day for you, because more than anything, I want you to be happy, and I am so afraid that you will not be happy by me. I never stop thinking of you.

I would go to meet Meho after his shift at the foundry. He would run to the car, kiss my hands, still with his work gloves on, then run back inside to shower, his grimy, sweaty factory day over. Then we would pull to the back of the lot, where trees grew in clumps. It was warm the day I brought the letter, and I had on my silky red and white print dress. Meho ran his finger along the low-cut neckline. I caught his hand and held it a moment. "I have written you a letter," I said, drawing the sheet from my skirt pocket and handing it to him. "A letter?" he smiled, surprised. His smile changed to an expression of perplexity, as he slowly deciphered the alien words of the text.

"Do you understand?"

"A little." He looked stricken. "I take it home and read again."

"Do you understand my question at the end?"

"Yes."

"Do you have an answer for me?"

"Do you need of me, Ellen?"
I paused. "Yes . . . yes, I need you."
"I don't know then . . . perhaps, you leave your husband for me?"

If I wanted you to sacrifice yourself, Meho, then I had not taken the right tack. Should I have told you I didn't need you? Then I would have lied to you.

For the time being, it was still easier for me to deceive Jacques. I drove home, undelivered from my lies, my lust, and my disarray.

Once again I lay in Meho's arms on the double bed, tired and satisfied. He slipped away from me to reach for his jeans on the floor, pulling two sheets of paper from the back pocket. "Me too, I write you a letter," he said. I sat up, intrigued and pleased that Meho too could wield a pen when he wanted to.

> *My beloved Helena,*
> *You have shattered my soul, for I understand from your letter to me that you are anticipating a time soon when you will leave me physically and spiritually. You gave me the courage I needed for my life, Helena, and I cannot even tell you the spiritual joy you brought me. Now you are losing the warmth and fire that you used to have for me, and perhaps even it is all gone, or does it give you satisfaction to play with my heart as your husband has played with yours? When we met we talked about our disappointments and aspirations, and you were like a wounded bird. We gave compassion to each other, so that now you are a saved bird, and I am in the place you used to be. I thought my love would stay with you, because I gave you everything from myself both physically and spiritually to make you happy, though I do not know now if you are really happy in your marriage. It is good that you have found comfort with your husband, despite what you told me about how unhappy you used to be with him. Our souls are the same, Helena, and*

our characters are alike. Have you not obtained enough of my love and my manhood, do I not touch deep enough in you that you cannot forget the rest now?

You are deep in my heart and you cannot get out. I cannot be without you, because you are my soul, and I cannot live without you. My nights are restless, my thoughts are with you. Wherever I go you are with me, and I cannot understand what can separate us from our love. I can understand, my darling, only if you do not love me and do not want me or do not need me anymore, so never speak of humanitarian love because it is false love.

Ever since you gave me that letter, my Helena, I cannot find sleep, I am anxious and nervous, and can hardly wait to call you and for you to come to my arms. Never before in my life have I wanted to see somebody so much, look for somebody so much as I do for you. You asked me about my son, Nadir, but when you are in question, no one else comes to my mind. Now you tell me you will soon be leaving to go to America for your summer holiday, and I am full of sadness. Once you are gone, I do not know what will happen to me. I will probably go mad.

If it is your wish not to continue our relationship, my darling, then, as you wish. When you need me, I will be with you, because you are a part of my heart and more. I would risk anything in my life for the kind of person you are. You are not wood or a stone that cannot feel love, so why did you not obtain love from your husband? Now, I do not understand your situation with him. What will happen later if you stay with him? Your letter is very hard on me, I do not understand how you change your mind. Je t'aime, Meho

To write to me, Meho had chosen what to him was the language of the *gadje*. Not only did he know I would never find a translator for Romany, but he clearly associated me with the non-Gypsy women of his country and chose his language accordingly. At the time, I couldn't read Meho's letter in Serbo-Croatian. After weeks of searching, I finally found, thanks to the Internet, a Serbian translator willing to take on a personal letter.

As I lay next to him then on the bed, the mysterious letter in hand, Meho was able, however, to explain some of his thoughts in French:

how he had seen me as a bird with wounded wing and brought me back to life with his warmth. The handwriting was difficult, and I put the scrawled sheets aside, falling back into his arms. What did the exact meaning matter? It was a love letter, and I knew he loved me. The emotion I felt crystallized into a warm pool of tension between my legs, spreading into a yearning that engulfed the rest of my body. My need became imperative: I seized him and drew him into me again. *Me mangav tu, moj Rom, moj cigno phral,* my own Rom, my little brother.

Jacques wore the expression he'd had the day I'd returned from Champrichard. Strain and anxiety had left deep gray-black shadows under his eyes. I sat reading in my usual russet-colored armchair. He was on the chocolate-brown sofa, near me, his book lying forgotten on his knees. "Ellen," he spoke abruptly, "are you happy with me?"

"Yes, yes I'm happy." Fear seared through me. We were in for a discussion again.

"There are still things . . . things left unsaid between us."

"What do you mean?"

"I don't know exactly what there is, but I just feel that you don't tell me everything. There's some secret."

I made up my mind in the instant. I would tell him, out of respect for him, for his overwhelming efforts, out of respect for myself, a truthful woman. And if I told him, it would embolden me, perhaps. There was strength to be found in truth.

"All right. All right, then, I'll tell you everything. Only . . . it's not so easy to say. I wrote to Thérèse the other day, and I kept a copy. If you want, you can read it. It's simpler for me that way, I mean, writing things instead of saying them." I got up to get the letter and placed it before him. Thérèse was the first person beyond Melisand in whom, in guarded terms, I had confided. She would understand me. Her own marital shipwreck would make her sensitive to my distress. Moreover, she had met Meho, and, possibly, her intuition had spoken to her. Before, I had never told her plainly about Jacques' long night of solitude, and the ravages it had brought to our marriage. In the letter, it poured out.

> ... Then enter my Rom musician, who, unlike Jacques, was able to see. I am deeply involved with him, and I try to avoid remorse, because I realize now that all this was inevitable. I might even have thought of rebuilding my life with him, if he were not thirteen years younger, with an artistic career before him, a totally different culture, and the responsibility of a family.
>
> But then, my butterfly started to emerge from his chrysalis. The anti-depressant treatment began to take effect, and, moreover, the complicity he guessed at between my friend and me made the scales fall from his eyes. Not only has he begun to see me, but to see me to the point of suffocating me, as if he had to catch up ten years in ten days! He wants to reconstruct our life together, and, of course, I do too. I still love him in a way, and I realize that my life is not with this Balkan refugee, but I am completely torn in half.
>
> He, too, has known so very much suffering, and I don't want to inflict any more on him. He has invested himself totally in our relationship; it is not superficial, and it is not over. Duplicity is not a mode of life that I can bear easily, and yet Jacques must know nothing of what I'm going through. I have to help him find his life again. So here I am with the responsibility of these two hearts, plus my own, and my worst fear: that I will hurt someone. The doctor and Melisand tell me to think of myself. I do try to, but it's hard when other people's happiness depends on one.

Jacques put down the letter, still not understanding. "Well, yes, but I asked Meho to stay away from you, and you said you were willing to work on our relationship. You said you would tell me when I was unkind to you."

"Of course I did, Jacques, but I can't just stop loving him overnight. Don't you see that? I can't turn off my feelings like a faucet. And you understand that I can't talk to you about that."

"Did you think I would hold it against you that you have fallen in love with someone else?" Jacques' words stunned me; was he then so tolerant?

"I can't just suddenly say, 'I won't make love with you any more,' either..."

"Make love?" He was dazed. It was as if I had suddenly reached out and struck his face. I thought the letter was sufficiently clear, but it had not been. I would need to speak words after all. For years, Jacques had shunned language, and now it was I who could not speak. We would both have to learn.

"I thought you would understand that from what I wrote."

"Not really." I had never seen him so pale. Suffering was written all over his face.

"Well, yes. I'm sorry. Now you know."

"I should have realized that time when you said, 'This is not going to be easy.'"

I had not desired to confess in order to assuage my own conscience. I was willing to bear my guilt. But he had pushed me to it, and I had seen the reasonableness of transparency. The air would be cleared. The secret, as he said, would be unveiled, and we would have to find a way of living with it. His knowledge would give me strength, perhaps, to fight my own inclinations. How curious, though, that the most terrible blow was the avowal of my sexual betrayal. He was willing to accept that I should love another man. That I should give my body to another man was more than he could bear.

"I never would have thought it," he said, "I never would have imagined it possible."

Neither would I, Jacques, but neither you nor I knew my Gypsy streak, did we?

He made me promise faithfulness. "If he wants you to meet again as lovers, will you tell me? In that case, I will go and see him."

"It will take some time for my feelings to change, that's all. You'll have to give me time."

"I will be patient for however long it takes. I will be waiting for you."

I gave him my word.

Jacques and I decided on a weekend together, at an inn in the country. It would be the beginning of our new construction together. Something was broken between us, but we would build anew. The foundation remained. We would sweep away the ruins and begin a new structure, brick by patient brick, building in pain and truth, but building together.

I agreed to make an appointment with Meho to explain the situation and to break with him. Some time before, when our passion was first unfolding, we had sworn there would be only truth between us. If one was no longer willing, he would tell the other, and we would separate good friends.

> *Weren't we naive, Meho, to believe this possible? There could be truth between us, indeed, but separation could never be so simple.*

We met in front of the cathedral and walked to the park, where he had kissed me on that sunny afternoon during our first times together. We sat on a bench some distance behind the archives building where my librarian friend worked. A path led in front of the bench, but trees in full leaf of summer now surrounded it on three sides. Jacques had trusted me to meet him alone like this. He had asked no questions about our affair, whether from natural discretion or unwillingness to hear details that could only pain him, I did not know.

"I only want what is good for you, Ellen," Meho said, when I told him what Jacques had asked me. But he didn't seem to register that our encounters were over, that I was announcing the end.

"I want to give you a present for your birthday," he told me. "I have something for you." Our birthdays were two days apart, at the beginning of September, and we had long planned to celebrate together, if the Kozić family obtained refugee status. It was a goal I had set in my mind. But what money could he possibly have to buy me a present with? Meho touched the heavy gold chain he wore around his neck and looked at me.

"Your chain, Meho? It's not possible. I can't possibly accept that."

"You don't want it?"

"It's not that I don't want it. But when could I wear it? What would Jacques say? Not to mention Gordana."

"All right. But then, maybe you'll take this?" He showed me the silver ID bracelet he was wearing. It wasn't the one with Nadir engraved on it. "Gordana picked it up on the sidewalk. It has an 'E' on it, like for Ellen, but there's a 'B' too." The bracelet bore only two initials, "E" and "B".

"Well, the 'B' could be for my middle name. My middle name is Barbara."

"That is wonderful!" He was pleased with Gordana's find. "I give it to you in September. I try to see if something more can be engraved, maybe my name too."

He doesn't understand the importance of what I am telling him. And he hasn't thought of Gordana. As if she wouldn't notice the disappearance of his gold chain. I had never seen him without it.

"How is Gordana?"

"Still very nervous. Can't stand *Château*. She wants apartment."

"I understand that. Listen, Meho, if I write you a check for the three thousand francs for your papers at the *Préfecture*, then you can get your French ID papers and speed up the process. Would she be shocked if I did that?"

"No. She would accept that."

I took my checkbook out of my purse and wrote a check for the sum. Jacques would approve. Gordana would be relieved and in better humor, which could only help their marriage.

"Thank you, my Ellen. How can I ever thank you enough?"

Meho placed my cardigan on my short skirt, over my knees to cover them, and, while he kissed me, in full view of the path, he slid his hand under the sweater, under the skirt, to the warm place between my legs. He felt me clench with the flood of orgasm. "Ellen, I want to come to you. Please, I need of you."

"No, no, we mustn't, it's finished." I had taken pleasure in spite of myself and given none. I had sinned against Meho, sinned against Jacques.

"How did your meeting go?" Jacques asked, when I returned home.

"Oh, fine. We parted the best of friends."

Château Lore
Smaïl

What Smaïl liked about the home he had been assigned to in France were the coffee smells in the morning, wafting all the way upstairs and bringing him back to drowsy life, the way it used to be when he was in Sarajevo. He shut thoughts of that time out of his consciousness and contemplated the day awaiting him. His roommate, a lanky African, lay sprawled on the bed, still sound asleep, half of the bedclothes dragging on the floor. Smaïl would get up, make his way down to the kitchen where he kept his little store of powdered Nescafé, but, more often than not, one of the women would serve him some hot, black coffee from her own pot.

His good nature had got him more or less adopted by the matrons of the *Château,* while he fit in with the men, too, talking about soccer in the half-French half-Slavic jargon they shared. They taught him how to play chess, and he spent hours hunched over the board with them in a corner of the dining-hall, while the television droned on in the opposite corner. When he was not out playing soccer at a youth center, he was trying to learn the language.

Marie-Toussainte had worked two lessons per week for him into the Catholic Aid schedule, Tuesdays and Thursdays, except for school holidays. His name, Smaïl Berković, was posted with the others in the list on the pane of Elizabeth's office.

If he could have, he would have written to Aunt Maja and to others he knew in Sarajevo, God willing, they were still alive, and to his uncle in the suburbs, but the post didn't work. The mail piled up, undelivered, tons of it, they said. The fear of letter bombs was so great, that layers upon layers of hopeful script were left to rot. He had taken no telephone numbers with him, when he'd left Sarajevo; it hadn't occurred to him. Smaïl rather liked his limbo of chess and soccer and coffee, so long as it wouldn't last. Once he had obtained his papers and could muster enough French, he would go to a special school to learn auto bodywork; it was a reasonable dream.

Thirteen

*M*arie-Toussainte frequently praised Elisabeth to me. "She doesn't just take care of them while they're waiting for their papers," she said. "She even follows up on all the administrative rigmarole afterward. They'd never get through it without her."

Gordana had to undertake endless procedures to obtain government-subsidized housing. Accompanied by Elisabeth, she climbed in and out of buses, opening up the folding stroller each time for Veronika. She told me how lost she felt in the meanders of the French bureaucracy, where impatient secretaries, unused to slowing their speech for foreigners, only increased her feelings of frustration and strangeness. It was Mademoiselle Elisabeth of the pulled hair (forgiven at last?), who patiently helped her fill in forms and explained the arcanes of family allowances and municipal aid.

> *Gordana, you never asked me for help, no matter how difficult it all seemed to you. Did you hesitate to bother me? Or did you not want me around? If only you had asked for my friendship, it would have been so much harder for me to betray you. But you didn't seem to care for me.*

"Write, 'for my brother' on back of photo," Meho said. I was at the *Château* again, with oboe reeds from Jeremy. He had obtained them for Meho at a good price in Aiguebonne and was sending them through me. I did not mention the cost. He had got them from a friend, I said, without further explanation. After sighing over her administrative tribulations, Gordana disappeared momentarily into the kitchen. I did as Meho asked and gave him the small identity photograph of myself, my blond bangs brushed to one side, my American smile broad. He slipped it into his wallet. A little remembrance to tide him over during my summer vacation time in the United States.

My car, too, he said he would like to have during that time. Could it be arranged? After all, we had two, and both would rest unused.

"But you need a license to drive here," I said.

"I think I can get," he answered. "Not a big problem. I was talking on phone with my cousin in Skopje, you know, in Macedonia. This cousin, he like a brother to me. Someone I need, I need to see." I wondered how he could possibly see his cousin and what the need could be.

"Some day, maybe you agree, get visitor papers for him at town hall?"

"Sure, Meho." I thought that some day was very hypothetical. I tried to imagine myself telling Jacques I was going to vouch for Meho's cousin, so that he could obtain a visa to France. I could worry about that later. Asking for the car would be enough for now. I was in the process of acquiring a new, small car. My own rust-eaten Peugeot would only sit in the driveway, and, if Meho could get his license, as he claimed, Jacques' refusal would have little grounds other than ill will.

"Cousin's daughter coming from Skopje soon," Meho continued. "There is big international meeting of Roma people in Paris, and she will represent young people of our community. She come and visit us here, but it's not allowed we keep guests overnight at *Château*."

"So, you would like us to put her up?"

"If OK with you."

"Sure. That will be fine."

"She coming for national *fête* in France, fourteenth of July, Bastille Day. You come too, with Jacques. We see fireworks from the home, then have lunch the next day."

I accepted. More than anything, I wanted things to be as they were before, our two families friends, our relationship cheerful and relaxed. I wanted the impossible. The knowledge of what I had relinquished weighed heavier each day on my morale. My relations with Jacques were affectionate and strained. My promise to him both relieved and pained me. There are renouncements which tear the soul asunder. I began to experience moments of depression, when everything turned colorless and tasteless. The summer green of my yard, as I observed it from my kitchen table through the French doors, blurred and took on the color of mourning. Tears rose to my eyes, as the hot tea I drank burned my throat.

He would call from the foundry after work, as usual, and I would tell him, no, I will not come, no, I will not meet you. There is nothing in the world I would not give you, except my health and my marriage. He didn't want to understand. He, too, was waiting.

Jasmina arrived from her conference, a short, dark-haired twenty-year-old, with a brilliant smile and only slightly accented English. She was going to be a lawyer, she told me, once she was accepted at Law School. In the meantime, she did volunteer work with Gypsy children in Skopje. "Aren't they just the cutest things you have ever seen?" she said of her little cousins, who hung on her jeans in adoration.

Here was my Rom family in all its splendor, I thought, as I watched them together. This young woman would do something for her people. I could see what a fine family Meho had, indeed. I felt deprived, the outsider now.

Jacques could not refuse the invitation to the *Château*. He didn't want to dispossess me of my Gypsy brother for fear of alienating me. He could not justify his refusal to Gordana, either, for Gordana remained ignorant of the heavy secret we three shared. We would keep up a pretense of good humor at all costs.

The cost was high, indeed, as the unspeakable hung in the air among us. On the evening of the national holiday, the boarders of the *Château* brought out chairs to the scraggy patch of lawn in front and settled down to wait for the town display of fireworks. The hill where the home stood overlooked the rooftops of the town center and the river in the distance. The air was chill and damp, and I shivered.

Gordana ran to get me a pair of white cotton socks, brand new. "A present," she said. "You keep." Her hair was caught up in a short ponytail. She still wore her apron and a shapeless sweater. The children climbed on their father's lap and hung on his shoulders. He spoke to them fondly. I tried to empty my mind of this family harmony, but its warmth chilled me further. Suddenly Gordana said, "Why picture for Meho? Why not one for me?"

"You didn't ask me for one," I replied with a smile, surprised at my own repartee. "We'll bring you another one tomorrow." I sat close to Jacques, as the fireworks exploded in tiny, multicolored bouquets in the distance, wondering how we should ever bear the next day.

The two older children pleaded to come with their big cousin, and so we loaded our Gypsy girls into Jacques' car and drove them to our house. "This is a real house," said Suada, pleased to escape from their close quarters. Still, they huddled together for the night, the three in Jeremy's former double bed.

Jacques coaxed Amina into drinking her bowl of hot chocolate in the morning, playing the kind uncle. His rival's child; how he must hate doing this, I thought. He outdid me in attention to the children. I barely dared show interest in them. I could chat with the young Jasmina, however, show her our village, as I would a foreign student.

Taking the little girls in tow, we all walked around our suburban development. Smart, shuttered houses with well-tended flowerbeds and lawns stood in rows along the winding street. A French village, on the outskirts of a big town, was not to be compared to a Macedonian one, Jasmina remarked. Goodness, the streets were paved, and no chickens ran up and down them! We spoke English together, explaining, pointing: the hosts, the foreign visitor, each leading a child by the hand. Their innocence grated against our knowledge, and shortly our Bastille Day gathering would be our *Dies Irae*.

Jacques had autographed a small picture of himself for Gordana. "Ah, at last! A picture of my brother!" she cried, seemingly satisfied. He and I sat opposite Meho at the long table she set up in the chapel room this time, a white sheet serving as tablecloth.

My hands were clammy, my stomach tense. I couldn't swallow the mountain of dry rice Gordana served me. Jacques pretended to eat and barely looked up from his plate. Unspoken words whispered among us, mocking our masquerade. Meho once again brought down his cassette recorder with the songs of his Gypsy friends and danced with Jasmina, a slow jitterbug. They raised their held hands at arm's distance. He pulled her toward him, then they pushed apart, while Gordana looked on, smoking. I had expected the volts of tension among us to snap into thunder and lightning, but no storm came.

Finally the subject of the car was broached. Meho and Jacques spoke cordially about it. It was an object, after all, a hunk of metal and mechanism, thankfully exterior to our tense and passionate exchange. It was dumb, solid, and neutral. The 205 was in a considerable state of disrepair, Jacques pointed out, but Meho promised to work on it.

> *Jacques, you never knew how great was my hurry to replace that old green Peugeot, did you? I was so afraid it would break down some time when I was in the country with Meho. I could never have explained that to you.*

Meho assured Jacques his driver's license would come in the mail any day now. Jacques remarked that the car was so old, he could never sell it for more than scrap. Meho might as well keep it after our vacation. He would actually give it to him. Meho smiled broadly in gratitude.

"The car will be yours definitively," Jacques said, "once it passes the technical inspection in December. At that time, I'll turn over the *carte grise*, the gray registration card, to you on an official basis, and I'll pay the inspection fee, since I'm not allowed to sell or donate a car that has not passed. But, once it's yours, then you'll have to insure it and pay for the new papers at the *Préfecture*. It could add up to quite a lot." Meho agreed, content. The car was nearly worthless, but still quite a fortune for one who has nothing. A car, in the Balkans, meant one had arrived.

Meho had certainly had his eye on my car ever since I'd announced that I was looking for a new one. "Ellen, you must get BMW," he had said one day, excitedly, as we met behind the foundry.

"Do you think I'm so rich, Meho? I can't afford a BMW!"

"But I see ad in paper for BMW. It say ten thousand francs." That was about seventeen hundred dollars.

"Oh no, Meho," I shook my head. "That must have been the discount they were offering, depending on the car you turned in. Or some commercial lure. It can't possibly have been the price." Meho was rarely naif, but this time his keen interest in cars had made him jump to a wrong conclusion. After all, Western Europe was the fairy tale land of plenty, wasn't it? In his mind, it apparently still was. "I'm going to get just the simplest little Fiat," I said.

"Well, your Peugeot fine for me," he said. "If you lend one day, I treasure it, if only for good times we have in it!" He gazed at the driver's seat that so willingly reclined when he twisted the handle.

Meho had once again got his way. Jacques was telling him now that he could not only borrow the 205 but keep it. The price he mentioned for the registration and insurance, three thousand francs, didn't appear to faze Meho. He nodded to show he understood, and I wondered at his self-confidence. The money would fall from heaven as it had before, no doubt. Moreover Jacques and I told Meho and Gordana they would be welcome to stay at our house on weekends while we were away. They would pay us back by taking care of the lawn, the plants. We would expect them the following Saturday to see about the practical details.

As we left the *Château,* descending the steps as usual, admiring the view, walking close together, I felt a bolt of energy pass from Meho to me. A wave of desire unfurled against me, like a breaker that surprises at the seashore, leaving one dumbstruck and gasping. No, and no again. You have renounced him. The world spun gray and sank before my eyes.

"Well, it went all right," Jacques said, when we were home. "Are you satisfied?" Incapable of answering, I burst into a Niagara of tears, shaking with sobs, as I had never done in my life. Jacques guided me to our bedroom, soothing, bringing me water.

"How lucky you are to be able to cry like that," he said simply. "I so often feel like weeping, but I cannot do it." I knew my tears were one more betrayal, but they would not be stanched.

Jacques could never bring himself to put the snapshots into the album. They showed the Kozić family in our garden on the day Meho and Gordana came to pick up the car. She was holding Veronika in her arms, her expression tense in the sunlight, her cheeks hollowed. Meho was standing straight, the good father, as Amina and Suada leaned on either side of him. Another snapshot showed Jacques and me together against the dark green backdrop of the high hedge. Meho held the camera and caught our forced cheerfulness. Jacques, pale but smiling, was leaning slightly toward me. We were wearing the light-hearted clothes of summer.

"I have no desire for nothing," Gordana confided to me in the kitchen. "I have no appetite, can't eat."

"Gordana, you're depressed. It's only natural. Think of the year you've been through. If I give you some medicine for anxiety, will you take it?" To my relief, she acquiesced. I counted out the shiny pink and white capsules, the five milligram ones, half of what I usually took. There was no milder dosage. "Take two or three a day. It depends on how you feel. And if they do you good, ask a doctor for some. You really ought to see a doctor."

Why were you so depressed now, of all times, Gordana? Was it because you were, indeed, exhausted from a year of anguish? Was it because you were now well on your way to settling in this foreign country which you were unable to adopt? Anticipation and desire could be borne, but the certainty and the finality of acceptance? Or was there something in your husband's attitude that did not satisfy you? Some turning away that you could neither define nor explain?

I brought cool drinks and potato chips, while the children chased a tennis ball in the yard. Without preamble, Meho pulled a shiny, new-looking driver's license from his pocket. It had been issued in Sarajevo. Was it his Skopje cousin who had got it for him or another in Sarajevo? Gypsy networking, I thought, swift and efficient. The ID photograph showed a dark, scowling Meho, his bearded chin thrust forward. It was a Meho I recognized but didn't know. I had never seen him with a cigarette, either, but on this day, he shared Gordana's pack. "I thought you didn't smoke," I said.

"Well, now I do," he replied, gloomily. A cigarette instead of my Ellen, he seemed to mean. Then, on an impulse, he got up and stroked my cheek. Gordana looked on, indulgently. She surely took it for his way of saying good-bye before our vacation. Jacques had gone to get the papers for the car.

He took them from the secretary drawer in the hall: the insurance, the registration card. "Here's a second key," he said to me, turning over in his hand a key I no longer used. The black plastic top was cracked, and it twisted in the ignition. "I might as well give him both."

"No, we'll keep the old one," I said. "You never know. He might lose the other key or something." Meho drove deftly off with his family piled in the back, Gordana clutching Veronika on her lap. The children waved cheerily.

You were at ease now, a real man with his automobile! What premonition made me keep that key, Meho?

Château Lore
Aslan

"You are not a man!" Marie-Toussainte had never spoken so harshly. Aslan hung his head, while her reproach rained on him in a chilly hail of pelting French words. Leila had gone hiccuping and wailing to her, and now she was at their apartment, playing the wicked mother-in-law. Leila had noticed what he felt for Mademoiselle Nathalie. Why should she be jealous? She should know he had never loved her, even though he had finally taken to forcing himself to perform his conjugal duty. Yes, he had responsibilities to Leila; yes, he had made the child, but as a divorced man, he would pay alimony and be done with it.

"I am going to marry Mademoiselle Nathalie if she will have me," he told Marie-Toussainte.

"And I who took you for a saint," Marie-Toussainte sighed, disgusted.

"Well, I am not one. Enough is enough."

"You brought your wife to this country in the face of great danger, and now you must stand by her. She and Marie have no future without you. A man accepts his responsibilities."

Aslan let her rail on, all the while thinking how one day he would no longer depend on half-way houses and Catholic committees, where people felt they had a right to lecture him and teach him morals. What did they know of what he had to endure?

Leila was rocking Marie on her lap in a corner of the living room, humming softly, almost moaning, while Marie-Toussainte sat with him on the stained, overstuffed sofa that came with the flat. He agreed to everything, nodding like a repentant schoolboy called to the headmaster's. Just let them wait till recreation rings, he thought to himself; just let them wait!

Fourteen

I had to make it up to Jacques: my tears, my uncontrollable distress. "We could have a session of *glasnost*, transparency," I suggested that evening as we prepared for bed. "He knows that you know. You know that he knows you know. And still, we are silent. When he comes on Monday to say good-bye, we can have a talk." Of course, Meho had found an excuse for one last visit, a farewell in due form.

Jacques welcomed my idea, and I felt glad. He could see my good will, my resolve. Moreover, if this were aired among us three, it would make us stronger. Breaking the invisible barrier of hypocrisy and play-acting would make it harder to break promises.

I awoke before dawn in a sweat on the Sunday morning before our departure. I kept talking to Meho in my mind. I climbed the stairs to my computer alcove and began to type my thoughts in a letter to him. If I took it to the central post office, it would be sorted even on a Sunday and distributed the following day. I would address it to the foundry. As always, I wrote in the simplest French I could command, adding terms of endearment he had taught me.

> *Dearest* digo *Meho,*
> *When you get this letter I will have left. You'll see, it won't be for very long. You'll come with me in my thoughts.*

I feel very badly, because I hurt you. I hurt myself too.

But I know you can understand. I want and I have to continue in my marriage with my husband of thirty years. He has been very generous, very understanding. It made him suffer terribly to think I had given myself to you. When he sees us together, he feels frightened. He did not play the jealous husband. On the contrary, he has been very good to me, so that I will return to him. Everything he has given you, the car, for example, was actually for me. We are trying to repair our relationship. We talk to each other.

I saw how depressed Gordana was on Saturday, when you came. That is why she is not kind to you. She needs a lot of calm and rest and to see a doctor. Take good care of the children, so she can rest a little.

You are so strong, Meho. You are still young, and you have so much talent. You have succeeded in everything you put your hand to in France. You have four beautiful children. Your little girls need you, and they need two parents who get on well together. You have friends here. Isn't it wonderful? Be brave, moj cigno phral, *my little brother!*

Meho, unsuspecting, arrived at the end of the day with presents in hand. I ushered him into the living room, where he sat on the leather sofa. He had a string of plastic beads for me, another for my mother in America. "For mama," he said. Mamas were important, and mine, as a part of me, had to be honored. Family was family. Meho still apparently imagined that he could slip into mine.

"Let's have a talk, the three of us, all right?" I asked.

"Of course," he said, mildly surprised at my solemn tone.

"And, so, what are we going to say?" I turned to Jacques. I had prepared nothing, and my heart was pounding. I felt oddly empty, weak, unnerved.

"Listen, Meho," Jacques said, his face entirely drained of color. "Do you remember when I asked you to stay away from Ellen? Do you?" Meho nodded.

"And you didn't do it. You didn't respect me. I went to see you at the home, and I was ready to help you and your family. But you continued with Ellen." His voice was strained; the sands of the desert in his throat were audible.

Meho blanched, as the realization of what he was in for came over him. He was in the dock now. Large drops of perspiration formed on his forehead, and he reached into his shirt pocket, drawing out a white, cotton handkerchief. Then he pressed his face into its folds and wept.

I was seized with compassion. I didn't hate Jacques, but I loved Meho. I restrained my one overwhelming desire, which was to take him in my arms and tell him it was all right. When he had regained his self-control, he lifted his dark eyes to Jacques'. "What happened between Ellen and me was not my fault," he said. "It was only nature." I sat as far back in my armchair as I could, willing myself to disappear through the floor.

Jacques wasn't enjoying his position of power. He began to find excuses for Meho. All right, he had been lost in a strange country. He had seized a helping hand and got carried away. He, Jacques, was guilty too, for he had not loved his wife as he should have. He hadn't seen how abandoned she felt. Meho began to relax slightly. He was being forgiven before having to plead. Jacques turned to the question of Meho's marriage. It had to be repaired. Everything must be done to make Gordana feel better.

"She always so nervous. She only think about her child in Macedonia, even ready to leave the three she has here for that one," Meho told us. "To me, she turn her back every night. Yesterday, we had a big fight. I do everything, always, to make that woman happy, but never, never she is happy." Meho sponged his forehead again. "I tell her I pay for her way back to Yugoslavia to go get her daughter. But she just scream and say hateful things to me. I went into the other room, and I cried, and my three little girls came to comfort me. I adopt Latifa, no problem, but Gordana, she say Nadir not her son, not her girls' brother. I always tell the children, 'all together, you are five,' but Gordana refuse that."

Jacques was moved by this narrative in spite of himself. "Do you really want to leave Gordana?" he asked. Meho shook his head. He didn't look at me.

> *Did you or didn't you, Meho? It was comfortable staying with her, wasn't it? But you suggested that I leave my husband for you. A harem was perhaps to your liking.*

The costume jewelry necklaces lay on the coffee table in front of us. "Your little brother is good to you," Jacques said to me, glancing at them. "But what did you buy for Gordana?"

He had bought nothing for Gordana. I found a beautiful, hand-painted barrette for her in my dresser drawer and wrapped it in the paper from my own present. "Take this to her. Tell her it's from you, and that you love her, please!" Meho agreed, reprieved.

"From now on I will be interested only in you," he told Jacques, "not in Ellen." They shook hands like old friends.

I stood before Meho in front of the car, as Jacques went into the garage for an anti-rust chemical. "Why, Ellen, why you not warn me?" he asked.

"I'm sorry, Meho. We just decided at the last minute that we ought to bring it all out into the open. Wasn't it a good idea?"

"Yes, good, very good," he said, nodding his dark head slowly. On the following day, we left the country.

Had I had some inkling of the force of depression that lay in store for me, I would have consulted a doctor before leaving. But I had underestimated the price of my renouncement. Time came to a standstill. The past forced itself on my consciousness, the present nonexistent, the future unthinkable. Vivid images of the moments I had spent locked in passion with Meho imposed themselves on my retina in a continual parade. Over and over I heard his voice as he came, repeating, as if it pained him, his ardent "I love you, Ellen, I love you!" When I slept, the images were gray and barren. I ran down long, cobblestone streets, calling his name. He did not answer, and I would awake, bereft, the sinking, dying feeling washing over and through me.

Jacques would take me in his arms and we would make love for hours, but I could not come. "I have to give you pleasure, Ellen," he would say, anguished. "I want to and I have to."

"The other man . . . I mean . . . it doesn't make you not want me any more?"

"On the contrary." *My price had risen.* "After all, you could have had sexual encounters before our marriage."

"And that wouldn't have changed anything?"

"Of course not, if I loved you."

"I haven't said 'I'm sorry.' I can't just yet. I can't get to feeling that it was wrong, what I did."

"You don't have to. I'm the one who was wrong for years. I'm grateful to him, you know."

We lay together in the early morning humidity of the New York summer, listening to the huge, black crows screech outside the bedroom where I had slept as a child. As the sun rose higher, the cicada would begin their hum, rising in excited crescendo, then falling to a prolonged, vibrant tremolo.

I thought of the plastic beads Meho had given me for my mother and that had remained behind in a drawer. How could he ever have imagined I could give her these from him. From whom, in fact? From a family friend? Certainly not from an admirer.

> *And that cheesy plastic. My mother does not wear a kerchief and hoop earrings as yours must have. I do not say that out of snobbery, but they are from two different worlds, Meho. Don't you see that?*

And how did he think that Jacques could have tolerated this appropriation of his mother-in-law? He had, in fact, never been so overtly affectionate with her. When he hugged her slender, seventy-eight-year-old form, I saw how threatened he felt.

She's still yours, Jacques, be reassured. And this country, where you come each summer to vacation. He won't take them from you, I promise.

My mother came and went in her own world of bridges and teas, oblivious to anything we were feeling, to anything amiss with her daughter or her son-in-law. Had I told her myself, she would not have believed me. "Come now, Ellen, your imagination is getting the better of you!" she would say. Hadn't she brought me up to be a lady? To wear white gloves to church and write thank-you notes? I had moved to another world since those days, more recently, to another planet. We continued to see each other during brief summer visits to her house, where only proper, happy topics were discussed.

Melisand and Julien, winding up their own vacation, were there during the first days of our stay, rushing off to tennis courts and swimming pools and cocktail parties. In between times, Melisand applied herself to soothing her father, now that the floodgates had opened, and she realized he was aware of her own knowledge of the story. She reported their conversations to me faithfully, coming to comfort me in the afternoon, as I lay in sweaty misery on my bed.

"You will win Mom back," she had told him, "if you do not ask her to love you again right away. You have many years to repair, and it isn't because you suddenly feel in love with her all over again that you can expect her to feel the same about you. If you don't give her time to forget Meho, you won't have her back, because she's going to be smothered, and if she needs air too much, she'll leave."

He told her how the letter left undeleted on the computer had shaken him more than any electric shock treatment could have done. Since the Prozac, he had been better, but not better enough. "I thought it might take a death in the family to reawaken our relationship, something drastic, something dramatic. I didn't know what, but this, I never imagined."

"So then, it has been a good thing, a miraculous thing," she had told him. "But if you want to be sure to get her back, admit that she is still in love with Meho, continue loving her as you have, and wait for the scars to heal. After all these difficult years, how do you expect her to believe you're going to be nice to her forever? Keep on being a hero,

Daddy, because I know now that you truly are one! I am so, so proud of you."

At times, I would see him rest his hand gently on the nape of her neck. They hadn't known such complicity since her childhood.

"Let's go into Manhattan today," I would suggest, inventing one activity after another, so that life would seem *as if*, so that things would continue *as if*. No one among our relatives or our American friends must suspect what we were going through, and we ourselves must work on the hypothesis that it was only a difficult passage, a time for smashing worn foundations and rebuilding. Only the vibrations of the breaking continued their devastation, and the new edifice could not be realized overnight.

In every crowd, I instinctively sought out his face. In spite of myself, I was constantly looking for him, and the sight, on our arrival at the airport, of a square-shouldered, dark-bearded man had sent an irrepressible shock through me. In shops the idea of what souvenirs I could buy to please him never left me, and it was myself I was depriving of gifts, when I turned my gaze away from the myriad objects and inward.

"Are you depressed today?" Jacques would ask, and I would have to admit the truth. "Anyway, I can feel it," he would say. "Depressed enough to want to die?"

"Yes, enough to want to die," I would say, and he would tell me that he, too, felt that way. I would clutch his hand, begging comfort, but the suffering flowed back and forth between us.

I swallowed quantities of the mild pink and white capsules I had given Gordana, the only medicine for nerves that I had with me. The respite was brief, and when I was not miserable with depression, I was miserable with guilt for imposing my depression on the wretched, steadfast husband I had at my side, so little known in recent years, so forgotten.

Sometimes bitter memories of the hurtful times we had spent together rose up in me, and I lived them over and over, begrudging him his reclaiming of me, when he had neglected me so much and so often. How dare he demand that I have eyes only for him, when only a few weeks before he had been totally blind to me!

Innumerable postcards of the Statue of Liberty, the New York City skyline, the twin towers and the Empire State building lay on my desk. I wrote them to my friends and acquaintances in France, and Jacques signed them all, even the two for Gordana, Meho and the children.

I knew I was asking him to make still another effort, and yet the longing was too intense in me. I would have written every day, if I could have. I watched the narrow mail slot at the bottom of the oak door, spewing forth each morning its lot of bills and catalogues, but never any message, scrawled in the uncertain French of the Kozić family. What were they doing? How was he feeling? Was Gordana in a better mood? Had they received any news of their future apartment, or were they still captives of the *Château?* These questions and others intermingled with recollections of pain and passion. Jacques, seeing me distraught, fell ill.

He suffered a feverless influenza, his limbs weak, his breathing labored. The asthma attacks came more frequently, and in each I read the suffocation I was inflicting on him. We sought an explanation for this nameless illness, but humiliation and anguish were the plausible ones. The interminable days of our three-week absence were coming to their conclusion, and in this aching, feeble state we faced the long return trip.

Jacques, exhausted from the hours spent in waiting and on the plane, was sleeping soundly when the doorbell gave out a quick bark. I bounded from my bed, dressed in my flimsy summer nightgown, opening the door ever so slightly to see who might be at our house at nine in the morning. Meho's skin was darker than ever from the sun, his slightly jagged grin flashing. He was thinner and more muscular than when we had left, radiant with health.

"What are you doing here?" I asked, aghast. "If Jacques wakes up and sees you, he'll be beside himself. Go away!"

"I left extra tire in your garage. Want to get it," he said, unperturbed by my hostile greeting.

"All right, I'll open the garage for you. Then you'll have to go."

He held out his arms to me, as I stood petrified in the dim light of the garage, the near-transparent material of the nightgown barely covering me. His gesture spoke for him: At last you have come home to me, and I have been here waiting for you. Come to me! I know you want to.

"Nooo!" I hissed. "You've got to go away. Go away!" I nearly pushed him out. Half a minute after I had re-entered the house, Jacques came out of the bedroom, smiling.

"Up already?" he asked.

"Yes, I've slept enough," I replied. "I was just going to get breakfast."

I sat with my legs crossed, jerking one foot nervously, behind the psychiatrist's wide desk. The doctor was a slight young woman, hazel eyes snapping intelligence behind her slanted glasses. "You are someone with a strong superego," she said. "You have to be in control all the time. You don't like to be carried along by events, as some people do."

"I guess that's true. The unknown and the unexpected upset me."

"That letter you forgot on the screen; don't you think it was an unconscious cry for help?"

"Heavens, no! I would give anything not to have left it."

"Well, at any rate, try to see the good side of this affair of yours. Look at what it has brought you in terms of personal fulfillment and in terms of your marriage!"

"All I know right now is that I can't cope. I've made my choice, but I feel miserable, and I'm making my husband miserable."

The little, white, anti-depressant pills, twice daily, stopped the parade of pictures short. They stopped also the long, gray dreams, the fruitless calling. But the beseeching desire and the desolation, those they could not stop. Jacques knew of my treatment, but I did my best to make him forget it, the rectangular package out of sight in the medicine cabinet.

"You asked me to be patient," he said, "but I may tire of being patient." I was seized with fear when he said this, fright stricken, too, each time I caught a glimpse of suffering and questioning in his eyes: When will you be over him, when will you be entirely mine again? If his reason let him accept my transition, his heart would not. How could he possibly imagine that three or four weeks could douse the burning that had consumed me for months and smoldered still?

Jacques returned to his office, his vacation time used up, while I remained at home until school should start again. My own aging Peugeot brought me Meho in the afternoon. He had repainted, repaired, and refurbished it. It hadn't looked so presentable in years. He no longer needed to call, to ask me to get him at the bus stop. His rival had granted him the means to court his wife and trusted him not to, but Meho wasn't one to torture his mind with scruples.

He subjected me to a barrage of attentions, while I fought against myself and him. Sitting next to me on the shiny coolness of the leather sofa, he would run his hands along my bare calves. "Stop!" I would command, but Meho, smiling, would slide them up to my thighs. "Just to here, please, Ellen?" he would grin.

"Meho, can't you understand? I can't have two husbands."

"But I am not your husband!"

I told him how ill I was, how much medicine I needed, but he would simply shake his head and tell me to let *him* be my doctor. The niceties of my inner conflicts escaped Meho. Moreover, it was clear that if one of us had gone mad during our separation, it was not he.

"I felt good," he said, "because I came here weekends to your house. I was living among your things. I looked at your books. Even waste basket in your room! I was with you. I read parts of books you marked for Jacques. I understand them. He, he didn't understand." Meho was referring to a chapter by Karlfried Graf Dürckheim, on the subject of lovemaking. Indeed, Jacques had understood nothing of the passage I had marked for him. Graf Dürckheim tells how important it is for a woman to know that her husband can see her inner being, and that he finds it beautiful. A man must tell his wife that she is beautiful to him, if he wants her to desire him. In those underlined sentences was yet one more call for help which Jacques had ignored. Meho, however, knew such things instinctively.

"And Gordana, was she well during the three weeks too?"

"Better. A little nicer to me."

"So she's happier with you now?"

"Yes . . . it's better that way, no?"

"Of course."

"Helena, I love you more than Gordana."

So you did love her then, at least a little.

"Did she let you make love to her?"

He nodded, smiling. "What would you say if Gordana and me made a baby?"

"A baby, Meho? You know she doesn't want one. Don't do that to her!"

"Why not?"

"She's exhausted, and she doesn't want one is why not. Just look at her! She even lost her tooth when Veronika was born."

"She can get another tooth."

"Meho, you won't do it?"

"I want you to choose the baby's name," he said.

That evening, Meho returned with Gordana, the children, and a pile of papers for the housing office, where they would put in their request. An apartment was soon going to be available, and they might be able to benefit from it.

Gordana was transfigured. Meho had cut her hair, and the heavy black waves were piled above her forehead in a youthful, rakish style. She was made up and wore a purple hue of velvety lipstick, a miniskirt, and, around her neck, Meho's heavy, gold chain with the "M" pendant visible.

> *My birthday present, Meho. But you are right. It is better for her to have it.*

I presented her and Meho each with a tiny souvenir, a miniature bottle of liqueur from the airplane for Meho, a Statue of Liberty pin for Gordana. Meho thanked us warmly, but Gordana barely glanced at her pin and tossed it carelessly into her bag, without a word.

> *You didn't care for gifts from me, Gordana, did you? You had entered a new phase of your life. You were elsewhere, now, as if your vital forces were concentrating inward, and the outside world didn't count. At last, you had your husband's full attention. Or at least, you had had it, when Ellen was away. That was undoubtedly better for you than the medicine she'd given you to take. Ellen had no place in your world.*

Jacques took his fountain pen and filled in the forms for Meho and Gordana, the dates of their marriage, of the children's births. It was she who spoke them each time, with certainty and a measure of pride.

The apartment was granted at last, a sunny four-room flat with a kitchen and a balcony, from which one could look over the roofs of the town toward the *Château* in the distance, on the hill, beyond the river. The former refugees could look with triumph at their old home of transition. Suada and Amina were each to have a room, while

Veronika would sleep in her mother's arms, as she was accustomed. Meho and Gordana spread a wide mattress on the floor of their room, and a paper Chinese lantern covered the light bulb. Throw rugs of vivid colors were tossed about the rooms, and pictures of flowers and landscapes brightened the walls, even before furnishings were brought in from the second-hand store. Gordana's gaze rested on these small details of luxury, more important to her well-being than chairs and shelves. For the poor, the superfluous is more urgent than the necessary.

"Is the apartment nice? Do you like it?" I had asked Meho, before seeing it. They were busy moving. From morning until late at night, Gordana scrubbed and tidied their belongings, making packages that would be transferred from the *Château* to the flat in and on top of my old, green car.

He shrugged. "It's all right. Not very nice, really."

I hadn't often heard Meho ungrateful, yet his tone surprised me. "Would you have had something so nice in Sarajevo?" I asked.

"Oh, no, not in Sarajevo. Impossible."

On the first day of school, they entered their new housing. After my own classes, I stopped by to see them. The apartment block was five minutes from my *collège*. I climbed to the last floor and knocked, but no one was at home. Suddenly Meho came up the steps, astonished to see me on the landing.

"You, here, Ellen? I didn't expect to see you!" He took my hand and motioned to me to sit down beside him on the step. "I don't have the key. Gordana has the key. She went to the school to get the children. We wait." He kissed me quickly on the lips, like a child stealing a treat. What electricity did he generate, that I felt so irresistibly magnetized by him? It burned through me with a force I could never have predicted. Gordana's voice was audible in the stairwell. We drew apart.

She served me fruit juice, sweets, peanuts, while the children buzzed around the snacks on the makeshift table like bees around a jar of honey. They smeared their sweet, brown faces with streaks of chocolate. *"Pivo, Tato?"* Suada asked her father. "Would you like a beer, Daddy?" A miniature Gordana, she was her father's servant, opening the refrigerator, which, for the time being, stood in the middle of the living room.

"We see you for birthday dinner Saturday at our house," Gordana said, as I left. Our joint birthday celebration was to take place after all, in the triumph of their acceptance, in the joy of their newfound home, in the agony of our unspoken longings.

"How old is my daddy?" Suada asked me, as, together, accomplices in the kitchen, we put candles on the chocolate birthday cake I had made. "Forty-one," I told her, but she didn't react.

"And you?" she added.

"Thirty-nine." I lied easily to the child.

"You are younger than me," Meho had said. What difference did numbers on a birth certificate make? The celebration I had so dreamed of and willed when the Kozićs were in the throes of their requests, refusals and appeals was now taking place, but how bitter now was the taste! Jacques, at my side, was stiff with restrained tension, while Meho overplayed the host. He drank too much and plied Jacques with whiskey.

"Here's to your young years!" Jacques toasted him, as Meho opened the oboe concerto I had ordered for him especially from the music store. From his pocket he pulled a lumpy object wrapped in newspaper for me: an ornamental trinket from the secondhand shop. It was a pink and white china statuette, a peasant boy and girl carrying a bucket together, an amorous Jack with his Jill. Gordana bent her knees as if curtsying and handed me a bouquet of orange marigolds. She had made no effort for her appearance this time, and her black hair was brushed back without style. Her sweater had grease spots on it and clung to her plump middle, plumper than before, it seemed to me.

When Meho ate, he casually brushed crumbs off the table onto the floor. Jacques and I looked at him in shocked disapproval. "Look at what you've done! Now the floor will have to be cleaned," I cried out.

"No problem," he said putting his arm around Gordana's thick waist. "I have my own vacuum cleaner."

You didn't respect her, Meho, did you? Or was it cultural, this subjecting of the wife to menial tasks? Some of your relatives, you said, were married to non-Muslim women, and they had changed. But you were at ease in your role of man-of-the-house. Weren't those crumbs on the floor an atavism from the time when your forebears traveled the world in horse-drawn wagons? So easy to sweep outside? But Gordana did not live in any Gypsy wagon.

Meho brought his heavy red and gold accordion into the room. The theater company must have made it fully his, now that he had his papers and was settled to stay. He serenaded us: variations on "Happy Birthday", then a cascade of Yugoslavian and American folk songs. Amina took out the little half-size violin I had lent her and scraped the bow across it. She was playing at being Madame Ellen.

A year had gone by now since I had first seen Gordana in the doorway of the parish schoolroom, twelve full months of anxiety and battling and unforeseen relief at their miraculous acceptance. With my Rom family I had traveled the roads of despair, of hope and, unexpectedly, of passion. When one asylum finally presented itself, another withdrew. They had reached their port of good hope, but now that they were there, the scars of the struggle remained, unhealed. A year was nothing; a year was a lifetime. A year was the lapse of time necessary to gain a new country, a promise of life and of a future for their children. It was also the time to lose themselves in a sea of fear, of foreignness, of homesickness. Ellen had been Meho's buoy. Gordana had had none.

Meho sat across from me at a table in the cafeteria of a shopping gallery on the outskirts of town, where I had agreed to meet him. He fingered the silver ID bracelet with "E. B." on the small plaque. He had scratched his own name next to it with the point of a sharp tool.

Did you forget you were going to give it to me? I wasn't supposed to want it, but I did.

I begged him not to come to the house, for I couldn't trust myself. The large cafeteria was nearly empty in the middle of the afternoon. We bought our coffee at the counter and carried the small espresso cups to a table in a corner, far from the wide door, which opened onto the gallery. "She is pregnant," he said abruptly.

"Little brother, what have you done?"

When you had an idea, nothing stopped you, did it? Let others pay!

"It is the child I could not have with you."

I put my head in my hands and cried. He waited for the flood of emotion to pass. "She doesn't want it," he said. "She wants to . . ." — he made the gesture of sweeping from his middle down toward the floor— ". . . clean out the house."

"No! She won't do that?"

He shrugged. "She says, if doctor say it's a boy, she'll keep it, if another girl, then *abortus*."

"No, Meho, please don't let her! What difference does it make if it's a boy or a girl? *A little Gypsy child, his, mine*. Besides, the doctor won't know the baby's sex before three months are up, and, in France, she's got to decide if she wants to have an abortion before the three months. Promise me you'll talk to her! Meho, I could be the godmother!"

"I told her, you do what you want. But I'll talk to her." He seemed surprised at the vivacity of my reaction. "It is my passion for you that inspired me this child."

"Love me less, Meho, and try to love your wife a little more!"

"My heart is very big," he said. "In it is room for Helena and also room for Gordana."

Meho, why did you do it? You didn't withdraw, as you knew so well how to do. Each child you had with Gordana bound you more strongly to her. Was it true, as you told me, that you didn't love her very much? Was your desire for another son so great? Or did you just want a good way to tie her to the house and to her chores? Were you really thinking of me when you gave her that baby?

Château Lore
Smaïl

Smaïl was luckier than most, in the labyrinthine world of the bureaucracy at least, for he was accepted at the first Appeal. When Marie-Toussainte heard the news, she pressed him to her buxom breast and waltzed around the dining hall with him. Even Monsieur Lenoir, who was not really a bad sort, had gone teary eyed.

"I have a job where there are not many satisfactions, you know, Smaïl," he said, as if to excuse himself. "Good news doesn't come very often."

Good news was more likely to fall into the hands of a healthy eighteen-year-old orphan than into those of a forty-year-old African widow with five children or a Gypsy musician with four mouths to feed; this, he knew, and he did not gloat, but his satisfaction was profound. The stiff prose of the letter granted him ten years' refugee status and invited him to present himself at the *Préfecture* of his region, to put in a request for his new identity papers.

Monsieur Lenoir explained about applying for citizenship later, but Smaïl was undecided about that yet. Wait and see how things evolve in Bosnia. For the moment, there was nothing to go back to there, and much to do here. His parents would approve of auto bodywork; it was a solid, respectable, useful trade.

France-Sanctuaire was sending him to Lyons, where he would take an intensive language course. Before going, he'd throw a little party for the people he liked at the *Château,* his French tutor and Marie-Toussainte, and the guys from the soccer team. Maybe that Rom from Sarajevo would provide the music, since he had an accordion now. He was affable enough, and his family somehow looked familiar.

Fifteen

The orchestra began preparing for its fall season, after the summer break. Evenings were cool now, and the sun set early. Driving to rehearsal in my new Fiat, I turned the corner on the boulevard leading into town and caught sight of Meho, signaling to me from a bus stop. He'd parked my old 205 in a parking lot and had been watching for me. He sprang into my new, silver-gray car, so we could finish the drive into town together. I was pleased and annoyed at the same time.

"Why you not kiss me to say hello?" he asked, a bit peevishly.

"Did you kiss me?" I countered. Then, remorseful, "I'm sorry, Meho. I'm just a little bothered, because we're bound to arrive at the same time at the rehearsal room, and everyone will see we've come together. We'll have to space it out."

"OK," he agreed.

Yvonne was at the stand to my left. "Your Croatian oboist is a conceited twerp," she whispered, leaning toward me. It was true, he had been interrupting constantly, giving the conductor directions, holding up the orchestra, as we waited for him to express his criticism in halting French. Gérard hadn't respected the dynamics; the tempo wasn't suitable. I had never seen him like this.

"Yvonne, I think he's annoyed, because Gérard has given him the second oboe part."

"Well, that's all he deserves to have. Who does he take himself for? He never could have played in the Sarajevo National Symphony. You heard what he did to the dotted fourths in the third measure? He's a fraud, as far as I can see."

"Be fair! He hasn't played in six or seven years. There was a war over there, for God's sake."

She shrugged. *"Solfège* is *solfège.* It's not something you forget. Ever since he got his papers, I've noticed he thinks anything goes for him." Her words stung, but his attitude hurt me more. I didn't know this insolent, obstinate, and vengeful Meho.

"What have you got against Gérard?" I asked, driving him back.

"He doesn't trust me. Why did he give me second oboe part?"

"He wasn't sure you'd be back, that's why. He asked someone else to do it, and he couldn't change afterward. Stop interrupting him all the time! It's rude, and it gives a bad impression of you. He may be an amateur, but he's the conductor, you know."

"OK, my Ellen. Whatever you say. You know best." The warmth of his confidence erased the unease I felt.

After this first evening drive, Meho asked me to stop a short distance from his apartment block. "Please, Ellen, just feel what you do to me," he said, pressing my hand against his lower abdomen. I could feel the hardness of him, shoving up against the inside of his pants. "Ellen, please . . ." he began, but I held back, biting my lips, trying not to feel the heat rising in me too.

"I've got to go."

Jacques glanced at me anxiously, as I entered the house. He had surely kept his misgivings to himself when I had left, but now they surfaced, irrepressible. "Ellen, are you sure there is . . . there is no one between us?"

I sat on his lap, needing to be forgiven, needing him to protect me from myself. "No Jacques. I've already told you. There's no one."

When I entered the teachers' room the following day, I checked my pigeonhole as usual, for mail or other papers. On a wide, white envelope was scrawled *"Za Helena",* for Ellen.

My little Helena,

I am very, very sorry. You know I do not want to hurt you or my brother Jacques, but why do you hide and run from me always? You tell me you are worried about your job, beginning of school year very hard, but I know you are good at this, your profession. Besides, you are young, only 36 years! Please do not get sick like Jacques! Do not deny yourself what you need! Do not hurt yourself by refusing! I believe in you, and I know you believe in me. I want to be your foundry; we could melt into each other.

I know we are different, because I am Rom and you, you are American, but, I don't know, I think you are a Gypsy too. It is as if you are hiding another person inside you. Be brave and strong, my Helena, I love you, my darling, my heart, my life. My heart beats so hard in my chest, I think it will break. Volim te. Je t'aime.

Meho had found his way back to the staff room I had shown him in the spring. He had put the note in my box and then slipped out. Now I sat there reading it with tears streaming freely down my face. By luck, I was the only teacher in the room. I went to the drink machine, put in two francs and pushed the tea button. I had to get control of myself. My students would be waiting.

I decided to prepare an answer and slip it to him at our next rehearsal. I chose a photograph of myself taken during our American trip. I looked young and happy, dark glasses protecting my eyes from the hot July sun.

Malen'kii Brat, *Little Brother,* I began in Russian,

I found your letter at the school, and it upset me. I was very touched. But, don't you see, I am much too fond of Gordana and of Jacques to be anything more than a sister to you now. I do not want to hurt you, but I cannot hurt them either. Here is a picture of your sister during her vacation in America. This way, you can see me as I was in New York. Love from Ellen

Another note from Meho found its way into my mailbox at school. "Your eyes are hidden behind your sunglasses," he wrote, "but I know you are looking at me. Why don't you contact with me, my darling Helena?"

He came to the house once again in the afternoon, as I napped upstairs, worn out from too much emotional strain. "A visitor for you, Madame Aubert," said Ginette, the neighbor who came to do my ironing. She showed him into the living room and discreetly closed the door leading to the kitchen.

"What are you doing here?" I asked, still groggy with sleep. I didn't want to see him.

"What does she know?" he asked contemptuously, nodding his head in Ginette's direction.

"Nothing," I said, "and she is to know nothing." He didn't seem to find it serious if the entire neighborhood knew that Madame Aubert was entertaining her lover.

Meho was beside me on the sofa. "You find my answer to your letter in schoolbox?"

"Yes, I did."

"I stay up till midnight writing to you."

"So Gordana must have seen my letter to you?"

"Yes, she see."

"You showed it to her?"

"No, she pulled picture and letter out of my pocket after orchestra. Don't worry, she don't understand enough French to read it!" She had asked him why he was writing to me. "Because she is my sister, and I love my sister," he had answered her. "You can write to her too. After all, she's your teacher, isn't she?" Gordana had scoffed at this correspondence, but Meho was proud of his defiant reply: "Anyway, one day I will go to America with her!"

Gordana, he said, had huffed off, slamming the bedroom door. "Then go! What are you waiting for?" she had barked at him.

You had begun to understand, then, Gordana, hadn't you?

"Helena, you say no to me, and when you say that, you make me dead," he said. I shook my head, sorry, at a loss.

"Don't worry, I don't want to hurt you. I will leave you alone." He took my hand. "But it is you I need, a gentle, sentimental woman like you. Why couldn't I have found you earlier? Without you I have no life, Helena."

I smelled the leathery, animal scent of his jacket, the warm workday odor of his perspiration. Desire gripped me, while my reason fought on. Nervous exhaustion was taking its toll. I put my head down on his knees and sobbed, long, noisy, drenching sobs. He had wiped away my tears before, but never had he seen me give way to despair.

"You are not well, my Ellen," he said, surprised at such a violent show of emotion. "It proves that you are not happy with your husband."

"No, Meho, it's not that, not that at all. But can't you just stop coming to me? Can't you understand what you're putting me through?" It was obvious he could not.

I still gave an occasional French lesson to Gordana at her apartment. I could barely look Marie-Toussainte in the face any more, and Gordana was too angry with her to go anywhere near the Catholic Aid Committee. She now took Marie-Toussainte for a meddling, maligning creature, spreading rumors of thievery and prison.

"When you come on Monday morning," she said on the telephone, "I want to speak to you about something." I had no peace that weekend. What had she guessed? What could this something be? Perhaps she had read more of my note than Meho thought. She wasn't stupid; she would have put two and two together.

I kissed her on each cheek, twice, half expecting the skies to open and spew forth brimstone, yet vulnerable, unprepared. I placed my books on her living room table, but she pushed them aside. "I need to talk to you, Ellen," she said.

"Yes, Gordana?" My blouse jumped where the heartbeats made the material quiver.

"When you leave after birthday party, I get so sick, dizzy, you know, then throw up."

"Ah? I think I understand," I said, light-headed with the relief of one who has just received a stay of execution. She touched her stomach, already as round as an egg up to her chest. "Meho, he don't care how many babies I have." She spoke bitterly. "The more children, the better. But I don't want this one. Maybe, if it's a boy, I keep, but only boy. I feel sick, so sick."

I stroked her arm. "You'll be better soon. It's the first three months that are hard."

Feigning feminine solidarity. Weren't you ashamed, Ellen?

"Did Meho tell you about my daughter in Macedonia?" she asked.

"Yes," I admitted.

"I never tell them at *Préfecture*. They ask, how many children you have; you sure? And I say, yes, only three, no others. Now it's too late." She shook her head, close to tears.

"I don't think so, Gordana. Do you have legal custody of her? After the divorce, I mean? Who is responsible for the child?"

"Me," she said. "My mother has paper of divorce judgment."

"Then, surely, you can do something. Meho should go ask them. Won't he do that?"

"Yes, he's very nice about it." I hadn't often heard her say her husband was nice. "But not now. Not good time to ask for more family to come. Foundry closing, you know? Maybe no more job for Meho."

I nodded. "Have you had the pregnancy test? Have you seen a doctor?"

"No, no test."

"Then I'll drive you to the laboratory. Before you see the doctor, you'll have to have a test. I can take you to my doctor, if you want."

"Thank you, Ellen." Gordana followed me obediently, and I paid for her blood test. Like a child, she let me lead her. She walked quickly behind me, her head down. Her face was livid beneath its sallow tinge, her translucent, sea-green eyes dimmed to two brackish pools.

The results came in the mail two days later, positive. Gordana agreed to make an appointment with my gynecologist, a kind doctor I had known for many years.

> *Dear Dr. Duplessis,*
>
> *I take the liberty of sending you a note concerning the patient you will be receiving this Friday, October 10th, at 5 p.m., and whom I will accompany.*
>
> *She is a young Bosnian woman, a war refugee I am helping.*
>
> *This woman, mother of four daughters, one of whom remains in Yugoslavia, is pregnant with her fifth child. Because of her fatigue, the difficulties she has been through, and an anxiety state due to her long wait for the regularization of her status in France, she is not sure to want this child.*
>
> *She says she will not terminate her pregnancy if the child is a boy. This woman is in particular need of physical and psychological support. Certain of your understanding, I thank you in advance for your attention to her case.*

The foundry where Meho had been hired through the compassion of the director had been having financial difficulties for some time. In recent weeks, it had begun to turn a profit, but it was too late. The personnel knew they would be laid off sooner or later. They demonstrated in front of the building, but Meho avoided participating. He didn't appear to understand the seriousness of the menace. Cédric gave him the address of another employer.

"He's got to call for an interview," Cédric told me on the phone.

"He doesn't seem to understand it's urgent. He seems to think his job will go on forever," I said.

"Well, it won't. The last to get hired are the first to go. Anyway, he only has a three-month contract. It won't be renewed, that's all."

When his contract expired, Meho had to face reality. He hadn't taken the precaution of seeing the other employer. When at last he did, he discovered that jobs were not to be had simply for the asking in France, even the most menial of factory jobs. Not everyone got teary, either, at the sight of a Bosnian war refugee with four mouths to feed.

Cédric called again. "I've been in touch with the employer. Meho went to see him, but he can't use him."

"Why not?"

"He couldn't read the technical instructions for the operations he would be required to carry out. He's got to work on his French. He understands things backwards!"

I didn't dare say I would help him work on his French, although I knew that was what Cédric was expecting.

"At any rate, tell him he's got to get off his bum and get with it. He'll never get anywhere here if he doesn't learn the language right. It's the key to everything. It's going to be a downward spiral from now on, and they'll start losing everything they've gained. In the meantime, he might as well apply to moving companies. He ought to be able to carry furniture. You don't have to talk to tables and cabinets."

Gordana opened the door to me on the day of her appointment. "Are you alone?" I asked, surprised. I knew Meho had free time on his hands now, and I assumed he would want to see me, but the apartment was silent.

"No, I am not. Meho is at home," she answered in perfect French. Her language was improving faster than his, thanks to the many hours she spent in front of the television. I felt hurt. He was at home but hiding, then.

Suddenly, he appeared, yawning. "Hello, Ellen," he said. "Forgive me. I fell asleep." His morale had clearly plummeted since he had lost his job, and since his American mistress would no longer sleep with him. His hair was greasy, his face pale and slightly puffy.

Gordana snapped at him. I couldn't understand her words, but her tone was that of the shrew untamed.

"*Dobro, dobro,*" all right, he said, conciliatory, "whatever you prefer." Her words struck him like sharp-edged stones. His shoulders were slightly stooped in his black jacket, and he did not seek out my gaze.

"Meho will want to come with us, perhaps?" I asked.

"No, he's got to baby-sit for Veronika."

"She can come," he put in. "Vera, don't you want to go see the doctor with Mama?" The child held out her little feet to have her shoe laces tied. Meho tousled her black curls and hoisted her onto his shoulders. "Mama go see doctor. Mama don't feel good," she said sweetly.

"Madame Ellen has been my teacher," Gordana told the doctor. He smiled approval; he had not known anything of my humanitarian concerns.

"And so, do you already have any children, Madame Kozić?" he asked, beginning his medical inquiry.

"Yes, three daughters!" Gordana replied quickly. When he disappeared for a moment into his examination room, I whispered to her, "Why did you say three? What about your child in Macedonia?" Her eyes filled, and she shook her head furiously. "No, I won't mention her!"

"But it's just for medical reasons."

"No!"

Her tone admitted no argument. The subject of Latifa was a delicate one. What difference, anyway, so far as this birth was concerned? Latifa or no, the new child would come. Gordana told the doctor she didn't want this child.

"And your husband, Madame Kozić? What does he say?"

"My husband, he wants, but not me."

"Did you use any contraception?"

"Never contraception . . . at least, not yet." Her voice grated on the last words.

"The problem is, you will have to make up your mind before we know whether it's a boy or a girl. We can't know that in the first three months," he explained gently. "And if you do decide on an abortion, then you will have to return to see me, or, if you prefer, you can go directly to the center at the hospital, but you'll have to speak to a counselor there." He invited her into the examination room. I heard him say, "You must remove your underwear for the examination, Madame," then her voice, uttering a little, frightened cry. She came out with a shiny, black and transparent sonogram of the minuscule embryo in her hand.

Gordana's blood pressure was very low. When we told Meho this, he patted her head, but she cringed. It was all his fault, she seemed to be saying, and she would have none of his comforting. Meho studied the tiny picture of his child, round and curved like a kidney bean, as I drove them to a pharmacy. Gordana needed medicine to relieve her vomiting and her violent headaches. Still, she seemed heartened by the medical attention.

"I'm not afraid give birth to baby," she said suddenly. A little shock of hope stirred in me.

Please, Gordana, it is my child you are carrying. It is my indelible, living tie to him, his flesh and my spirit.

"Listen, Gordana, I know how tired you are. Don't you want to come and spend some time at the house with us? Jacques and I will take care of you and spoil you, and you can just rest." I had spent some time working out this offer in my mind, e-mailing Melisand and discussing it with her.

"What about the children?" she asked, surprised.

"Meho is at home now. He could take care of them, couldn't he?"

Meho said he would. "If I were you, Gordana, I would accept what Ellen offers." He looked toward her in the back seat. We had come to a stop now in front of their apartment block.

"Thank you very much, Ellen," she said, "but I prefer to stay with my children. And now, I say good-bye to you . . . to the . . . what is the word? . . . the godmother?"

Jacques did not like hearing about Meho and Gordana's child. At first, he had taken it for a sign of healing in their marriage. Then, he began to suspect otherwise. "Ellen, there are some things I don't understand," he said, in the tight-voiced tone I had so come to dread. "You worry about her keeping that child as if it were yours. I know I have a place in your heart. All right, but what bothers me is that I feel I'm not the only one there." For once, he looked me directly in the eye. For so many years, Jacques had looked away when he spoke to me. I hadn't realized it was because he was somehow ashamed of himself. I had wrongly assumed it was I he couldn't bear to look at. I met his gaze, painfully. He had struck a sore point all right. I was at a loss.

"And tell me, how is it you have so much libido? You never used to. What did he awaken in you? Just exactly who are you making love with, when you make love with me?" His voice grew accusatory, almost angry. "And if you're over him, as you say, why do you still need those anti-depressants?"

"You should know it yourself, Jacques. Depression doesn't go away overnight."

I realized that referring to his depression, which had little in common with mine, was not exactly fair play. But I had no defense other than his fundamental gentleness and vulnerability. He did not continue his litany, and I knew I was getting off easy. When Jacques spoke to me like that, I would suffer long, white hours of insomnia, and only the chemical magic of pills could restore my sleep to me.

This dependency too, he watched. If I arose in the night to swallow medicine, it didn't escape him. During the darkest moments of his own depression, he had slept like the dead. Now he was attuned to my every movement.

His intuition pierced my soul, when before I had been an opaque curtain to him. Had he become a mind reader? I felt spied upon, my innermost thoughts violated, denuded. I could struggle against Meho, struggle against myself, but I could not win the fight against my own mind. Jacques must be patient longer, and I must accept that I was the cause of his suffering. I could not carry the whole world.

Each time Meho called, I felt the same mixture of anguish and pleasure. "There is something here for you, Ellen. Can you come by on Monday after school?" I said I would. His tone was warm and enticing. What excuse had he cooked up now to see me? Meho liked mystery.

It would be Gordana's birthday in two days. I had a pair of silver earrings for her. One small disk hugged the earlobe, while another, pendent, bore a tiny French inscription: *Je t'aime*. I had found them on sale, a giveaway.

"Oh, Superrr!" she cried, rolling and snapping the "r", as she always did. She did not say thank you, but there was a small note of triumph in the sound of her "superrr". She got up to try them on in front of the mirror. On the television set, Jacques' and my identity photographs stood in miniature frames. On the wall, stuck in the corner of a still life, was my summer photograph with my sunglasses.

Meho got up without a word, his expression closed, almost grim, and took a second snapshot from the frame. Still silent, he handed it to me. Did I imagine he glanced briefly at Gordana? It showed a stocky, adolescent boy with medium-long, black hair. The boy resembled him astonishingly. I understood who it was but decided I had better play innocent. I looked from the photo to Meho and back.

"Is that you, Meho, at twenty?" I asked.

"No, not Meho!" Gordana put in, in a disgusted tone. I chose to look perplexed and say nothing. I was not supposed to have heard of Nadir.

"Who is it?" Meho asked little Veronika.

"It's Daddy's boy," she chirped.

Meho disappeared momentarily and returned with a bag of clothes from the second-hand stand at the marketplace. From his bag, he pulled a number of garments in varying states of disrepair.

"For you," he said, pleased with himself, showing me a plaid blouse with a worn collar. Then he pulled out a bright red skirt, three-quarter length and flared. "I'd like to see you in this," he said. Gordana shook her head in disgust again, glancing at my dark, tailored suit. He had chosen a turquoise-colored apron, too, appropriate for a *hausfrau* at her chores, and a wide, shapeless, polyester smock in fuzzy, gray material.

"Looks like something for a pregnant woman," said Gordana, holding out her hands in front of her stomach. Then came a pair of violet, suede boots. "These for Gordana," he said, "but she don't want." They were high-fitting and impractical. Suada, watching, laughed to think what was coming next. Meho had chosen for me a pair of black, patent leather pumps with extremely high, pencil-thin heels. I nearly fell over, trying to fit my long feet into the narrow shoes. "I'm sorry, Meho, they're just not my size." He took his disappointment in stride.

"What will Jacques say?" asked Suada, more insightful than she realized.

"Oh, he'll just think you're all nutty," I laughed. I knew he would think nothing, because he wouldn't hear about these streetwalker's shoes, nor this flashy, red Gypsy skirt. I accepted the plaid, cotton blouse, unwilling to hurt Meho. Gordana sulked before this display of apparel.

"And what will you have for your birthday, Gordana?" I asked, trying to change the subject.

"I don't want anything for my birthday, not from Kozić, I don't!" She spoke vehemently. I was embarrassed, clutching the plastic bag with the worn blouse in it. Suada was listening but seemed unaware of anything unusual in her mother's tone of voice.

"Oh, come on, surely you like presents?"

"No, I don't want any presents. Besides, my husband forgets my birthday every year. Why should he think of it now?"

I left as quickly as possible. Meho followed me downstairs, catching at the lobe of my ear. "Meho, you're crazy. Why all this stuff for me? What will Gordana think?"

"Think what she want."

Why was he doing this? Was it intentional or not? What covert signals was he sending Gordana? He was too clever not to realize the impact of his acts. Did he want to force Gordana into a fit of jealousy? Did he want to hear from her that she really loved him and wanted to keep him? Or, on the contrary, was it a sort of revenge for her indifference to his lovemaking? He couldn't be thinking of abandoning her, could he? He had made the baby, after all.

"Will she keep the baby?" I asked.

"Hasn't decided yet."

"Be good to her, Meho! Help her with the children! And get her a present for her birthday!"

"She has lots of presents. New apartment, appliances, furniture, everything."

"It's not the same! Get her a bouquet, anything, just for her! She's expecting your child, and here you are, spoiling me!"

"I never get her birthday present before, so why now?"

"Because now is very important."

I met Meho after our rehearsal the following Wednesday. I had asked him not to wait for me any longer at the bus stop, but still we usually walked out together, once the playing was over. That, after all, would evoke less suspicion than coming in together, I thought.

"I must tell you something, Ellen," he said, solemnly.

"What, Meho?" I asked, alarmed.

"Gordana very sad tonight."

"Why?"

"She understand all of a sudden that I am in love with you."

"How?"

He shrugged. "She says she's decided to go back to Yugoslavia and live with Latifa. I told her, OK, go ahead. You'll gain one daughter, but you'll lose three others and a husband. Then I told her she's got to iron my shirt for tonight, but she wouldn't do it."

"And so?"

"I insist, and she finally do it. But she very angry with me all the time. She leave mess from children all over apartment on purpose. She ask me, why birthday present for Ellen and none for her?"

"Meho, what did I tell you?"

"Now she say she wants to call you tomorrow. I'm just afraid she say something to you that hurt you."

"OK, Meho. It's all right. Thank you for warning me."

"And now, we go for a little walk in the park?"

"You know I can't! How can you even suggest it?"

He sighed, resigned. "Ellen, you give me life, do you know that?"

"I give you life? Am I your mother then?"

"You are my mother and my wife, my sister and my daughter. You are everything to me."

I drove him back to his car quickly, touched by his words and disturbed by what he had said about Gordana. I had seen their relationship deteriorate before my eyes, without realizing to what extent I was responsible. What mixture of maternal instinct, compassion, emotional need and physical attraction bound me to this asylum seeker? So long as I would feel his imperative need for me, I could not cut that tie.

> *Meho, was I your asylum, or were you mine? And now, were we not being rejected together on the road?*

"Please, Ellen, just give me a kiss," he begged. "Make it a long one, all right? It has to last for a few days."

The next morning, the telephone rang as predicted. Gordana's voice was taut with repressed anger. She dispensed with salutations. "Ellen! Give me *telefonnummer doktor,* right away!" I dictated the gynecologist's number to her, knowing her decision had been made.

"And now, Ellen, do you have just a little time for me this afternoon?"

"Of course, Gordana. School is over for me at three today." I fought to keep my voice even. "What time shall I drop by?"

"Four o'clock."

The children would not be home from their study period after school until six.

I didn't kiss her as usual, when she showed me in. The air was crackling with high voltage. She pointed to a chair opposite her, the cat-green lanterns of her eyes flashing. Meho sat at the table, to one side, frowning, silent. Gordana set her cordless telephone down hard in front of me.

"You dial doctor's number for me," she said. "Make appointment to talk about abortion!" I fumbled, not knowing how to turn it on. She pressed the button for me, as though she were dealing with a mental retardate. The pink capsule I had swallowed, ten milligrams of self-control, helped me keep my composure. I spoke to the receptionist calmly, asking for the appointment and for more information on the formalities preceding abortion.

When I hung up the receiver, Gordana attacked. "I do not want this baby, because it is you who decided on this baby!" I was thoroughly dumbstruck. I hadn't expected that.

"No, Gordana, you are wrong."

"Yes, it was you! You and Meho, you decided it together."

All I could do was shake my head in denial. From her pocket, she drew out the letter I had written to Meho with my vacation picture, now gone from the picture frame. "And this? What does this mean?" She detached each word in staccato. She held my own handwriting up to me. In the letter I had told Meho that I could be nothing more than a sister to him, that I was too fond of Gordana and Jacques to be otherwise. What had she understood? It was damning for Meho, but not for me.

"I . . . I guess it means Meho was becoming a little too attached to me. Gordana, please understand! This past year was hard on him too, as it was on you . . ." She elaborately tore the letter in two, drawing out the movement of her hands. Gordana had a fine sense of drama.

"Well, so be it," she said. "You continue with Meho! As for me, I am going back to Yugoslavia. I take my daughters and go back home. I thought you were my friend, like family to me," she added. "You say so yourself. You too from a foreign country. You say you know what it's like. I have deprived my own children of food in order to give you things to eat." She also had a remarkable flair for embellishment. In a crisis, Gordana rose to the occasion. Her command of French was greater and greater. "Tell me, does Jacques know you wrote a letter to Meho at his work?"

"Yes, he does."

"Does he know you gave money to Meho?" I nodded yes, although I had never mentioned the eight hundred francs.

"Always, you do everything for Meho, never for me. I should have reacted earlier. I noticed a lot of things. But I kept them to myself. I was wrong. I should not have waited."

"Do you love Meho?" I ventured. He had persuaded me she did not, and I had believed him. It suited me to believe him.

"Not any more, I don't." She spat out the words. Her emerald eyes glinted, as she looked at him squarely.

> *Had I really never done anything for you, Gordana? And those weekly language lessons that I prepared with care each time? The meals I invited you to? Had I really taken the food out of your children's mouths? Aren't you forgetting the little gifts, too, and the visits? The friendship I offered? It was you who hesitated to accept it, you who never showed any gratitude. It is not too difficult to deceive an unwilling friend.*

She rose from her chair, picked up the French books I had lent her, and set them down brusquely in front of me. Then she handed me the pair of silver *Je t'aime* earrings I had given her. I gathered the things, standing straight, my head up. Then I walked out, touching her hair lightly as I passed her. "I never wanted to hurt you, Gordana, honestly," I said, then let myself out of the apartment.

Jacques was relieved that Gordana finally knew. It wasn't right for us three to share the painful secret that excluded her and maintained her in an illusory innocence. Meho, on the other hand, didn't want her to know everything. He spoke to me from a telephone booth, after Gordana's scene.

"Does she know we've slept together?" I asked him.

"No, but she suspects. She even told the children, 'We are going back to Yugoslavia together, just the four of us, because your father has made love to Ellen.'"

"She said that to the children?"

"Yes, but I'm not sure they really understood. I called them all together when the girls got back from school. I said to Gordana, 'What have you done, now? You have sent away our best friend, our benefactress, the only friend you have in this country. Where would you be without Ellen? Would you be living in this apartment now? Would you have seen the doctor? Would you have your medicine?'"

"And that letter?"

"First, she asked Suada, 'What does *love from* mean?' Suada tell her, it's to finish letters; it's like kisses to say hello or good-bye. Then I told Gordana it was my fault. I sought you out for making love, because she always turns her back to me. She said I should know that's because she's worried about Latifa. I told her you refused me, anyway."

"Oh, God, thank you, Meho. Thank you."

"Now she wants to call you again."

Château Lore
Murat

Marie-Toussainte was surprised to hear Murat's young voice over the telephone. In fact, she had given up any hope of hearing from the Osayin family months ago. They had disappeared one day from the furnished apartment a charity had lent. When the neighbors finally looked in, they said there were still curtains at the windows, still milk and yogurt in the refrigerator. The furniture was untouched. But there were no clothes left in the chest of drawers or in the armoire. And no notes or messages for anybody.

"*Bonjour!*" said Murat's voice, unchanged.

"Where are you?" asked Marie-Toussainte, stupefied. "Wherever are you calling from?"

"From Bulgaria."

"Bulgaria? You're back there? But why . . . ? How . . . ?"

"Maman and Papa got fed up one day, and we just decided to come back home. France didn't turn out to be what we were hoping. Papa thought life would be easy there, but he couldn't get a job."

"And in Bulgaria? He has a job?"

"Sure, at the bakery."

"But . . . I thought . . . in your *own* bakery?"

"Yes."

"Then it never burned down?"

"No, my grandmother kept it for us"

"And how did you get home?"

"With the Deutsche marks Papa had. The ones Mademoiselle Elisabeth changed for him at the bank. So anyway, my parents just wanted to say hello, and thanks for everything. Oh, and if you see Mademoiselle Antoine from my school, tell her *'bonjour'* from me, all right? I'm still good at French!"

The lawyer, the journalists, the demonstrations, the newspaper articles, the audience with the Prefect were all Marie-Toussainte could think of. So much effort, so much good will mobilized. For this. She sighed, and then she laughed, wryly. I'm the sower in the parable, she thought to herself. So many seeds by the wayside, so many among thorns. But if I've sown one, only one, in good ground, then it will prosper one hundredfold.

Sixteen

"*Allô?*"

"*Allô* . . . Ellen?"

I'd sprung up from the table to answer the telephone. It had rung as I was eating lunch with Jacques, opposite him in our country-style kitchen, my back to the window. The room was drenched in autumn sun. Gordana's voice was tremulous this time. "Ellen, about yesterday . . . I was nervous, a little upset, little bit conflict with Meho . . . you understand, yes? I didn't mean it. Please forget what I said! All right? Will you forget everything? Will you?"

"Of course, Gordana, it's all right."

"Come tomorrow! We talk again, OK?" I heard her voice catch; she was close to tears. Now, Gordana was asking my forgiveness, and I was a sorry hypocrite, playing the magnanimous soul with her. But I couldn't tell her, no, you are right. I did deceive you. I have slept with your husband and taken great pleasure in it. I hung up the telephone and burst into tears myself.

"Poor Gordana, poor little Gordana," I choked, as Jacques waited for my emotion to subside. We had returned to our realm of lies, and there was nothing he could do.

The first thing I noticed, when I entered their living room, was my photograph, which had been violently crumpled, then flattened and spread out again. It had regained its place in the picture frame, near Nadir. Meho was silent again, as Gordana presided. She began to recite thanks.

"Ellen, you have done many things for us. I do not want you to think I am ungrateful to you."

"I don't think that, Gordana, but you misunderstood sometimes. When I gave Meho the three thousand francs, it was for all of you to be more comfortable here together, it was for all the family." My eyes filled with tears, as I recalled how I had, indeed, made this attempt at mending Gordana's misery at the *Château*. Where was the truth? How much of this aid had been for all of them, how much simply because of the love I felt for her husband?

Gordana reached for a box of paper handkerchiefs and handed me one. "Now, now," she said briskly. Then she spoke of her marriage to Meho. "You must understand, I am very . . . what is the word . . . of Meho . . ." She sought in her vocabulary, pronouncing a word which sounded to me like "realistic". "I very *réaliste* of Meho."

"I think you mean 'jealous', perhaps?"

She began again. "That's it! Jealous! When I got divorce, I thought only of my daughter, Latifa. I never think to look for another man. But Meho, he came to get me, he sought me out."

Here was a version I hadn't heard before.

"Beginning of my marriage with him: superr!"

"Thanks," Meho interrupted, ironically.

"But then come other wife!" She spoke the words furiously. The wound was still smarting. Gordana had spent so much of her time ruminating over the hurt Samira had caused her, that for some time she had not measured the extent of the threat posed by that American woman, Ellen. "Meho make big mistake with Samira. Now, he make mistake with you. If third mistake come, then I go. Besides, the door is always open. My house is not a prison. He wants to leave? He can leave." She gestured toward the corridor and door in back of her.

"With Nadir, I get on very well. We have cigarette, cup of coffee together, he call me 'Mama'. But that woman, now she have fourth man, and I don't know how many babies. It's very hard on Nadir. He tell me, my mother have baby with Algerian man, then Swiss. Now she's with a Yugoslav."

Meho studied the tabletop. "I don't understand," he said. "She used to be a good woman."

"Gordana, do you write to Latifa?"

"No! I have address, *telefonnummer*, everything, but I don't want to write."

"But why not?"

"Her father like me, remarried now. Other wife, other children. I think other wife, she . . ." She made the motion of tearing a letter in half. I could understand her distress at their separation, but her refusal to keep in touch, even at the risk of a torn letter, was beyond me. And why would Latifa's stepmother have wanted to tear up the letter? Undoubtedly that is what Gordana herself would have done, had a letter from Samira come to their address. "Ellen, what happened with Meho, it's not your fault." I said nothing. Meho's little lecture had been convincing.

"Are we still friends then? Shall we continue seeing each other?" I asked, rising to leave. She nodded yes, but without enthusiasm. How could she have shown pleasure at the prospect of seeing her rival again?

Two days later, on a Friday, I went to meet Meho for lunch at Quick, a fast-food restaurant near the shopping gallery, where we had sometimes met for coffee. He took my arm with pride, raising his head slightly to look up at me, as we crossed a rotary circle. The midday traffic was heavy, and cars whizzed around. He pulled me close to him, protective.

"How beautiful you look today, Ellen," he said. "How is it that you are so very beautiful?" I smiled at him, pushing the hair back from my ears. I was wearing the silver earrings Gordana had returned to me. Some virus of defiance had bitten me. If she wouldn't sport the *Je t'aime* I had offered, I would. I forbade myself to say it, yet it burned my tongue and now swung from my earlobes. My behavior was bound to puzzle Meho. I was confused myself: desiring, denying, deluding myself with this friendship game.

We made an odd couple, I thought, although no one in the restaurant seemed to notice us: a smart woman wearing glasses with a bearded, truck driver sort. "To me, you are a *grande dame,* a great lady," he said, gazing at me. Then he pulled off his wedding ring and handed it to me. "Ellen, when are we getting married? When are we going to live together?"

"*Rom dilo!*" I laughed, crazy Gypsy. A recent movie, "*Gadjo Dilo*", told the story of a French boy in love with a magnificent Gypsy girl. I had longed to see that film with Meho, but it was Jacques who had accompanied me. To the Gypsies in the Romanian village, the young man was *dilo,* crazy. I remembered the word, and Meho laughed to hear me tease him in his language.

"We go sit in car, give each other a little kiss?" he said, clearly uninterested in hamburgers.

"No, Meho," I protested. "It will only heat you up, and then you'll be miserable. When are you going to become a gentleman, anyway?"

"All right, for you, I'll try," he said, "but I love you, Ellen. What do you make of that?"

You always disarmed me. What could I say?

"How is Gordana now?"

"Always feels sick, headaches, constipated. Too tired now to play her little dictator, but as soon as she'll be better, she'll be bossing everyone again."

"I've been thinking about that child, Meho. I hate to think of abortion, and yet I'm so afraid she'll never be able to love it. That would be a tragedy. Maybe she's right about not bringing it into the world. Every child needs love. It's better not to be born if you're not going to be loved. Do you think she'll reject it?"

"No, she wouldn't do that." He seemed sure.

"Does she know where you are?"

"She thinks I am at hospital this afternoon to see friend I met at chorus about job for her."

Meho had joined a choral group in Laudes. He'd met a doctor there who had shown interest in their situation. He'd said he might be able to get something for Gordana at the hospital, if only she could get a copy of her diploma. "I'll tell her doctor wasn't there today." Meho lied easily, as always.

> *Did you lie so easily to me, too? You told me Gordana didn't love you, but without love, there can't be so much jealousy. You said it was she who insisted on your marriage, but she told me you had run after her. You told Jacques and me she didn't accept your son, and yet she was proud he called her Mama. You said she wasn't affectionate, yet now you were assuring me she would accept and love this new child. You arranged the truth to suit circumstances, didn't you, Meho?*

I reminded him of Gordana's words. "You 'made a mistake' with me, Meho," I said, but he would have nothing of that.

"No, Ellen, I made love with you," he corrected. Then he smiled sourly as he thought of Gordana's growing pregnancy. "We can't *faire sexe* anymore," he said, "she is too big." For me, he used the word love: *faire l'amour*; for Gordana, *sexe*.

"But she's only two months along," I said. "How is that she is so big?"

"Like that for each pregnancy. Very, very big. Last time, she started it, the day you came to the apartment, but I said no. I didn't feel like it."

"Meho! Give her what she wants, or she'll be even more suspicious of our relationship! Why did you turn her away?"

"She do it to me hundreds of times. Me once!" He sounded like a child, wronged on the playground.

> *You'd told me, too, that she didn't enjoy sex with you. But now I understood that she sometimes demanded it, even when she was angry with*

you. You had a tempestuous relationship that I would never be able to fathom.

"What has she decided about the baby, finally? Time is running out." I was becoming resigned to the fact that Gordana was sole mistress of the decision. I realized that the birth of the child, especially if I were to be the godmother, would only be one more thorny complication in my relations with Jacques. I was as ambivalent now about the child as Meho had been, when he had first announced its conception to me.

"She asked me to call abortion center, but I said, 'No, it's your decision, you take care of it.' But she didn't." Meho was clearly unhappy. Gordana applied herself to making his life miserable. "I don't like her," he said glumly. "She always finds just the right word to hurt me."

"Why did you marry her?"

"Because was nurse."

"Because she was a nurse?"

"Yes. I was so sick over Samira. And because she went to see my mother. My mother told her, 'Get yourself pregnant, if you want Meho to stay with you.' Before, she wanted children. Now, she doesn't want." He spoke dryly, as if this contradiction of Gordana's were beyond him.

Gordana, you wanted to take your revenge on Meho, didn't you, and what better way could there have been than getting rid of his child? Still, you hesitated. Why? Was the child a way to keep him, nonetheless? Religion was clearly not a preoccupation of yours. Was it some primal dedication to life that made you hold on?

I called Gordana on Sunday to ask how she was feeling. "Shall I come for your lesson on Monday?" I asked.

"What?" she exclaimed, mildly surprised. "Didn't Meho tell you on Friday, when he was at your house, that I don't want a lesson this Monday?"

I didn't know what to answer. Had he told her, after all, that he had seen me on Friday? But he hadn't come to the house. I stuttered an answer, "Why no, I guess I didn't understand that. Honestly, no. Well, you know, his French isn't so good." I didn't deny having seen him, nor was it clear that I had. The issue remained cloudy between us.

"You should have said, 'I didn't see Meho on Friday,'" he told me afterward. "Couldn't you see it was a trick? She wanted to know if I spent Friday afternoon with you. She is a cunning one!"

Now, you were setting traps for us, Gordana. And I, indeed, was naive.

I was still trying to convince myself that Gordana and Meho could find a common ground and be reconciled. The latest film by the Yugoslav, Kusturica, was showing in our town, and its subject matter was the humorous and colorful goings-on in a Gypsy community. There was Gypsy music, and the actors spoke the Romany language. I knew the Kozićs longed to see this movie, but they had no means to treat themselves to outings. I slipped the cinema program into their mailbox with money for the tickets.

Gordana, I was still trying to extricate myself from Meho's hold and yet incapable of simply leaving you alone. The attachment I felt to him had to express itself in gifts, in attention; it was an imperious need. This gift was not insincere. I wanted you to go out with him, to be happy, if only for an hour and a half of escape in a movie theater. But I couldn't stop doing things for you.

The film was prolonged, and the little art cinema where it was showing put out a new leaflet with dates and times, which I went to drop off at the apartment after school. I hoped to see Meho, and, at the same time, wanted Gordana to be sure I was thinking of her too. I was fighting to convince myself that it was the two of them together that I loved. I still had illusions that I could convince Gordana of this as well.

Meho was seated at the living room table, eating a piece of elaborate ice cream cake, while Gordana grilled pumpkin in the kitchen. It was five o'clock, their dinnertime. He was careful to show me no particular warmth, and, in fact, he appeared quite dispirited, his head bowed over his plate. Without asking my opinion, she brought me a piece of the same cake. I knew they had little money for food. This pastry, in fact, might have come from the *Restaurant du Coeur,* the charity grocery, where French people in dire circumstances could buy food at cheaper rates, or, in some cases, qualify for packages. Humanitarian aid again: It was their habit. But to buy such a cake at a normal store? That seemed like folly. I did not ask, eating my serving politely, forcing myself, for I was not hungry. Then Gordana, always standing or busying herself at something, served us each a chunk of boiled pumpkin, which she had grilled afterward on the stove. I had already coaxed down the cake, and I could not swallow this too, but she wouldn't take no for an answer.

"*Allez!*" she cried, come on, but her voice was shrill and hostile. This was not courtesy or generosity, but something like a cry of war. If I was my own dupe about my good intentions, Gordana was not. Her tone frightened me.

"May I take it home, please, Gordana?" I asked her. "I really can't eat anything more now."

"Yes, wrap it up for Ellen, so she can have it later!" Meho was trying to humor her too. I left quickly with my grilled pumpkin in hand, tossing it in the garbage as soon as I got home.

Marie-Toussainte had not insisted, when I made a pretext of too much work to volunteer again for her in the fall. She must have felt the unease she had created by referring to Meho's past. Gordana retained her grudge against her and refused adamantly to see her. Meho told me he had suggested that they invite Marie-Toussainte once, "to say thank you", but Gordana, intractable and unforgiving, had replied, "Never! Never I see that woman again."

I stopped by at the Catholic Aid offices in town one afternoon with a book to return, both fearing and hoping at the same time that I would run into Marie-Toussainte. She was there between phone calls and visits, ready as always for a chat. I tried to press her for more information on her earlier revelations about Meho, but she remained vague. "Oh yes, he really did do time," she said, "but, then, I don't know if it was in a real prison or a detention camp, you know, like they have for illegals in Germany? He wasn't exactly caught stealing. You know what it was? He did over stolen cars so they could be resold."

"Is that it? I know that's big in Eastern Europe. It's part of the survival game."

"Sure, I know. What's delinquency here is just a way to feed your kids over there."

Why did you have to mention it last spring, then, Marie-Toussainte? Who were you helping?

"You've noticed how the TV set is sealed into the wall at the *Château?*" she went on. "And you know why the washing-machines break down now and then? Some of the refugees steal the parts and sell them. Here, teenagers steal to buy Nike running shoes. Whereas those people are used to doing that sort of thing to put bread on the table!"

Playing the oboe in the Sarajevo Symphony must have been lovely, Meho, while it lasted, but all's fair in war and poverty, isn't it?

Monday morning was Gordana's lesson time. In theory, at least, all had been repaired between us, and, so, I stopped by at the apartment, ready with my French grammar book. On this bright October Monday, Meho had been vacuuming. He wore trousers and a sleeveless, V-necked undershirt that exposed his muscular upper arms.

"Shh," he said, "Gordana sleeping in bedroom," as he led me into the living room. He glanced into their room, where she lay sprawled on the mattress, just off the living room. Then he turned on the television.

"Why the TV?"

"Shh," he said again, "background noise."

I sat at the table by him, spreading out papers in front of us. "Then I'll teach you," I said. I was dressed for school in heels, stockings, and my narrow-skirted red suit with the fitted jacket.

"I get some breakfast for you?" he offered. "Some eggs, maybe?"

"No, Meho, I've had breakfast. Let's just talk!"

He sighed, overwhelmed by too much marital strife. His wife kept up an atmosphere of reproach and tension; he had lost his job; his beloved Ellen would not provide the comfort he wanted.

"Has she decided now, about the baby?"

"She wants to kill it," he said, grimly. "She take scissors and cut up sonogram."

"Oh, no, Meho. She can't do that. It's our baby." Suddenly, his unspoken distress was more than I could bear. "I do love you, you know, Meho," I said. For two months I had done my best to respect my promise, but my feelings had become too much for me to keep in. The words were out before I realized it.

"Me too, I love you too!" he said, as though seizing a life-rope. "Helena, my darling, *donne l'amour,* give me love, please!" he begged. I shook my head, mute, chagrined.

Gordana entered the room, her features crumpled, like her clothing. "I am too tired for a lesson," she said in a chilly voice. Meho slipped on a cotton shirt and accompanied me downstairs.

"Come down one more flight with me, Ellen," he said. I realized he was taking me to the basement. "Give me love, here, please, I can't wait for you any longer!" He took me in his arms in an unlit corridor of the apartment house cellar, undoing his trousers hastily, pushing up my short skirt, groping to pull down my panty hose. Defeated, I let him do it. He came immediately, thanking me profusely.

I gathered my dignity, adjusting my skirt, picking up my attaché case, walking swiftly out into the sunlit parking lot. I could feel Meho's wetness seeping into my underwear.

"Just a little present for you, this morning, little brother," I said, as I got into my shiny, bullet-gray car and drove to school.

Dear God, what have I done now? But it is only this once. I will not fall again. Please, give me the strength not to fall again!

Meho called me soon afterward. "Gordana, she understand everything now," he said. "All of a sudden, she see us together in the morning. She says, 'Now I know! You have an intimate relationship with Ellen.' I asked her why she says that. It's because she saw me there in undershirt. I explain I was cleaning apartment, then you came. Was I undressed, I asked her? Was Ellen undressed? Did you see us doing anything together? No, she said, but she knows. Why was I so long in coming back upstairs, she wants to know. Because I talk to Ellen, I said. But now she says she is sure."

My anxiety returned in nauseous waves. I was becoming gradually less depressed, thanks to my frequent conversations with Meho. I was busy feeding myself the illusion that we could carry on as friends. Then I had relapsed, and Gordana's intuition had spoken the truth to her. The sight of us together at the table, he in his cotton mesh undershirt, had been the light of revelation.

"I told Gordana, yes, I want another woman, because you, you are always nasty to me. One day, God will punish you for your nastiness, I told her. But that other woman will not be Ellen. When I went to chorus yesterday, she stayed up and waited for me. But she did not say anything. Then, I went to bed, and she got into bed with Amina. Then, a little time later she come into room with me and cry and cry. 'Now I have lost everything,' she said. Cried very hard."

"Did you comfort her, Meho?" He ignored my question. "Then today," he went on, "she make a mixture with chlorine bleach, try to drink it, but I stop her. She was hysterical. Wants to get rid of baby."

"Meho, she's a nurse. She must know you can't abort by drinking bleach. She wanted to poison herself, maybe? What did you do?"

"I called emergency squad. They came, nothing serious. She'll be all right." He took this incident very lightly, I thought. Or was he used to Gordana's talent for staging?

"Next, it's me she'll be wanting to kill."

"Don't worry, Ellen," he said sardonically. "Her only pistol is her tongue."

That evening, Jacques took part in another theater production, a staging of extracts from Nathalie Sarraute, called *"Tu ne t'aimes pas"*: You Do Not Love Yourself. The title was fated. For so many years, he had not loved himself, nor, in fact, anyone else. It was all word play, verbal pyrotechnics, the nuances and color of expression. But I couldn't concentrate. Gordana's distress haunted me, as did the guilt of my relapse. I watched Jacques and his fellow actors come and go in the light and shadows of the stage, reciting jousts and pirouettes of language, while my mind was a haze of worry and distraction.

"You were bored, weren't you?" he asked me in a disappointed voice, as we left together.

"No, honestly I wasn't. Of course, it's all a little bit abstract for me . . ." This was my only plea. I couldn't tell him the thoughts that obsessed me: the new drama unfolding between Gordana and Meho, and Ellen in the middle. I couldn't voice the reason for my absent-minded staring. And this time, he didn't guess.

Meho said he was down to his last franc. He came to the house for help, but in the afternoon, when he was sure to find me alone. He couldn't receive the benefits that the government allotted to families with children, because he had no legal proof that Suada, Amina and

Veronika were his. For this, he needed birth certificates, and whatever declaration of birth had been made for his girls had long ago burned in the war. Suada's and Amina's births had been declared at a mosque in Sarajevo, but the mosque itself had burned to the ground. As for Veronika, it was simply lucky that she had been brought into the world at all.

The authorities would not accept a declaration on his honor. Too many before him had gathered together the children of the neighborhood to soften a social worker's heart, swearing up and down that they were their own. Meho was prepared to undergo a blood test for paternity, but the test was highly expensive and, of course, beyond his means. His daughters were thus a potential source of income, however modest, that he could only sigh after.

"I have nothing left, Ellen. Please, can't you lend me something?" I went to get him three hundred francs in cash, grocery money that Jacques would never notice. Then he showed me his telephone bill, one thousand francs. "Very high this month," he said, "because I call Yugoslavia all the time, try to get papers for children's birth."

"I can't do anything about that," I said, shocked he would ask me. "What would Jacques say if I wrote a check to the phone company?" He folded the paper and put it back in his pocket.

Why were you always so unrealistic?

"Gordana does everything now to make me miserable," he said. "She sleeps on pile of blankets in living room. She never picks up after the children. I do everything for them, feed them, give bath. She's doing her best to drive me out, but I have no place to go. Can't I come stay here?"

"You must be insane! What would Jacques say? You know he'd never want that!"

"Then, I am lost." He pressed his high forehead into his hands, his fingers combing back his black hair. I could hear the tears in his voice.

"Meho, there's no reason you should leave the apartment. It's yours too. Without you, she'd never have been able to get it. Why can't Amina and Suada share a room and you take the one that's left? You could put your things in it and come and go as you like." He seemed to consider this. "Suada is not well," he said. "All this stress and fighting too much for her. Sleep walks now."

"Poor child! Gordana does nothing to spare the children, does she?"

"Nothing at all, she do just the opposite."

"Listen, I'm willing to ask Jacques if you can stay here with the children and Gordana too, if she wants, while we're away for fall break."

> *Jacques, you and I will be away together. You won't mind, will you? One more indulgence?*

"That way, you'd have the big house, the yard for the children. Maybe Gordana will relax some if you're out of the way with the girls."

I was still trying to write the script of a play and make it come true. We would all be friends and there would be a happy end. Gordana would believe in our good will. Jacques wouldn't tire of lending his rival the lovely house he had put the best of his skill and energy into renovating. My role in the play would be something like fairy godmother, orchestrating conviviality.

"And now, let's look at the job ads in the paper together," I suggested to Meho. He desperately needed something to boost his spirits.

"Thank you, Ellen." I had never seen Meho so close to depression himself, a lamp extinguished, too disheartened even to flirt with me.

"Come back this evening, and we'll talk to Jacques together, all right?" He left, telling me I was saving his life one more time.

The following day, he called. "My darling, Gordana has gone out to a telephone booth to call you. She's furious."

"Why?"

"She went through my pockets yesterday, and she find the three hundred franc notes you give me. Tell her you did it to help us buy food. Explain everything to her nicely, please!"

"I'll see."

Actually, I had no stomach to explain anything at all to Gordana. Meho could tell her the money was for groceries, which, indeed, it was. Her fury intimidated me. Why had she left the house to call me? Was it because she was so angry that she didn't want the children to hear her? That didn't seem like her.

The phone rang again and again. I ignored it, although each new series of rings made my skin crawl. I could imagine her raging in the narrow cage of the telephone booth, wondering why I wasn't at home at lunchtime. I could hear her anger in the incessant ringing. Did she suspect I was there, lying low, that her husband had warned me? If so, then she might well have thought that I had some reason to hide from her. Still, I lacked the courage to pick up the receiver.

The following day, Jacques and I would leave Laudes for a short holiday, and, little by little, she would calm herself. School was breaking for midterm, and we were leaving for Brussels again. After forty-five minutes of sporadic, stormy ringing, the telephone fell silent.

Jacques agreed once again to the Kozićs' staying at our house during our absence. Meho had come, as planned, that evening before our departure and earnestly explained Gordana's nervous condition to him, as well as Suada's, if not the exact reasons. Before leaving, I had prepared a note for Gordana, forcing a light-hearted tone:

Dear Gordana,

I hope that you are feeling better now, for Meho has explained to Jacques and me how tired you have been these past few weeks. Perhaps you will be able to come to the house a little for some fresh air. When we return, I will not resume our French lessons, as I realize this is too much for you. However, if you want me to, just let me know.

These were the last friendly words I addressed to Gordana. Brussels would shield me from her now for a blessed time of respite. I couldn't foresee that I would return from my trip weak and tired and broken.

Château Lore
Oleg

Notification of their expulsion came for Oleg and Sveta, first from the Foreigners Bureau at the *Préfecture,* then from the mouth of Monsieur Lenoir, obviously much distressed by this errand. Their last recourse had been ineffectual; they had already overstayed their time at the *Château,* reserved for those in the course of the asylum procedure. Hope had dwindled out for the Petrovs. At home, the Military Tribunal loomed, and the horrors of prison after it; return was unthinkable, yet staying impossible.

Oleg remained self-possessed as he always did in crisis and telephoned Monsieur Dobrinine. He spoke about Meho Kozić's employment offers and how the Prefect might be swayed by self-sufficient asylum seekers, even deserters. Shortly after that telephone call, the Petrovs disappeared from view.

They resurfaced briefly in a village nearby, where a mattress manufacturer was persuaded to sign an employment promise for asylum seeker Petrov. Oleg went about learning the trade quietly, on a volunteer basis, gliding soundlessly home evenings to the room he shared with Sveta and their little boy in the country house of the Dobrinines' best friends. They continued to bide their time. Gordana wondered where they could have gone.

Seventeen

Mental images of Gordana accompanied me to Brussels: Gordana brandishing the bleach bottle and threatening to pour the contents down her throat. Gordana suspiciously rummaging through the pockets of Meho's black jacket for some, any damning evidence, fulminating at the empty, incessant ringing of my telephone, sobbing one desperate night that she had lost everything, then rebounding and setting sly traps for me. I swallowed my anti-depressants and tried to think of other things, yet the same images played themselves over and over like feverish dreams.

Jacques and I went out with Melisand and Julien, and I playacted my role of mature, happy wife, and mother. We drank toasts to one another of Belgian *wittebier* and warmed ourselves before the open fires in the cafés of the *Grote Markt,* dipping our spoons into thick dobs of whipped cream on apple tart and watching the crowds hurry past in the chilly November dusk.

On our last day, we went for a bicycle ride in the *Cambre* Wood. The trees still wore their red and gold leaves, shading the dirt paths that cut through the forest, and the air was pungent with the tang of autumn. My bicycle ran up against an unexpected rock, and I fell swiftly and hard on my head. I didn't hear the bicycle smash to the ground. At the instant I struck the ground, a wide, black curtain, punctuated with sparkling silver dots, filled the field of my vision. Then, once again, my eyes focused on the dull, gray sky above me. I lay without moving, feeling the cold, hard earth beneath me, supporting me. Jacques and Julien were bending over me in a second. "Leave me alone!" I whimpered, like a petulant child. "I don't want to get up."

"We aren't helping you up, sweetheart, don't worry." Jacques, unnerved, spoke gently. He took off his jacket and covered me with it. "Melisand is off to call someone. How do you feel?"

"All right. Nothing hurts. Just tired, so tired. I don't think I can get up yet."

"There's no rush." He sat beside me, holding my hand.

My body had turned to icewater, so weak I felt, and so utterly cold. *Thank you, God. Perhaps you will send me death, and I am ready. You have seen my wretchedness and all the misery I cause around me.* I had always feared death, but at that moment, on the chilly ground of the wood, I felt it would be the sweetest, kindest thing that could happen to me. I felt perfectly calm, reassured, even, that this accident should have come to me at this time when I was so incapable of facing my life. Whatever was wrong with me, I would accept gladly. I would not have to return the next day to my work, to my worries, to the relentless revenge of the stalking Gordana. Suddenly a tremor ran through my body. I was going to be prey to convulsions; I breathed deeply to welcome them, but they did not come. I let myself be carried off on a stretcher to an ambulance waiting in the street.

"X-rays," the young woman doctor said, touching her head and smiling in complicity. She slid a tube into the blue vein inside the crook of my elbow. "Plasma, for shock," she said, "just in case."

"The neurological examination isn't normal," I told Jacques, after they had wheeled me back into the corridor where he sat waiting. "On one side, I see double. They say I have to go to Ophthalmology next." The doctors decreed I must stay there under observation, undergo tests. Jacques said it was all his fault. I hadn't been eager to go riding, and he had insisted.

I wanted to tell you how relieved I was, how thankful, but I could not do that. Normal people do not rejoice in concussions.

The hospital sheets were crisp and neutral. An odor of disinfectant floated in the air, and a dim light filtered into the room from the busy corridor, where white, thick-soled shoes padded back and forth. I slept easily, freed for once from the thoughts that habitually obsessed me. A good blow to the head was what I had needed.

At two in the morning, I awoke to see the room spinning. I had never experienced vertigo, and, for a moment, forgetting how blissful was my injured state, I panicked.

The night nurse on her rounds looked in. "Madame, excuse me please, but I had a dizzy spell," I whispered to her.

She immediately strapped her blood pressure instrument around my forearm, squeezing it tight, reading with a thin, pen-like flashlight, which she then pointed at my pupils.

"Everything is OK," she said, reassuring. "After a fall, it's to be expected. Tell the doctor in the morning!"

The hospital was a cradle of security to me, sheltering me from a world I no longer had the strength to face. I hoped for some sign of insidious injury that would keep me there for weeks, but, three days later, I was released, all my tests normal. I was shaky on my legs, hanging on to Jacques as we climbed on the train at *Bruxelles Midi*.

No sooner was I settled in our own bed at home than the telephone rang. I heard Jacques' voice, forcedly jovial. "Oh, Meho, it's you. No, everything's fine. We just stayed a little longer than planned."

Why didn't you tell him? You had no reason to, of course. Why should you share your wife's injury with another man, any more than you should share the rest of her?

He came of his own accord to find out. The following morning, I still lay in bed at nine, while Jacques had left for his office. The doorbell let out its little yelp, and I got carefully up, catching onto the windowsill in case of dizziness, opening a crack the heavy shutters that kept my room in darkness. "I'm sick, Meho," I said. "I had an accident."

He let himself in, walking swiftly down the hall to my room. "My darling, my Ellen, what has happened to you? What did they do to you there? Why didn't you come home? I have been so sick with worry." He stroked my hair, stringy and unkempt as it was, and wiped the little sands of sleep from the corners of my eyes.

"I'm sorry. I haven't been up yet; I haven't washed yet."

"Why didn't you call me?"

"I couldn't! I was in a hospital, and I had no access to a phone. Besides, I didn't have your number with me, and I don't know it by heart. You don't think I could have asked Jacques to find it out for me, do you?"

"I thought I would go crazy." His voice was reproachful. "Even Gordana, she finally felt sorry for me. She said, 'Here, take the phone and call them!' I was calling and calling until Jacques finally answered yesterday. But he never said you had an accident." He enfolded me in his arms. "I am so famished for you." I let him hold me, burying my injured head in the warmth of his shoulder. "What do you think if I tell Gordana about us? She could understand that I love someone else."

"What? Gordana understand? Please don't do that! That would be the end of any chance we might have of all staying friends together. Don't, Meho, don't tell her anything!" I felt ashamed and pained. Gordana would be sure to think I had done everything in my power to steal her husband from her. Never in a million years would she believe my spasms of conscience. The idea that she would see my guilt in all its hideous extent brought tears to my eyes. She would hate me more than she did already, and, moreover, I would never see Meho again.

> *What idea entered your head, Meho, when you suggested that? Were you tired of dissimulating? Did you underestimate Gordana's capacity to react? Hadn't she given you enough proof of her gift for anger and jealousy?*

Meho drew my bath and picked up the clothes I left on the floor behind me, then made coffee for me. I was moved at the sight of my Gypsy macho, humbled by love.

In the following days, he returned from time to time, preoccupied by his job seeking, asking me to type letters and résumés for him. "Couldn't you return to Sarajevo?" I asked. "You must still know people there. You wouldn't feel so strange. You speak the language."

"And what could I do there?"

"I don't know. Play the accordion?"

"People are mourning their dead, and I should play the accordion?" he said, bitterly. "Ellen, sometimes when I am alone, I just sit down and cry, thinking of all the friends I lost there."

"I'm sorry, Meho." I had been horribly indelicate.

"It's all right, Ellen. You have given me the courage to live. You are my sunlight."

He came once at the end of Jacques' lunch period. The municipality might be able to offer him a *Contrat Emploi Solidarité,* a subsidized part-time position intended to help put the unemployed back on their feet. His résumé had to be typed, with an accompanying letter. Jacques left for the office, left him with me.

I trust you Ellen, do you see, and I know you will not betray my trust.

I received the unspoken message. But soon Meho was beside me, upstairs, next to the computer, as on that first warm day in May, when we had made love. He looked at me questioningly.

"Jacques is so jealous and worried, Meho, and yet he has gone out. He doesn't say so, but I know he is. It even upsets him when I get e-mail from my colleague, Philippe."

"You have a new lover, Ellen?"

"How can you say that? What do you take me for? Look! I'll show you his message." I clicked it onto the screen, all in English. I translated it for him. It dealt with the organization of comprehensive exams for the *classe de troisième*.

You did believe me, didn't you, Meho?

The doorbell rang. Ginette, the cleaning woman had arrived; she let herself in. I didn't care for her to know that Meho was upstairs with me. I led him into Melisand's former bedroom, transformed now into a little upstairs sitting room. We would wait until Ginette was firmly settled in the kitchen. Then I could let him swiftly and quietly out the front door.

"I could plant a tree in your garden," said Meho, glancing out the window. I looked at him, not quite understanding.

"A sort of present." Was he serious or was it a metaphor? Meho rooted himself within me, and I could not bring myself to stop him. Still in his leather jacket, he held me to his warm body on the wide, blue, brocade armchair, where Jacques often liked to read. When we had done, a spot damp with the salty smell of sex remained. Meho slipped down the stairs, while I, a harried Lady MacBeth, rubbed desperately at the stain. I could never tell Jacques I had had a glass of water there. I went to get the hair dryer.

Is this a soap opera you are living in? A comédie des boulevards, *as the French say?*

I felt demeaned, and helpless, and hopelessly bound to him.

How, Ellen, how are you ever going to get over him?

The pattern of my sin and my treason re-established itself, and Meho would make love to me again on certain afternoons when I finished work early. He would gather me to him on the living room sofa, and I could not find the heart to refuse him, even though Jacques' strained features would impose themselves on my vision. I could see him like an apparition in the armchair opposite, telling Meho how he had trusted him, only for his friendship to be deceived.

"I love you, I love you so much," Meho repeated on one of these occasions, while I remained silent, passive and accepting. "Ellen, please," his voice was supplicating, "please tell me you love me!" I could not bring the words forth, hating myself, yet not daring.

"I don't know, Meho," I said slowly. This hesitation was the best I could muster just then, to honor fidelity. "I know I desire you, but I don't know if I love you."

Indeed, I did not know. It was when I could no longer tell you anything, that I realized how much I loved you.

"Can I see you on Thursday?" Meho was calling. "There is something I want to explain."

"Just tell me now, on the phone."

"No, not here on telephone."

I had additional meetings at school on that particular day, due to the end of the marking period. I tried to explain this to him, but he didn't seem to understand. He knew I usually finished by four o'clock and undoubtedly imagined I was putting him off. I gave up trying to explain why I was not free. "How is Gordana? Is she all right?" The bleach episode still haunted me.

"*Tranquille*," he replied. Tranquil. That meant she was appeased, reassured.

I was relieved. How good to know that you had soothed her.

I picked up the receiver again, still warm from my own hand. "*Allô?*"

"It's Gordana." Her voice was cold and threatening.

"Gordana, how are you?"

"Perfectly fine!" Her tone proclaimed victory. Was this the tranquil Gordana?

"Now you listen to me! Today, Meho showed me everything from you, the letters, the photographs . . . ah, the photographs! What a fine lady you are in the photographs!"

Those snapshots you insisted on taking of me, of us in the bathroom, Meho. What folly!

"Now you listen to me well!" She repeated the words of her injunction like the shots from an assault weapon. "It is over with Meho."

"Yes, Gordana, it is. Honestly, it's over."

"You are . . ." she searched for the words. "You are a woman who takes money from men in the street!" I let the hammered syllables beat down on me.

"Oh," she said, "I am not an *Amerikanische* lady, I am a *Musleemish* lady."

Scorn, scorn for the infidel. American, French, Muslim, Christian, are we not all human beings, Gordana, all fallen short of the glory of God? Why put a label on people? But you needed to brandish your own label just then.

"And the next time you take someone's man, don't take a Muslim!"

Naturally, Gordana, I spend my life stealing other women's husbands.

I leaned against the wall, my heart pounding wildly. I deserved this, but was she incapable of understanding anything?

"I know Meho just called you from a phone booth. He told me everything today, how you met him after his work at the foundry for sex, two times a week!" She was nearly screaming now. "And how Jacques went and spoke to him. I know that too. I know your husband is sick, and that he doesn't make love to you."

"It's not exactly true, Gordana. He was depressed . . ."

"I know that your daughter, Melisand, knows about Meho."

The height of depravity. The women in our family are sick.

"And I know you are also sleeping with your school colleague."

"What? What colleague? That's not so!" I was horrified. I had shown Meho my e-mail from Philippe. Had he really imagined that Philippe was my lover? Had he transformed that into scandal in order to blacken my name a little further with Gordana? That would have been a tactic of self-defense. I was an easy woman in need of attention, who had tempted him.

"I thought you were like a mother to me."

"It's true I wanted to be. I wanted to help you . . ."

"Help me?" She cried her outrage. "You took my husband from me!"

It was he who took me, Gordana. I wanted to say that to you, but I kept silent.

"And now I know," she added, her voice low and bitter, "why we can't get our allowance money for the girls. Jacques said he worked for taxes, but I know he works for social council. It's to get revenge on Meho that he has blocked our file."

"No Gordana! It's not true! You are absolutely paranoid. How can you even think such a thing? Anyway, Jacques has forgiven me, and he has forgiven Meho."

"Forgiven?" This word was utterly foreign to her. She did not want to believe it possible. "I was so well for awhile. Meho and I, we made love together normally. And now . . ." She was adding self-pity to insult. Still, there was no denying that the only time in that year when I had seen her actually blooming was at the end of my three-week absence.

"We all get together and talk about this. Not at my house. In café, maybe."

You want a neutral ground. I will never cross your threshhold again, of course. But you have to bring us together in order to shame me in front of my husband. You know, in spite of it all, that I am not really a loose woman. You know how susceptible to shame I am.

"All right."

I will show you that I am brave and forthright. Besides, I have a weapon.

"Then, at that time," I said, "we'll take the car back, and my half-size violin. There must be no unresolved business between us."

"I do not understand." She was nonplussed.

"The car isn't yours, Gordana. You didn't think it was, did you? Jacques lent it to Meho. It was a loan until December, until the technical inspection. It's ours, in our name, and we insure it."

She remained silent for a moment, stunned. Meho must have returned from the phone booth, for his voice came on the line, speaking gently.

"Hello, Ellen?"

"Yes?"

"I think it's better if we don't see each other any more."

"Of course it's better."

Gordana snatched the receiver back. "Did you hear what Meho said? Did you?"

"Yes, I heard."

"You are dead!" she said, *"morrte! morrte!"* Her tone dropped menacingly on *morrte,* while she drew out the trilled "r". Had Gordana been capable of black magic, I would certainly have shriveled and died on the instant.

"Listen, Gordana," I said, suddenly rallying to my own cause. "Just ask yourself one question before you hang up! Ask yourself why Meho came to me for love!"

Jacques found me exhausted when he returned from work. I had been torturing myself about my spiteful conversation with Gordana, about my missed chance for an appointment with Meho.

Why, Meho, why didn't you tell me over the phone that Gordana had found the photos? Why did you always have to be so cryptic? Why did I put my meeting before you, that Thursday? I didn't know how important it was, that "something" that you wanted to explain. You thought I was annoyed and indifferent, didn't you? That I was making up excuses. Everything could have been different, perhaps, if we had met. You wanted to tell me gently that it was all over. As for Gordana, did you really believe you had calmed her, that she wouldn't strike out against me? You were incredibly overconfident. Had you forgotten how artful she could be?

I had found some solace in whiskey and tranquilizers, sitting blankly in my armchair, while her words echoed and re-echoed in my mind. "Gordana knows now about my affair with Meho," I told Jacques. "She called this afternoon to insult me. She was upset, obviously. We won't be having anything more to do with one another. I told her we would take the car back. What do you think?"

"You did well," he said, relieved that this time everything was truly out in the open, and that Gordana was ready to apply her scalpel to the infection.

"But she believes you are to blame," I said, "if they don't get their family benefits."

Jacques was horrified at Gordana's delusions. "I will write to her," he said. "I will tell her we must make peace." He put himself to it immediately, in the simplest terms he could find:

Dear Gordana,

I understand that you are unhappy. Everything that has happened is unfortunate. But it's finished, and we have to make peace. Ellen and I love each other, and we have made peace. We hope that you and Meho will also be reconciled and be happy together.

Yes, it's true; I have forgiven Meho. I forgave him because I understood my own responsibility. I forgave him so that your family could stay together. I forgave Ellen in order to save our marriage, and because I love Ellen. Only the future counts.

How can you think that I lied about my work? I really do work for the tax administration. How can you even think I would want to hurt your family?

If you accept, Ellen and I will continue to help you. If you do not accept, we will understand.

The last line must have pained him, but he had added it valiantly. Jacques' suffering had brought out the very best in him.

Your wife is a common adulteress, poor Jacques, while you are a prince, generous to a fault.

Melisand, I wrote, but mentally this time, there's a reason for that commandment about adultery. It's not just finger wagging in the face of Mother Nature. It gets you in too deep; it's just too much, too soul-quaking. How could I ever have believed you, that no one would suffer?

Gordana had not finished calling. The following day, she rang at noon, certain Jacques would be at home. "It's me. I want to speak to Jacques!"

"He's not here."

"What, not here? And *le déjeuner?*" She didn't know whether to believe me or not.

"He's not coming today. He's having lunch with colleagues."

She didn't insist, but she had been thinking about the question I had concluded our conversation with the day before. "All right, so I am young," she said.

"Of course you are young." I didn't understand her gist.

"I am young, so I do not make love well."

"Ah, that's what you mean."

"Meho very interested for sexuality, I think you know."

True enough, but you were implying that that was my only value for him. I wanted to tell you that he needed affection first, but I held my tongue.

"I have made copies of the snapshots and photocopies of the letters." She was bragging, sure of her moral position, honing her arms.

> *What would the copies change, Gordana? Were you thinking of sending them to the local newspaper? I doubt they would have been interested. Perhaps to show a divorce lawyer?*

"We are going to give you back the car."
"All right. Meho can bring it to the rehearsal tonight."
"Ha!" she scoffed. "Don't think Meho will ever go near that orchestra again!"
"Whatever you say."
Gordana began a new tirade, fury unleashed. "He doesn't care for you. It's me he loves!" She shrieked "ME" like an angry child defending her own toys.
"I hope so, Gordana. I really hope so. Because don't think it has been easy for me! I'm ill, you know. I have to have a treatment now, of sleeping pills, tranquilizers, anti-depressants. Do you think it's easy for me always to have your husband coming to me, when Jacques and I have both asked him not to, always seeking me out to make love?"

> *What possessed me to say that? But it was out. The truth and not the truth. I didn't want him to come, and I couldn't bear it when he did not.*

She hung up abruptly.

Two hours later, as I sat in the dining room writing lesson plans with Danielle, a fellow teacher, the phone rang. This time, it was Meho. "I am coming tonight. You really want me to bring the car?"
"Yes."
"You have decided that?" He sounded surprised and uncomprehending.

> *Couldn't you see that I was reacting to Gordana's attack? Couldn't you imagine that I would be upset and shaken after her insults and imprecations?*

"Yes. That's all there is to say. I don't think we have anything else to say to each other." I didn't recognize my own voice, hostile, aggressive. I myself couldn't understand why I had spoken to him like that. Danielle was at the table, within hearing range of the telephone. This was no time for explanations with Meho. I wondered if she had heard my tone but put it out of my mind. Even if she had, there was nothing to be done about it. I felt considerable relief that I could recover the car without having to undergo the confrontation Gordana wished for. Meho could drive the Peugeot to our house after the rehearsal and leave it there. Jacques would take him back home, and that would be the end of it. Shaken, I returned to discussing schoolwork.

He wasn't there when the rehearsal began, and I threw myself into the music. In the middle of the first piece, I glanced toward the back of the room to see him standing near the door in his leather jacket. He beckoned to me, and I nodded irritably toward my music stand. The piece wasn't over; Gérard raised his baton again. Once we had played the final chords, I looked back again, but Meho had disappeared. Caroline, a first flute, tiptoed over to me.

"Meho asked me to tell you he had to go, because he left his children alone at the apartment. His wife is in the hospital."

I got up quickly, shoved my violin into its case, and hurried out, while the strings attacked the next movement.

Meho came to his door, then out onto the landing, while the two elder girls pushed forward, curious. He sent them back in abruptly. "You left the rehearsal?" He seemed surprised.

"Yes. What has happened to Gordana?"

"She lost a lot of blood, hemorrhage. I drove her to hospital."

"Did she lose the baby?"

"No, not yet, anyway."

"Jacques has written a really nice note to Gordana. He's asked her to make peace. She'll get it tomorrow." Meho looked at me hopefully.

"Now, tell me, why did you hurt me like that?" I was caught between fury at him and a desire to re-establish our old complicity. "Why did you tell her everything, show her everything?"

He shook his head in disgust at my gullibility. "I didn't show her anything. It's her. She rummaged and looked through all my papers, until she finally found the things."

"Why did you tell her I was having an affair with another teacher? You know perfectly well it's not true."

"I never told her that. She thought, that's all. We were just talking about the electronic mail you have."

> *Perhaps, indeed, Gordana had looked until she found your keepsakes, Meho, but I couldn't believe what you said about the e-mail. Of course you made that up about my fellow teacher to damn me.*

"Now, you must calm yourself," he said.

"Gordana wants to talk to Jacques," I told him.

"Jacques knows anyway."

"But not everything! You know I promised we would never start again. It will be the end for me, if he ever finds that out." I drew my forefinger across my throat, shaking my head fearfully.

Suada and Amina pushed the door open and nearly toppled out. Meho scolded them sharply, sending them in again. "Do you want the car?" he asked, resigned.

"No, not now. She's in the hospital. You'll need to go and see her. Keep the car for awhile."

He came closer to me. "Were you . . . were you clean, when we made love?"

"Of course! What do you mean?"

"They tell her there at the hospital she has an infection."

"Well, it isn't from me. I never had any infection."

> *My dearest Ellen, give me AIDS, you said that day in the botanical garden.*

"Gordana was very upset. You shouldn't have said that about you being ill from my come to see you."

"But you know I didn't want us to sleep together any more, Meho."

"Why did you sleep with me last summer?" He sounded hurt and suspicious.

"Because I loved you!"

"And now?" he asked, the bitter lines at the corners of his mouth visible again.

"Like a brother . . . !"

I couldn't say, I love you, but I do not have the right to love you.

"Let me know how she is!" I kissed him on each cheek, then sped down the stairs, fighting back tears.

Château Lore
Aslan

Aslan had been working steadily now for three months. He'd started substituting at the hospital as an auxiliary, rolling people around on stretchers, and they'd kept him on. He wore a white tunic, a cap, and special shoes, and it was he who helped the patients onto their beds, after they had awakened from anesthesia. Some were like logs that had to be shoved, and others were as light as birds, especially older people, with their bones so brittle and fleshless; he handled them like boxes of crystal.

He thought he'd caught sight one evening of that snappy-tempered, little Gypsy woman from the refugee *Château*. She came into Emergency, her face all sullen and tear-stained, and then they sent her to Gynecology and Obstetrics. Her husband was half carrying her, but it was hard; she was big out to here. He must have been nuts to go and make another baby, when they didn't even know if their papers would be renewed. Then again, maybe that was why, in fact. A baby born here could do the trick. But he would never play that card, not with Leila.

He knew Meho Kozić, and he'd been one of the lucky ones. Everyone knew it was that woman from the Catholic charity who'd helped them. She and her husband lent them their house when they went on vacation, and he cut the lawn in exchange. Imagine, leaving your house key with a Gypsy! And, of course, he knew she'd given them her car. The guy had come to him for a loan.

"The battery's dead," he'd said. "I just need a hundred and twenty francs to get a new one. You'll get it back as soon as I find a job."

Aslan had lent the money to him, given it, more probably. Could you expect a Gypsy to repay you? But he'd felt sorry for him. He'd told Leila, and she'd said he must be crazy. She would say that; she was always bitching. But he was still with her. Nathalie had someone. Someone she lived with, in fact. At first, he couldn't believe it; she seemed so fond of him. She was, she assured him, but not that way. Not that way at all. At least he had a job, and that was more than many.

Eighteen

Each gray, late November day that followed brought its cortege of wait, hope, worry, and heartache. When would he call to tell me how Gordana was? I didn't dare telephone the apartment. She might have been released quickly and answer herself. Was she seriously ill? Had she kept the child? If not, had she been relieved that nature had delivered her of that unwanted burden?

I drove past the apartment block and saw my pistachio-colored car parked in front. I restrained the urge to slide a note into it, some gift for Meho. I would not do it. I had broken enough promises. Now, if he was helping me to keep one, I must submit. It was better that way. Still, it hurt so much, the need to give and to give again, and to refrain from it, to bind my tongue and my heart. They smarted and bled.

Ten days later, still without any news, I left for Brussels to do my pre-Christmas shopping with Melisand, my child who was mother to her mother. At the train station I dissolved in tears when I hugged her, gracile and sleek in her long, fitted coat.

"I'm just a little depressed, dear," I told her. "It'll pass. We'll have a good time together, and it will pass." It did not, of course, either in the fabricated, commercial cheer of the shopping centers or the luminous folklore of the Christmas Market, with its multiethnic stands of gifts, decorations, hot, spiced wine and gingerbread. I fingered the shiny Christmas balls, the candles, the handcrafted jewelry, choosing presents for each member of the family, clutching at these baubles, at this glad tradition like a shipwrecked woman at the side of her lifeboat. On the second day, Jacques called.

"Mel has been spoiling me so much," I said, "I'll probably come home with two extra pounds!"

"That would be a shame," he said.

"So you wouldn't want me, then?"

"Yes, I want you. Just come home!" Something in his voice sounded hollow, bleak. When I found myself in the street again with Melisand, I burst into tears.

"Mom, what is it?"

"It's your father. He says it's a shame if I gain two pounds. Two pounds, can you believe it? To think I gave up a man who always found me beautiful for a husband who will never find me beautiful!"

In my dream that night, the baroque Christmas stands spread out their charming wares before me, but they were foreign, all foreign, and I couldn't touch them. A voice told me these tempting trinkets were not for me, that I must return to my own country. I understood well enough. My own country was named Jacques.

I soon discovered the reason for his dreary tone. "Come sit by me," he said. "I have to talk to you." We settled on the sofa. I had no idea what to expect. "Gordana called while you were gone. She called on Saturday afternoon."

> *How like you, to know just when I was not there and to distill more poison from your cauldron.*

"How is she?"

"She said she was well. She was very poised, and she spoke very good French."

"Did she keep her baby?"

"I don't know. She didn't mention that. She said she wanted me to come over, she wanted to show me letters and pictures. I would have gone, but she said not just then. Saturday evening they were celebrating Veronika's birthday.

A family celebration. You wanted to be sure we knew that.

She told me I was very nice, always kind, but she said, 'Ellen is nasty.' I told her if she had something to say about you, she had to say the same about me. Then she told me it's not over between Meho and you."

"What? Not over? How dare she say that!"

"She said she had proof, and she would show it to me when I came."

"She has no proof at all. I'd like to see that proof! Don't you see she's bluffing, just to get revenge? She wants to hurt me and to destroy us. We don't have to go see her, if we don't want to. She'll be on her own ground, and that will make her stronger. Why should we let her hurt our marriage?"

"Ellen, I have to know. For my part, I have been doing everything in my power to repair our relationship, haven't I?"

"Yes, that's so," I admitted. He had been more considerate and attentive than even the young, newly married Jacques had ever been. He looked at me closely. Gordana had efficiently sown the seeds of doubt.

"Is it true you have been lovers again? I want the truth, no matter how painful it is to me."

"No, Jacques it is not true." I lied boldly, for I would not let him go. I lied to save my skin, to save my relationship with the man who had accompanied me faithfully for thirty years, the only man I could conceivably spend my life with. Meho was not mine and never would be, except in some mythical land of Gypsy reveling. Anyway, Gordana had no proof this time. There were no more photographs and no more letters, except the scribbling I had found in my school mailbox.

"It's true he has been after me. You can see the notes he wrote me, if you want to." I went to one of my school drawers and pulled out the envelopes. Jacques glanced with disgust at the impossible handwriting, the illegible French. He looked at the latest date: the end of September.

"That's all, I promise you."
"But you let him visit you? You let him kiss you sometimes?"
"Yes, sometimes." I lowered my eyes. He didn't press me further.
"You see, if it had been true, I would have just left."

You didn't want it to be true, did you?

Jacques led me into the bedroom. My fear gave way to the fulguration of bursting suns as he claimed me, as I cried out in release. For whom the suns burst, I could not tell.

"Let's write to Gordana again," I suggested. "We can tell her it's no use meeting. We'll tell them what they have to do about the car. If they want to keep it, we can do as we said, pay for the technical inspection, pay for the required repairs, if there are any, and then give it to them. They'll have to pay for the new registration in their name and the insurance."

He agreed, and we sent the letter the following day. They would have to return the old *carte grise* to us, the registration card, so that we could write "ceded to Meho Kozić" on it, with our signatures.

Gordana herself returned a note, addressed only to Jacques. "*I want to inform you,*" she wrote, "*when you write new registration for car, make it out to my name. I send you my identity card number if you need. I want to say thank you for car. I know you can understand me for everything, because of all the pain your wife make to me. I thought she was like a mother to me, and now look what she has done! But it's all over now. Thank you, Gordana*

She wanted the car in her name, although she couldn't drive. This was, perhaps, her way of saying the car was a present from Jacques to her, and not from Ellen to her husband. Might it also have been self-affirmation before Meho, the assurance that in case of separation, this one modest possession would be hers? Jacques, at any rate, insisted he would write both their names on that fateful, gray card.

As I reread her note, I was stricken with remorse. I could hear her tearful tone, *"all the pain your wife...."* I had hurt Gordana, wounded Meho's pride, too, when I had cried out that I couldn't stand his coming any longer. More than anything, I feared I had hurt him. Whatever pain his silence might inflict on me was nothing compared to the torment of my own self-reproach. I would do the noble thing, humble myself before Gordana and ask her to forgive me. I had worked for the Catholic Aid Committee, hadn't I? I had been brought up with Christian values, and, if I had ground a number of them underfoot for months, it suddenly pleased me to remember them.

Gordana hadn't understood about the registration, for apparently she thought it was up to us to take care of it. I would write and explain again. I added a paragraph onto the end of my letter.

> *Dear Gordana, I know that I am dead for you, but, I would like to ask you to forgive me for all the hurt I have caused you. I never wanted to hurt you, but I wasn't always strong enough to say no to your husband. I think nature was very strong between us. I hurt my husband, too, but now we have repaired our hurt. I wasn't always happy with him, because of his chronic depression, and he was often hard on me. So, he thought that what happened was a little bit his fault too. Each of us hurt the other. Now we understand that we are better off together, and I hope it is the same for Meho and you. My greatest desire is to see you happy together and happy in France. I hope everything will go well for you. When I think of you, I cry. All I want is for you to be happy together. Yours, Ellen*

I couldn't admit it, but I wanted their friendship back. Even though I sensed my own hypocrisy, I dared hope Gordana would not. I was using Meho's own argument about the force of nature. I intimated that he had sought me out, as he had at first had the gallantry to do himself, before Gordana had found the evidence of our affair. Secretly, I longed to see Meho again. Above all, I wanted him to be touched by my note. Hadn't he said once that he needed a tender, sentimental woman? At the same time, I realized that the tender woman was rubbing salt in Gordana's wound. I was accusing Meho of being the instigator in our relationship, and indeed he was, although I knew my part of guilt.

This letter brought Gordana's voice back to me. The telephone bill must have been paid somehow, high as it was. My heart leapt to hear her. Had she been moved by my apology?

"I don't understand about *carte grise,*" she said, without any preamble. I began to explain once more, slowly, patiently.

"There will surely be repairs before the car can pass inspection. Take it to Bertrand's Garage, opposite the foundry," I told her.

"Why there?" She was clearly suspicious.

"Because they know us, and if Meho asks them to send the bill to us, they will."

"Then you go to *Préfecture* and get registration!" she commanded.

"No, Gordana, we've already told you. It's up to you to do that."

"And I have to pay?"

"Yes." She was trying my patience.

"How much?"

"Jacques told you. Five hundred francs."

"But you know I haven't got that," she said, obviously hinting. "I still don't get family allowance."

"Then leave it in the parking lot until you can afford it. It's a nice enough present as is. After all, Meho can take it to be repaired, and we'll pay for that. That was always his agreement with Jacques."

You thought I owed it to you, didn't you? Well, you could have chosen another tone then, to make your request.

"You have finished with Meho," she said, in her menacing witch's voice, "but with me, you have not finished! I will do everything I can to hurt you! You ask me to forgive you. Never will I forgive you, never! I have forgiven Meho, because he is my husband. And because he is a man!"

"Does that make a difference?"

"Of course it does! It's natural for a man to look for sex. Meho, if he could, he would sleep with a different woman every day."

'Men and women equal,' you'd said before, Gordana. You said what suited your purposes. And 'a different woman every day,' really? Some husband that would be! Anyway, try to persuade yourself of that. Go ahead, tell me I was just a sex object to him. Do your best to belittle me, to deny what your own eyes told you.

"I have copies of those photographs," she said, as though I should grasp some innuendo. She wanted to threaten me with them but wasn't quite sure how.

"It's your husband who took them, you know," I said.

"That's normal too!" Her tone was vindictive. "And you? Wouldn't you do like me? Keep the photographs?"

"Whatever for?"

"I have note here from you in Russian too. It says, '*Ia khochu* . . . I want to sleep with you.'" My condemnation had been pronounced. I could still see Meho scooping up the crinkled paper, his eyes sparkling, insisting on keeping it. What better proof now that it was I who had run after him?

"All right, it's true I wrote that. But Meho wanted to so much . . . I finally gave in."

Now I remembered how you had answered, Meho, when I asked you why you fed the children so many sweets: 'because the children, they wanted . . .' I sounded just as weak and foolish.

"How many times you sleep with Meho?" she asked me brusquely.

"I don't know."

"Hmph, you don't know. And how many women did he sleep with?"

Go ahead, try and tell me I was one of many.

"How should I know? Ask him!"

"Do you know what Suada and Amina said about you, after you left that evening?" Her voice was dark with implication. I ignored her question.

If they called me slut, bitch, whore, then they learned those words from you.

"You know, Gordana, Jacques has a few reasons to be angry with Meho, too."

"Ah? Jacques? You are thinking of your husband now?" She dripped sarcasm. Her talent for repartee floored me. I was no good at this.

"If you understood those letters you have, you'd know I never ceased thinking of Jacques."

"You wrote in one of those letters that I should see doctor. I am not crazy!" She was reaching a feverish pitch, nearly screaming now. I held the receiver at a distance.

"I never said 'crazy'! I said you were tired and depressed." Gordana was working herself into a frenzy. She sputtered French words I could not make out, and, when I asked her to repeat, she seethed with annoyance.

"Meho never love you, you know."

"That's not what he said."

"He told you he loved you?" Her feigned surprise was laden with sarcastic sympathy: *Poor deluded thing!*

"Well, he told me so, but maybe it wasn't true." I played at being conciliatory. I could be dishonest too. I wasn't going to stoop to a fishmonger's fight over Meho.

"I told *doktor* you gave me that infection," she went on. "Meho, he has the infection too." She left time for this to sink in. "I gave *doktor* your name and address."

"Gordana, I never had an infection. It's the truth."

She floundered for a word that I assumed must be miscarriage. "My . . . my . . . baby!" she cried, as if she had been wounded in what was most precious to her, the baby.

"Did you keep the baby?" I asked, hoping at last to know.

"Yes."

You would have preferred to call me murderess of embryos, wouldn't you?

She began a long, muddled outburst that I couldn't follow, except for the tone of her voice, self-righteous, then accusatory, closer and closer to hysteria. Suddenly I asked myself why I was listening to her rant. I hung up on Gordana, banging down the receiver. The telephone jangled forth again in two tempestuous spurts, then was mute.

Was it Doctor Duplessis she had spoken to about me? The thought made me sick. But why would she have gone back to consult my doctor? And a doctor at the public hospital would never know me. It was probably a bluff anyway, aimed at shaming and frightening me. I was beginning to understand Gordana's tactics. Would she have admitted her husband had deceived her with another woman? After all, she might have, perhaps to shame him, too, before the doctor.

> *You are treading on dangerous territory, Gordana. If you embarrass me publicly, if you break my marriage, as you are now trying to do, are you sure I will not then do my all to take your Meho? What makes you so certain you have him back now? Anyway, if you want war, then you can have it. I am a citizen of this country, and you are not. I have university degrees and a respected position here. I can tell the Foreigners Bureau at the Préfecture that a paranoid little Rom woman is harassing me, that it might be wise to think twice before renewing her family's papers in the spring.*

I suffocated at my own thoughts, then broke down sobbing. I had loved nothing so much as my Gypsy family, cared for nothing so much as their acceptance and success. Now I was ready to undo the work of a year's passion.

Jacques came home to find me red and pale, blotchy from tears. "Am I a wicked person, really?" I asked him wearily.

"No, not at all," he soothed. "You are probably not wicked enough." He went up to the computer and typed a long message to Gordana. It was no use speaking harshly, he told her, because when she hurt me, she hurt him too, and she only hurt herself. He reminded her he had asked her to make peace. If she was still bent on being so vengeful, what could she hope to gain, other than destruction? If Ellen and Meho had found each other, it was because they had each felt a lack in their marriage. He told her Meho hadn't found the love and affection he needed at home. He reminded her that he knew of our relationship, and that he needed no photographs, no written proof. Besides, Ellen could show Gordana her own proof: a love letter, for example, written in Gordana's own language.

> *You never thought I had my evidence too, did you Gordana? Yes, it was I who asked Jacques to add that sentence. Revenge breeds revenge.*

We each had our part of responsibility in this unhappy business, wrote Jacques, she no less than the rest. He pointed out how Meho had disappointed him and deceived him. Yet he didn't seek revenge. He regretted that their friendship had been broken.

As for the automobile, Ellen had explained to him what Gordana hinted at obtaining. She should understand that it was not and never had been a gift from Ellen to Meho, but a loan from him, *even when he knew of our adulterous relationship*. Moreover, he had already explained to Meho that he could keep it, but he would have to pay for the registration, five hundred francs, and insurance, at least two thousand more. If they didn't accept our conditions, they should return the key to us, and we would pick up the car. He wouldn't change his mind.

Jacques carefully placed a copy of the letter in a second envelope, addressed to Meho, in case Gordana should hide this missive from him. He had to know that her terms and behavior were unacceptable.

Exhausted from the storm, I clung to Jacques now, my own asylum. Like a child in need of parenting, I clung to him, begging refuge as I never had. Balkan passion was more than I could withstand, Balkan fury more than I could face. Jacques, in these unleashed winds, was sure and steady, and, unbelievably, he loved me. My wedded husband, *havre de grâce,* home port, haven of grace. He was my history, and so he would be my future. I would love him again one day, for it was his language I spoke.

What Gordana and Meho were able to understand of Jacques' letter is a moot question, for the cultural and linguistic barriers that separated us were incommensurable. They thought in terms of retribution and revenge, we in terms of pondering and forgiveness. Lying, for Meho, was a survivor's reflex. To Jacques, it was inconceivable, an affront to self-respect and dignity. Gypsy life in the Balkans had taught them ruse and deceit. Integrity was Jacques' second nature. He was attuned to moral and intellectual subtleties whose existence Meho did not even appear to suspect.

The practical instructions concerning the car, at any rate, were clear to them, for Meho proceeded to have it checked and repaired. The garage called: "We have a gentleman here with your 205, Madame. He says we are to send the bill to you. We would like your confirmation on that."

"Yes, we are agreed," I told the secretary. "Send us the bill, but only do the repairs required for the technical inspection, please!"

I could imagine Meho standing there, his head slightly bowed, his shoulders covered in black leather, awaiting the verdict. Did he take it for granted I would say yes? Had he any gratitude for that yes? Did he wish he could hear my voice? Why did he not call me himself? Why did he not walk past the junior high school when he knew I would be coming out? Why did he not happen to be in the old town on Wednesdays before orchestra rehearsal began? Had Gordana so tyrannized him? Had he no free will any more? He had been clever enough at tricking her before. Was it possible he had renounced that forever? Or was it Ellen he had renounced forever?

So quickly, Meho? How could you pass from the most heated passion to complete indifference, if not hatred, overnight? Is hatred really the inner lining of passion? What were the workings of your mind? 'I will always love you more,' you had said, yet now it was I who remained ensnared, despite all my resolutions.

I should have understood how demanding and imperious Meho could be. Occasionally, in the first moments of our passion, when I was reticent to grant him the time he felt entitled to, he had flared up in irritation. I remembered one incident when he had demanded to get out of the car, as I drove him back to the home on a Wednesday evening. "It will be five minutes together or nothing," I'd said. The rehearsal had lasted late, and Jacques was expecting me. I should have been home already.

"Then it will be nothing! Let me out here, Ellen!"

I was relieved for a fleeting instant. Were you going to free me from the bondage I felt toward you, so suddenly, so easily? But it was I who couldn't free myself; I cajoled you into staying, and you let yourself be persuaded, for that was what you wanted. Now I could cajole no longer.

The dreams dogged me: Meho calling, continually, telling me how he was, how Gordana was, if he had found work, if the child was the boy they wanted. I heard his voice as clearly as if he were standing in the room beside me. Then I would awake and live over and over again the scene between us on the landing. I would hear my own nervous, overwrought voice, hear the hard words I had had for him, while the bitter waters of self-reproach washed over me.

If he had broken with me in a snap, as a twig breaks in a strong wind, then it could only be because of my own selfishness. I had failed to make him comprehend that I was only reacting instinctively to Gordana's assault, putting out claws I never knew I had.

I wasn't brave and generous as you were, Meho, when you first took responsibility for our affair. And I couldn't expect you to do so forever, although I would have liked you to.

And you, Gordana. I told you that I was wearied sick of Meho's constant solicitation, but this was a partial truth, indeed. I was weary of my own weakness in the face of it. And you had hastened to repeat my harsh words to him, hadn't you? Only too pleased, of course. How could I have imagined I could hurt you and not him? If I had admitted my love for Meho, you would have flaunted it in Jacques' face. I wasn't strong enough to face that. You forced me to a choice I didn't want to make, not that way.

I knew Meho was never mine for the taking, but this was not the separation I wished for. Was it, stormy and uncivil, the only effective way to cut the cord? I had to accept it as such. I turned again and again on my bed. Acceptance was a road to be traveled. I couldn't think of one time I had ever had a hard word for anyone in my life. Why, now, did I have to suffer so for it? Others could spend a lifetime in cruel words, even deeds, and pass unscathed through disgrace and rebuke like the innocent through fire. I could forgive Meho for anything he had said or done; myself I could never forgive. Silent tears would stream down my face onto my pillow when I thought these thoughts, and I would turn my back to Jacques, so that he would have no knowledge of them.

You still travail in exile, Ellen, astray from your own world of decency and propriety, the world where people live day after day. Do not make your loved ones pay the price. Take the path back. That world is yours; you were born to it. The cost of exile is too high for you; it is beyond your means. But first, you must pay your pound of flesh, for there will be no dispensations.

I put on a facade for my children, for it was the holiday season, and we must make merry. We met in Jeremy's apartment in Aiguebonne, where the dampness made the sidewalks gleam red and green and yellow in the Christmas lights, as we did last minute shopping, joining the crowds on the busy, twilit streets. I sought consolation in trivia, a new pair of shoes, champagne for the evening. The wide shop windows poured forth light and warmth and the temptations of fashion.

Pain can be shoved to the back of the mind for awhile, where it lies in wait for us in the quiet times when we are in company with ourselves. I looked at my new, satin pumps.

A year earlier, Meho had held little Léo in his arms, while his own curly-headed Veronika had looked on, fascinated. Suada had skipped about in cheap, high-soled shoes with gold specks shining through the plastic. "She is my daughter, and I want her to be the prettiest!" Meho had said, and his fatherly pride had touched me. Santa Claus would bring her a Barbie doll, she knew, and I had been pained at the thought that this childish faith would be her first disappointment in her new country. The *Comité d'Entr'aide Catholique* wrought miracles, however, for it organized a party for the asylum seekers, where the Christmas dreams of little Muslim Gypsy girls came true.

The *Comité d'Entr'aide Catholique* was now a dirty word in her family's vocabulary, and their benefactress a whore. For having loved too much, she had loved badly. For having given too much of herself, she had lost herself and them. Did Suada and her sisters hug new dolls to their narrow chests this Christmas? I could only hope so, for I would never be told.

On our return home, a letter from Meho was waiting:

> *Monsieur and Madame,*
> *Today I had technical inspection done on car. If you want to do things right for registration, write a check. I don't know how much it cost, really, you ask at Préfecture. I thank you. Here is old card to make exchange. Make the contract. Kozić, M. Good Christmas!*

I was chilled through and through. Now we were "Sir and Madam". Was it a parody of respect, or did he think we expected this distance? Moreover, either the meaning of our previous letters had been entirely lost, or else he and Gordana were densely stubborn. Their blind obstinacy angered Jacques. We were having *un dialogue de sourds,* a dialogue of the deaf. In my mind, a litany was forming, which I put to paper:

Gordana, Meho,
We received Meho's letter. We were surprised.
We did not find our names but only 'Monsieur and Madame'.
We did not read 'thank you' for the repairs or even for having lent the car.
We did not read that Meho apologized to Jacques as Ellen did to Gordana.
We did not read that Gordana was sorry for calling Ellen a prostitute.
We did not read that she has stopped seeking revenge.
We did not read that you regret what happened.
We did not find the word please.
All we read was, 'If you want to do things right, write a check'. We heard orders. That shocked us. We will not write any more checks.
Please read our other letter again.
If you do not want the car on our conditions, please return the key to us this week.
Ellen and Jacques

We held the *carte grise* now, for he had returned it to us. Our relationship was degenerating into a petty, ugly dispute over the payment of five hundred francs for a registration card. Was a car so important? Was it a convenience for Meho or, indeed, a symbol of manhood and survival? A memento of our love trysts, it was clearly no longer. In any case, what authorized him to think he could take that arrogant tone with us? Or was this once more a cultural misunderstanding?

He had added Christmas greetings; was that an attempt at softening the rest of the message? If it had been, there were other ways. He could have pointed out his need for the car, appealed to our sympathy and understanding, said only *s'il vous plaît,* and he would have obtained what he wanted. Meho had thrown diplomacy to the winds. He preferred a duel, apparently.

The letter had lain in the box while we were celebrating in Aiguebonne. No sooner had we found it and mailed our reply than the telephone rang. "It's Gordana."

"The dead cannot speak. Here is my husband."

Jacques took the phone from me. I heard him, brief but courteous, "Yes, we got your letter, and we have answered it. You will get the reply tomorrow."

> It will not be the reply you are expecting, Gordana. Too bad for you. You cannot insult, all the while holding out your hand for alms.

This time, the answer came from Meho, addressed only to Jacques on the envelope. He was borrowing our tactics.

> *Hello Jacques and my darling Ellen,*
>
> *I forgot that I love you, Ellen. That's why you made up plot for car. Because I don't invite you, I don't call you, because I don't sleep with you, because I don't kiss you, I don't give you chance to realize your fantasies.*
>
> *And I don't want to do all that, because you are sick with terrible infection you gave me in December. Anyway, you, Ellen, take good care of Jacques and tell him all the truth about you and me! I don't find things in good order, it's you who find, Ellen. I won't give you any more. For car, if you decide to give us, we agree, if not, it's yours, I will send you key.*
>
> Notre amour est mort. *Our love is dead.*

There was no signature. Had he not dared put his name to that venomous scrawl? *"Morrt!"* Dead! I wondered if I was hearing Meho's voice or Gordana's. I felt nauseated and seized with panic. Would Jacques ask me about his insinuations? At any rate, it was plain I hadn't seen Meho in December. Why had he written that? Had he made the mistake on purpose? Jacques blanched on reading the letter, while I sat stupidly at the kitchen table, staring at the paper between us, my mind numb.

I had yet to learn the Flamenco couplet, "If you are a Gypsy, so then am I. If you shatter my soul, so will I yours!"

"I guess he addressed it to you, because he wants to hurt you through me," I finally brought out.

"Well, he has succeeded." Jacques looked incredulous. Here was the wild fox biting the hand that had fed it. "However could you have loved him?"

"I don't know," I said slowly, wounded to the quick by the savage thrust of his letter, yet knowing, even as I said it, that I still did.

That evening we took from the secretary drawer in the hall the half-broken key to the Peugeot, that we had kept. We drove to the Kozićs' apartment block, hoping, above all, that there would be a minimum of gasoline in the tank. At first, the car was out of sight, parked on the opposite side from where he usually left it, shining modestly, unsuspectingly in the electric street lamps that lit the wide parking lot. It sputtered and balked but finally started.

Before we drove back home, Jacques in my old car and I taking his, I ran into the entryway of the building and slipped a note I had written myself into the Kozić mailbox, which Gordana, curiously enough, had labeled "Mademoiselle KOZIĆ Meho":

> Meho,
>
> We thank you for your letter, because it showed to us what sort of man you really are. That way, we have no regrets about taking back the car. We are taking it ourselves. You do not have to send us the key. We wish to give the little violin to the children, because it is not good to mix children up in the problems of adults. Good-bye to you and Gordana, and good luck. Jacques and Ellen

The trunk of the car, to our dismay, was loaded with belongings: scraps of metal and machine parts, junk and tidbits collected by

Meho. We found a pile of leaflets inviting people to join the chorus he sang with, a lone, black leather glove, a roll of pink toilet paper, its top delicately stained along the edge with bright, red blood: Gordana's blood, on her way to the hospital.

Jacques found a large carton in the garage and filled it with the unwieldy mass of paraphernalia. Meho was a pack rat, and his careful collecting of spare parts harked back to a well-acquired habit of laying hands on anything that might serve, might sell, might bring in the few dinars, marks, or francs likely to put some food on the table.

Our carton loaded, we started back to their apartment building, stealing into the vestibule with it like thieves. We left it near their mailbox with *Monsieur Kozić* written clearly on it, down to the respectful diacritic on the "c". What would he think the next morning when he found the carton, opened it, realized where the things had come from? Would he be dumbfounded? Would he swear in Romany? Would he understand the note? "He understands things backwards," Cédric had said. Would he show it to Gordana? We glanced up at the window where their bedroom was, and, as we got into the car again, suddenly the light snapped on behind the lace curtains, pulled slightly askew. We sped out of the parking lot like culprits.

You never thought we had a key, did you? We could have done this long ago.

Château Lore

Oleg

Oleg had a confused vision of a border crossing. There was no inspection, and he and Sveta were motioned to go on. It was a mythical sort of country with a king, and he saw himself and his family established there in a great castle that made the *Château* look like a cabin.

When he talked to Sveta about his dream, she said the country must be Belgium. In Belgium, there was a king, and everyone knew there was a huge refugee center in Brussels that looked like a castle. It was surely a sign, and they must go there. Hitchhiking would be fine. At any rate, they had no alternative now, for the employment promise had brought no results.

They packed their belongings into huge backpacks, and, after emotional good-byes to the Dobrinines, they set off, little Vania in his father's arms.

A Gypsy trailer pulled to the side of the road. The man who leaned out had sunburned arms and a black, handlebar mustache. "Where to, brother and sister?" he asked cheerfully. Sveta and Oleg sighed with relief. "But you're already so loaded down!" they said.

"Naah, when there's already room for five, there's room for three more. My brother can take a couple in his van. Move it over in there!" he shouted to his tousled children.

"Will you be stopping in Brussels?" they asked. "We want to go to the central police station. If we're lucky, we'll sleep at the refugee castle there tonight."

"Refugees, eh?" the driver laughed. "That's what we *Gitans* are, from birth. The eternal pilgrimage! We never can seem to do enough to catch up on all our sins!" His sins did not seem to overburden his conscience, for he chuckled and chatted to Oleg all the way, while Sveta rode in the back with Vania. "Lots of us in that castle in Brussels," he said. "They leave Slovakia and the Czech Republic in droves. No work for them there, nothing. Substandard housing, prejudice. Black hair and eyes, and that's the end of it for you. Not long ago, I drove a Yugoslav family in that direction, picked them up right about here too, met them at an encampment. They'd been around: Croatia, Germany, France. Out of money, out of luck. She was pregnant, could hardly walk. Another girl she said, and they already had three. But you people are as blond as the wheat in the fields. Maybe they'll have you in Belgium."

"Who knows," sighed Oleg, "but it will be time gained. They can't expel us right away. And when they do, then we'll go to Germany. The one place I can never go is home."

"That's all right, boy," said the driver. "Home is where you *are*. It's the blue sky over your head, and the fresh air, and the smell of woodfire in your clothes." He breathed deeply and laughed again.

Nineteen

For weeks, I awaited a new flood of invective which never came. The mailbox was a wasteland, the telephone still and brooding. We had spoken the last word; they punctuated it with silence.

Gordana always comes to me in my dreams now as a spider, and she is watching, half-hidden behind a door, just as she was on the day I first met her, while I creep into a parking lot at night to steal my own car. Sometimes the dreams end well, and Jacques delivers me from her sticky grasp. I listen to his regular, reassuring breathing beside me and feel infinite gratitude that I have escaped some personal form of shipwreck, the shadow of certain death.

"*Tu es morrte!*"

No, Gordana, do not delude yourself; I am not dead, for we cannot kill the past. The past never dies but nourishes our present and informs our future.

The last view I retain of the Kozić home is that bedroom window, with the sudden burst of electric glow through the paper lantern that covered the lightbulb, through the flimsy, polyester lace of the dime store curtains. I have driven past many times since that cold January evening, but the curtains keep their secret, sometimes pulled wider open, sometimes less, always at the same angle.

Life goes on for you, life without Ellen, incredibly: an already shadowy existence that is now a sheer, black hole.

For months, I scanned the city register birth notices in the local newspaper, but no Kozić child, son or daughter, was ever announced there. Was that unfortunate child finally lost in the ashes of his father's burned out passion? Was he born on the never-ending road, under the light of some other country's skies, amidst the sounds of one more foreign tongue? The dagger of Meho's final letter turns again and again in the unhealed wound, his stubborn silence more painful than any words written in anger, but, most of all, it is the knife of my own words that turns against me, piercing and scraping.

You made your choice Ellen, if, indeed, you had one, and there's no turning back. A bout of fever cannot end in a handshake. Passion is of the moment, and you know that, but you have yet to see how long the aftermath lasts.

'An American woman, a free woman,' you called me once, Meho. Free to wound myself, but not beyond. Pray for Gordana and Meho, now, Ellen, for that's all that remains for you to do. Be happy, little brother, and remember only that your name has been engraved with the stylus of pain on a free woman's heart.

Now, as Jacques and I sit close together in front of our television set evenings, huddled and slowly healing, watching the flood of refugees stream painfully out of the Yugoslavian province of Kosovo, they, too, in desperate search of some asylum, I commune with Gordana's anxiety for Latifa. Will Macedonia in its turn burst into flames? Will the Rom quarters of Skopje, where Jasmina lives and studies her law books, be pillaged and martyred and broken?

Your asylum among us has been tenuous and angst-ridden, yet you live, somewhere, you live, and your children will live. May they thrive and all the youth of your people! It is I who have been expelled from the Garden, banished forever from the perfect happiness of innocence. Like the true peregrine Gypsy that you are, Meho, you will continue your route, Jelem, Jelem, singing on your way, for where can the pariah rest his head? Wherever you may be, know only this: In spite of yourself, you left a golden-haired gadji *pregnant on the side of the road. Pregnant with this story...*

ACKNOWLEDGMENTS

A hug and warm thanks to Susan Tiberghien for her intitial encouragment at the Paris Writers' Workshop, to Paulette Bates Alden for her enthusiasm and advice, and to Holly Gruber for her faith and her astute editorial hand.

A number of books and articles fed my imagination and personal culture in the elaboration of this story, and I am grateful to their authors. Among them were, on the Bosnian war: *Bienvenue en enfer: Sarajevo mode d'emploi* by Ozren Kebo (La Nuée Bleue, 1997); *Blood and Vengeance: One Family's Story of the War in Bosnia* by Chuck Sudetic (W.W. Norton and company, New York, 1998), and, on Gypsies: *Les Tsiganes, une destinée européenne* by Henriette Asséo (Découvertes, Gallimard, Histoire, Paris, 1994); *Paroles de Gitans* by Alice Becker-Ho (Albin Michel, Carnets de Sagesse, Paris, 2000); *A History of the Gypsies of Eastern Europe and Russia* by David M. Crowe (St. Martin's Griffin, New York, 1996).

I would also like to thank my family for their patience with the absent, glazed-over look that regularly stole into my eyes and signaled to them that there I was, off in my own world again. My husband, François, deserves a special mention for his forbearance, when, once again, in the middle of the night, the light would be snapped on, so that some fulgurant, embryonic idea might be jotted down and thus survive until morning.